I0676288

A Fiction

The Slave
and the
Book Keeper

Discover an ancient journey

Four Thousand years ago

Daniel of Susa, almost sixteen, is about to begin his first adventure.

A magical journey through the ancient land of Edin and the love and loss of youth and innocence.

It is not what he expected.

The Author

Yeo Sola was born in
Fort Johnston in British Nyasaland.
This is a first novel.

YEO SOLA

YEO SOLA

The Slave, the Book Keeper, the Dreamer, and the Orphan

Book 1

The Slave and the Book Keeper

PRINTFIELDS LTD

YEOSOLA.COM

First Published 2014,
Published by Printfields Ltd, London, N13 5UD, UK.

Copyright © 2014 Yeo Sola

CreateSpace

ISBN 978-0-9576859-3-2

Genre: Fiction; Spiritual; Travel

YEOSOLA.COM

DEDICATION

For an Angel

YEO SOLA

ACKNOWLEDGMENTS

The Camino in this book began on another Camino in Spain, and the story came to life in the hills, mountains, valleys, and deserts of Syria, Oman, Jordan, Palestine, Turkey, Israel, Spain, Italy, Qatar and India.

My gratitude to William for the initial inspiration.

My thanks to friends and family for their unlimited support and encouragement.

Most of all, to those who have already read the book and shared the journey, and to those about to do so, thank you for walking the book with me.

Your support is greatly appreciated.
I invite you to leave a review at yeosola.com.

YEO SOLA

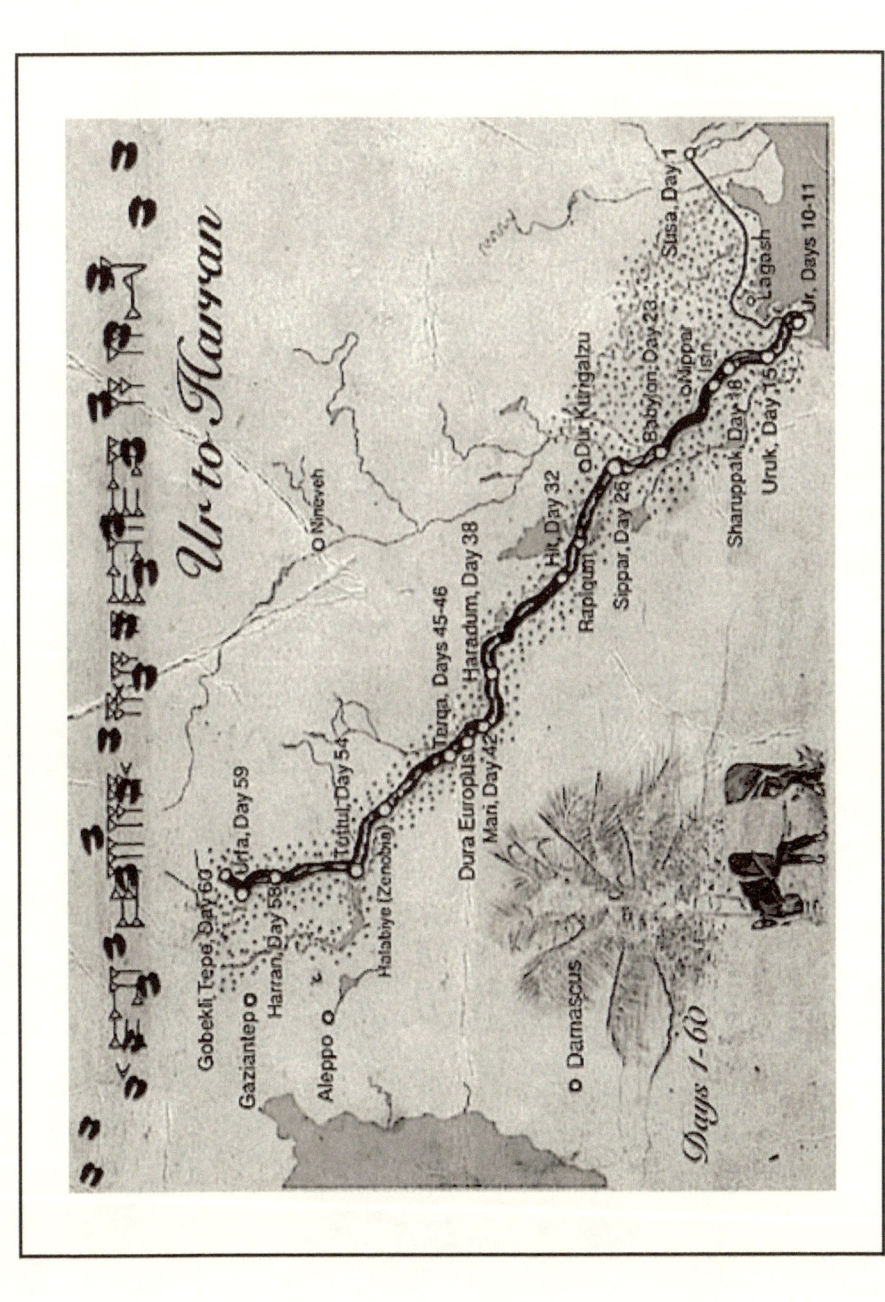

Ur to Harran

Gobekli Tepe, Day 60
Gaziantep ○
Urfa, Day 59
Harran, Day 58
Tuttul, Day 54
Aleppo ○
Halabiye (Zenobia)
Dura Europus
Terqa, Days 45-46
Mari, Day 42
Haradum, Day 38
○ Nineveh
Hit, Day 32
○ Damascus
Rapiqum
Sippar, Day 26
○Dur Kurigalzu
Babylon, Day 23
○Nippur
Isin
Shuruppak, Day 18
Uruk, Day 15
Susa, Day 1
Lagash
Ur, Days 10-11

Days 1-60

YEO SOLA

INTRODUCTION

An ancient scroll, translated and published in 1887, describes a gathering on the night of a birth almost four thousand years ago:

Chapter 8: 2-4

"2. And when all the wise men and conjurors went out from the house of Terah, they lifted up their eyes toward heaven that night to look at the stars, and they saw, and behold one very large star came from the east and ran in the heavens, and he swallowed up the four stars from the four sides of the heavens.

3. And all the wise men of the king and his conjurors were astonished at the sight, and the sages understood this matter, and they knew its import.

4. And they said to each other, This only betokens the child that has been born to Terah this night, who will grow up and be fruitful, and multiply, and possess all the earth, he and his children for ever, and he and his seed will slay great kings, and inherit their lands."

(Trans. J.H. Parry, 1887)

If the birth is well known, the astronomical phenomenon described in the passage is not. Yet, the fear generated by the interpretations of the movement of the stars – a warning, a danger, a threat to "great kings" and their realms – would end the lives of many newborns entering the world on that particular night.

According to a paper in a recent edition of the Bulletin of the American Astronomical Society, five visible planets - Venus, Mercury, Mars, Jupiter and Saturn - aligned with the Earth on Feb 26, 1953, BC, and were still visible on the night of the new moon on March 5, 1953, BC. It is unimaginable that the astronomers and astrologers in the city-states of the lands that would later be known as Mesopotamia did not witness the event. The administrators of the region were known to be meticulous record keepers: even the times of the risings of the moon and individual stars have been discovered on tablets. It is strange then that amongst the records of Sippar, Nippur, and Ebla, no alignment of five planets is recorded, yet the astronomers of China not only saw the heavenly event and recorded it, but also they used the day of the new moon, a Monday, to begin a new calendar.

This novel is a story of fiction, set against a fictionalized backdrop of the events that led to a Messenger being thrown into the fire almost four thousand years ago.

Distance: For the purpose of this novel
one Beru is equivalent to two hours travel
(5.25 miles or 8.45 Km)

PROLOGUE

If it is conceivable and even believed that the book was not satisfied where it lay, then it would not be a surprise to learn that when Alizer entered the bedchamber after the customary knock, given as a sign of respect even though he anticipated no answer, his attention was immediately imprisoned by the discarded, skin-sheathed papyrus scroll on the otherwise empty floor next to the bedding, catching the only light from the single high window of the room. Momentarily forgetting the purpose for which he had entered the room, Alizer made a decision he would never remember making. He stepped forward, knelt down, carefully picked up the sheath with both hands, and gently removed its contents. He unrolled the unusually long scroll that Taros, the Egyptian trader, had commissioned in Memphis on Alizer's behalf almost two years ago. Alizer had first met Taros in Harran, and the same Taros who had become one of the wealthiest Egyptians after selling, at hugely inflated prices, rare tablets and equally rare animal skins purchased in Harran to owners of palaces and noble homes in Memphis. Alizer glanced across the columns of writing and smiled as he reached the end of the scroll, realising that the entire book had been scribed.

As if this moment was preordained, and with the scroll returned to its sheath, Alizer produced and unfolded a large piece of finely woven temple cloth from his tunic pocket, the one he had been given moments earlier by the tailor as an inspection sample for the temple gowns ordered by the High Priest of Ur in whose house Alizer now served. The book was gently placed on the cloth, wrapped, and then securely tied with the string Alizer had carried from the store room with the intention to tie back two fast growing branches of the highly scented Night Lady Yasmin shrub, which looked untidy at the main entrance of the courtyard. If anyone had seen Alizer, his behaviour would have been described as ceremonious in the way he picked up the wrapped package with both hands, paused, and then placed the book in his shoulder bag. As he made ready to leave, Alizer wondered what the author of the book would say if he learned of Alizer's actions.

'He will not even realise it's gone,' Alizer justified his actions – maybe for his own peace of mind.

Suddenly returning to himself and remembering the purpose of his entry, he quickly surveyed the room, satisfying himself that the room was in good order. Without another worry, he stepped back into the courtyard.

Strange as it may seem, the book too felt satisfied.

1 FAREWELL

Days 1 to 10, 35.5 Beru.

Today was their last day of travel together. Having known no other travel companion since his coming of age at eleven, five and half years ago, Iannas would part from his father, Appa, at dawn, and Iannas would continue the remainder of the journey to Ur with his young friend Daniel.

With a peculiar feeling that this was an extraordinary time, Appa had already handed his son to the earth, the wind, and the sky. Each of his other children had embarked on their own journeys, and his wife was into her own in the next world. He felt, for the first time in his life, truly alone. The thought made him wish to be with his young family all over again, and live his life all over again to experience the joy of that time, for he had received so much love. And he wondered how he would feel to live all that love again, along with the regret that he could have given so much more.

Appa had spent the morning watching the waking eyes on the half-sleepy faces of the two teenagers, the young men they wished to be, as the first light gave life to slowly brightening heavens of fresh blue. The first flourish of renewing dew that gently settled on the exposed, soft morning skin on their faces and arms had created an enchanting early dawn beginning to today's walking. The day had passed too quickly for Appa. He took solace in the memory of the walk through the huge oak trees that welcomed visitors this morning by releasing dewdrops on the unsuspecting Iannas, more than on Appa or Daniel, much to their amusement. Remnants of the recent rains were still apparent in the brilliant green of the life-giving scarf that wrapped the land around the rivers being followed and crossed by the travellers. The trees proudly flaunted their little green acorns as if to announce the new beginnings for the next season; Appa wondered where the new beginnings would lead tomorrow. The caravan was always voiceless in the mornings, allowing the congregations of birdlife to pray on behalf of the world as the travellers passed through the decreasing wild forests and increasing arrays of planted orchards, currently resplendent with red, palm-sized pomegranates waiting to be savoured whilst nestled in their new woodland.

For Iannas and Appa, this morning's silence drew a culmination of emotions and memories that both had been navigating through ever since they had left Susa in preparation for their imminent parting. Iannas was excited and did not hide his excitement too well. Appa was melancholy, and very successfully hid his sorrow from his son, Daniel and fellow travellers.

Daniel had kept the conversations alive although they may have been a little one sided today. 'I cannot believe it's already our sixth day on the road from Susa,' Daniel remarked and waited for a response from Iannas, but he did not expect the one received.

'You have reminded us all day, Daniel!' Iannas felt obliged to point out after having heard Daniel repeat the phrase at least four times since dawn. Appa found this amusing and fortunately, Daniel did too. When the laughter had finished, Daniel continued to entertain by describing the aching utterances of his teenage feet at the end of each day and the protestations each morning of his recently engaged muscles. Daniel, in his excitement, had overlooked that it had been almost a year since his last journey, and his arms and legs were beginning to recall that memory with cramps and pains and he had commenced to reply with morning stretches.

Daniel was allowed to meander into reminiscences of Susa and the exhilaration of the past days in the caravan. While Iannas engaged with Daniel, Appa listened, enjoying the youthful enthusiasm. He was very aware their banter successfully buffered any attempt Iannas and Appa made to share their feelings between them today. Daniel was still preoccupied with the excitement of Donkey's first trek as well as taking responsibility for his very first journey, having already made it clear he was nearly sixteen and would soon be the same age as Iannas. Appa already appreciated that Daniel did not wish to talk about the special task granted to Daniel by Azhar, the High Priest of Ur, the reason for the journey that would take Iannas and Daniel to Harran. While recognising Daniel's apprehension, Appa laughed as he watched the two companions argue about whose turn it was to hold the ropes for Donkey. Somehow Appa had been comforted with the knowing that during the last six days, the times Iannas and Daniel had kept a distance from his ears, they had found quiet moments and granted themselves permission for their emotions to surface. Appa had a sense that Iannas remembered his mother with Daniel, and Daniel in turn used these opportunities to share his own anxieties for the journey ahead. While Appa was grateful that the journey from Nineveh had allowed him and his son to grieve, his only remaining wish was that Iannas and he would remember mother together.

Today, even unspoken, Appa and his son had made sure to walk together. When the cart and camel owner carrying Appa's stock for Lagash market began to draw alongside at the third checkpoint, no one could help but feel concern for the long suffering camel pulling the full cart containing the goods of three other traders in addition to Appa's. The camel owner wondered if the young strong donkey next to him would be able to manage the load his camel was pulling.

'If he looked after his camel, the camel would pull a larger load,' Daniel commented. Iannas agreed and Donkey was thinking the same.

'There are more checkpoints along this section of road than all the way from Nineveh,' Iannas exaggerated.

'It is not the checkpoints,' Daniel corrected patting his pocket containing his coin pouch handed to him by Alizer in Susa before Alizer had travelled. 'It is the taxes at each checkpoint I object to.'

'At least the roads are patrolled,' Iannas offered and looked at his Appa, 'and we can enjoy the evening campfires, the food, and Appa's stories without worrying about bandits.'

'The bandits?' Daniel exclaimed surprised. 'What about the millions of biting insects? That is what I worry about every night.'

Iannas laughed and reminded Daniel, 'You worry about everything.' Although Iannas and Appa found Daniel's comments amusing, they had to agree with him. The mites were tedious, but it was hard not to enjoy walking, resting, and camping amongst the pomegranate orchards, olive trees, cedar trees, and the wild forests. The itchy, irritating bite marks, presented as gifts and mementos of the road by the feeding mosquitoes that took full advantage of the end of the rains and the daily new flesh arriving with the caravans, were part of the experience of the journey.

As the shadows grew longer, the caravan leaders navigated successfully to the river-raft crossing, repositioned up the river to a safer location and replacing the bridge that had collapsed only the day before. The well-rehearsed river crossing teams had been known to move floating toll bridges to safer locations within hours whenever the river's height posed a threat. The caravan leaders made it their business to be well informed, so there had been no delay at any of the crossings. But the few remaining muddy sections from the recent rains had yet to dry and were effective in slowing the heavily laden carts and supply animals. Daniel was not overly worried. He knew that Alizer would learn about any delay from other caravan leaders and would still find him in Ur Market where they had arranged to meet. Anyway, Alizer had travelled the same road three days earlier so he knew the conditions.

'The walls of Susa are always washed away at this time of year, you know.' Daniel was still reminiscing about his birth town and making conversation. Daniel's family lived on a simple holding next to the artisan district outside of the walled city. The morning of their departure, Daniel had watched the silhouette of Susa's crumbling mud brick walls and the soldiers with their campfires perched along the broken sections as the first light lit the sky behind the city.

'Did you know,' Daniel continued, 'we have a local story in Susa that many years ago, someone made a decision to build the city wall with the good supply of local mud bricks rather than the stone from the far mountains? The king at the time must have been a miser or a very poor one. The result is that after every rainy season, wall repair teams have to be employed to rebuild all the washed away sections. The new ruler of each generation has had to spend a fortune rebuilding almost the entire wall with new mud bricks or earth. The people in Susa think this is great because every year, without fail, those who need work have jobs but everyone dreads the day when someone will think of upgrading the wall to stone like the one in Ur.' Iannas and Appa laughed, sometimes truth was stranger and more comical than the ancient legends Appa was particularly fond of.

'I wonder how Ur has changed since we were last there. It has been more than a year,' Iannas thought out loud. Being still considered the largest city in the world, Ur was a city always full of anticipation and always changing. With almost half a million residents and thousands of other travellers passing through every day, it was a hectic, bustling place, and having never been designed for so many, the huge beautiful floating Ziggurat in the centre of the walled city was no longer the main focus of conversation.

'I hope they have done something about the stench of human-' Daniel paused as he noticed Appa's glare, '-*waste* and the piles of uncollected smelly, fermenting-' Daniel wanted to use a more colourful expression but negotiated his way through very successfully, '-*rubbish* inside the city. I have seen it collect and flow through the squares and the streets and turn into a channel of putrid liquid mix, battling with everything living until it eventually and successfully claims the sea.' Daniel got a round of applause for his animated description from Iannas, and Daniel felt like stopping and bowing, but he was leading Donkey and did not want to stop the rhythm of the pace.

With so many residents and travellers, Ur should have amassed the largest city tax fund and things should never have been allowed to get this far, but ever since Ur had been taken over by Susa, bureaucracy had increased, no department would take responsibility for the rising towers of rubbish, and the newly imposed increased taxation to pay for more soldiers to patrol the empire had resulted in a very unsettled Ur populace. More alarmingly, the number and size of the protests were growing, and their voices were becoming increasingly outspoken and critical of the Governor of Ur. This, however, was a time when such politics and unrest were the very nature of the city-states of Edin and, not surprisingly, the people of the land and the travellers had learned to ignore the protests and continue with their lives as normal.

As the sun began to prepare for its nightly adventure, the sound of the caravan horn, a melodic chant particular to this caravan's horn blower, traditionally announced the longer shadows and the ensuing camp. Appa had quietly feared this moment, the last horn of the day. The caravan leaders slowed to a stop at the often-used site marked by a lone oak tree, and the activity began in preparation for the evening rest.

Tonight the caravan prepared camp within sight of the evening smoke rising vertically from the city of Lagash into the calm, salty sea air before being blown horizontally inland by the higher air currents, creating a long streak passing over the camp. The caravan would divide at dawn. The main caravan would continue to Ur, and a smaller group form a new little caterpillar to cover the short distance to Lagash.

Any fear the sound of the horn had agitated quickly dissipated when Appa heard the word dinner called by Iannas and Daniel as they quickly fell into the pattern of unpacking Donkey and preparing the night's camp. They were hungry, and tonight Iannas would cook the three fish they had purchased at the last river crossing.

His mother would have been proud of her son, Appa thought, having resolved to let Daniel and Iannas have their own adventure together. Tonight he would enjoy his time with the two young friends. There was dinner to eat and more stories to tell.

As darkness fell, the travellers settled, and the security teams were already returning from their first of many night patrols that would continue at regular intervals until dawn. In the circular camp centred around the oak tree, Donkey was being fed with the other animals in the holding area, and Daniel's orange, hot, crackling wood fire was already in charge of the evening's roasted fish in eagerness to feed its hungry hosts.

Iannas was already at an age where he was learning to appreciate the moments and cherish the memories of the stories that were shared when his parents, brothers, and sisters would sit together around the evening fire after the meal, and Mother, it was usually Mother, would tease and say something like, 'You were named after your great, great grandfather, Iannas. He was lost at sea in the great ocean beyond the known lands, and it is told that he cried and cried to be found. You cried so much when you were born we named you after him.' The intended mirth was then allowed to cascade amongst his siblings who would tease him for the remainder of the evening. Mother would then turn to her husband and ask him to narrate the story of their ancestor being lost in the great ocean at the time of a great flood, which would subsequently enfold the entire family into a huge embrace.

Since ancient times, stories have been used to bind and unite families and communities. These chronicles kept the family history, tribe, and community culture alive, although sometimes not for the right reasons. Appa had kept the tradition alive with his family, and Iannas was beginning to feel very grateful as these moments had given him recollections of a complete family joined in a bond. The union allowed him to remember the scent, sight and feel of his mother, for being the youngest, it was often he who sat next to her.

'You are named after my great grandfather, my son,' Appa began as the three sat together for the last time around their campfire sharing roasted fish, sweet corn, grapes, and pomegranates and sipping the hot date drink Appa had just boiled. This time of year was the season of plenty. The fire, not so long ago, was worshipped as a divine god-creature for the heat and warmth it provided and the miracle it possessed in turning meat and other ingredients into delicious food, but this story was not the one in Appa's mind tonight.

From just the first line Iannas knew the story, but he never tired of it, for his father always had ways of adding new pieces to the story, and Iannas wondered what extras he would discover today.

'Have you noticed the young woman from India in our caravan?' Appa asked.

Iannas, Daniel, and most of the young men in the caravan had noticed the young lady in question travelling with servants from the very first day.

'Her name is Sai Tang,' Appa continued. 'I spoke with her and her group yesterday, and she mentioned she had travelled from north eastern India with tea and many other goods. She described a great calamity in her native land. The whole of the north of India has been flooded. Nothing has been left it seems, and it is one of the largest disasters any of them have ever seen or heard of. She is from a village in the mountains and had to follow many difficult mountain passes to reach the safe trading routes. It appears that one generation after another have to face their disasters.

'Your great, great grandfather, Iannas, was caught in the great flood that hit this region during his time. In his time, it was considered the greatest flood the world had ever seen. He had sailed the seas before so he was not afraid of the water, and he knew what he had to do when the floods from the mountains came and the rain did not cease. There were many boats in these harbours, and in one of the harbours was a large boat already carrying many hundreds of families. He secured a place on it for himself, his wife and their child of two years.

'The storms continued unabated, and the boats could not sail very far because the wind and the waves were too powerful. My great grandfather's boat was not designed to carry so many people and more and more people who were caught in the water tried to rescue themselves by climbing onto the ship. As more and more people clambered on board, great grandfather's ship slowly began to sink; it could not hold the extra weight. The ship had smaller boats, rafts of woven wood for emergencies, and some of the families close to these rafts, including great grandfather's family, found their way onto one of the three rafts that survived the sinking ship. All the other passengers perished.

'Everyone on great grandfather's raft was exhausted and the rain was relentless. Great grandfather started to pray to his God. His God was none of the ancient gods of the time, not Inanna, Utu, Nanna, An, or even Enki the Earth God; he believed and worshipped his own God, but I never learned who this God was.

'He prayed loudly and boldly, and the other families in the boat became scared of this man. Everyone started yelling at him to stop and it was raining, it was windy and the waves made them ill. They were cold, very cold, but your grandfather had such belief that he prayed even louder barely noticing the people screaming around him and the anger of the sea.

'Then came a short lull in the wind and the waves, and another raft appeared nearby; it was half empty. With so many people in great grandfather's raft, and so many scared of his chanting and praying, they shouted at the other boat to come closer and take them away from this madman.

'The rafts approached each other and when they were close enough the survivors moved into the new raft until it was full. Still, the last few squeezed on because they did not want to be on the same boat as my mad great grandfather; so the only ones remaining on the raft were great grandfather, his wife, and their child.

'The rafts released themselves from each other, the wind grew strong again, and very quickly, the waves grew larger than they had been before. Great grandfather saw the other boat move farther and farther away until it was almost out of sight. He watched with great distress as the other raft caught a large wave and capsized hurling everyone off the raft - all that could be seen were the remnants of the raft amongst the waves. He was too far away to help anyone. He had watched everyone fall into the sea, and he could not save one. He grieved for them, prayed even louder, and gave thanks to his God for saving him.

'He stayed on the boat for one entire moon. They survived by harvesting floating fruit and vegetables, any scraps they could find on the water, and asking for food and water from passing ships, some of them were happy to give them a small portion if they had something to spare. There were many boats and rafts on the waters, and everyone tried to watch out for one another. When larger boats came by and offered great grandfather a place, he always declined. He wanted the freedom to pray to his God and did not feel that he would be allowed to do so on board a larger ship amongst other survivors.'

Daniel and Iannas had finished their food and were already pulling their blankets over themselves. Daniel was really absorbed by the story having never heard it before and wondered for a moment why his family had chosen to leave behind the tradition and lose the memories of their histories.

Iannas' father took a pause as he finished his dinner, put some more wood on the fire, gathered his blanket over him, and continued. 'One moon later the raft found some solid ground. They had lost their little daughter and had already allowed the sea to take her small body. Great grandfather and his wife had grown weak, for there had been less and less food to collect from the sea and no more rainwater to drink with the clearing skies. They had actually fared better than many of the other boats that had either sunk or run out of supplies and then fought each other over a few morsels of food, chewed leather and even the wood from the boats.

'The raft came ashore on what was once a mountain region, and a very elderly, mountain-dwelling woman who was searching and rummaging through the shoreline debris for food discovered it. Her family had perished during the floods as they were tending their sheep and goat herds on the lower slopes. She had survived alone in the cave which, she explained, was once at the very top of the mountain but was now as if it was in a small hill.

'While she had grieved for her family and wished for the water to rise further and take her too, this angel rescued and nursed great grandmother and great grandfather. But great grandmother died in the cave and great grandfather recovered to watch the water recede and a new land appear. The flood had carried the raft across the sea and beyond to another land, which the old woman called Arabia.

'When his strength returned he left the cave each day and made short excursions to survey the land around him, collecting food from wherever he could and harvesting fresh water from the rock pools. Each day he watched the water line recede as if it were escaping into a bottomless hollow somewhere out at sea, and soon vast expanses of land began to reveal themselves leaving behind lakes of fish and more debris from the floods. The time came when he decided to set off on his journey to explore the lands, maybe find other survivors, and promised the angel who had saved him he would return with news. When he came back half a moon later with news of other survivors, she was gone, the cave was empty, but he saw new tracks and expected that other survivors who were now gathering and forming new communities had probably rescued her.

'Great grandfather travelled through the Arabian lands. He reminisced about beautiful white beaches caressed by new emerald green seas from where giant sea turtles would emerge to celebrate the moonlight and lay their eggs in the sand. He discovered valleys with new communities and so much beauty, trees, and pools, little pieces of heaven after the deluge and where he fell in love with great grandmother, a place that the locals still call Salalah in a region called Majan from where they bring the frankincense to Ur. He told me it is a wondrous country with a gentle culture and a peace that his soul absorbed casting out the trauma of the flood.

'On his way back to Nineveh, he went through many lands and met many tribes, some peaceful and some filled with war, and he claimed to come across a tribe of people so tall, almost twice as tall as himself. I never believed him until one day, soon after you were born, I met a trader who described long graves he had seen himself in the south of Majan when he went to trade his goods for the local frankincense.

'It took great grandfather and his new wife two years to return to these lands. Great grandmother was renowned for wearing the most colourful clothes with pride. She made sure my grandmother and my mother, when they were young at least, wore the same style of bright clothes. The purpose, she explained, was so that her tribe and the village residents could always see their children and women in their valley, and always come to their aid if needed. Their clothes were an identity with the village and also a torch light to their community.'

Appa concluded, 'And so you see, my son, we named you after your great, great grandfather who cried to his God for help, and your mother and I heard you crying so much when you were born, we thought you were calling on God to take you back to the heavens because you did not want to stay with us!'

Appa's last words brought smiles to Iannas and Daniel's sleepy faces shining in the firelight.

'What about my mother?' Iannas asked. 'She always wore colourful clothes. Where was she from, Father? How did you meet her?' This was a question Iannas had never thought of before and one his father had not expected.

'You are asking because she wore the same bright colourful clothes as Grandmother? My mother taught her well, and she adapted. She loved the clothes. Actually, she was from Ur, in fact, from the same tribe as Daniel's Uncle Terah. I noticed her on one occasion when I went to visit a new client in Ur. I remember I was late for the meeting, and she came to the door to tell me her father had waited but had already left. Later, as I came to know her father and family, I grew to love your mother, married her, and brought her to Nineveh.'

'Did you ever find out which god he was praying to in the boat, Uncle?' Daniel asked referring to Iannas' great, great grandfather.

Iannas answered casually, but regretted his words straightaway, 'The same God as yours and mine, Daniel. There is only one force in the world.'

Puzzled, Daniel looked at Iannas. He had never heard such a thing. Iannas looked apologetic and realised he had allowed the atmosphere to take control of his thoughts.

Father looked inquisitive, 'Where did you learn this, Iannas?'

Iannas stayed silent; he did not want to say what his father already knew.

'Your mother used to say the same thing to me,' his father came to the rescue, smiling at his son and remembering his wife. When Iannas saw the contented memory on his father's face, he felt more relaxed.

'It's time to sleep,' Appa declared.

'One more story, Uncle,' Daniel protested. He loved listening to Appa's stories.

'No, it really is time to sleep. We have to wake before dawn and say our farewells.'

'Wake us, Appa,' Iannas called. 'Good blessings,' he added.

'Good blessings,' Daniel called to Appa, and they allowed Great, great grandfather's adventures to dress the night and journey them into sleep, but Daniel could not sleep. The apprehension of watching Iannas and Appa say goodbye in the morning brought back more memories of his last few days in Susa and his own farewells. He dived into the comfort of his memories of seven nights ago remembering first the contentment of his father sitting in front of the fire, remembering his father's touch as he placed the gold amulet into Daniel's hand, and then the memory of the sound of his father's voice.

"Carry this seal as an amulet for your first journey, Son. It is a golden talisman. I understand, it has no other purpose or value. Alizer presented it to me in Harran as a token of his gratitude. I have no use for it. May it bring you back safely."

Daniel moved his right hand to under his pillow, feeling for the pouch containing the seal and grasped the pouch tightly as if to confirm the memory was a reality and bring him once again close to Papa. But he did not dwell in the goodbye, Daniel's mind quickly moved to watching the priest in the Temple in Susa perform the Full-Moon Blessing Ceremony the night of his leaving. She was a very beautiful woman, or at least Daniel's heart had spoken this way ever since his eyes had been mesmerised by her at his first Full-Moon Ceremony at the age of eleven. He had already decided that when he was older, he would marry her or, more realistically, a woman like her. Her face had always been hidden behind the priest's moon mask, and Daniel would not have recognised her had she been standing right next to him in the central market or the Susa caravanserai where he spent most of his spare time mingling with travellers and traders.

Under the clear starry sky just outside of Lagash, Daniel remembered the ceremony. The familiarity of his thoughts calmed him. He pictured the priest in the white flowing dress made from prized soft cloth finely woven in the temple garden sanctuary by the equally resplendent assistants. The priest in smaller temples like the one Daniel attended was always a woman, and for Daniel, this priest was the most beautiful and perfect representative of the God Sin. She raised her left arm slowly and let her sleeve fall as she guided her hand to the full moon directly above her with the palm facing the congregation and five fingers pointing towards the moon above. Her moon mask looked directly at the congregation as her right hand came up to the centre of her chest and rested with the palm facing her heart. The fact the priest was probably twice Daniel's age and was already married with a young daughter of her own had not been a deterrent to Daniel's affections. But then again, he was only just becoming accustomed to the feelings of a fifteen-year-old going on sixteen. Daniel tried to hear her soft hypnotic voice inviting those ready for the Blessing of the Full Moon to make their way towards her.

Like the others stepping forward, Daniel was leaving at dawn, but it was not for success and profit that blessings were being offered or sought this night. Tonight the prayers were for safety and a smooth journey without incident. Of course, Daniel was confident in his belief that the Moon God Sin would comfort and watch over the traveller at any time. However, this extra blessing on the night of the full moon would provide added protection, and Daniel did not want to leave anything to chance. The youngest and smallest blessing seeker, Daniel gazed at the moonlit radiant priest from the front of the group as she stood with the altar behind her. Daniel was always moved by this moment, which he conjured up vividly while turning his face towards the warmth of the still burning campfire he always enjoyed sleeping next to. He used his senses to try and recollect the sight, scent and sound of the priest's blessing, the representation of the divine God Sin serving to strengthen Daniel's faith. Daniel consumed the memory through his mind and his heart as he mouthed the words of the priest inviting the Sin God to bless, watch over, give strength, and protect the souls standing in front of her. The words, a song from an ancient time in a forgotten language that very few understood, reverberated in their melodious sound, the meaning lost in the moonlight of the moment but clearly touched by the scent of frankincense that absorbed the atmosphere releasing holiness and peace for all to embrace.

'Thank you, oh God Sin,' muttered Daniel silently to himself as he lay on his bed warming his face and listening to the crackle of the burning logs. 'Thank you for watching over me. This is my first journey without my father. Look after Iannas as well even though he does not pray in the temple very often.'

Although the last six days had gone well, Daniel, complete with his new blessing, remained nervous but also confident that he had made all the necessary preparations for his first journey. Before he fell into a slumber, the smoke and smell of the burning fire, mixed with the cool night and the starlit sky, recreated the moment he stepped out of the temple into the still late evening Susa market square. For a fleeting moment Daniel even smelt the market air scented by roasted grain and corn where he had grown up and come to know almost every local trader. Daniel fondly absorbed his last memory of Susa and remembered how he had used his eyes to repeat his farewells and leave-taking in the moonlit shadowy activity of the square as the traders packed their unsold wares, ready for the routine of the market to begin again at dawn. From his warm bed Daniel allowed himself to watch as he stepped into the folds of his future from the streets of his past. The comfort of the memory allowed him a few hours sleep. Unbeknown to him, Daniel would not see, smell, or feel the streets of Susa under his feet again until the autumn of his years.

2 THE ZIGGURAT OF UR

'Remember everything I have taught you, Son,' Appa looked at Iannas and smiled warmly before turning to his son's companion. Appa had just put out the fire, Donkey was packed, and the caravan was ready to separate. 'Do not compromise on this journey, Daniel. Obstacles will come your way. You have seen your father work his way through many troubles. Always remember how he tackled these difficulties when you are faced with yours.'

'Yes, Uncle, I think you know his advice. "Follow the laws of the land" he always says, "and if there is trouble in front of you…"'

'"Walk away from it, think how you will get through it and never rush your steps." Iannas had heard Daniel's father use the phrase so often. Iannas and Daniel finished off the sentence together and, catching each other's eye, they instinctively knew they would be fine.

'Thanks, Uncle, I know, he has taught me well, and I know you have taught Iannas well'.

Appa nodded in approval. 'Travel peacefully, calmly and with a care for your fellow travellers. This is the way of our family and this is how we travel,' Appa paused. 'We may be very distantly related, but we are the same tribe, Daniel's family and ours.' Neither Daniel nor Iannas had heard him speak this way. 'Our tribe represents a way of peace, a way of goodness. It has been our way for generations. Never forget that, Son,' he said to Iannas. 'And you, Daniel, find your destiny. Travel well together.'

Appa took out a small bag of coins. 'I know Daniel already has coins for the journey. This will last you a while for the extra things you might need. You have your seal with you?'

Iannas tied the bag of coins to his waist belt, dropped the bag into his pocket, and lifted from under his shirt his clay seal that had been prepared for him by his father when Iannas had come of age.

'Let me give you this seal to add to your own,' Iannas watched his Appa untie a seal from around his neck and tie it onto Iannas. 'It belonged to my great grandfather. If you look closely, it even has a big fish marked on it. Keep them both together.'

Iannas looked at his father one last time and Appa understood what his son was thinking.

'You are right of course, Iannas. It is time you made your own way in the world. I love you deeply and have selfishly wanted you next to me all the time; it is not fair to put the burden of my loneliness on your shoulders.'

Iannas was thinking how alone he and his Appa had felt without mother. He missed her so much. He looked down at the ground to make sure his Appa did not see his thoughts through his eyes.

'You are scared of leaving us, Appa,' Iannas looked up and replied with renewed confidence and a broad smile for his Appa. 'We are grown up now. You told me you completed your first journey alone at the age of twelve. I am already sixteen. Go and finish your business in Lagash, Appa. Daniel and I will travel very well with each other, and we will see you soon. The moons will pass quickly.'

The way Iannas and Daniel had spoken to him gave him comfort. Appa knew he had to release his son. They embraced each other and with a final 'I miss her so much too, Appa. God be with you,' from Iannas, the first and last time he mentioned his mother's passing to Appa, they parted and faced their new futures. Appa was, for the first time in his life, truly alone.

For the next few days, unusually odd without Appa walking with them, Daniel and Iannas both became preoccupied in their thoughts about having left their respective fathers behind. Iannas used the time to share with Daniel his journey from Nineveh to Susa.

Iannas could have stored the events and memories of each day in each of the caravans from Nineveh to Susa in little raindrops, for when they fall to the ground they shatter into a million tiny particles and disappear into the earth. Iannas had so intensely wrapped himself in his thoughts that he could not assemble the fragments of any of the memories. Iannas could only describe to Daniel his embarrassment when travellers in the caravan expressed concern over his melancholy and asked questions of Iannas' father and eventually learned of his mother. Iannas' news spread through the caravan just as silently as words are written on papyrus.

The only part Iannas remembered well and described in detail was the unexpected flash flood that had taken the caravan by surprise as they crossed a dry river valley eight days out of Susa. When it came it washed away three women, two teenage children from two families, and a number of sheep belonging to shepherds who had hoped to sell them in Susa for a good price. The women and children were found alive and unharmed perched on some higher ground further down the valley. They had survived after holding on to one another as tightly as they could and refusing to let go until a large boulder blocked their onward path, injuring the oldest, but they were able to help each out of the water. Only four of the sheep were found alive while the recovered dead sheep provided the caravan with a fresh supply of meat for the remainder of the journey. Iannas did not remember at all the only other notable event - an early morning bandit alarm raised by the lookouts on the road to Sippar from Nineveh. The raindrops of each day had become one large pool of emotion, and Iannas had been glad to reach Susa.

Iannas and Appa had travelled through the motions of the journey without many words, and Iannas wondered if he should have made more of an effort to talk with Appa. But, like his father, he appreciated this wordless time, for there seemed to be no words to convey their feelings to each other; it felt enough to be with one another. In all, they had originally planned to spend a moon trading in Ur, Lagash and Susa before returning to Nineveh with new goods and enough income to fulfil the needs before the next season's trade journeys. Soon their plans changed, and now Appa would return to Nineveh without Iannas.

It had been a year since Iannas and Daniel had last met and both were so excited to be in each other's company again, Iannas more so than Daniel. Without realising it, Daniel pulled Iannas out of the melancholy that had already consumed him, and only with Daniel did Iannas begin remembering his mother, Ha-Tima, as she would have wanted him to – with the joy of a mother's love.

Ha-Tima discovered her illness very soon after her return from Harran nine moons ago. This had been the only trading journey where she had accompanied Iannas and Appa, having wanted to visit Harran for a long time. The memories of his mother Iannas would remember most intensely would be the time he had spent with her in Harran and how excited and happy she had been.

It was an unhurried but increasingly weakening illness, which if it were a blessing gave Iannas and Appa time to come to terms with the possibility of losing Ha-Tima. The illness soon became acute, and when the deep sleep overtook her from which she did not wake except for one moment close to her death, the illness chose to hurry and half a moon into her deep sleep she passed away. It was strange how the world around Iannas continued as normal after the passing of a mother, a loved one who had given so much love. 'How do people get used to a passing, Appa?' Iannas had asked the day after when the pain was so strong and physically sickening deep within his body.

'No one can, and no one ever will,' Appa had replied finding the words inside his own profound grief.

What Iannas could not permit himself to say to Daniel, were the words. The words that his mother "had passed" had finality; and he could not utter them. The other thing he could not share with Daniel was his dreams. Throughout his young life, Iannas could only remember two dreams; one a fire and the other a touch of a hand, both so insignificant. He was happy not to dream in an era of dreams. One moon before his mother died, Iannas had the two new dreams which arrived on two successive nights, in the same bed, in the same room, and he thought at the same time of night. He remembered waking up on both occasions with a heavy sweat, as if he had actually travelled to that place and moment in the dream, and when he looked out of the window the moon had been in the same position.

In this age of dreams, powerful dreams had a meaning and the dreamer could not escape the dream once dreamt until the significance of the dream was established and the consequences accepted. This was a time where the universe was still able to touch the human soul, and the soul would reply through its ability to dream in the language of the universe.

When Iannas had the first dream, the memory of it, the feeling in his body, his ache, and his soul spoke to him that he had been transported to a new place and he had been in the presence of something too powerful for him to even try to comprehend. Iannas was convinced it was a divine being, too holy to describe. Sixteen year olds did not dream of God. The divine asked a question, and the audience was the world. Iannas was listening from the back, at the very back. Had he crept in uninvited? Was he supposed to be there? Why him? Moreover, what was that sense of vulnerability in the voice of the divine?

The manner of the asking, the emotion of the asking, and the setting, the power and passion it had evoked in Iannas was too heavy for him, and he had no idea what to do with all this complex web of senses and feelings. The next night, his second dream, as holy as the first, saw him enter a room in the presence of a messenger, not a divine being. The messenger, sitting on the floor in the corner of the room next to the small window through which the sunlight had lit the room, was dressed in what Iannas thought were white clothes, but then the entire room was a white recollection. As Iannas approached the messenger from behind his mother, father, and sister, the messenger looked up to his parents and gave an answer to an unasked question,

"Do not worry; everything will be all right."

The words, when spoken, had so comforted Iannas that his fear of the power of the dream of the previous night was also calmed. Iannas would remember these two dreams for the rest of his life. In this era of dreams, dreams of power were extremely rare, he could have done much with them, but Iannas chose not to. No one knew and he had no intention of revealing the dreams to anyone. On the night Ha-Tima passed away, she woke for a brief moment just before her passing from her deep sleep. Iannas was alone with her, his father being outside tending to the animals. As she tried to speak with him, he put his face next to hers, his cheek on her cheek as she had done to him when he had been a baby.

'Your dreams,' she whispered, 'seek the answer to your dreams.' She paused. 'Have no fear. Make the journey. Everything will be all right.'

Iannas was shocked that his mother had awoken after all this time, shaken that she had spoken to him, and in absolute turmoil that she spoke to him of his dreams. So when his father entered and witnessed his tears and then realised that his life companion's breath had left her, he fell into an ocean of sadness, and Iannas' tears in that room at that time were simply passed, assumed, and never questioned or explored.

Iannas once remembered returning from a journey to Babylon with his father, and before the two of them could even say hello to mother, she enquired if something had happened to the two of them the week before on a particular night. Iannas and his father had indeed had a stomach illness that night from having eaten food prepared at a roadside station; both had been violently sick. He never understood a mother's connection with her child until he had children of his own in his later years.

Iannas used these few days to Ur without Appa to describe the melancholy and heavy heart with which he had arrived in Susa. He apologised to Daniel for not telling his friend who only learned about Ha-Tima from his father that night, and even now he still did not utter the words. But Iannas carried good memories of the days that followed in Susa. The days he spent with his friend, and the day Daniel introduced him to two beautiful one-year-old Egyptian donkeys, one male and one female. And what beautiful gentle creatures they were.

It was on the last day of the journey to Ur, when the caravan had made its way across the final river crossing and was barely half a day from Ur, that they crossed paths with a caravan heading to Susa, and almost immediately rumours began to circulate describing some unexpected troubles in the old city the night before. With protests being a common occurrence in recent moons, many ignored the news as usual. The troubles in Ur rarely stopped the caravans, but they did mean more soldiers and more thorough checkpoints. Unbeknown to the travellers, however, the news on this occasion was more serious. The local people of Ur knew, or at least believed, that the uprisings were in protest at the unreasonably high taxes, the many layers of unnecessary bureaucracy, the mountains of rubbish, and very poor unmaintained putrefying contents of the drainage, all of which had amplified since the takeover of Ur by Susa. "Where is the Glory of Ur?" they were shouting.

The Governor of Ur, on the other hand, preferred to believe that the protests were an uprising against the rule of Susa. A delegation to inform the King in Susa had already been sent, and word was spreading that the empire would do everything in its power to put down this treasonous behaviour deemed a threat to the security of the land. The Governor of Ur, a spokesperson for the empire of course, blamed forces from outside of Ur, insurgents from Babylon, and the immigrant Amorite community from Mari and Ebla were accused for good measure as attempting to unsettle Ur for their benefit. Intent on diverting the blame for the protests away from his palace, the Governor inflamed an already delicate situation, and now the Amorite community of Ur were rising up against the Governor whereas before, they had been neutral. Had the Governor of Ur studied history, he would have known that he had made a terrible mistake in attempting to apportion blame to a minority tribe and settle old tribal scores. So began the final step in his decline. The Governor had enjoyed the power. He had neglected his responsibility.

The caravans had yet to receive the news of how serious and ugly the protests had become overnight. The increasingly charged protests had so scared the Governor, and he felt so personally threatened, that he mobilised all his soldiers and closed the city gates on the very day Daniel and Iannas' caravan was due to arrive. The Governor left strict instructions that no one was to be allowed into the city, under the pretext of securing the city from any more insurgents entering Ur and intending to create more havoc. Residents and travellers could leave the city, if they wished, but only during a strict one hour window at dawn. A huge crowd of more than one thousand people had now occupied the city market square the previous night and were refusing to leave until their demands were met. Demonstrators had been beaten, soldiers beaten by retaliating crowds, and in the chaos, a small, young girl and her mother had been trampled on, and both were fighting for their lives. The crowd had now surrounded the Governor's palace and were baying for the blood of the soldiers responsible, and for the Governor, who they believed had ordered the soldiers to strike the protesters.

As Iannas and Daniel's caravan approached, the Governor of Ur had already made use of the secret palace exits, gone into hiding, and was now waiting for reinforcement troops to arrive from the garrison between Susa and Ur. The arrival of the soldiers would likely provoke an already delicate, but in fact resolvable, problem.

The sight of the royal walls of the city of Ur in the distance with the huge floating Ziggurat, or Temple, resting on its own huge monolith at a height above the city wall so it appeared to be crowning the city, meant the caravan would soon disband. But any relief was short lived. As they began to near, numerous soldiers at checkpoints were already in place informing the approaching caravans that the port was open, but the city was on lock down; a curfew. News of the curfew caused some panic among a few, but the veteran travellers were resigned to the circumstances having experienced temporary curfews, if not in Ur, then in other cities on their travels. There was always a power struggle, sometimes in and often between the cities. The lack of worry amongst the seasoned travellers kept the novice travellers calm.

The normally quiet, dilapidated rows of stores and stands for basic supplies and caravan bookings at the east station within sight of the East Ur Gate where the Susa caravan always disbanded already resembled a refugee camp. The profusion of travellers, some waiting, some selling, some buying, and some setting up for the night wherever they could while other caravans were arriving from the north with nowhere else to go, was quickly swelling the camp like a camel's stomach at a watering hole.

Three service stations were located outside the old city: one to the north, one on the west, and one on the east. The southern gate led straight into the harbour. Iannas and Daniel had already put aside any sentiment regarding their fathers and found a quiet place outside of the horde and near a lone small olive tree to discuss their options.

Iannas was worried but did not show it. 'The soldiers say the city is closed, Daniel. There will be caravans heading towards Babylon from the north station. There is much anxiety here. The protests could escalate further and be the start of a very serious problem here in Ur. No one is allowed into Ur, but the soldiers at the checkpoint said that tomorrow morning the gates will be open for city residents and travellers to leave at dawn and only if they have exit permits.'

While Iannas described their predicament Daniel had cast his eyes at the distant city wall and the floating, shimmering Ziggurat in the sky above as if waiting for an offering. Daniel had already thought about his answer. Donkey was temporarily tied to the tree, and both companions had found seats on the damp but firm ground.

'We have to wait for Alizer, Iannas. He told me to wait, and that is what we have to do.' Daniel too was nervous about the situation and was less successful than Iannas at hiding it. Reaching Ur and meeting Alizer was only the first part of his task. The thought of abandoning everything at this very first hurdle was too painful to bear, and he was not going let it happen. He remembered his father's words, "Your task is simple, and once given to you, you are honour bound to complete it."

Iannas too remembered Daniel's father's words, "Think how you will get through and never rush your steps." Iannas was preparing a compromise. Their safety was, at this moment, his only concern.

'Daniel, there will be another caravan heading back to Susa tomorrow and then another the day after. Let us secure a place in one of them for now so, if needed, we have a way out. If Alizer leaves the city to meet us, I cannot see how he will be allowed back in. If the soldiers are right, and a whole troop is making its way from the garrison, it is best to be away before they arrive.'

So many thoughts were going through both minds.

'There has to be something we can do. What if Alizer and the family are trapped inside?' Daniel worried.

'Considering who Uncle Azhar is, the family are probably well protected, Daniel. We need to make sure we stay out of trouble and be safe.'

Daniel reluctantly agreed with Iannas who had said the right words, which reminded Daniel of the sight of his Uncle Azhar stepping into Papa's shop in the main street in Susa and this thought, much to Iannas' relief, brought a smile to Daniel's face.

'Did I tell you how it all started?' Daniel asked knowing full well Iannas had heard the story at least twice before.

'Go on, tell me again if it makes you feel better!' Iannas conceded, sensing his friend would feel more at ease after sharing the story again.

Daniel allowed a calming pause to pass between them and began.

'It was midday, and it had just started raining. Actually it was a downpour.' Daniel laughed, and they both felt good to ease their worries away so quickly, even for a short time. 'Uncle Azhar was getting drenched as he walked hurriedly through the main street of Susa and the street being so narrow, even the water from the shop roofs was draining over him, so he was a sight when he arrived at our doorway. A walking puddle! He is always so particular about his appearance and likes to present himself well with Papa, but on that day, his wet thinning white shoulder-length hair and water-soaked dark green coat complete with muddy feet did not make for the impression I suspect he hoped for.

'I watched him remove his muddy sandals and was pleased to see him glance at the freshly painted shop sign, an image of Donkey, above the door that I had only finished fixing earlier that morning. That is when I saw his face painted with his aura of seriousness. He made no attempt to acknowledge or smile at me, so even as Uncle Azhar was stepping in I quickly called Papa.

'Papa knows I hate being called little one or young Daniel, but that is exactly what he did and in front of Uncle Azhar as well. I am nearly sixteen, you know!

"Thank you, little one!" Papa called out loudly. Papa was in the rear storeroom where he had been examining the small leak that had appeared that day. I did not wait to hear his report of the leak. I left the shop leaving Uncle Azhar to settle, and when I returned with three cups of hot date drink, they were already in conversation, and Papa was in the middle of a reply. He paused as I offered the drinks and sat next to him. We all sipped the warming sweet liquid and through the noise of the downpour outside I listened to Papa's reply.' Daniel tried to imitate his father's deep, mature voice.

"Look, Azhar, I am always at your service. We have looked after each other for as long as I can remember. My first memory of you is when a cart in this very street nearly trampled me, and you rescued me, I was only five years old but the moment has stayed with me. We have treated each other as brothers, and our families are one. But," Papa paused, "how old is your son now?"

'Uncle Azhar answered, "Forty, Fifty? Sixty? We all stopped counting when he got married! What has age to do with this?"

'Papa slapped the table and made me jump, and then in a raised voice, he answered, "I think we can safely say he is old enough, and," Papa emphasised the next bit by saying it loudly and slowly as if he was scolding Uncle Azhar, "he does not need looking after!"

'I thought for a moment Uncle Azhar was going to get really angry at Papa but instead he laughed, I thought it was very funny so I started laughing too.'

'That is a better imitation of your father. You are improving. And you are sure you do not know how old Uncle Azhar is? If his youngest son is as old as that, your uncle must be ancient! Older than Appa! I told you there are rumours about your uncle!' Iannas interrupted excitedly.

'I have never asked him, and you should not be listening to rumours!' Daniel enjoyed the compliment but was otherwise dismissive. 'Anyway,' Daniel continued encouraged by Iannas' interest, 'and then just when Papa started into his loud happy laugh, Uncle Azhar's serious demeanour found him again, and Papa too quickly became serious.

"Daniel, wait." Uncle Azhar always calls Papa Daniel, I find it confusing sometimes but I have got used to it. "Wait until I tell you what this baboon has done." Uncle Azhar said again. Daniel now tried to imitate his uncle's voice. "He has decided that we must all move to Harran. The entire family!"

Iannas stared at Daniel. 'He called his son a baboon? You did not mention this in your previous versions!' Iannas feigned disapproval that a father would call his son such things.

Daniel continued, 'Papa laughed, but Uncle Azhar did not. I remained serious and sided with my uncle. Uncle Azhar was clearly troubled, and I guessed that it might have something to do with news from Urfa, only a short journey from Harran.'

'I know,' Iannas interrupted again. 'The king there has declared himself a god, and no one trusts him. They do not know what he will do next. But like I said before, Daniel, it does not affect us.'

'I agree,' Daniel replied and continued.

'Papa tried to calm Uncle Azhar's worry by saying that his son was probably just bored and needed a change, a new place to revive him.

"Look, Daniel." Uncle Azhar replied, still sincere, serious, and apart from the first time, not another smile covered his face for the remainder of this conversation. I think Papa sensed there was a deeper worry. "I do not care how old he is. He has some madcap ideas of his own, and this King of Urfa will make soup out of him if my son starts opening his mouth. My son is disorganised, gives away pretty much all his money, has no idea how to make money, and is the worst business man I have ever seen, yet he always seems to be making money! His animals multiply overnight! He has been a tragedy since the day he was born, do you remember? We had to hide him for eleven years before we could get him out of the town." Honestly, Iannas, he really did say all that! Papa started laughing again, and if Uncle Azhar had a smile, he successfully hid it from me, and I knew better than to laugh with Papa. Uncle Azhar stared at us with his stern face. I had not heard this eleven years thing before. I am not even sure I was supposed to hear it.'

'I told you,' Iannas reminded Daniel, 'Appa used to tell us stories of a generation of newborns a long, long time ago hidden from the authorities for fear of being put to death. All because the king at the time believed one of the newborns would grow up and become a threat to him. Just old tales, Daniel. No one believes them for real.'

'Well anyway,' Daniel continued as Iannas had intended, without the worries of Ur, 'it was the first time I had heard that Uncle Azhar had a son born at that time. I always called him uncle as well when we met, but we never spoke about anything in particular, and I never spent time with him. Then Papa said, "He was a handful, wasn't he? And how did he end up with the most beautiful girl in town? He must be some sort of a wizard." Papa started laughing again, his deep laugh. Really, he could not keep a straight face even though Uncle Azhar just listened and looked at him seriously. I do miss Papa.' Daniel slipped in the last statement and Iannas noticed but did not comment.

'That is when things turned serious.' Daniel described. 'Papa then referred to Uncle Azhar as "Terah," his formal name, something he only does when they are very solemn with each other. I like the way our languages and tribes translate and alter our names. "Terah" is such a foreign sound in Susa.

"We are brothers, but I have a family of my own, Terah. I have children, and they have their children. I have responsibilities, and, right now, you know I cannot abandon them. Tell me exactly what you want me to do. Let me see if I can help you find a solution." Daniel was still imitating his father. 'That is when things got interesting and Uncle Azhar described the task and insisted a number of times that the task would secure his family's safety. Papa paused and thought for a minute, probably less than a minute, and I knew the moment he looked at me what he was thinking. Papa asked, "And you say this is a journey to Ur, Harran and then straight back home to Susa?"

'Uncle Azhar would trust only Papa with his family's safety. Being Papa's son I knew this trust was to be extended to me, and I always worry that my mistakes will reflect on Papa. I think Papa knew I was ready. I thought I would be able to wait patiently, but then in my excitement I blurted out.

"When do I leave, Uncle?" I just could not wait, Iannas. Uncle Azhar turned to me, still serious and gave me a wet hug. Papa looked at me, nodded, and gave me his blessing.

"I trust you, little one." Papa instructed. "Your task is simple but it will have a great many challenges and once given to you, you are honour bound to complete it. You must not be diverted by anything or anyone else. You are to complete your task and return home. First, find yourself a companion whom you trust and whose company you enjoy. The way to Ur you know. We have been every year for the past six years. To Harran, I have taken you before and our family from Nineveh trade there every year. They will be here tomorrow. I will make the arrangements for you to travel with them as far as possible once I know their arrangements."

'I knew you would be arriving the next day and hoped immediately that you would be allowed to travel with me. There would be so many preparations to make and much to do. Would I be in Susa for the Full Moon Blessing Ceremony? My mind was racing.

'Papa then turned to Uncle Azhar and asked the obvious even though he and I already knew the answer. "What about Alizer? Why not send him ahead?"

"Alizer?" Uncle Azhar replied. "He is the only one I can rely on to hold the family caravan together. The whole family is moving, Daniel. He cannot leave us."

"And there is no one else?" Papa asked again to reassure himself. I was worried for a moment that he would change his mind about me. There were many people in the town that would accept payment for a task like this, but I knew Uncle Azhar was not going to trust his family's safety with anyone. Tradition and honour! You know what it is like. So just to make sure, I stepped in again "When do I leave?' I asked looking at both Papa and Uncle Azhar. I promise I asked in a much more gentle way this time. Then the answer came.

"At the latest, ten full days from today," and as if Uncle Azhar knew what I was thinking, "the day after the Full Moon Blessing Ceremony." And that is how it all began.' Daniel finished and smiled.

Iannas was glad that Daniel was relaxed now. 'I like your father,' Iannas said. 'I can tell from his face, his smile, that he is so contented.' Iannas was in fact thinking about his own Appa who for a while now had lost his usual happy smile. 'You told me he is a member of the town council and even advises the local governor. Do you think that is the reason your papa did not agree to make this journey himself?'

'I am sure it is one reason,' Daniel was wondering the same. 'Uncle Azhar and Papa are brothers, and I know Uncle really wanted Papa to lead the journey for him. There was no one else in Susa, Ur, or anywhere else Uncle Azhar said he would trust.' Daniel paused as if to remind himself and also add drama to what he was about to say. 'Now it is we who are responsible for the safety of Uncle Azhar's family!'

Recounting the meeting with Uncle Azhar gave Daniel hope and optimism again. He had arrived in Ur, and he was not going to give up. 'If residents are allowed to leave at dawn, then Alizer will do his best to come in the morning - or at least he will send a message.' Daniel could not accept that Alizer would let him down.

Iannas agreed but still pushed his compromise, 'Yes, I know. We have to try, but he will need to think of his family first, Daniel. If he cannot leave, he will expect us to make our own arrangements and stay safe.'

Iannas thought for a moment and realised he needed to grasp the options. 'Let's commit to stay here two nights and book the caravan back to Susa the day after tomorrow. That gives us time to find out what is happening. We can camp here well away from the city or the roads. We have to book a place away from here, Daniel. We cannot afford to travel without a caravan. The bandits always pick those that are travelling without protection.' Iannas felt obliged to remind Daniel what he already knew. 'We have always been taught never to venture ahead on our own.'

'I know you are speaking sense, Iannas,' Daniel saw the concession being offered and always thought of his friend as a good diplomat one day. For now, there did not appear to be another option. 'We have to try and we can always extend our stay if the situation calms.' Daniel was disappointed but still hopeful.

'Come on, let's go and book our caravan. We can purchase some food, set up camp, have dinner and then we wait for Alizer. If he looks for us anywhere, it will be here at the east station,' Iannas said, taking the lead.

They settled under the same olive tree after paying the deposit and registering their names at the caravan stand for Susa for the morning after next. The prices were fixed in Ur, unlike Susa where bartering would have been essential.

Both Daniel and Iannas were quietly relieved at having secured a way out if needed but still remained anxious and frustrated as they prepared dinner. There was much to talk about, but little was said. Hoping to start the next day with renewed energy and optimism both nodded off to sleep in front of the fire soon after dinner.

Donkey had already made his allegiance. Once, on the farm, a snake, a rather large one, had suddenly surprised Donkey and Daniel had arrived and taken it away. He trusted Daniel and would protect him with his life. He took delight in being on the road where he knew he belonged. He enjoyed being with Daniel and Iannas, watching them laugh and their light-hearted fights over him. He sensed their deep joy for the world that he shared. He was proud of being Donkey, and proud they were his companions.

3 UR

Day 11.

Even before the sun crept up and caught the top of the olive tree that had been waiting patiently all night to be wrapped by the sun's rays, the birds in the distant lush forest were already awake, washing themselves, drinking the dew on the leaves and making ready for the calling. Soon the sun even seized Iannas and Daniel's rugged morning faces, which shone as if they were moons themselves.

Iannas and Daniel had woken, but remained in their camp bedding listening to the voiceless sound of the nearby departing morning caravan to Susa. It seemed an age for the entire train to pass suggesting a large caravan today. Then as a celebratory roar from the waiting horde in the distance signalled the opening of the Gates of Ur, Daniel and Iannas were serenaded by every variety of bird on Earth. Today would be a waiting day and the birds were already answering two fathers' prayers to watch over their sons. Both fathers, if they had not yet done so, would hear all the details of the curfew in Ur before the end of the day. For now, with the sunrise blessing ceremony concluded, the birds completed their prayers and dispersed to look for food.

It was too early for any conversation between Daniel and Iannas. Mornings were always a time for silent packing routines and walking. Today there was no packing to do and nowhere to walk, so the pattern had been broken, but the silence remained. Both would leisurely enjoy the hot date drink this morning and savour the rest that had unexpectedly presented itself.

Even as Iannas and Daniel were waking and nudging their camp fire back to health so as to be able to prepare breakfast in readiness for the long day of waiting, and while Daniel wondered if Alizer would find a way to get a message to him, Alizer was standing behind the huge gathering of people looking to exit the city at the Gates of Ur.

There was much jostling in the queues at the gates. Exit tablets were being thoroughly inspected and validated with identities, each person was interviewed, asked to proceed for goods inspection and finally make the payment of the current hiked exit tax. The gate would remain open for only an hour, but there were plenty of soldiers on duty and the queues began to dissolve quickly.

Alizer kept his distance from the crowd. He had made a point of dressing in travel clothes today to blend in with the crowd, but unlike most of those keen to depart, he carried only a shoulder bag. He had made Daniel promise to wait for him at the temple steps in Ur in the main market square. With no one allowed to enter the city, it was now up to Alizer to find Daniel, and that was exactly what he intended to do.

He was excited for Daniel. At Daniel's age Alizer was still living on his family farm near Damascus. The farm was a legacy from his grandmother who had purchased the land after learning the husbandry of Egyptian donkeys along with growing crops along the Nile in Egypt. Grandmother had used these methods with so much success on her new farm that she developed a reputation for the best produce and the best animals, especially the highly prized young Egyptian donkeys in the entire region that stretched as far as the Dead Sea to the south and Emar and Mari to the north.

Alizer's entire family lived a life of wealth and privilege. Alizer loved growing up on the farm, which happened to be, not without coincidence for his grandmother had been both formidable and talented, on the trade route where citizens of the world passed by heading to Kanaan and Egypt to the south and Ebla and Antioch to the north. Travellers are always short of supplies for the next stage of their journey, so the farm became a station providing even a bed and place to rest for the night.

After listening to the stories and adventures from the daily travellers, and they always had stories of great cities, cultures, wars, animals and even new gods, Alizer, unlike his siblings, could not bring himself to be interested in managing the farm. He yearned to explore the world but he was never encouraged. He was always told to contain his discussions with the travellers. He felt trapped and spent his teenage years brooding and growing distant from his family.

One day an elderly traveller, Enaqim, heading north to Antioch from Memphis, arrived at Alizer's farm to view the legendary donkeys. He was so delighted with the animals he saw, he ordered four of the special Egyptian donkeys, and requested they be delivered to his farm in Harran, and he was willing to pay extra for the privilege. Alizer, by now a man in his early twenties, immediately volunteered to make the delivery.

Alizer felt guilty as he remembered. His father had been so pleased that his son had at last taken an interest in the business, and fearing that

Alizer would change his mind, he agreed the sale at a bargain price and ensured Alizer was on the road the very next morning.

Alizer greatly enjoyed his journey to Harran and savoured the city of Harran even more. He was mesmerised watching the strange styles of clothes on the travellers from around the world, the assortment of languages, cultures, foods, faiths and traditions. He remembered almost immediately falling under the city's spell as so many others had done before him. He smiled as he remembered Daniel's father teasing him, 'You were more enamoured by those independent, highly educated, and opinionated young ladies of Harran than the city itself!'

For Alizer, it was the city's freedom that captivated him. Everyone was allowed to walk freely without permits and openly worship their God no matter how strange to others, discuss any subject, be it politics or art, publicly and without fear, unlike Damascus. After only one day, Alizer had decided to stay in Harran and Enaqim's elderly wife, for Enaqim was still in Antioch, without hesitation invited Alizer to work for the family. When Enaqim returned from Antioch he was delighted with his wife's choice. He trained Alizer, taking him on all his trading journeys and introducing him to his contacts, and within three moons Alizer had taken over the running of both the business and the family household.

Alizer even made time to continue his studies in the temple libraries and museum collections in Harran and soon became a tutor to Enaqim's three adopted children. The oldest was half Daniel's age. The three had been orphaned during a violent robbery at a nearby village.

Alizer never regretted his decisions, but as he waited at the Gates of Ur amid the nervousness of the city, he wondered what course his life might have taken had he accepted Enaqim and his wife's proposal to be adopted as their oldest son and heir, in keeping with local traditions when an individual or a couple wanted to ensure their inheritance was well looked after.

Although Azhar, the High Priest of Ur, never knew it at the time, he had been the reason for Alizer's decision not to accept Enaqim's proposition that would have made Alizer one of the richest men in Harran.

Azhar had visited the temples of Harran as their guest speaker and prayer leader for a particular holy period of fasting. The High Priest had delivered a particularly fine speech in which he had described Harran as "a blossom, a beacon for tolerance and peace in a world of greed, envy, power and violence". Azhar always used the phrase when describing Harran. Enaqim and Alizer had been at the temple to hear Azhar speak, and they had talked of nothing else for the rest of the evening. Alizer felt something that night, a force that he would later describe as a window into the future. There and then, he had decided that being adopted by Enaqim, while a privilege, was not his destiny, and there was something else, a greater purpose, waiting for him.

That was the last evening Alizer spent with his employer and friend. Life sometimes reflects the greatest of adventures and the greatest of tragedies, just like in the stories of the travellers, Alizer thought, as he remembered how, the morning after Azhar's speech, Enaqim unexpectedly became acutely ill and died.

The sun was only just rising in Ur, and as the dawn light was reaching the Gates of Ur, so Alizer remembered the dawn light streaming through the window of his room in Harran when he was called urgently to Enaqim's bedchamber. Enaqim was still conscious and patiently described severe pain in his thigh and chest; then his speech began to slur, Enaqim seemed to know he was about to pass, and very quickly he could not speak at all. It all happened so suddenly. Enaqim in his last act pulled a golden amulet from around his neck and placed it in Alizer's hand while his wife watched through her tears as her husband breathed his last.

The grief overtook his widow, and within a few days she sold the entire business, the house, packed and moved with her adopted children to her family home in Sogmator. She could not spend a moment longer in the house so full of memories.

She gave Alizer a handsome purse of precious stones as her parting gift with instructions to close all unfinished household and business commitments, and in her grief, she never uttered another word to him.

Alizer watched the nervous crowd jostle its way through the gate, and as the crowd reduced, he too stepped through showing his exit permit and making eye contact with a senior soldier on gate duty who nodded in recognition. He headed towards the eastern station, but as he scanned the scene before him, even he was surprised at the mass of travellers heading in all directions outside the city of Ur. As usual, he kept his composure and did not worry. He knew the language of the world, and he knew Daniel was safe.

The market in Harran had been very packed too the day Alizer first met Daniel's father. Alizer only had one more donkey to sell from Enaqim's estate, and he was already settled in the Harran animal market just after dawn at the time when the more serious buyers came to trade. Daniel's father was attracted to buying a second Egyptian donkey after having made so much money from the first, the one he and young Daniel had bought on their journey to Harran together. Papa, as Alizer soon began to call him too, wanted to renew and take pleasure in his son's joy after having seen young Daniel look after their first donkey. This she donkey was gentler but smarter and tougher than the first.

When the deal was done and in the days following, Alizer and Papa became not just good but close friends. Papa and Alizer quickly became like brothers, and through this relationship Alizer came to know Papa's other friend and brother, Azhar, the High Priest of Ur locally known as Terah, the same priest that Alizer and Enaqim had heard give his rousing speech on the last night of Enaqim's life. During the remaining moon and a half in Harran, Daniel's father, Azhar, and Alizer spent so much time together they became inseparable, and Alizer became family.

There were too many camps around the east station of Ur. Alizer had already identified a camp with two young men and their familiar Donkey in the distance under a tree, but he was still too far away to be sure. Alizer continued to make his way through the busy station until he recognised Daniel; they were family after all, and he quickly headed towards the tree.

Iannas and Daniel had noticed the light becoming louder to the senses, and the new sounds of the latest arrivals to the station looking for new caravans and destinations. With them, the peace of the morning was quickly consumed, and the atmosphere changed as the new visitors unpacked their anxieties carried from the streets of Ur. Iannas and Daniel were now sipping the sweet, hot date drink and Iannas was warming the pan ready to prepare his special scrambled eggs. Iannas knew very little of Alizer and asked if Daniel had any stories of Alizer. Daniel had been remembering Alizer too and did not hesitate.

'Alizer told me how he found it strange and sometimes funny that in our culture, the same as in Harran, everyone was a brother or sister. When he first met them, he thought Uncle Azhar and Papa were brothers because that is how they introduced each other. Alizer told me the story of a first-time traveller from a place called Enkomi. I remember the name because Alizer told me it was on an island far away to the west and gave me a small copper bracelet as a gift from Enkomi. I cannot imagine what an island is like, a place with water all the way around it!'

'One day, you and I will travel there!' Iannas interjected, and Daniel agreed straightaway.

'On his first day in Harran, the trader from Enkomi fell in love with a woman in the market to whom he had been introduced as a sister of a market trader. The very next day, he proposed marriage only to discover, to his great embarrassment, that the 'sister' was actually the trader's wife!'

Iannas laughed as he broke the eggs into the heavily used pan containing the melted warm fat. 'I can understand it happening. I like calling everyone brother, sister, uncle; makes you feel safe sometimes, but I can see strangers being confused and embarrassing things like that happening.'

Daniel agreed and continued, 'The traveller was so mortified by his behaviour. Alizer always says that all travellers should pride themselves on their sensitivity and awareness of local customs, and he said that that the traveller knew his humiliation would stay with him forever. He made his apologies as best he could to both the woman and her husband, and that very afternoon made a quick exit from Harran never to be seen again.' Both Iannas and Daniel laughed until tears were streaming from their eyes.

'So how did Alizer end up running Uncle Azhar's household?' Iannas asked as he stirred the now ready scrambled eggs with his secret ingredient of local Ur hard cheese he had bought from the service station the previous day.

'You will have to ask him yourself when you meet him, Iannas.' Daniel replied confidently. 'If you understand him that is, he is always speaking in riddles. He rarely talks about his past.'

Just as Daniel was beginning to enjoy his eggs, Daniel startled at the gentle tap on his shoulder, followed by a joyous sound.

'I will answer your friend's question, Daniel. I told you I would find you!'

'Alizer!' Daniel recognised the voice. He put down his breakfast, jumped up with joy, and embraced Alizer. 'I thought Ur was shut down. We have even planned to head back to Susa tomorrow.'

They heard a quick rundown as Alizer sat down next to them around the fire and helped himself to the left over scrambled eggs and the hot date drink that Iannas was still topping up and boiling on the fire.

'Ur is locked down, a full curfew. Anybody in the street tonight after dark will be arrested. Last night after the temple prayers, I suspect there were no less than one thousand people marching through the streets to the Governor's residence and shouting for freedom for Ur and a new Governor. There were many clashes and some reports of deaths. Ur has seen many marches before. There is always some demonstration after the prayers, but it has never been as bad as this. It does not feel safe to remain in Ur for much longer.' Alizer hesitated thinking he may have said too much. 'Lovely breakfast,' he added.

'What about Uncle Azhar and the family?' asked a concerned Daniel.

'The family is fine for now. Some of the local priests are being accused of causing the uprisings, and I am keeping an eye on that.'

Daniel and Iannas knew that city governors often blamed priests for using their influence on their congregations to stoke personal agendas. Most of the time the governors were right, but not always.

'I have heard that at least one priest has been arrested for allegedly supporting and inciting the protestors,' Alizer was enjoying the eggs. 'I am still going to make sure that the family leaves in three days as planned. I knew you would be here, so I came to find you and to arrange a caravan for the family.'

'But you won't be allowed back into the city, Alizer?' Iannas was uneasy and also intrigued with Alizer. They had been introduced in Susa, but he had spent no time with him.

'And I see you have found a good companion, Daniel, who cooks very well. You and your young friend will not be returning to Susa.' Alizer announced. Iannas looked at Alizer and smiled at the inference of being young. He was older than Daniel by more than half a year and Alizer knew more of Iannas than he let show.

'You are to go to the town of Uruk four days north from here. Find Rabi, the lapis lazuli trader next to the Chapel of E-an. It means "Heaven" in our language. Take this,' Alizer handed Daniel a small bag of coins, 'to buy more supplies when needed and to book a caravan for the onward journey. I am relying on you, Daniel, and you too, Iannas. When I arrive in Uruk with Terah and the family, it will not be safe for us to stop so I will pick up the supplies you will purchase for me and depart with the caravan you will have booked for the family. Leave any message with Rabi, and I will make sure the family is three days behind you all the way to Harran.'

Alizer took out two identical seals, and a small wet bag of clay. 'When you gather the supplies and book the caravan, prepare a clay tablet like this.' Alizer took a small wet piece of clay and Daniel watched as he shaped it with a sharp writing tool. He wrote his name, 'Alizer of Damascus', underneath, he wrote a makeshift name of the caravan leader and then finally he wrote the destination, 'Uruk'.

'Once you have prepared the tablet, turn it over and with the seal I have given you, press the tablet. Leave the tablet with the supplies. Make a hole and tie it with string to the supplies. It will dry and harden quickly.'

Alizer made a hole in the centre of the tablet to show Daniel.

'When I arrive, all I have to do is show my seal, identical to the one I have given you, press it in some fresh clay which I will carry, and they will match my tablet to your tablet on the supplies you have left for me. That is how they will release the supplies to me, so you must make sure to carry good quality wet clay, press the seal clearly on the underside with the information I need, and tie it securely. You can always prepare two if you think one might break off.' Alizer had been slow and methodical in showing Daniel the procedure, and both Daniel and Iannas had watched and learned and would remind each other if needed.

Alizer gave his bag of wet clay and writing tool to Daniel. Alizer hesitated and then continued, 'It is not safe for the family to spend the night anywhere where they will be noticed.' Alizer repeated. 'Tell me you understand this. Do not talk about your task with people you should not. The family is a good family, Daniel, Iannas, and they need your help right now.'

'How will I know what supplies to purchase and how much you need?' Daniel asked thinking he might have missed something.

'Rabi will tell you. He will provide you with additional coins and a list of the supplies I need.'

Iannas and Daniel looked at each other and looked at Ur in the distance. It looked calm and peaceful. The sea and the port were probably busy as usual and looked as if, from afar anyway, that they were ignoring the demonstrations and the local politics going on in the old city.

Alizer watched Iannas stand and walk to the Donkey. 'Donkey and I are with you, Daniel, all the way. You can rely on us, Alizer, and later you can tell us how you came to run Uncle Azhar's household.'

'It is a beautiful Donkey. He is from one of mine, isn't he?' Alizer remarked. 'Agreed, Iannas. I will tell you tonight. After we have concluded the day's business and made ready your departure for the morning.'

Iannas and Daniel packed Donkey and Alizer accompanied them as they attempted to reclaim their deposit from the Susa caravan stand. Having brought them to Ur in his caravan the day before, the caravan leader looked at them with an element of concern.

'Are you sure you know what you are doing? I know your father, Iannas, and he asked me to keep an eye on you.'

'We are not returning to Susa,' was all Iannas replied by explanation.

The caravan leader reluctantly handed back the money. There was no shortage of customers, and he knew that at some point he would bump into Iannas' father. 'I do this for your family because I know your father, Iannas.' Iannas thanked him and rewarded him with his cheeky smile. Alizer had a quiet word with the caravan leader which Iannas and Daniel assumed was a personal thank you, and they headed towards to the north station from where they would book a caravan to Uruk.

'What will you do, Alizer? How will you get back inside the city? The soldiers told us there was a curfew so I thought it would be impossible.' Iannas asked trying to understand Alizer better.

Alizer gently ignored the question. 'First, we secure a caravan to Uruk for you to leave at dawn and for the family to leave in three days' time. Tell me about your father, Iannas. How was the parting between you?'

Iannas and Daniel described their journey from Susa, and they talked of Appa's stories and his parting as they walked to the north station amongst the masses of travellers heading in both directions. Who would have dared to say that the marks left by each step on the wet ground by two teenagers from Susa, a servant from Damascus, and a donkey outside the ancient city of Ur would last for eternity and would lead the world into a new history, a new chronicle?

Donkey knew.

4 THE STATIONS OF UR

Approaching the northern Ur station, Daniel noticed that Alizer was staring at someone ahead with a look of surprise. When Daniel and Iannas looked in the same direction, neither expected to see the same young lady trader, Sai Tang from India who had travelled in their caravan from Susa, talking to Husha the slave. Husha watched in surprise as he noticed Daniel and Alizer and recognised Iannas too. The last time he had seen Daniel and Iannas was in the Susa Caravanserai learning about looking after donkeys. Sai Tang had spoken to Iannas' father in the caravan and seemed pleased to see the friendly young travellers again.

'Daniel?' Husha called out first and added, 'Alizer?'

Iannas had noticed Sai Tang first, recognising her from the caravan from Susa. He smiled and waved at her before noticing Husha. He hid this well but the wave did not go unnoticed.

The warmth in the welcome between Alizer and Husha and their embrace drew more surprises. Husha began asking, as was his way, a string of questions of Alizer, but Alizer stopped him.

'I have some important things to do first and little time. Let's meet for lunch at noon, and then I will answer your questions, Husha. We can take shelter from the midday sun over there.' Alizer pointed to a quiet place about two hundred steps from the travel path and where an oak tree was happily sized to provide shade for all of them. He handed Husha some money to buy food for the group. Having seen some familiarity among Sai, Daniel, and Iannas, and in recognition of the customs of his family, he turned to Sai, although she had not yet been formally introduced, and added, 'You are most welcome and you must join us,' so that Sai could not refuse.

Sai, who had still to decide what to do with Ur being closed, introduced herself to Alizer and graciously accepted Alizer's invitation to the quiet delight of both Iannas and Daniel. She hid her nervousness well, but there were two who noticed it. One was Husha, who had unloaded Sai's goods in the Susa Caravanserai. Husha had spoken with Sai and her servants for some time in Susa only to see her again that morning at the north station alone, and struck up a conversation with her. Husha gave her a reassuring glance as if to say that she had made the right decision and that these were good people. The other who noticed her nervousness was Donkey, but no one paid attention to him.

Daniel had known Husha for as long as he could remember and had many dealings with him in the Susa Caravanserai. But in the last year he had become increasingly uncomfortable in Husha's company because of Husha's constant need, or was it desire, to uncover everything about everyone he met. Daniel felt suspicious of Husha's motives and nowadays tended to avoid him if at all possible. While Daniel was very indifferent about seeing Husha, Alizer had embraced him and invited him for lunch. If Alizer trusted him, Daniel would also.

Leaving Husha and Sai behind, Alizer, Daniel, Iannas, and Donkey headed towards the caravan booking stands where Alizer took the lead to make his booking for his large family group to travel from Ur to Uruk in three days' time. Alizer was again methodical, and Iannas and Daniel listened and watched attentively, learning everything they could and asking questions when something was not clear. Daniel also booked a place in the caravan to Uruk for himself, Iannas, and Donkey to leave at dawn confirming the caravan stands where they were now as their point of departure.

The next caravan booking from Uruk for themselves and Alizer's family would be Daniel's responsibility.

Iannas was more relaxed when the caravans had been booked. He and Daniel now knew the full scope of their responsibility and the details of the family and the animals that would be following three days behind. Both he and Daniel took on a new aura of maturity and responsibility. They noticed it in themselves and in each other. They had aged and even noticed that people around them treated them differently. Young ones but equals, Daniel thought. They also realised quite independently that they were all they had in this moment of time – each other and Donkey. Friends were precious when you needed them. Too easy to take them for granted, Daniel pondered as he developed a new respect for Iannas and the commitment his friend had made to accompany him.

Alizer felt Iannas and Daniel's thoughts and said, 'This is the best gift your parents could have given you young ones, a gift of responsibility, choice, an opportunity to learn about the world and be free to make mistakes.'

Iannas and Daniel liked what Alizer said, and they shared their apprehensions and hopes. They also hoped that mistakes would be few and not affect Alizer and the family.

'Only me,' Alizer corrected. 'Your job is to make sure I have everything I need. Do not worry about the family. They are my responsibility. I cannot put the burden of the family on you.'

But Iannas and Daniel knew that the responsibility for the family was theirs too. Alizer was trying to be tactful. Alizer changed the subject and pointed out to Iannas and Daniel that they would continue to talk about their first journey for many years. 'Your first journey is always special, Daniel, and the two of you will always remember it and talk about it until you are old in years to your great grandchildren.' Daniel and Iannas laughed, 'Each step you take will connect you to the ground that you touch; this earth that gives us our sustenance. Your eyes will open your heart and begin to fill it with the experiences of a new world. Before now, you relied on your fathers. Now you will learn to see everything happening around you, make decisions, and take responsibility. Learn to love the world that you see through your new eyes, and you will receive from the world so much more in return.'

Daniel and Iannas gathered that Alizer had a way of talking which sounded graceful, but maybe it was their age, for neither could grasp the meaning of some of these words. Alizer probably knew he was not always understood, but it did not stop him speaking in his, sometimes, very reflective way. Deep down, both Iannas and Daniel appreciated his words and the emotion with which Alizer had offered them.

Soon they arrived back at the tree and settled, as Husha and Sai had already prepared a rest area in the shade where they would eat lunch. Husha, patient but persistent as always, gently asked Alizer a second time why he was there with Iannas and Daniel. He already connected the conversation he had overheard between Daniel and Iannas in Susa and was putting the little pieces he could remember together.

When the answer came, they understood why Alizer had chosen a tree well away from the service station and away from prying ears to rest under. They sat in a circle under the tree, eating dates, fresh yogurt and labneh, a local sour cream delicacy, bread, olives, and pomegranates. To top it all there was olive oil and wine for dipping bread and a pot of hot date drink to quench the thirst.

Alizer congratulated Husha on the choice of food. 'The family is moving to Harran, Husha. The decision was made many moons ago, but the family only agreed the date for moving last moon. I had thought I had a little more time to organise the last few things for the move. No one expected that the uprisings would start right now. Terah, Azhar as you call him, Daniel, wants to retire, but no one officially retires from the temple at a time of uprising it seems, so he is having to explain himself to the Governor and the court officials. Everyone is suspicious now, and instead of leaving freely, we look as if we are fleeing. It is not a good situation for the family, but the son has insisted that we stick to the plan. He is right of course.'

Daniel and Iannas were surprised by Alizer's openness with Husha, and in front of Sai, a stranger. Alizer had his reasons.

'I had already arranged with Daniel's father to help with the move. We need to move as fast as possible between one caravan and the next and cannot afford to be delayed. Daniel's father could not commit his time to the task so he has sent young Daniel. And what a fine choice. This is Daniel and also Iannas' task now.' Alizer smiled at the two young men.

'Daniel will always be three days ahead of us. He will buy the fresh supplies needed at each place, mark them as I have shown him, and leave them for us so we do not have to enter any town or city and stop to buy the larger supplies or even find shelter in the cities. He will also arrange for the next caravan to take us onwards.'

'How will we know where to go after Uruk?' Daniel asked.

'On my last trip, six moons ago, I made all the arrangements. Rabi will give you the next set of instructions. It has all been arranged. Trust yourselves and trust me; it is better for you that you do not know the full details in case things go wrong. It is also not the right place or time to discuss the entire journey in case our voices carry. You will need to learn and make decisions along the way.'

Daniel already knew his responsibility, and for him the task was very simple. He had helped his father buy supplies the last few years, so he knew what to buy and from where. He and Iannas had a greater understanding now, and they continued to grow into their deeper selves. They were impressed with Alizer who was living up to his reputation as one of the most reliable, organised and steadfast people in the land. Daniel and Iannas were already awed with how much they had learned from him in such a short space of time. What an amazing first journey to be taking by themselves they were thinking. A dream trek!

Both Sai and Husha were also impressed with the task given to these two young people and acknowledged Daniel's first undertaking for a journey. It was plain that Husha wanted to express his reservations, but Alizer did not give him the opportunity.

'Iannas and Daniel, if everything goes according to plan, I will see you again in Harran. I anticipate two moon cycles of travel depending on the route you choose, the weather, and I have no doubt you will get through the challenges that will come your way. The fastest I have completed the journey is fifty days, but I was much younger then and travelled with the smaller, faster caravans. I have heard news of a drought in the west, north of Damascus. It should not affect us but let us be alert.'

'When will you head back to the city, Alizer? Will they let you back in?' It was Husha asking the question.

'I have time, in fact the remainder of the day and night. The doors do not open till dawn, so I have the whole day to make more arrangements from this side. I will leave you in the middle of the night to make sure I am at the gate when it opens. I have made an agreement with one soldier at the door, and he will make an exception and allow me to enter as long as I am discreet.'

Iannas was worried about his father. Both his and Daniel's fathers would soon hear about Ur; they might already have done so. Daniel shared his concern.

'How can we send a message to your fathers, Iannas, Daniel?' Husha was thinking ahead.

Alizer answered and was clearly pleased at Husha's concern. 'Not to worry, I have already sent a message with the caravan leader to Susa. He knows the family, and he will tell Daniel's father that they are both with me and safe.' Alizer had done this discreetly after the deposit had been refunded so as not to appear patronising; he now realised he need not have worried.

They all wanted to know about Sai and Husha, but Alizer cautioned them that there was still much to organise and suggested they continue after he returned from organising some extra supplies. Daniel and Iannas supported the motion, as they too had supplies to buy for the next stage.

Alizer did not waste time. He thanked and complimented Husha on the food and headed in the direction of the new improvised station market that appeared to be growing with the refugee invasion that morning.

Alizer had not shown any anxiety about the journey or the roles that Daniel and Iannas had to play. This had been extremely reassuring to Daniel and Iannas. When Alizer returned and saw that they had already purchased and sorted their supplies, even bought some extra for the evening meal that Husha and Iannas were now preparing, he was pleased, but had not expected anything different. Alizer filled his clay beaker with hot date drink that was boiling on the fire, sat and relaxed.

'Where is the young lady?' he asked and just as he finished asking he noticed Sai in the distance heading to the camp from the direction of the caravan stands.

Sai was just in time for the performance of the twilight colours, the prayers of the forest birds as they gave thanks for the day's cuisine and the disappearing sun, which they all watched muted, lost in their own thoughts. Husha called the group for the fire roasted chicken, rice, bread, yoghurt, and more laban, and Sai unwrapped olives, more bread, and a large basket of pomegranates as a way of returning the welcoming hand extended by Alizer and the group.

'Be the first to extend your hand,' Iannas was thinking as he remembered how Alizer had invited Sai into the group and how Sai was now expressing her appreciation. He was impressed with Sai's grace and her sensitivity.

The meal distracted Iannas and Daniel from any apprehensions of the adventures to come. The clear sky gave warning of a cold night, but the waning moon and the stars welcomed the night with ease.

Over dinner, to eager young ears, Alizer told the story of Ur during the time of its majesty, a hundred years ago when, he claimed, it had been the greatest city on Earth, and indeed he was probably right. He apologised that Sai would not see the city and the old magnificent buildings and temples from the time.

After dinner, with the relaxed atmosphere created by Alizer, Husha reminded everyone that although he was an Egyptian slave, he ran the caravanserai in Susa.

'It is strange being here. These are the very shores where the gang of slavers, who attacked our quarry in Egypt in the middle of the night taking all the stonecutters they could catch, brought us to be sold.'

Husha was a particularly large man and how on earth the slavers first managed to trap him and hold on to him was always a mystery. But Husha's renown in Susa, as Daniel knew, was not his size but for his continuous chatter; most people had very little time for him. In fact, Daniel was surprised at the brevity of Husha's description. He had heard the story told many times and was surprised Husha did not take advantage of the captive audience in front of him.

'You are not going to tell us again about the slave ship with the rats and cockroaches?' Daniel could not resist. 'How your constant talking drove your captors to near madness? That is the best part of the story.'

Husha, however, did not see the value in repeating the story tonight. Daniel wanted to hear the version where the slavers attempted to be rid of him by throwing him overboard only to be saved at the last moment by the ship's captain who pointed out the good price he was likely to bring in the Ur slave market and assured them he would be the first to be sold.

'The Ugibi family!' Husha attempted a response. 'They owned most of the businesses in Susa including the caravanserai. They now owned me. There is not much more to tell.' Husha did not mince his words, and he continued in his very confident manner that might have been interpreted as very pompous and offensive for a slave by a different group of people.

'When I told my new owner that my name was Djadsefptah, he could not pronounce it and immediately wanted to name me Ahu-Shina. He told me it meant friend, but I knew enough of the language to know it meant foreigner, and I did not like it. So I suggested Hushina, which sounded more Egyptian to me. By the time we arrived in Susa someone had shortened it to Husha and the name has stuck ever since. I was such a good purchase for the family, almost eight years ago, that for the last five years I have been running the family's entire caravanserai in Susa.'

'Very unusual for a slave and often frowned on by most people,' Alizer pointed out.

'Ugibi or Ubi, as he prefers to be called, did not care. The traders got to know me, and I learned to have access to the information they wanted. Through me, everyone knew what goods had arrived and what goods were on the market well before the Susa tax clerks. As long as I made money for both Ubi and the traders, nobody cared.'

Daniel and his father had dealt with Husha in Susa too and Daniel quickly mentioned how it was Husha who had found a mate for their donkey when she was in heat.

'The same donkey that Papa bought from you in Harran, Alizer. It was Husha who found us a beautiful Egyptian he-donkey.' Daniel knew but did not want to say that as a slave Husha made no money for himself; he assumed everyone already knew, and he was right of course. But that was not the complete story. Money was not Husha's interest. Husha's currency was information. Even when Daniel and Iannas had talked of travelling to Ur and Harran and then ran off, Husha knew he had to find out more and if this information would benefit him.

Iannas was surprised to hear Husha talk about his enslavement without any emotion. Iannas wanted to explore further but decided he did not know Husha well enough.

Alizer was particularly interested in Husha's family ties in Egypt and asked many questions. How did he end up working in quarries in Aswan? in Thebes? in Memphis? Then Daniel asked how he came to be in Ur that day.

'Before I tell you, let me describe for the others the chaos that you and Iannas created in my caravanserai the day Iannas arrived with his father.'

Iannas and Daniel knew what Husha would say and listened with smiles on their faces as Husha described the series of events with his own dry sense of humour that not everyone appreciated.

'I had just finished showing Iannas' father to the storeroom where his goods would be unloaded and recorded for the tax clerks when the next thing I hear is a loud scream! I turned and there I see this brazen young man standing on a stool, which I could see had been made vacant momentarily by a young woman who had stood to help her younger sisters with their food. The young ladies, along with everyone in caravanserai, watched in astonishment, but I must say without any derision as Iannas shouted for the second time, as loudly as he possibly could, one word to the whole world. "Daniel!"

'It was a loud scream; I think he must have been saving his voice for this moment. There were at least two hundred young, old, and extremely middle-aged people in the courtyard. They all stopped their business of ordering drinks, drinking, and sharing the news with one another and, as if in a temple choir being led by the priest, turned their heads together towards this messy upstart. What they saw was a sixteen-year-old young man with shoulder-length dark hair, dust covered well-travelled and ready-to-be-replaced sandals, and an equally dustcovered well-worn plain tunic. His only redeeming feature was the cheeky grin that he held as he waited for the reaction that only came after the obligatory pause, and then everyone smiled. Even his father laughed loudly. Of course, almost everyone in Susa is called Daniel, but that is another story.

'Then I see young Daniel walking over to Iannas and I notice that my stone bench, where I always have my break, is free. But did I get any peace? No. I hear a huge fuss and turn to see these two running through the crowd of two hundred, previously well settled customers, being chased by five hunting dogs, who in turn were being chastened by three young waiters. And they were heading right towards me. Where did these two want to sit? Right where I was about to sit myself.'

The description brought good laughter into the group. Husha was glad his humour was being appreciated.

'A little quiet corner I normally reserve for myself. Of course, they ignore me, sit, and start their conversation, keen to tell each other their news. All I heard was something about donkeys and also about some journey.

'When I tried to talk to them, they looked at me as if I was some interfering old man – which I am of course, stood, and left without another word. How rude they were.'

Alizer, Sai, Iannas and Daniel were still laughing at Husha's narration; most of it was quite accurate.

'Anyway, that is when Sai arrived in the caravanserai with her cart full of tea from India. I left and organised the goods for her and even arranged the sale for the tea on the same day.' Husha finished.

'So what brought you to Ur?' Daniel reminded Husha.

'I travelled with my master from Susa to make a first delivery in Babylon and then a second in Ur. Ubi has a small home in Babylon and many business interests. Ubi is elderly but usually very healthy and strong. In Babylon, he became sick. In fact, too sick to travel. The doctors said something about the food he had eaten. At my suggestion, Ubi prepared a permission tablet so that I could travel with one of Ubi's business partner's who was travelling to Ur so that I could make the delivery as planned. I arrived here last night only to find the gates already closed. Ubi's business partner decided to continue to Lagash this morning and told me to wait here until he returned. A slave is not allowed to travel without an overseer, a custodian, and so here I wait. I have sent word back to Ubi with a caravan; maybe he will send other instructions.'

Husha's clothes, simple and drab and clearly a slave's attire, would attract attention at the checkpoints, and there were plenty of them. If he were caught, he would be arrested very quickly. The empire was already scared of troublemakers.

'It is probably not safe for you here alone either, Husha,' Alizer pointed out. 'What were you delivering to Ur?' he asked.

'Very valuable paints and pigments for temple restorations to be delivered to the Office of Restorations in the main square,' Husha explained, pointing to the two large bags attached to the pole under the tree.

'I will take them, Husha,' Alizer offered. 'I know the manager in the office.' Husha was grateful; at least he would not have to carry them back to Babylon.

'Tell us more about the pyramids in Egypt, Husha,' Sai asked. The others were collectively glad at hearing her voice and that Sai had felt relaxed enough to take part in the discussion around the campfire.

'They are glorious,' Husha claimed. 'They will be the greatest human-built structures ever - mark my words - and Egypt is going to be the world's most powerful and richest country and empire. The Gods have blessed the Egyptians with a strong culture, ambition, and greatness,' he added boldly and continued his descriptions.

When Husha completed his glorification of Egypt he finished off, 'After I unloaded the tea sacks in Susa, I did not see this lady again,' he pointed to Sai, 'nor did I expect to. Then, to my surprise, I saw her here alone this morning and only just began talking with her when you arrived.'

Husha motioned for Sai to take over and she began with what was foremost in her mind; the closure of Ur and how it had left her at a loss. She had not yet decided where she would head to next. She was seventeen years of age and had married less than one year ago to an adventurous, young, wealthy landowner from a village close to her own in the mountains on the China-India border. Having recently married, her husband had no intention to leave her alone for such a long journey. So she undertook her first journey away from her mountain with her husband and their servants almost half a year ago. They travelled through the mountains to avoid the great floods in India and reached Afghanistan carrying tea from their mountain plantations. They did not sell the tea in Afghanistan, as the prices would be higher in Mesopotamia. Instead, they bought lapis lazuli with the extra gold her husband had carried. The cities in the south were always looking for new supplies of blue lapis for their temples, palaces, and nobles' homes. Her husband had made this journey before and prices for lapis in

Mesopotamia, with the high demand and low supply, were a lucrative prospect.

Almost as soon as they set off with their new load her husband became seriously and violently sick. They stopped in a village in Afghanistan to care for him, but there were no medicine men the like of those in India or China. The sickness was short, less than half a moon, and he died in the village, where they cremated his body according to his custom. The locals said that his blood had become poisonous from the mosquito bites, and there was currently an infestation in the region. Sai had little time to grieve and very quickly she had become the lady in charge; her servants looked to her for guidance. They helped her by teaching her everything about her supplies, her goods, the accounts, and the caravan. She learned quickly, she had to. Rather than go back, she took counsel from her servants, who respected her for this. They recommended that finishing the journey and selling their wares was the best and only option. One servant, the accounts keeper, knew exactly where the lapis lazuli was to be sold, as he had made a deal with a trader from Babylon on a previous journey.

After selling her lapis lazuli in Babylon for a record price, she and her servants went onwards to Susa, where the value of her stock of Indian tea was the highest in the region. In Susa, she paid her servants handsomely and released them from any further obligation to her. She and her servants knew that for Sai to return home as a young widowed woman would put her in great difficulty. On her mountain and according to the local tradition, widows never inherited anything after the death of their husbands. Occasionally, widows would marry an unmarried brother of the deceased husband if there was one. All the land would be distributed to her husband's brothers. More often, the widow would be turned out of the household to fend for herself. The servants knew Sai's predicament, and they also knew that they too would be out of work if they returned, so they rallied round their new mistress and helped sell her wares at the highest prices possible in the hope of a bonus. They had been fortunate; the price of lapis had more than tripled since the previous year as a result of the high demand caused by the rivalry between the city temples and the reduced stocks due to the increasing numbers of bandits on the northern route.

Sai left Susa with a few of her former servants who hoped to catch a boat to India or China from Ur and look for new work. Sai had planned on staying in Ur to decide the direction of her next journey in life. One thing she was sure of, the mountain was no longer her home. She had hoped to make time in Ur to pray and find her way. She knew she needed to invest her new wealth, and make a new home, but she did not yet know where that would be. Now that Ur was closed, she needed to find another place to stop and seek guidance from her God. Whatever her circumstances, she had enjoyed these lands and felt good discovering new places and cultures.

It might have been her voice, her posture, her confidence, and her independence, with the combination of her simplicity in dress and manner that had mesmerised her listeners, so no one noticed that she had finished. Each was lost in his own reasons for wanting her to succeed. The most likely reason for this pause was that a wealthy, recently widowed young woman was expressing her gratitude to the world for having succeeded in reaching this point in her journey and in her life, regardless of the continuing obstacles.

Iannas realised that the confidence she exuded was not certain. It was still young with a hard edge and that it had emerged as a result of events of the last six moons. While he could see her strength and admired it, he also felt the reasons for her intensity and experienced a deep sadness that he connected to the loss of his mother. Catching a glimpse of how Sai had dealt with her adversity enabled Iannas to transfer his grief into a new vessel, this time filled with hope and inspiration.

Alizer asked himself a different question. How did she happen to be in this place at this time? What was her place in this universe? He did not know of India or China, of women on her mountain, and wondered how Sai had found the courage to make it through in this new land. Alizer knew something else, something Terah believed in and taught him - destiny. Alizer believed in a world of natural forces that always shifted or, he thought, conspired to bring events together. It was her purpose, here with them, at this time, that he was contemplating when she reached the end of her story.

They may have guessed that Sai did not share her complete feelings. Sai was alone in a strange land, amongst a strange people and could not reveal her weaknesses, fears, and uncertainties to anyone. She had protected herself from them ever since her husband had become ill, and she could not bear to be prepared for the worst. The journey had been her medicine. She had walked her fears away. Her silent grief and pain had leaked slowly into the soil with every step through the soles of her feet. She walked her shyness away, learned to walk into herself, and realised she was capable of so much more. She walked and discovered she knew how to learn, and whatever she learned, whether it was the accounts, the inventory, managing the servants, or the art of negotiation, her new knowledge filled her with hope and a new realisation of endless possibilities with every step she took.

The fire was still burning strong, and Iannas took the moment to remind Alizer to tell his story of how he happened to be running Azhar's household.

'Daniel's father and I first met when I sold him a purebred Egyptian donkey in Harran. This donkey's mother as a matter of fact.' Alizer pointed to Donkey who was already resting on the ground but appeared to be listening intently. 'When the deal was done and in the days following, your father and I shared a thirst for knowledge and wisdom that endeared us towards a deep friendship, and we became brothers very quickly. Through him I came to know your Uncle Azhar, the High Priest of Ur, who is known as Terah in Harran. While in Harran, the three of us spent so much time together we became inseparable.

'Your Uncle Azhar is considered a very wise man, and his teachings have a huge following in Harran. He was there at the invitation of the temple. Did you know his very presence almost doubles the congregations?' Alizer wondered if Daniel knew.

Iannas squeezed in. 'I thought his popularity was due to the rumour that Uncle Azhar is descended from a tribe who are known to live almost twice as long as other people.' Iannas laughed. Appa had told him a story about a 'mythical' tribe, the ancients, the first tribe.

'It helps his popularity, and Uncle Azhar does little to dispel the rumours, that is true.' Alizer admitted, joining the laughter. 'I was looking for a new position, for my previous employer had passed away and I was settling his estate. Harran had been a gift; it gave me so many opportunities. I was even fortunate enough to spend one moon in the Harran Royal Palace recording and studying the palace art and tablet collection. I learned a number of languages and to read and write the languages of Antioch, Mesopotamia - two ancient languages found only on the tablets in the museums of Harran - and Egyptian. I learned so much knowledge in the libraries and museums as well as from the many different travellers I came across in Harran that I became confused. I could not put the pieces of all the world's knowledge together. I was even becoming perplexed about the purpose of the world and our purpose within it, but your uncle had a way of blending different perspectives and knowledge together into a concept he called "united humanity with a single wisdom and one source of knowledge". It had a huge impact on me.'

Daniel and Iannas looked at each other clearly mystified by the phrase, but said nothing.

'When your father and uncle were ready to return to Susa and Ur, Azhar persuaded me to work for him and run his household. I finished my obligations in Harran and placed myself in his service and mentorship.' Alizer said this with deep satisfaction, and everyone noticed.

Alizer quoted a poem from an ancient tablet he had studied. 'Wisdom and nature are one and the same. They have their own power, their own force which compels seekers of knowledge towards them as if it were sustenance, and once the seekers have absorbed and become intoxicated, they allow the drunk to disperse, carried like the wind to new lands, dressed in new voices and new tongues so that wisdom may be shared and new knowledge explored.'

Again, Daniel and Iannas appeared completely baffled by the words and caught each other's eye, but as before stayed silent.

'Choosing to follow and serve your uncle's family is the most honourable thing I have done, and it was a decision that has transformed my life. Your father, Daniel, continues to treat me as a brother, and I will always be grateful to him for introducing me to your uncle. I have learned to follow the voices of the world with my heart and my eyes and translate them into the language of the world. My advice to each of you is transpose the beauty in what you hear and see into your own music, and that music will connect your soul to the soul of the world.

'This is now getting way too confusing for me," Iannas admitted at last, not able to hold himself while enjoying the pomegranates. Daniel quickly nodded in support.

'When I was younger,' Daniel reinforced, 'Alizer used to speak like that to me all the time, and I would just nod. I never understood a word of it either.'

Alizer laughed with Husha and Sai. 'You never told me that before! I have to admit, living with your Uncle Azhar, I have been able to understand spirituality, destiny, and what the ancients called the 'The Laws of Goodness'. I learned more of the Gods from your Uncle Azhar, and I also taught him about the ancient kings and the ancient knowledge as described in the archived tablets of Harran, found and studied by the famous Queen Zugalum many centuries ago.'

Daniel added, 'Papa told me he watched how the journey from Harran bound you and Uncle Azhar together.'

'Your father is very perceptive Daniel.' Alizer welcomed Daniel's thoughtful comment.

While Husha felt at ease with the group, he did not shy away from his concerns and voiced them confidently, 'Do you not think they are too inexperienced, Alizer, for a task like this? There will be so much for them to do at each stop to make sure everything is arranged for you and the family. This is not an easy undertaking.' He wanted to say they were too young but instead had chosen the word 'inexperienced' to make a stronger case.

Iannas and Daniel did not like being referred to as 'they', but wisely did not rise to his bait. They were confident too and were glad to have this conversation in the open. They had also wanted to know why Azhar had been so quick to accept young Daniel as the one for the task when Azhar had specifically approached Daniel's father.

Alizer answered as if reflecting Daniel's thoughts. 'Azhar chose young Daniel. I trust his choice with my life. I trust Daniel, and now Iannas, not only with my life but the lives I am responsible for, Azhar's family. Look at Sai, Husha, she is not much older.' Sai seemed embarrassed to be brought into the conversation. 'She is in charge of her own wealth, she trades, and she knows the roads already at this young age. She learned and you learned at their age, I am sure.' Sai now felt better at the way Alizer has complimented her. 'I wish I had had the opportunity and trust at that age and been set free to have my own adventures, make my mistakes, and learn in my own way about the world.' Alizer was remembering his protected youth.

Husha's reply expressed his own personal circumstance. 'They have more hope than I do.' No one commented but listened to his pause.

'There is something else,' Alizer continued. 'Sometimes the right people are in the right place for a task, and for this particular task Iannas and Daniel are not to be faulted. They will realise this along the way and when they arrive in Harran.'

Iannas and Daniel did not understand what Alizer meant, but they felt stronger hearing Alizer's remarks and felt closer to him.

Sai used the moment and told the story of her God, Krishna. She viewed him as the father of the world and how it was said that he too had journeyed to these lands many years ago. She was glad at least that these lands were not strange to her God, so she was not entirely a stranger. Alizer had not heard of the tradition of Krishna and asked if Krishna might be known by a different name just like some of the local gods had different empires of the region, but there was no other name that Sai had come across.

Then as the stars reigned over the darkness, Donkey was fed, and each began to find a place around the tree and fire to sleep. Sai asked if the group had any objection to her sleeping in the safety of the group. She had slept in the safety of her servants the night before and did not wish to be alone. The camp was already her camp, they all insisted. The welcome left an impression on Sai and she selected a spot next to Donkey to sleep, where she knew she would feel warm and comfortable and away from passing eyes.

Many years later when Iannas was to watch the fireworks in the city of Manali near Kullu in the Himalayan Mountains in Northern India with his eldest and most loved, he would remember this day at the Station of Ur when he met his first beloved. He would ask himself how the decision to join Daniel on his mission had changed his heart and his mind. He would ask his eldest if he had loved enough and had he lived his life well? Had promises of young love broken his heart, or had they make it wiser? They would talk of each other's destinies, and his daughter would listen and tell him that 'everything had unfolded just as it was supposed to.' She would also make her Appa recollect everything he could about her mother for the rest of the day and night.

5 THE ROAD TO URUK

Days 12-14, 10.2 Beru.

The birds had not yet gathered for the sunrise celebrations, and the night was still firmly in charge when Alizer awoke Daniel. Alizer spoke quietly and softly, and Iannas, who was next to Daniel and having not slept too well, was alert. Sai and Husha's heavy breathing, including some gentle snoring from Husha's direction, were the only sounds to be heard.

'I have a precious item for you to carry and put away before the others wake up.' Daniel may have been asleep only a short moment ago but he was already listening intently. 'It should not be seen by anyone until you meet me again in Harran. You must not unwrap it or show it to anyone,' Alizer repeated. 'It is a book of thoughts and stories. Hide it well. If anyone discovers it, claim you know nothing of its origin or its contents as you are only delivering it. I know you can read, Daniel, but if pressed claim you cannot. In these times, everyone is afraid of something they do not understand and will consider this book a threat.' Daniel and Iannas knew the paranoia of the world and both their fathers had separately lectured them on this subject.

'If anyone asks who you are delivering this to, tell them you are delivering it to Ibi-Faru of Harran. He was the brother of Enaqim and also a local artist, and,' Alizer paused and clearly had not finished, 'if anyone asks who gave it to you, say "Alizer of Damascus". This will absolve you of any responsibility, but it is better if you hide it and nothing more is spoken of it.'

'What is in the book?' Iannas asked. Alizer knew, of course, Iannas had been listening.

'In Harran I will tell you, Iannas. Whenever you camp, make sure you tie the donkey well. I would suggest you tie a long rope to both your feet, Daniel. If someone tries to steal him you will know straight away.' Alizer, who had spoken softly all this time, said this last statement more loudly and smiled but did not know if Iannas or Daniel had appreciated his humour. It was too early in the morning, he guessed.

Daniel had already slipped the well-wrapped and tied cylinder-shaped package into his shoulder bag intending to transfer it into Donkey's saddlebag when Sai, who was still sleeping between Donkey and the supplies, awoke.

Alizer strolled over to the other side of the tree where Husha had slept a distance from the others. 'Time for me to go, Husha.' Husha stirred as Alizer woke him.

Soon everyone was awake in the still dark of the night. Alizer made his farewells, having so quickly endeared himself to the group. There was something on his mind, something he wanted to say to Husha and Sai. He thought better of it. If they want to travel with Iannas and Daniel, let them ask, he thought. This is Daniel and Iannas' journey.

They watched Alizer disappear into the darkness carrying Husha's supplies for the temple across his shoulders and leaving behind a mixed sense of anticipation, excitement and uncertainty. The sun had still to signal its morning ritual, so nothing apart from the travellers stirred. Alizer was in good time to reach the gates before they opened at dawn.

Daniel and Iannas packed the supplies, and Donkey was made ready for the next stage of the journey. While everyone was busy clearing the camp, Daniel slipped the package given by Alizer into Donkey's saddlebag, which was by now already well-hidden and camouflaged by the large sacks of supplies. Sai packed her bedding into her small bundle of personal items that she would carry on her shoulder, having sold, discarded, or given away everything she did not use or need to her former servants. Husha made a last check of the camp, ensuring nothing was forgotten and all the rubbish had been burned in the campfire.

Packing completed, they sat briefly and silently around the warm fire to sip the date drink prepared earlier by Iannas, and as they were finishing, Sai made a declaration. 'I would like to travel to Uruk with you.' Iannas and Daniel looked at her with some surprise as she explained. 'There is nothing for me here. Would you mind if I travelled with you?' Sai had been thinking about what to do and clearly did not want to stay in the refugee camp outside the walls of Ur on her own. Iannas and Daniel both smiled broadly and Sai could see the delight in their faces.

'Great!' she replied even though her two chaperones had not said a word. 'You will have to help me make a reservation in your caravan.'

Husha looked at the three of them and they noticed his despair. Each was fearful of being the first one to say the wrong thing and make the situation worse for him.

'I have a suggestion, Daniel,' Husha himself came to the rescue. 'Let me give you my ownership and travel permit. Let me travel with you to

Uruk and then onwards to Babylon. I can travel as your property. It is meaningless for me to stay here, and I have no other option but to return to my owner, Ubi.' Without even hesitating, Iannas and Sai looked at Daniel with a plea on their faces that Husha saw and was embarrassed by; equally quickly all three smiled together. Daniel had misgivings, but also knew that everyone trusted Husha. He was not going to leave Husha at the station.

'I am glad you asked, Husha. Of course, we were not going to leave you here. Give me your tablet. If anyone asks, I am now your steward, and you are accompanying us to Babylon to look after us young ones,' Daniel stressed the two last words with sarcasm, 'and to ensure our safety.' Husha understood and returned Daniel's sarcasm with a frown. He was in a better situation than he had hoped for and better than it was only moments ago. While Husha should have been pleased, he did not feel it deep down. His heart was heavy and it was slowly consuming him.

Husha's despair was not for himself. It was despair, maybe a melancholy, for the world. The short time spent the previous day with Daniel, Iannas, and Sai, and their joy and hope for life had reminded him of his own hopes as a youth and how he would change the world. The despair that had grown inside him these past years was now surfacing, and the pain and guilt was consuming him. He had made sure he learned everything he could about different people, traders, places, tribes, priests, and governments. His skills in connecting information had been so useful and profitable for the Ugibi family in running the caravanserai in Susa, and he knew he was appreciated, but it was not enough.

He had been seeking something in particular, and he had been close. And just as a bird flies when someone gets too close, the gates of Ur had closed the very day of his arrival.

It was the astrologer in Susa who had first put him on the trail to Ur by asking Husha, who had already established himself as the archetype of discretion, to find out everything he could about five elders from a particular tribe residing in the eastern district of Susa. The request, the subsequent information Husha collected, and the relationship with the astrologer slowly led Husha to connect pieces himself without the astrologer realising. Nothing seemed clear at the time, but there was always a thought, maybe a conclusion, that kept returning the more he learned, and the conclusion was not one he was expecting or even ready for.

If only Ubi had not fallen ill in Babylon, he would have been here earlier before all these troubles. Husha's intuition was still not confirmed. His despair, however, concerned what the world would do with this knowledge. He did not admit it, but his despair was also a realisation of his place and his role in the darkness he had become joined to. He tried to shrug it off, but he had lost his trust and faith in the human condition, and everyone with power now appeared corrupt to him. Last night, as he listened to Sai, her words and her story reminded him how much he had loved life once and the hopes and dreams of his youth, which only served to cast a light on the treachery, fraud, lies and wickedness that hurt his very soul. And yet his own life was also a lie, even now, as he was standing ready to move with the caravan to Uruk. The manner of Alizer's greeting and the warmth of his welcome haunted him. He had not touched such kindness and compassion in his years since he had left Egypt casting his despair deeper into an abyss of his own creation.

Iannas and Daniel had made good with the caravan leader after informing him of the two extra travellers and paying their fares. They all absorbed the atmosphere as they watched the activity, heard the sounds, and felt the weight of the huddle of travellers, carts, animals, caravan guards and very relieved families from Ur slowly stretch into a meandering living chain that each was giving life to.

As the sun rose and blessed the birds for a good day's food hunting and delivered its warm gift to all the creatures of the world, for a fleeting moment the sunlight created a mood and feeling that existed only in that instant and entered the hearts of those souls already unlocked to the world. The land showed its gratitude to the sun for returning and in turn warmed up its progeny.

Husha took an interest in Donkey with his three white feet and white tipped ear. 'You have looked after your donkey well,' he said, and Daniel and Iannas, who were taking turns to look after Donkey, appreciated his praise.

'We learned from Papa and the many travelling donkey owners in the Susa caravanserai,' Daniel replied knowing that they had been frequently noticed and watched by Husha the slave.

'We heard an interesting story from one trader,' Iannas added, 'who owned an Egyptian donkey he had bought in Mari. He told us that the best donkey teachers were the Egyptians who could talk to animals. He also claimed they even had a religious sect that associated many qualities with animals that later became only and specifically related to humans.'

'It is an Egyptian cult,' Husha recollected. 'Not everyone took them seriously. I think they have some evidence for their cause. This group believe that animals actually think, learn and solve problems and even talk to one another. Donkeys do not talk with a language,' he explained. 'Donkeys talk with their bodies.' Husha described how each ear movement, each eye movement, each movement of the tail, each hair, and even a twitch or the speed of the heart beat was a word or a sentence or a feeling or an emotion, maybe even a story that a donkey was conveying. With this knowledge, the Egyptians learned from and trained their animals.

'How do you know this?' Iannas enquired further.

'I knew them from the quarries. The people of this sect led the way as the most advanced donkey and animal trainers in Egypt.' Husha described how the Egyptian donkeys developed a reputation for carrying the heaviest of loads for some of the longest and toughest of journeys. In fact, their feats of endurance through deserts, up hills, and over mountains and their firm hold of any load, including the huge stones in Husha's quarry, had given them not just a legendary reputation, but some even said "god-like" divinity. Iannas and Daniel found all of this fascinating and were even surprised with the extent of Husha the slave's knowledge. Of course, Husha insisted on adding a few barbed comments about their youth and how misguided Daniel's preparations for his journey appeared given his lack of experience. Iannas and Daniel quickly thanked the slave for his advice and knowledge and promptly left, dismissing Husha's personal remarks as nothing more than envy. And how close to the truth they were.

For the remainder of the day, Daniel and Iannas quietly practiced what they had been told by Husha and noticed almost immediately that Donkey was calm when they were calm and responded to them differently depending on their own mood and frame of mind.

It was as they were discovering this new language that Iannas had a thought about Husha and Alizer that he shared with Daniel when the two were walking alone.

'Alizer treated Husha differently,' Iannas remarked. 'Not the same way others deal with Husha.' Iannas attempted to clarify. They had only ever known Husha as a slave in Susa and had seen him treated according to that station. Iannas and Daniel were no different. Yet here was Alizer regarding him an equal. Iannas and Daniel spoke freely about their embarrassment as they admitted how they had been speaking and behaving towards Husha.

Sai was walking behind and overheard the conversation. She kept her distance recognising it for a private conversation, and she too thought how so accepting she had become to the different forms of slavery in India. She listened as the two young people in front of her resolved to try and behave differently towards Husha. Sai thought how much she was blessed to be here in this time and this place listening to this conversation. She thanked Lord Krishna for sending her these two wise, young protectors. She felt comfortable with them, at least for now, and remembered that she had not yet grieved alone or reflected on her situation. Narrating her story around the campfire the night before, the first time she had done so since her husband had died, had allowed the reality to bombard her without the protection and distractions of her servants and the goods that needed to be sold.

She quickly parked her thoughts and moved them back to Husha, resolving to be more aware of her behaviour towards him as she continued listening to Iannas who had been inspired to ask, 'Why do people need to have power over one another?'

Daniel provided a different perspective in reply. 'Why do so many people allow themselves to be told what to think and what to believe?' Sai liked this conversation and gently plucked up enough courage to join them, freeing her soul from her past life that had only ended, it seemed to her, in that last step she took to catch up to Daniel and Iannas, and they were thrilled to have her company.

At this moment, Donkey was thinking how free he felt and how beautiful today, this morning, and the world were as he walked through the gentle hills having left the trees behind only to be replaced by flocks of sheep and goats with their own shepherd companions. He had never felt better, and for some reason, ever since the sun had risen and Daniel had finished packing Donkey's load, it felt so light he did not even feel it was there. His feet did not even seem to touch the ground. He felt so strong. 'Let's go faster,' he thought.

Iannas was particularly impressed by their joint efficiency over the next three days and nights, for each, without discussion, fell into completing the various tasks of travel: leading Donkey, setting up camp, tending to Donkey in the evening, collecting firewood, starting their fire, preparing food, making tea and hot date drink (since Sai would only drink tea), and reorganising the supplies every evening ready for the morning. Daniel appreciated how they reminded one another when needed, making sure nothing was forgotten.

The rapidity of the caravan meant that its temporary citizens walked at his or her own pace, speeding up and slowing down but keeping within the meandering caterpillar they had created. Although Husha, Iannas, Daniel, and Sai tried to stay together there was very limited opportunity for conversation during the day. They took turns leading Donkey and often just walked in silence enjoying the sounds of the river, the passing herds of sheep and goats with their little bells and the scent and views of the hills. Husha was the only exception, taking every opportunity to talk with fellow travellers and asking all the right questions to learn about them while telling his story to those that would listen.

In the evenings, Iannas and Daniel wanted to know more about Husha and Sai, but Egypt and the pyramids was always the favourite topic, and the days and evenings passed too quickly.

As Uruk approached in the late afternoon on the third day from Ur, and the long shadows signalled that the caravan would soon stop for the night, Daniel found an opportunity to thank Iannas for his companionship. Iannas wondered if he should have had more faith and been more encouraging in Ur on discovering the gates had been closed. But it was a short conversation. The caravan leader blew his horn, not as melodic as the one from Susa, and sounded the camp for the night resulting in the usual hurried activity as everyone attempted to settle before the darkness took over; the sun had a habit of setting a little too soon when camp was being set. The caravan camped close to the city, but no one complained about not walking the extra short distance in the darkness to reach Uruk as bandits always ruled the night, and the city gates were often closed at sunset.

Husha took Daniel's mind away from the expectancy of the next day with talk of the legends of Uruk over dinner.

'There is a tale that Gilgamesh himself built that wall one thousand years ago,' Husha interceded everyone's thoughts as they looked at the flickering torch lights mounted atop the distant city wall, as high as ten adults, under the clear, starlit, moonless sky animating Husha's words. 'I have also heard another legend that the wall is so tall and strong because spirits, some of the locals call them Jhinn, helped to build and rebuild it, for it has been rebuilt and repaired many times following the wars.'

Sai had heard the name Gilgamesh, Daniel knew a little of the ancient poems. Iannas knew more through his father's stories. 'We will have to tell Sai the story of Gilgamesh tomorrow night,' joked Husha, adding, 'Like Ur, there is a Ziggurat here and the main Temple is to the God Ishtar.'

'We have Ishtar in Nineveh too,' Iannas happily announced. 'She is our warrior in Nineveh. The daughter of Sin, the Moon God.'

'In Uruk, however,' added Husha with the air of a knowledgeable tour guide unwilling to be outdone and enjoying that his description was being followed so closely, 'Ishtar is the daughter of Anu, the Sky God and the Goddess of Love.'

'The same Ishtar?' quizzed Iannas.

'Yes, the same God,' Husha lectured. 'She has been dressed especially for this city or region. We do the same in Egypt when we introduce new gods from distant lands. We give them Egyptian qualities, making the gods more acceptable and more in touch with the local people and their needs.'

'It seems that Gods find it easier to adapt to different cultures than people!' Iannas exclaimed with his usual cheeky smile, but his comment did not find any response so he gave up quickly enough. Iannas, Daniel, and Sai were very impressed with Husha's knowledge. 'Now you know why I am always asking questions and listening,' Husha said, attempting to justify himself.

'Tomorrow will be a long day, and we do not know what to expect. Let's get some rest.' Iannas suggested but only succeeded in returning Daniel to his anxieties of the next day as everyone settled down in their bedding for the night.

Donkey was thinking of his new companions. He had grown to like Sai. He liked her heart. He liked the sound it made. She had very little fear inside of her, and there was little to fear inside her. He also wondered why the older one had been nervous and anxious. He had tried to calm him, but the old one had not listened to Donkey or did not understand Donkey's language like Daniel and Iannas. He decided he enjoyed the daytime more than the night times. He was not tired and was keen for the sun to return. One day he would follow the sun and find out where it travelled to every night.

6 RABI AND THE TEMPLE OF ISHTAR

Day 15.

'The Mesopotamians must have invented queuing,' thought Husha out loud as the five stood waiting to be allowed into the city of Uruk. They had stood in the queue from early morning when the caravan had arrived and disbanded, and it was now almost midday. When their turn came, the officials were less interested in the supplies on Donkey and much more curious about the travellers. They scrutinised everyone's identification tablets and each had many questions asked of them. Where did they come from? Where would they stay in Uruk? Would they be trading? Did they know anyone in the city? Where were they going to next and when? What was their hometown or city? Did they have a second citizenship? Did they know anyone in Uruk? All their answers were recorded at the gate and this was contributing to the delay.

The polite but firm interrogation was unusual, and the cause for the extra vigilance had occurred at first light when the gates had only just opened and a Minister from Babylon presented himself on an unofficial visit to spend, he claimed, a few days with his wife's family. The gate duty soldiers were caught by surprise. Being under strict instructions to inform the city Governor in case of any official or important visitor, they summoned the official protocol welcome committee of Uruk despite the Minister asserting he was there as a private citizen. Of course, he could not refuse for fear of offending the local Governor.

At the same time, a known, violent thief was attempting to enter the city as a trader at a different gate using an identification tablet and a supply of frankincense, both of which he had stolen from Ur and unbeknown to him belonged to a local Uruk trader. Worse still for him, the soldier guards happened to know the owner of the stolen identification particularly well, for the trader and his family supplied them with regular deliveries of fruit and wine. Arriving in Uruk with a stolen tablet of an Uruk local had not been one of his best ideas but the thief could not read, otherwise he would not have done so. Matters escalated quickly when they searched him at the gate and discovered a vial of poison as well as a blade, both of which the soldiers would, a short time later, realise was meant for the Minister from Babylon, who at that moment was waiting for the protocol welcome committee at the main gate. For now, the discoveries caused much commotion and delay as the amateur assassin proclaimed his innocence and accused the soldiers of framing him for good measure as he was being arrested. It did not take long for the Head of Security to make the connection, and immediately, all the gate entries were suspended in case another assassin was at large.

The gate soldiers, after they learned the details of the assassination attempt, remained edgy for the remainder of the day. It was not that they had avoided a potentially serious diplomatic crisis between Uruk and Babylon; they were far more concerned that they would all have been blamed and, at the very least, lost their jobs had the assassin made it through unchallenged. The queues on all the gates had grown long while extra security for the Minister was arranged, and when the suspension was lifted, the soldiers were on orders to make sure everyone was thoroughly questioned and any suspicious person was to be held for questioning.

Having established that Sai, Iannas, Daniel, and Husha - who had his identification and ownership tablet checked three times - were legitimate, they were all welcomed by the gate tax officials where Daniel paid today's entry tax for everyone which, as a result of the incident and the increased vigilance in the city, had been doubled. Finally, they received a one-night pass for the city, a small tablet they had to carry on them and return on their last exit.

Apart from the exhausting wait and endless questions, they congratulated each other on their patience when they made it through the final check. Daniel, however, would be satisfied only when they reached Rabi. Half the day had already disappeared.

The news of the assassination attempt was already the topic of conversation in the streets even as they walked towards the old historical centre, through the narrow streets with the narrower tall homes on either side, crossing the city canals over delightful stone and wooden bridges. The canals, with their mini islands of discarded rubbish with at least one dead guest rat, crisscrossed the entire city. Each bridge was beautifully crafted and gifted the city with a cultured appearance. A city with waterways instead of roads.

The shadows were still short and beginning to lengthen when they reached the lapis lazuli market and quickly found Rabi's little shop in the small square, next to the chapel of E-an just as Alizer had described. They could see ahead the busy and bustling main city market square, which they were glad at not having had to navigate through, although the Temple of Ishtar at the entrance of the square looked colourful and inviting. Husha volunteered to look after Donkey while Sai, Iannas, and Daniel headed towards the shop. When they realised it was busy with customers, Daniel suggested they take a quick look at the Temple of Ishtar with its majestic lapis lazuli decorated, tiled and gated entrance promising a beautiful welcome while they waited.

They made their way to and up the countless steps and, as they entered, they were taken aback, for none of them expected the interior to also be covered wall-to-wall and floor-to-ceiling with lapis lazuli tiling, artwork, and carved pieces. None of them had seen anything like it. Iannas and Sai watched Daniel head to the altar at the front and perform a short prayer and prayed in spirit with him. Sai realised for the first time why her lapis lazuli had sold for such a high price and thanked her husband for the legacy he had left behind and the hope for the future it would provide. There was no doubt the temple was a beautiful reality, as more visitors were constantly arriving to admire the majesty of Ishtar while the priests were busily and happily offering drinks and a blessing. But there were things to do, and Iannas nudged Daniel along and suggested they should try Rabi again.

Daniel had rehearsed the moment, and while he was confident about meeting his first contact Rabi, he was also particularly nervous. The shop was empty this time, and Sai paused as she stepped in first followed by Iannas and finally Daniel. Young fledglings ready to soar.

It was Sai who approached the shopkeeper first on the pretext of selling some lapis lazuli and finding out what was the latest market price. During the interaction, making sure that no one other than them was in the shop, Sai introduced herself and asked the very elderly shopkeeper his name.   When Rabi introduced himself, Daniel stepped into the conversation.

'Rabi, my name is Daniel, son of Daniel from Susa.' He spoke with confidence and also respect for his host. 'Apologies but I needed to make sure you were Rabi. Alizer asked me not to talk with anyone else.'

'Daniel, my friend, I have been expecting you. I am glad you confirmed my identity first. These are strange times indeed with the events in Ur, which is still under curfew, and today's attempted killing of the Minister here in our very own city.'

Daniel tried to apologise again, but Rabi was insistent, 'No need to apologise. You have chosen your companions well. You and your friends must join me for dinner, and I have a place for you, I mean all of you, to stay. Alizer told me all about you.'

'Don't you mean my father? He was supposed to be the one. I only came because my father could not leave.' Daniel tried to correct.

'No, it was you I was expecting,' Rabi confirmed with greater confidence.

'We are four and a donkey,' Daniel replied clearly but he could not understand how Rabi could be expecting him when his father had been the one Azhar had wanted originally.

'Leave it with me. First, let us have a small snack to see you through till dinner. There is much to talk about, much for you to prepare, and I expect you will want to leave tomorrow morning? Your next destination is Babylon.'

'In that case, we have supplies and passage to Babylon to arrange,' Daniel confirmed.

Daniel was briefed on what to buy and given a prepared list on a small, red, clay tablet.

'Use this list until you become familiar with your purchases and then discard the tablet. It will be better and look less conspicuous if you are in the market without it. Alizer will have told you not to bring attention to yourselves.'

Rabi finished with instructions on where to leave the supplies, the name of the contact in Babylon, and where he was to be found.

'You will need this to pay the deposit for the caravan and to buy the supplies.' Daniel took the pouch of coins and secured it on his belt. 'When you book the caravan to Babylon, you will have a choice of routes. The journey is seven to eight days, and each route has a stop midway to purchase fresh supplies for yourselves and leave a set for Alizer. Tell me tonight which route you have booked, and I will give you more instructions. You should have enough money in the pouch for everything I have mentioned as well as other emergencies. Now let's go,' Rabi insisted. 'I have an area round the rear where you can leave your Donkey. It's secure.'

Rabi locked his shop as they returned to the street. Daniel settled Donkey in the rear of the shop where he made sure to remove a package from the saddlebag and place it in his shoulder bag before leaving. In the meantime, Husha had a short, private conversation with Rabi and then wondered off as a curious Sai watched, intrigued.

'Wait,' Rabi called to Husha, 'let me treat you to lunch!' But Husha waved and continued walking.

Bread and bean stew was the day's special in the little bar next to Rabi's shop and where Rabi fielded more questions.

'Tonight we can talk after your tasks are done. Eat quickly, you have much to do.' They could not argue with Rabi. As they set off together on their errands, Sai wondered if she had attached herself to Daniel and Iannas, or had they adopted her? Sai concluded that sometimes words are not needed for a feeling to be understood.

The market was busier than usual with extra soldier patrols, but very soon they had secured the supplies and asked them to be delivered to Rabi's son Wasi at the station outside the main gate. Sai, Daniel, and Iannas walked to the station past the still long line of new arrivals. First, they headed to the caravan stands where Daniel and Iannas discovered there were three caravans to Babylon at dawn; one travelled through Isin, one through Nippar, and one through Sharuppak. After a short discussion and a pause, Daniel made the decision.

'What about you, Sai?' Daniel asked, remembering she had only mentioned travelling as far as Uruk back in Ur. With the supplies and bookings, Iannas had not even thought to ask Sai.

'I will stay with you till Babylon,' was the short reply that delighted both young men, and Daniel booked a caravan for the four of them first and then Alizer's group for three days later.

Wasi's station was close by, and after a short wait they accepted delivery of the supplies. Iannas and Daniel organised the fresh supplies with the dried foods into a large pack and labelled it as Alizer had instructed. Local towns and cities had long ago set up a system of transferring food supplies to passing caravans as a way of ensuring caravan leaders had fresh provisions for the next stage of their journey without delay. The system was primarily used only for food provisions and rarely for other goods, for that would involve additional licences and high export taxes. Wasi warned that tax officials would sometimes check packages to make sure they contained only food.

When they thought they had finished, just to satisfy himself, Iannas checked whether Alizer's supply pack was tied together well and double checked that Daniel's handiwork on the tablet, which was already drying, contained the name Alizer of Damascus, the destination, and the name of the caravan leader for the next stage. He also checked to see if the seal was clear on the reverse side. Having made sure the seal was securely tied, Iannas left verbal instructions with Wasi for good measure. Daniel appreciated Iannas' caution, for they did not want anything to go wrong at this early stage.

Alizer had clearly organised things well. It was important to use the correct station supplier. Some unscrupulous ones made extra money by siphoning off supplies that would not be missed once collected. Suppliers had occasionally been known to 'lose' entire deliveries. One or two had made good money this way.

It was already getting dark as they returned to the market to purchase fresh supplies for themselves for the next stage of their journey. As well as fresh and dried food, Sai and Iannas also bought some extra utensils to cook with and wooden plates. The group had grown larger than first anticipated. On the way out of the market, the snack stalls caught their eyes just as they were designed to. Iannas found dried salted corn, Daniel some fresh local dates, and Sai could not resist the colourful honeyed boiled fruit specialities of Uruk. Daniel noticed he had much more money than he needed, so he quickly made a decision to buy more utensils, pots, plates and spoons. Then he ran back to Wasi's stand and left them in the supply pack for Alizer.

'I got the idea from you two!' Daniel credited Iannas and Sai for the inspiration when he returned. When they arrived at Rabi's store, Husha was already waiting, and Rabi led the way up the tel to his home. That night Rabi made sure to feed them well.

The caravan would leave at dawn from the service station, and Rabi would ensure they slept well and were woken on time. He was intrigued by his guests and wondered how they had met. Husha sat and ate by the door as was fitting his station and where he felt comfortable listening to the conversation. Sai, Daniel and Iannas shared their story while enjoying the food, but Daniel and Iannas also wanted to know more about how Rabi knew Alizer.

'That's another story, young ones,' is all he would say, which captured Husha's interest and played on his mind. 'First tell me which route to Babylon you chose and why?'

Daniel described the three route options he had been given at the caravan stands.

'Nippar seems to add an extra night, and Isin is a large and busy city and is midway. Sharuppak is a smaller quiet town, but any supplies we leave there will not be midway, they will be three days and then five.' Daniel paused while everyone listened. 'We decided on Sharuppak.' Daniel paused again and waited for a reaction, but none came, so as a 'get out' he quickly added, 'but since all the caravans are run by the same company, they told me we could change our minds in the morning.'

'I heard this from Wasi, you have done well.' Rabi seemed to reassure everyone. 'I would have chosen Isin. Isin will have a good market, and you can leave a good fresh supply for Alizer mid way through his journey.' Daniel was disappointed with Rabi's words. He constantly worried about making the wrong decision, but Rabi continued.

'By choosing Sharuppak I can see you are much wiser than I. The route will be quieter, and it means the caravan will bypass the big city of Isin. This is better for you and for Alizer; there will be less eyes. Well done, Daniel.' Daniel looked relieved. 'In Sharuppak, visit the library where they are restoring the "Instructions of Sharuppak" and ask for Rabiat. There is a family connection between us, and she is one of the restorers. She will guide you as I have done in Sharuppak. As long as you leave enough, and the right supplies, such as grain and dried foods, the five days to Babylon will not be a problem.' Rabi was satisfied and noticed Daniel, Iannas, and Sai catch each other's eyes with a sense of relief.

'Now,' he continued, 'being in Uruk, you must already know the stories of Gilgamesh?'

Both Iannas and Daniel had heard various and different versions of it before, but Sai had not heard any except Husha's comments the night before.

'So let me tell you the true story, not a version heard in some story time as told by some teller in the market square or some long lost poem on a tablet. I can trace my family back one thousand years to the time of Gilgamesh. My ancestors served in his court.'

Rabi explained there were so many legends from the time of Gilgamesh, and, much to everyone's disappointment tonight, there would be only time for one.

'Over a thousand years ago,' Rabi began, 'Gilgamesh was the King of Uruk. His empire and influence encompassed many cities and lands. He performed his duties diligently and built great city walls including the one you see here in Uruk. He was a warrior, so he focused his efforts on his strengths, and what he did, such as improving the security of his people, he did well. But he was not a man with the skills of society; therefore, he was a lonely man, and his loneliness hardened his heart. He began to rule his people by oppression and even tormented his subjects by passing rules and regulations that made their lives more difficult than they needed to be, and this made them angry. The people of Uruk gathered in temples and called on the God Ishtar, "Send us a companion for our King; spare us his madness".

'Enkido lived in the forest outside the city of Uruk. One night, he was watching the stars when he heard the people of Uruk call to the Gods. He listened and read in the stars that it was time to meet his destiny, so he entered Uruk and challenged Gilgamesh on behalf of the people of the city who wanted an end to the hardship and the difficulties. Enkido was a warrior of the forest, and Gilgamesh listened as Enkido spoke of the people of Uruk's suffering and challenged the King to end the oppression or fight. But Gilgamesh was a soldier of war and rather than listening to the words of Enkido, the challenge was accepted and a stage was set outside these very city walls, the same location you have walked and queued to enter the city.

'The battle began at dawn the next morning; it was long, terrible, and hard. It was a battle, not a fight. Both warriors battled with all their might and all their weapons. At the end of the day, Gilgamesh was defeated. As he lay on the ground with Enkido ready to strike the final blow, the people were hushed not knowing what would happen next. Enkido, instead of striking the blow, took one step back. The crowd gasped as Gilgamesh was allowed to stand. Gilgamesh composed himself and asked Enkido what he wanted. Enkido answered, "Only one thing, be kind to your people, nothing more."

'Thereafter, they saluted each other, Enkido bowed to his King, and the two became the best of friends.

'One day, the people of Uruk talked of a special bull rumoured to be from the heavens, which was running free in the forest not far from Uruk. On hearing this news, the two friends, Gilgamesh and Enkido, who loved the hunt and organised a chase every moon, quickly prepared a large party to accompany them to the forest to find the bull. It was a long hunt, for the bull moved between the desert and the forest, and between the days and the nights, at the end of it, the bull was killed. Gilgamesh and Enkido had not realised the bull had been sent by the Gods, and as soon as the Gods discovered that their bull had been killed, they became so angry they retaliated by killing Enkido who had struck the final blow.

Gilgamesh lost his one and only true friend. He was devastated and grieved, 'He who was my companion!' he cried to the Gods. 'You have taken him and he has gone forever.'

'Much of this you will have heard,' said Rabi, 'what many do not know is the next chapter to this saga,' Rabi whispered, as only a true storyteller knew how. 'There was one other warrior whose duty was to be protector of the King and his friend Enkido. When the Gods killed Enkido, the warrior and protector was so enraged that he had failed in his duty, that he drew his sword, ran out, and struck a blow against one of the Gods who had surrounded Enkido's limp body. The Gods were so shocked that a mortal would threaten them that they paused, stunned, and they did not strike him down. The warrior seized the moment and challenged the Gods so that all could hear. He asked them, "Who are you that kill so easily and can be harmed so easily by my sword. What sort of Gods are you?"

'His challenge shamed the Gods; the Gods looked at each other and withdrew. This one act transformed how people believed in the gods of the time. This warrior, protector, was from my family, my tribe. When Gilgamesh saw what the warrior had done and heard what he had said, Gilgamesh came forward, stood next to this man, raised his voice, and challenged the Gods to return from where they had come. The Gods were taken so much by surprise at these events that they left without a word.

Gilgamesh returned to Uruk and challenged the temples and the priests, asking them what sort of gods had they led the people to believe in? Gods that kill so easily? He opened his eyes to see that temples were being built before the public sanitation projects, before the clean water was brought into the city, before the services the people needed, and before the city waste was collected. He challenged his government, his priests, and the power of the temples. He reformed the temples to put the needs of the people of the city first.

'Gilgamesh, a King, abandoned his sword, and turned to forgiveness and compassion, and commanded the priests dress Ishtar as a God of Love and Protection and not war and fear. Gilgamesh even challenged the ancient laws and rewrote the tablets of law by replacing the act of revenge, an eye for an eye and punishment, with acts of compassion and forgiveness.

'But when Gilgamesh died, his actions and beliefs quickly died after him. My ancestor was there at the end of the reign of Gilgamesh. Our stories that passed down from him describe how the priests returned to the old ways very soon. Towns quickly filled with beautiful ornate temples with fabulous gardens, and the cities returned to their former state without sufficient funds for clean water, waste collection or drainage.

'The priests returned to the old laws and created new ones to forbid anyone to speak against the laws and put themselves under the protection of the new king and invited back the old gods of fear, for only the gods of fear could protect them from neighbouring armies and gods of peace.'

Rabi was pleased his last comment brought some amusement.

'What happened to the protector?' asked Iannas.

'He protected Gilgamesh till the end and on the King's death, he and his Order of Protectors continued to watch, some even mistakenly referred to them as "Watchers",' Rabi threw in the last comment in passing. 'The Protectors took an oath to continue to protect the land from fear and oppression and to protect those who came to bring peace into the world. The stories of Gilgamesh in our family have been passed down from the Protector himself and there are so many stories. It is a privilege of our family that we continue to live in this city of Gilgamesh, the city of canals, the city of spirits and the city of legends.'

The story had captivated them and none, not even Husha, had heard this version of Gilgamesh.

'Was it really true?' Daniel asked, a little cynical, 'Were the Gods really afraid?'

Rabi laughed, 'It is only as true as you want it to be. I hope I have opened your minds to new ideas. History has much to teach us. It is my family heritage so there is nothing more for me to add. Eat, finish the food. Tomorrow you start another long journey.'

Rabi had mentioned a phrase that Husha had not heard since his time in Egypt. He would try and recollect his thoughts. Strange to be hearing the phrase again now, he thought. What was the connection? Husha was good at making connections.

Iannas enjoyed this version of the story; he decided he would have to add it to his own collection. He remembered the stories of Gilgamesh Appa used to tell, and, as he expected, there were parts of Rabi's story that were familiar, but, as Gilgamesh was a much later King, he was not expecting to be reminded of some ancient legends Appa had once spent a particularly wet winter narrating when Iannas had been too young to remember them all. He knew, of course, that sometimes stories overlapped one another, or one story was familiar because it was an adaptation of another. If he could remember to remember, he would try and recollect some of the ancient legends of the first ten kings of the world his father had told. Right now, there were more important things to remember.

'Enough!' said Rabi. 'I will look forward to hearing news of your journey along the way. Let's get to bed. I will wake with you and see you out of the gate.'

Donkey had a very restful evening. He had watched the red sun set from the tel through the palm trees under which he had been resting. The garden was a lovely setting, and he found the deep red orange of the sun behind the palm trees mesmerising. He still wondered where the sun went and if he would ever discover its secret.

7 THE INSTRUCTIONS OF SHARUPPAK

Days 16 to 18, 7.8 Beru.

The pre-dawn morning welcomed its worshippers with its silence and freshness. The streets, canals and bridges at this time of morning created a particularly magical mood amongst the small group of travellers heading towards the main gates of Uruk with their donkey. There were no customs to go through as they left. The soldiers were beginning to extinguish the gate torch lights when they recognised Rabi. They were clearly happy to see him and greeted him warmly. Daniel presented the pass to the soldiers from the day before, and the soldiers waved the group through with a smile and morning blessing. They even offered them a hot, sweet, morning date drink, which had to be declined because of the time, but Rabi promised to return and share some with them. It had been a quiet night for the guards, and they would have welcomed the company.

Rabi had been the perfect host and watching him see them off and wave goodbye was somehow reassuring for all of them, but, Iannas thought, gave Daniel unrealistic expectations for the remainder of the journey.

Rabi returned to the gate to enjoy a hot date drink with the guards and catch up with the morning news, which was still occupied with the attempt on the Minister's life the day before.

Husha was relieved to be back on the road. Daniel remained preoccupied with how Rabi could have been expecting him instead of his father, and when he shared his confusion with the others they could not provide him with any reasonable explanation. Iannas was still enjoying Rabi's story and recollecting the details so that he would be able to narrate it some time. Sai was simply glad to be sharing this journey, still a stranger in new lands, with new friends.

Having seen that Iannas and Daniel had now been joined by Sai and Husha, Rabi set into motion his chain of communication so that all the

Protectors would know who to expect within the next days and moons to Harran. If the Protectors had understood the language of the world correctly, Iannas, Daniel, Sai, Husha and Donkey were, somehow, exactly where they needed to be at this moment. None knew the purpose of this unexpected fellowship, and even the Protectors would have to wait for the answers to be unveiled.

As far as Husha was concerned, nothing good would come from Daniel and Iannas' journey. He waited for the caravan to fall into its natural rhythm and then began sharing his concerns. As they headed north towards Sharuppak, the warmth of the day welcomed the caravan as the sun squeezed through the hills with its morning touch that made the land and the people appear as golden treasures. To interrupt Husha's tirade about how young and inexperienced they were, Sai asked 'Where did you disappear in Uruk, Husha. I saw you head towards the other tel?'

The question created the desired pause and they could see that Husha clearly did not appreciate being asked and nor did he want to answer.

'What's the matter?' teased Daniel. 'Normally you have so much to say.'

Husha began his diatribe about rude behaviour and how the current generation had no respect for their elders. Iannas, Daniel, and Sai walked a little faster, moved ahead of Husha, and carried on their own conversations while Husha, who was leading Donkey, decided at the same time to slow down a little and create a larger gap between them. Husha did not make it easy sometimes, but for some reason, which they had not yet understood, they felt safe around him, and Husha, although he did not express it, enjoyed their company. He had not enjoyed anyone's company for so many years.

Rabi had left all of them in good spirits, and Daniel and Iannas set their mind to Sharuppak and Babylon. Daniel pointed out that finding his contacts in the cities was not going to be as easy as it was in Uruk. Iannas was concerned about the short window to complete all their tasks at the various stops ahead of them. He felt they could organise themselves better and promised to put his mind to making the stops more efficient in future. They were both aware the caravan had a very short designated stop scheduled in Sharuppak. Daniel reignited his fear that he had made the wrong decision. 'Isin might have been the better option,' he would say. They were quickly learning that while they could rely on chance, fate, and faith, they also had to make the right decisions to give the universe a helping hand.

They followed the river for most of the day and soon crossed a new floating toll bridge to replace one that had been washed away. The water levels were settling down now after the rains of the previous moon. It was strange to think that while the rains in this region had arrived early, a drought warning had been issued in regions in the west.

On the third day, after an earlier than usual start, they arrived in Sharuppak not long after sunrise as planned. Husha quickly sprang into action and unloaded Donkey at the service stop outside of the walled town. Daniel had carried the book in his shoulder bag that morning allowing Iannas, Sai, and he to head straight up the ramp, through the main gate, and after Daniel paid their entry tax, were quickly let through. The market was just inside the gate, so Iannas and Sai immediately began to make the purchases. Daniel asked a guard the direction to the library and made a brisk pace towards the building. Daniel had only walked thirty paces when he thought he heard a woman's voice call his name. It was perfectly possible there was another Daniel here, but instinct and curiosity stopped him anyway, and he turned to look from where the call had come from.

Rabiat saw a very surprised young man looking at her and dressed almost exactly as she had expected. A welcoming smile was her gift to Daniel, which drew him towards her.

'Daniel, you are exactly as I expected you to be, and you need to cut your hair, young man.'

Daniel brushed his dark, below-the-shoulder length hair back with his hand and returned a shy smile to this lady who had to be Rabiat. Her face, or was it the shape of the nose, reminded him of Rabi, while the tenderness in her voice reminded him of his mother whose memory would now linger.

'Auntie Rabiat?' he stumbled but was courteous to give her the title she deserved. 'Rabi sends you his greetings. How did you recognise me?'

'I recognised you from your description that Alizer sent me, of course, and no, Uncle does not send me his greetings. You are too polite. He forgets his eldest cousin too easily.' She spoke with a warm smile, and Daniel knew Rabiat was just teasing. She pressed on, 'We do not have much time, Daniel. Where are your friends?'

Daniel quickly explained how they had distributed the tasks amongst each of them while they headed back to the market where Sai and Iannas could be seen choosing fruits and vegetables from the local farmer with whom they had already made an order of grain and dried fruit and seeds. Before Daniel and Rabiat reached them at the market stall, Rabiat whispered to Daniel, 'Ask for the supplies to be sent to Shari at the station.' She then discreetly placed a small bag of coins into his hands, and the two continued walking towards Iannas and Sai.

By the time Daniel and Rabiat approached, Iannas and Sai were already completing their order and settling the payment, pleased that one farmer was supplying both the dry and fresh food items, which meant there was no further shopping to be done and there was still time to spare. While Rabiat introduced herself to Iannas and Sai, Daniel gave the delivery instructions to the market farmer who nodded and explained he needed a short time to put the order together.

Daniel looked around the small market and noticed that Husha had found his own market trader and was making the purchases for the four of them. Iannas' plan was working.

Rabiat put everyone at ease with her words, and her warm welcoming smile that only Rabi and Rabiat could have provided made the three young travellers feel as if Sharuppak was their hometown.

'I am impressed with all of you. A great team you have put together, Daniel!' Rabiat invited them to the library while they waited for the supplies to be delivered.

'That is the building there,' she pointed to the one Daniel was originally heading to. 'We can make it a short visit.'

'What are the Instructions of Sharuppak?' Sai asked. 'Rabi said that you were restoring them.'

Rabiat asked them to wait until they saw the tablets and, conscious of the time, led them quickly to the library workshop; one large workroom in the basement of the main library lit by mobile metal mirrors reflecting the light entering through the long narrow horizontal window panels high up along two walls. Sai was surprised at the brightness of the room and counted ten large tablets, at least twice the size of Daniel's shoulder bag, each placed on its own wooden bench. Three restorers were working around one particular table on broken segments. One of the restorers was wiping segments with a damp cloth, piecing them together and reading the resulting inscriptions while another scribe was sharpening his tools to work on the faded areas and a third was preparing clay to bind the broken pieces together.

'These are the stones of Sharuppak,' Rabiat explained. 'They were found deep underneath mud as high as all three of you put together end to end. Half the words are so faint they can only be seen when you put your nose up against them,' she put her hand up to her face so that it was almost touching her nose. 'So each word is being gently impressed again so that we can read the entire script.'

'We believe they are one thousand years old. These Instructions, Sai, are an ancient code for the people of the world at that time. A code for life. Maybe they are the same as our rules and laws as we call them today but it is incredible to us that they had such instructions even at that time. They may be the first recorded history of our world, Sai. We are all historians here funded by the Governor of Sharuppak from the city taxes. These tablets are our heritage, and if we do not protect this culture, then who knows? In two, three or even four thousand years from now people might think we were simple minded savages roaming this land,' she laughed, and Iannas sniggered. 'I would like to think that if we pay our respects to the knowledge of the past and if we can learn from their history, maybe we will not make the same mistakes again. Since the floods wiped out so much history, many cities have been recording our traditions and our lives as historical documents for the future. If we stop for a moment and think, these are some of the very few documents left describing the world before the floods. When you are in Sippar, ask about the "History of the World" before the floods. They say it is still buried there.'

Sai had never seen anything as old as this before and tried to conjure the culture that would have written these tablets. Iannas and Daniel had never seen a library where they restored old tablets. They did not even know restorers like Rabiat existed and thought it wonderful that their culture was being returned and protected by people like her.

'Look,' Rabiat interrupted their imaginations, 'time is of the essence today. Let's get you back to the service station. I have some roasted grain for you to take on your journey, and we even have time to share a breakfast of some grain soup I have already prepared. You go ahead. I will follow you with the soup and the grain.'

Rabiat wisely declined Iannas' offer of help to carry the grain and breakfast suggesting he would be more useful sorting the delivery at the station. When they returned to the station next to the caravan camp, Husha had already taken delivery of their personal supplies and was in the process of packing while Donkey was still resting and feeding. Donkey was wondering why he was being treated to a long rest when he was not tired at all. Sai stayed to help Husha while Daniel and Iannas looked for Shasi to sort the supplies. They had no sooner left Shasi's stand, having carefully sorted, packed, and labelled the supplies for Alizer, when they smelt the most delicious mix of aromas. They saw Rabiat already with Sai and Husha with her rather large pot of soup, fresh bread, and bag of roasted grain as they approached. Needless to say this second breakfast was wonderfully delicious, and Husha asked for the recipe. He thought it was the best he had ever tasted.

'Roast the grain before you add it to the soup, Husha. That is the secret,' Rabiat confided.

Husha was impressed and promised to try it next time. There were no caravans to organise as they would continue with the same one, and Rabiat promised to make sure the supplies would reach Alizer.

Rabiat turned to Daniel, 'You did very well stopping here, Daniel. Do not enter Isin even if the caravan stops outside its gates. Someone high up from Ur has arrived in Isin with his own battalion, and a military struggle for the control of Isin has already begun. You do not want to be part of that.'

Daniel thanked her for the warning and her hospitality and wondered if the God Sin was guiding him after all.

'Can you tell us some of the things you have read in the tablets, Rabiat?' Iannas asked.

'Of course, but so much is missing we only have half of the writing. Let me give you a few examples of the code of life from two thousand years ago. I should explain that the tablets were written by a lady called Nisaba, a scribe I assume, while being narrated by Curuppag, obviously an ancestor of Sharuppak; maybe he founded this town. We know of at least three hundred instructions but let me share with you some of my favourite ones.' Rabiat was always excited to share the 'Instructions' with kindred spirits.

Rabiat paused and then recited as if a poem, '"The spoken word is a gift, use it to soothe the mind", I always say this to my harsh-tongued husband but he never listens,' she giggled.

'Here is another one, "Do not speak arrogantly to your mother, that will cause hatred for you, do not question the words of your mother or your God", one of my favourites,' Rabiat laughed. 'We think our young generation is troubled, but they had problems with their children even at that time. My son never listens to me!' She laughed again and they all shared her laughter. Husha seemed to agree more than the others.

'How about this one,' she said. 'Your fathers are traders, are they not?' She looked at Iannas and Daniel, '"Heaven is far, earth is most precious, but it is with heaven you multiply your goods, and all foreign lands breathe under it", what do you think of that one?'

'That is beautiful,' Husha exclaimed, clearly moved, 'and this was written two thousand years ago? It is so deeply thought!'

Rabiat was happy and proud that her work was being appreciated. 'Another one, "Who insults can only hurt the skin. Greedy eyes however can kill", one for all of you to remember.'

'Wow, I like that,' exclaimed Daniel and then tried to repeat it as he sipped another tasty spoonful of soup.

They all relished the breakfast. Husha had even found apples in the market for everyone. The caravan started stirring and they knew they had yet to load Donkey. They quickly finished the wonderful food. Husha and Iannas prepared Donkey. Sai hugged Rabiat in appreciation, as did Daniel and Iannas; they already called her Auntie.

As they prepared to depart Rabiat looked at Daniel and called, 'I have one more code of life for you, Daniel.' They all paused to listen, 'It is line 264. Maybe it will be useful to you one day. "It is inconceivable that something lost is lost forever".' Daniel looked at her quizzically and Rabiat only replied with her now familiar smile.

'I like the way that sounds,' he began, 'but I do not understand it at all!' he replied with honesty.

'You will when you lose something!' Husha commented a little dryly. They all laughed loudly and fondly bade farewell.

'Remember Sharuppak,' Rabiat said her farewell. 'It is a place of beginnings. There is much more here than we can see or know. It may be the beginning of everything.' With that she waved and headed back to the gate.

As the caravan headed north towards Isin, they were leaving behind a particular region which Rabiat and the locals called Edin. There was still so much to discover and Rabiat hoped she would learn so much more before the end of her time on this Earth.

She stood at the gates of Sharuppak watching the group travel away from her and noticed a particular sleight in the way Donkey was walking. It was as if he was effortlessly floating on the rocky path unlike the other animals that were steadily and sometimes clumsily making their way. She observed carefully for a few moments longer, for the sight was quite hypnotic; she waited until the group were out of view. She thought for a moment, smiled to herself recollecting Daniel's shoulder bag, and turned to return to the library, her task for now completed.

8 SARGON OF BABYLON

Days 18 to 22, 18 Beru.

'Apart from Rabiat, the Instructions of Sharuppak and the delicious grain soup, which I hope, Husha, you will try and make, I remember nothing of Sharuppak. It is all a blur.' Sai was disappointed with herself that she had not taken a moment to absorb the place that she knew was the setting for an ancient story of a king who had built a huge ship that carried all the animals of the world to save them from the flood. 'Why did none of you remind me? I might never come back here!'

The Sharuppak stop had been short and intensely packed, and sightseeing had been lost on the task list.

'Sometimes it is the feeling and the people you remember of the places you visit rather than the place itself. I am glad everything worked out as it did.' Husha was sincere. 'See the troops up ahead in the distance? I think we are approaching Isin.' Husha was ever observant.

In Sharuppak, the caravan leaders had been alerted to the troubles in Isin, and they kept the caravan at a safe distance as they approached and passed the road junction that led to Isin. The city could be seen on the tel in the distance to the east lit by the late afternoon sun as if announcing its existence and inviting those passing by to enter. A large troop of soldiers from Ur was already stationed at the junction, and although the soldiers appeared relaxed, the caravan increased its pace as it passed. It maintained the fast pace for the remainder of the late afternoon till the shadows were long and only when everyone felt at ease at having left a good and safe distance from Isin did the horn announce the evening camp. Daniel had felt a strange feeling inside of him as they passed the soldiers from Ur patrolling the junction to Isin. He could so easily have chosen Isin as their middle station to Babylon and gave thanks to the God Sin for guiding him.

The near miss of Isin and the Instructions of Sharuppak held the conversation for the next few evenings as they tried to imagine the society that two thousand years ago created such thoughtful writings. Iannas guided the discussions to the subject of Babylon when he sensed the timing was right. He noticed that no one wanted to be the first to mention Babylon, or that Sai and Husha would be remaining behind in the city. None wanted to be reminded of the impending farewells.

With the success of the organisation of the group in Sharuppak, Iannas was more relaxed but made a point of reminding everyone that they knew very little of Sargon, Daniel's contact in Babylon, and he was likely to be harder to find than Rabi or Rabiat.

What they knew from Rabi was that the Babylonian Sargon, named after an ancient king, was in charge of repairing the walls of the city. Rabi had made it clear not to trust anyone else including Sargon's family and not to discuss their business with any other even if they were not able find him. Rabi had warned that there were always repairs to the walls in Babylon, and Sargon could be anywhere in the city supervising a repair. In the last report Rabi had received, Sargon lived in the Babil district in the north of the city, but had a habit of moving his entire household to the area nearest to the main works that were being carried out at the time, sometimes taking many moons to complete, even after organising day and night shifts to ensure their quick completion. The walls were as high as sixty adults in places and took Sargon five days on foot to circumnavigate. So, if Sargon did not move his family to where he was working, he would rarely see them. The family had grown accustomed to the regular upheavals. Although his wife occasionally complained, his children always found it quite exciting living in different parts of the city. Rabi described Sargon as a perfectionist, and his standard of building was already a subject of legend. Sargon the Builder was the only builder Babylon would trust to keep all the walls in shape and secure.

'It is always strange,' his wife would scold him, 'I can never figure out if you repair the walls to keep us in or keep the people out. In any case, these walls are huge, and I feel like we are living in a prison.' She was always asking him to move the family out of the city.

Daniel and Iannas tried to organise themselves in preparation for Babylon but always returned to the matter of saying farewell to Sai and Husha in the city. Husha was proving invaluable with his contribution to the daily routine; his creative meals and his support in Sharuppak had been greatly appreciated. They all enjoyed and valued Sai's calm manner of travel, her wisdom, her experienced advice during the purchase of supplies, and her spirit for life. Daniel and Iannas particularly respected the fact that Sai had a better connection with Husha than they did and was able to say things to him they never could. In fact, Sai had become a friend, and although they did not admit to it, both loved her company, her smile and how she inspired them to get through the day and keep perspective of the larger task ahead. They briefly talked about convincing her to remain with them but both agreed they were being selfish; although this did not stop them returning to the subject later.

Donkey was now carrying a larger load, as the journey was longer on this particular stretch to Babylon. He was managing admirably and attracted good comments from all his companions.

Donkey and Daniel had settled into a good routine of carrying the book given to him by Alizer, concealing it from unwanted eyes. Donkey carried it in his saddlebag during the day. At the end of the day, Daniel made sure the saddlebag was unloaded first and the supplies from Donkey placed on top. The supplies were always kept close at hand, and since Ur, Sai had requisitioned them as the place for her bedding at night. Donkey slept in the caravan holding area if there was one or slept with the supplies if there was not, and Sai always welcomed his company. Only when Donkey was due to separate from Daniel did Daniel transfer the book to his shoulder bag. This minimized the movement of the book and did not draw any attention to the package, just as Daniel intended.

'Could Alizer really have organised all the contacts moons ago?' Iannas would ask Daniel in between their conversations about Sargon and Babylon. Iannas did not want Daniel to become too complacent because things had gone well so far. Iannas' mother had handed down a memory, "Always show gratitude when things go well", she would say, and he did not feel that they had shown enough gratitude for the good they had experienced on this journey. It always struck Iannas how people always remembered the temple in times of need and often forgot their God in times of plenty.

'How much of Babylon are you familiar with, Daniel?' Iannas asked.

'Three times I have been, and father always made sure he took me to the main sites each time.'

'Me too,' Iannas replied. 'My favourite area is the palace district.' As he described the splendour of the area through his eyes, Sai who had been listening to the conversation, disappeared into her own thoughts being reminded of her short stay in Babylon selling her lapis lazuli. Has it already been one moon? she thought. Her priority at the time had been to obtain the best price possible and having done so, the next morning was already on her way to Susa with her supply of tea, animals, and servants. Just like in Sharuppak, but for completely different reasons, the visit was a blur of memories. The lapis had secured such a high price and instantly transformed Sai into an independent, wealthy young lady who now grasped the new choices open to her. At this particular time of need in her life, she appreciated the magic of the world for guiding her to Husha, Alizer, Daniel, and Iannas in Ur and gave thanks to all the beings, spirits and forces of the world that might have been listening and responsible.

'You will show me around Babylon, won't you?' Sai checked with Daniel and Iannas, interrupting their descriptions of Babylon.

'Of course we will. And one more thing,' Daniel had now built up his courage to approach the subject, 'what will you do when we reach Babylon?'

Sai answered without hesitation, 'I know my mind and my body needs to stop and catch itself. It has been a difficult few moons, but as we approach I cannot say I have decided. I have enjoyed our journey together. Let me see Babylon and get a feel of the city; it will help me decide if it is the right place for me to come to terms with the past and see the future.' She already knew what she wanted to do, but she wanted to be sure.

'Husha?' Sai called, 'Will we be saying goodbye to you in Babylon?' Iannas noticed the hesitations in Sai's words but did not know what they represented. Sai was asking Husha so that he did not launch into another tirade about how Iannas and Daniel had no idea what they were getting into.

'Yes. I will return to Susa with my owner Ubi. Let me know if you have any messages for your father, Daniel.'

'Will you miss us? Will you miss me?' Sai felt like teasing him.

Husha tried not to smile. In truth he had grown to enjoy his time with them and the memories of his youth that they had stirred. The travel had been useful too.

'Yes, Sai, I will miss you, but as for these two know-it-alls...' Husha enjoyed winding them up, but Sai did not let it go further. Sai was enjoying her turn to lead the Donkey, but she was hungry too.

'Time for us to make camp soon, Husha, tomorrow we arrive in Babylon. What are we having for dinner this evening?'

Donkey saw the light was fading and was looking forward to the food and the stars of the night. He felt healthy, strong and had already sensed that this was more than a long journey; he now knew from Daniel that this was a particularly important journey. While he could sense Daniel, Iannas, and Sai well, he wondered if they knew his sense and being. In fact, it was Husha who could read Donkey better than the other three, but Husha did not let Donkey read him.

Early in the morning on the eighth day out of Uruk, they crossed the river in full sight of the Tower that grew larger as they approached, albeit an unfinished ziggurat, and locally known as the Tower of Babylon. The moving caravan did not pause but continued the short distance past the Tower to the main gate of Babylon where the excited caterpillar disbanded, and almost all the released individual units rearranged themselves to create a new one as they joined a long queue with at least one earlier caravan of twenty traders and families in front of them. The wait in the queue reminded Iannas and Daniel that this was the end of the journey for the group, and the end of the day would bring with it the time for parting. The wait and procedure to enter Babylon took the remainder of the morning and dragged past midday as it had in Uruk.

Daniel and Iannas blamed themselves for not expecting the long queues and the thorough questioning, which was more an interrogation. They had forgotten the attempted assassination in Uruk, and Babylon was still on alert. After the grilling, the soldiers in charge of customs insisted on seeing the inventory of their supplies and went through one of the large supply bags on Donkey, only to find the contents matched the detailed inventory prepared by Husha and Sai. The guards seemed disappointed and allowed the group to progress to the tax area where Daniel paid the entry tax for the group even though Sai was insisting on paying her share. Daniel received the passes, and then, with relief and hunger, as it was past lunchtime, they walked through the gate. The queue and entry procedures had been more tiring than the journey that morning from the night camp.

It was during the wait in the queue and the interrogations that Husha reflected that the Babylon gate marked the end of his journey with these young people he had shared the last twelve days with. He had remembered his youth. He remembered drinking the clear water from the wells around the Nile. Where had the time gone? Had it been so long? Where had the laughter been hiding all these years? He could not remember being as joyful in his youth as these youngsters. He would never be young again, and he would never be this age again, and yet somehow he was content. Content that he had fulfilled his purpose and learned the knowledge that, if he were right, would change the world.

Acutely aware that it was already late, they immediately headed to the Babil district and asked for Sargon the Builder at the busiest beer and wine bar in the small district square. They were quick to learn there were many builders named Sargon in Babylon, and most of them from the same family. The former king had clearly been popular. When they asked for Sargon, the Head of Wall Repairs they got a different answer; he had moved to the south of the city only a few days ago to take charge of a major wall collapse as a consequence of an uncharted underground stream. Everyone in Babylon was talking about it; it had caused the collapse of a number of houses too. The group was disappointed but knew that they had to find Sargon as soon as possible. Daniel hoped, at least, that if the wall collapse was as big as the people described, it might be easy to find.

The beer and wine bar owner suggested Daniel visit Sargon's previous home just around the corner from the bar in case the new address had been left there. Daniel ran to the house and quickly returned with the news that Sargon's family possessions had been moved to a villa in the gold district, not far from the wall collapse.

Heading to the gold district meant walking across the city through the narrow, busy main streets and although everyone knew Donkey would slow them down, they still tried, and Donkey did. Husha came to the rescue. 'You three go ahead. Let me follow at my own speed with the Donkey. The streets are too busy for him. I know some quiet back streets. I will meet you at sunset in the gold quarter at the southern gate. Look for a small private stable next to the soldiers' quarters and a beer and wine bar. The bar serves good food and that is where I will meet you.

After the gentle quiet travel of the countryside, a bustling busy city atmosphere did not seem to suit Iannas, Daniel or Sai, only Husha appeared to thrive.

It was now late in the afternoon, and they had not yet reached the southern part of the city. Sai slowed them down a little as they passed the Palace complex but it had been worth seeing her reaction. She had never seen anything as grand as this and coupled with the distant Temple or Tower of Babel as it was locally known, the views had been breathtaking, but their pace needed to quicken and now Iannas was hurrying them onwards.

Daniel firmly held on to his shoulder bag that he had packed while they were clearing the camp at dawn and wondered if he should have left the book in Donkey's saddlebag as they hurried through the artisan's district and entered the gold quarter. They walked through a small district full of compact and brightly-lit stores, little bubbles adorned with jewellery. The streets were much busier than any of the other areas they had walked through, announcing the extent of individual wealth in Babylon, but the streets were also narrower and blocked any view of the city wall. So, in the dimming light, as none of the torches had yet been lit, they had to ask for Sargon again. This time, a patrolling soldier guided them to a villa in a small quiet street immediately behind the main gold market street.

It was the right house, an oasis of peace, but Sargon was not at home. The young servant boy who answered the door gave them very precise directions to the wall collapse. The damaged wall was only a short distance away, but the new darkness and the crowded maze of dimly lit narrow streets were so confusing, they could not make any sense of their bearings until they caught sight of the newly-lit torches on the city walls, which drew them in the right direction. Once there, finally, they caught sight of the scaffolding being erected on a section of the city wall. As they approached, they saw the workers were following orders from what appeared to be an officer in army uniform, clearly in a foul mood, directing the various wall repair teams and demanding that all the torches be lit so the repairs could continue.

'We will be here all night if needed until this wall is secure, so get used to it,' he shouted at the workers.

Sargon was paying particular attention to the digging and underpinning at the same time as directing the wooden scaffolding system being built by another team. A third team was busy closing off the road for the night, creating more chaos on the road than was necessary. An accident involving an old man tripping over some of the building rubble caused a commotion in the street corner, and all this because the streets were now so packed that it was becoming almost impossible to go anywhere.

Iannas, Daniel, and Sai understood now why the streets around had been so full and chaotic but they had not expected that Sargon would be an officer in the army.

They approached Sargon, and Daniel introduced himself after catching his attention. While Daniel, Iannas, and Sai were relieved to have found him, Sargon was none too pleased to be found.

'Now you arrive? I expected you in the morning! We could have sorted all this before now. You have to wait. Part of this wall could fall at any time. I have to sort this out.'

He shouted more orders to the scaffolding team, turned his attention to the diggers, and finally told the soldiers to aid his men in closing the streets around the repair area, which they were actually trying to do without much success, as there were too many people interested in the work going on and the injured man. He returned his attention to Daniel.

'Look, I cannot leave the men. Come to my home later in the evening. Once this is under control I will make time for you.' He was a little more conciliatory, but there was nothing more to do to change his position. 'One of my men will tell you where I live. Just ask any one of them.' Sargon did not know that Daniel had already been to his home. Sargon focused his attention back to his men and continued shouting instructions to the teams.

'Let's find Husha.' Iannas quickly assessed the situation and realised they were in the way and did not want to be responsible for any problems caused by distracting Sargon. Sai and Iannas had to drag reluctant Daniel away, who eventually gave in to their insistence.

Daniel's spirits had now opened the door to misery and self-pity as they picked their way through the mass of people in the streets, only made slightly easier because of their smaller size and greater agility. When they reached the stables, Husha and Donkey were not there. No one at the stables had seen anyone matching Husha's description. If Iannas and Sai were exasperated, Daniel's misery was now replaced by desolation.

9 DEATH IN BABYLON

Day 23

Next to the stables in the beer and wine bar, hungry and thirsty, having not eaten all day, three lost souls took possession of a vacant wooden bench and table at the entrance, baring their souls for all to notice from the street but none of the passersby cared. The menu of the day was ordered, roasted lamb, boiled grain, pickled olives, bread, dates and, of course, pomegranates from Susa.

The markets would remain open late into the night, but the fresh food market farmers would probably have very limited supplies at that time of the night, and they would probably be stretched to find all the items needed for Alizer's group. It looked inevitable that they would have to organise the supplies and caravans tomorrow. Iannas took the responsibility of voicing their fears and preparing themselves for a second night in Babylon.

'A reduced gap of two days between Alizer and us is manageable, but it will become a major problem if we are delayed once more after this. If we find ourselves buying supplies for Alizer's group on the same day as their arrival we will have failed.'

Daniel started scolding himself, and Sai and Iannas attempted to calm him.

'We could not have anticipated the queues to enter Babylon, Daniel. Even if we had, there was very little we could have done.' Iannas tried to be reassuring without success and saw that Daniel was submerging himself in self-pity, so he decided to tease him instead. 'We cannot do anything now, we do not know which city we should be heading for and who our contacts are. Worrying does not make it better.' Iannas said all this quickly in a matter-of-fact manner with his cheeky grin and added, 'And we have shown Sai more of Babylon than she wanted to see.' Iannas looked at Sai who was feeling guilty that she had contributed to the lateness, but she too grinned as Iannas started to laugh, Iannas' way of dealing with the situation and letting go of any tension. Sai was concerned by Iannas' laughter, but then could not help but join in the mirth, seeing the impossibility of the situation.

'It does not take you long to slip into that half-empty world of yours, does it?' Iannas commented. Sai was watching and was shocked at how daring Iannas' words were to his hurting friend. She was still getting to know their different ways of dealing with things and saw now how well Iannas complemented Daniel.

Iannas had more to offer, 'Ok, have you finished so that we can start solving the problem, or shall we continue listening to your self-pity, and walk with you into that empty hollow world that you happen to be standing in right now?'

Sai was cringing and saw this last comment had caught Daniel's attention. She waited for an angry reaction from Daniel, but none came. Instead, Daniel watched Iannas for a moment or two, clearly upset, but seeing the grin on Iannas' face, he too started to smile at himself, eventually dissolving into laughter at the situation. Ever since they had known each other, more than seven years since they had first met in Nineveh on one of Daniel's father's trading journeys, Iannas always had a way of making Daniel laugh, especially at times when Daniel thought his entire world was collapsing. Here was his friend whose mother had passed away only a few moons ago, and Sai, who had lost not only her husband, but her entire world only three moons ago, and he was sitting in his pity. He smiled and for a brief instant contemplated that he should rise and hug his friends but quickly thought better of it.

Sai watched the two of them and burst out laughing. 'Now I know what to do next time Daniel has a crisis.'

'This is just learning, Daniel. Let's deal with it, and then I will leave you to worry about it. To start with, you stay here, let me look for Husha.' The food had not yet arrived and Iannas stood up and left Sai and Daniel more relaxed and smiling.

Iannas was making sure he did not express his disappointment and concern too much. He knew he had to move on, and maybe it was his mother's passing, he had learned to accept the journey of life for what it was, not what he would like it to be.

Iannas did not have to go inside the small stables. From the doorway, he could see Husha settling Donkey in the corner of the torch-lit stable next to three other donkeys and their loads. When Husha saw Iannas, the two greeted each other. Although Iannas was relieved, Husha seemed more moody than usual but Iannas did not comment. Husha and Iannas walked over to the table where Sai and Daniel were waiting. Daniel did not need to say anything for Husha to know that something was up. 'Bad day?' he asked as he sat down next to Sai with Iannas and Daniel facing them.

'The worst.' Daniel replied almost sliding back into his worries.

Husha would have normally started a lecture but he had not had a good day either. 'Sargon is too busy to see you?' he asked.

'How do you know everything?' Iannas quizzed him. 'Where have you been? We were worried.'

'The streets were too busy for Donkey, so I took him to a quiet place, gave him water and shade while I dealt with my business.'

Daniel was glad he had kept the book in the shoulder bag. He needed to find something to be cheerful about right now.

'Did you find your owner?' Sai asked.

'Yes,' then without any emotion he added, 'he died yesterday. They buried him this afternoon. I went to the temple service, which is why I am late.' Daniel was struck by the news; he knew the Ugibi family from Susa.

'The illness?' Daniel asked remembering that Ubi had been ill and why Husha had been in Ur on his own.

'The doctors were bleeding him to remove the fever and the sickness. They tried almost every day in the last period of his sickness without any effect. They told me he had a fever lasting four days after I left and much of the time since then he has been asleep. He only woke five days ago and then only for two days; apparently he was very weak. He was aware of his condition and settled all his affairs during those two days and then fell back into his sleeping sickness. He never woke up. He died in his sleep last night. The herbs, the bleeding, nothing worked.'

'I am sorry,' Sai tried to soothe everyone, but none could read Husha who expressed no sentiment.

'What does this mean for you, Husha?' asked Iannas gently.

'The family is in Susa, and his son is already on his way here. He knows his father is ill but not that he has died. Anyway, when I heard the news, I rested and waited for the funeral temple service. He was buried in the cemetery outside the main gate and I collected my thoughts. I made my way here as soon as the streets appeared to calm, but in Babylon the streets never sleep so it took a while reaching the stables. I assume you have not had a chance to learn anything about the next stage of your journey?' Husha already knew the answer. By turning the conversation, he had avoided Iannas' question.

He made a familiar face which the three looking on recognised as the 'I knew it! I just wish you would ask me to help sometimes' look.

'I made sure I found out as much as I could just in case.' Husha stated in his matter-of-fact way drawing looks of surprise and raised eyebrows from Iannas, Daniel, and Sai who did not say anything. It was a difficult moment, for none of them understood what his owner's death meant for Husha and they could not see how he felt, so they remained quiet and let him talk.

'Sargon works for the government in the security division,' Husha said. 'These people are usually attached to the army in some way. His family also has a number of businesses here but his main expertise is construction. He has the best reputation for building massive, solid, long-lasting buildings. His family have been building some of the larger structures in Babylon for more than a generation. I bet he has Egyptian blood in him. Anyway, that is why he is in charge of all wall repairs in the city. Sargon uses a service station provider who is based just outside the Ishtar gate. It is very likely he will ask you to drop the supplies for Alizer at his stand. The name of the person at the station is Ibi, son of Har.'

Daniel, Iannas, and Sai were already mesmerised, not just by what Husha was saying but that he had found out all this information while dealing with the death of his owner and attending his funeral.

'The Empire at the moment appears to be relatively quiet. The main trouble spots seem to be Ur and Isin. On the road to the north, bandits seem to be the main issue. There is also some friction between the temple priests and the Royal Courts, but their problems should not concern us on the road. Alizer and his family, however, will want to keep a low profile so as not to be embroiled in any local problems. We have two options tomorrow. Most of the caravans heading north go to Nineveh. At the moment, there are many reports of bandits and also soldiers unsettling the travellers along that particular route.' Husha turned to Iannas and Sai. 'Did you notice anything unusual when you travelled from Nineveh?'

'Only on one night,' Iannas remembered. 'The camp had to be woken extra early and pack quickly. There was a report of a group of bandits in the area.' Sai mentioned a few checkpoints but nothing unusual, but she admitted to not being too clear and being preoccupied at the time.

Husha paused; he was embarrassed at having asked Sai as soon as he realised that her husband had died at that time. He caught his breath and continued. 'Some of these bandits on that road it seems may be soldiers from the neighbouring cities trying to set up extra tax and customs posts. They have not yet succeeded according to today's reports. North to Nineveh and then west to Harran, nevertheless, is one option. You both have been on this route,' he looked at Daniel and Iannas. 'You will know the route becomes difficult through the mountain range, and the valleys will slow down the caravan. This is what I heard from my source, but I have not travelled that route.'

Both Iannas and Daniel who had travelled that route nodded and confirmed Husha's information.

Iannas had noticed a change from 'we' to 'you' but did not say anything.

'The other route to Harran is to head towards Damascus along the Euphrates through to Mari, Terqa, and Tuttul. In Tuttul you come away from the Euphrates and take another river valley north to Harran. This is your second option.

'If you take the Euphrates option, I am told there are plenty of caravans, and that the route appears quiet and no troubles have yet been reported. It is on the edge of the empire, and there is much desert on the southern side of the river. There are villages and stations almost every day for basic supplies. It is well-travelled but less so than the Nineveh route. There may be more movement because of the drought, but I did not hear anything about that today. Quieter does not mean safer,' he added. 'Sometimes this means more bandits.' Husha finished and asked if they would order him some food. There was still no emotion to read.

Daniel spoke. 'The food is on its way, Husha, and we can order more. Husha, you are incredible, your strength is what we need right now so thank you. I am so sorry for your loss and the situation you are now in.' Daniel paused. 'We have to wait to see what Sargon has to say; there may be a route already organised for us, but let me hear your opinion. Which route should we take if we have a choice?'

'I gave that some thought on the way here. I would not be worried about the two,' he paused and looked at Sai, 'or three of you travelling along the Tigris to Nineveh, you will blend in. I worry about Alizer's family. He has already warned us they need to be more discreet.' Husha paused.

'My suggestion?' he reflected. 'Before I answer, I have one more piece of information to add. It is my own opinion. Azhar is no stranger to these lands. He has travelled north to Nineveh and beyond many times. I am given to understand that many caravan leaders know him, and he is well known in most of the towns north of here. In fact, I also understand that some of his distant family even reside in the northern mountains, mainly shepherds and mountain people. Having lots of people who know the family could be a good advantage. The mountains to Harran will be a problem, not for Azhar but the larger group, some elderly, and since they are known on the route they will not be able to keep a low profile. My suggestion is to take the less visible route, so we should travel along the Euphrates and then head north. It will be safer for Alizer and the family.'

Iannas chipped in, he could not resist now. 'Do you mean "we" as in all of us, Husha?'

Husha paused. The food had arrived while he was talking. 'The food is waiting, let's eat.' He did not answer. He picked up a small clay plate, placed his food on it, and then walked over to a stone bench where some other slaves were picking at their food. Daniel knew better than to invite him to join them, which would cause a scene in the bar.

Sai, Daniel, and Iannas looked at each other and tucked into the food. Each had their own thoughts and, starting with Iannas, each in turn spoke animatedly of the options in front of them and Husha's role in getting all this information. They were all thinking the same, but it was Iannas who asked the unthinkable and the improbable, 'There is no way he can come with us now that his owner has died, is there?'

Daniel seemed to know the answer. 'Not unless he can buy his freedom. He is now the property of the son who can refuse to release him. He will have to wait until the son arrives to know his fate. If he is not needed, Husha would be sold or used to pay off debts to creditors.'

Sai immediately thought about making the money available so that Husha could buy his own freedom. She left that thought hanging for the moment. She had no idea how much would be needed.

Iannas observed, 'Let's see what Sargon says to you, Daniel. It's nearly time. Finish your dinner. It will take you a while to find him again. I think you should see him on your own. I will wait here with Sai and Husha.' Iannas added. 'When you come back we can make some decisions.'

Daniel ate quickly and rushed over to Sargon's villa where Sargon had already arrived for his family dinner. Their meeting was courteous, polite, and concise. Daniel did not enter the house. They talked in the courtyard.

'Here is the money for the supplies and the caravans.' Daniel received the bag of coins from Sargon and attempted to return to Sargon the left over money from the previous trips, but he would not hear of it. 'You will need it. There is still a long way to go. I understand Alizer left Ur as planned and everything is going well.' Sargon then surprised Daniel by asking him his opinion regarding the route they should take next.

'Have you thought which route you will take, Daniel, to Nineveh on the Tigris or towards Mari on the Euphrates?' Sargon had already assumed Daniel knew the way. It was a fair assumption, Daniel thought, and he knew not to hesitate.

'The Euphrates River will be better for Alizer and the family. It will be quieter, more discreet, and also, I think, quicker to Harran.'

Sargon smiled, and he had a kindly face when he smiled. 'You are right. Terah made a good choice. Time is short, Daniel, and today you were delayed. Alizer is only three days behind you. Do not be delayed again. Alizer and his family depend on you, and it is not safe for them to be slowed down. If you delay and the gap between you becomes too close you will be of no use to them. Book a caravan as before and leave the instructions with my service agent. His name is Ibi-Har. Head to Sippar and look for Udama son of Szamasz, the scribe who resides in Tel Abu Habba. Udama will guide you further. He is a good man.'

Daniel made sure to remember the names.

'The markets will remain open a little longer, and to help you I have already asked my servant boy to buy the supplies Alizer needs for the next stage of the journey. They have already been sent to Ibi. You do not need to spend the money I have just given you. It is my gift to them. I owe Alizer that much at least. Now go and hurry. Book the caravans, label the supplies, neither my servant nor Ibi know who the supplies are for. And do not waste even one day. Alizer's family are depending on it.'

'What do you mean you owe him that much, Sargon?'

'He saved my life, Daniel. Now go, we will meet again no doubt in another time and place.'

Daniel could not remember if he said thank you or goodbye, but he ran as fast as he could and almost tripped over several times to get back to the bar where his friends were waiting for him. He waved to Husha who approached with an air of resignation and sat with them while Daniel described the meeting. There was much noise in the bar, but Daniel was nonetheless careful that no one would hear.

At the end, he turned to Husha, 'You were brilliant, Husha; your assessment of the two routes ahead of us was perfect and we...,' Daniel paused as he looked as his friends, 'I... could not have done this without you. I was sitting here earlier thinking that we had already failed, and you came and saved the day. Thank you, Husha, and my deepest gratitude for looking after us. I will miss you.' He said this as a man with sincerity blended with genuine appreciation that only a young man not too jaded with age is able to convey. Sai and Iannas wholeheartedly agreed with Daniel. Husha was visibly touched.

Sai added. 'You are very special, Husha. I think you should stay with us on our journey. Please join us, will you?'

Daniel and Iannas looked at Sai with surprise, 'You made your decision, Sai? You will travel with us!' Iannas and Daniel both said this together, and did not hide their pleasure as they looked at Husha. 'I think the question is unfair on you. We know your circumstances, Husha.' Daniel tried to ease the response. 'We would love you to join us. Is there anything that can be done?' He did not want to add any more and make matters worse for him.

'My owner left a message for me before he died, "a gift" it said, for my "hard work, loyalty and the good I brought him". It was part of the will he made before he passed away. The will said that he knew I was not meant to be a slave, he wanted to thank me for running the caravanserai in Susa and he set me free on condition that I pray for him. He seems to think that my prayers, as his former slave, will mean more to him in the afterlife than the prayers of his family. He even signed the tablet for my freedom with his seal before he fell into his sleep.'

Iannas, Sai, and Daniel were amazed.

'How do you feel about his death now?' Sai asked.

'He is born again,' Husha shrugged. 'In my faith, we lay the body down to be born again in another world, maybe another place, maybe another time.' Husha paused.

Iannas and Daniel tried to understand this way of thinking but failed to grasp it, but Sai nodded with a shared emotion. The faith of Krishna had a similar approach to death.

'I will travel with you,' Husha declared, 'because I am free to travel and because you have asked me, and I believe you are sincere in your asking. You have not told me, and that is important to me, I have a choice and that is also important to me. You must know I have very little money at present, but I will pay my way. But mainly,' Husha paused, more for effect. 'I accept because you need me and you cannot complete this journey without me.' He said this last part so seriously, there was no alternative but to laugh out loud and as was Iannas' way, he started the laughter to be joined by both Sai and Daniel. Husha, having thought about what he said, joined them in the hilarity. They all stood and congratulated Husha while those around them on the other tables and benches looked at them and joined the mirth, not knowing what they were laughing at. There was nothing else to do. It was a beer and wine house.

Iannas quickly took charge. 'All right, Husha and I will go to Ibi-Har and check that the supplies from Sargon are already there and securely packed. We will take Donkey, set up camp and get everything ready near to the station. I will also book the caravans for us and for Alizer's group to Sippar. If this works we can leave on the first caravan out. Sai and Daniel, you go and look for anything extra you think they might need as well as our supplies for the next four days. You do not have much time. After you have completed the shopping, have it delivered to Ibi-Har where Husha will be waiting for you. By the time you get to us, we should have finished with the bookings and made the camp ready, and you, Daniel, can finish off by labelling Alizer's supplies.'

Here they were, all four together again. Iannas felt as if the world had refreshed itself and suddenly decided, without any reason, to change its mind and lift away all the obstacles that had attempted to keep them apart. He still had not grasped the sense of the world, a world that needed Daniel to proceed and would help when it could. It was late, and they were all already exhausted so they were grateful for Iannas' clear thinking.

Daniel paid the bill and gave Iannas a bag of coins to pay for the caravans, and they all headed off to meet their tasks. Donkey did not get much rest but more than his helpers. He felt better with the water, the straw, and the sweet fruit, and vegetables. When Iannas and Husha returned to take him away, he was ready to go, and Iannas paid for the use of the stable.

In the thinning market, some traders had already packed, others were packing, and a few were planning on remaining open till late. Daniel and Sai quickly completed their supplies purchase but had to pay extra to have it delivered to Ibi-Har where Husha was already waiting. At this time of night, all the delivery teams had gone home and a willing pair of hands would need to be found and encouraged. Sai and Daniel, by chance, passed a shoemaker in the market square who was clearly intent on working into the night. Daniel's shoes had started to wear badly so he knew Alizer and the family would be experiencing the same. He did not know what sizes would be needed, but he bought a number of pairs in different sizes, as well as fresh pairs for Iannas, Sai, and Husha.

By the time they reunited at the station, the camp was ready, Iannas had secured caravans for both themselves and Alizer's group, and Husha had checked and repacked Alizer's supplies at Ibi's station ready for Daniel to label. Iannas gave Daniel the name of Alizer's caravan as Daniel took out his wet clay and made his tablet. He also left verbal instructions with Ibi-Har who was sure he would be there for Alizer.

Daniel would never realise how many blessings were showered on him when the shoes and the other little items, like the extra plates and cups, were received by Alizer and the family.

It was a fleeting thought, but Sai began to understand why it was young Daniel leading this journey and not his father. She thought about it no more.

Iannas understood something else; they needed to be much more organised next time.

Husha felt a new understanding of his circumstances and his purpose. There was something incredible happening. A marvellous event was in progress, and he appeared to be at the very heart of it. How would it turn out? he wondered. But, for now, he knew that where he sat, is where the universe required him to be; next to Daniel, Iannas, and Sai.

When they finally rested in their camp, Iannas, Daniel, and Sai looked at each other and started laughing again, letting all their frustrations go. It had been a crazy day full of downs and ups. Husha could not help but smile as he watched them. Donkey heard their laughter as he rested, pleased that everything was good in the world, pleased that he was guiding his friends, and pleased they were all together as he had been worried for a while. He had been confused in the day when they had separated because together is what they were meant to be.

10 THE ROAD TO SIPPAR

Days 24 to 26, 9.2 Beru.

Even the river of Euphrates could not have created the turns and the variety of tides of emotions that had been experienced in Babylon, and today a silent recuperation was gently easing the marks of the surges of yesterday.

Iannas was leading Donkey and enjoying the day even more than usual. Yesterday had ended with a glow, and today he was delighted to be continuing with the company of Sai and Husha. A force was protecting the fellowship. Iannas could not help but wonder at the web that wove itself to reveal their present circumstances. He walked silently giving thanks to the God of the universe that was able to create such a scheme. Was it destiny? Iannas allowed himself to disappear in the mêlée of the caravan, lost in the calmness Donkey was sharing with him.

The new caravan united a very different mix of people. It was refreshing to see children and families instead of just traders and, highly unusual, a music band with their drums, harps and assortment of wind instruments heading to Mari for the Shortest Day Full Moon Festival. The caravan was so much more relaxed to walk in with the smiles and sometimes play of the very young ones accompanied with the parental love that was a pleasure to watch.

The clouds were being lit in the east by the still hidden sun when they had set off from Babylon. They had watched the early morning boats queuing to unload their cargos at the city harbour, which included construction materials such as stone and wood as well as different foods and even gold. With the soldiers on board, they could tell which boats held the precious cargos.

The river levels had begun to decrease, and the ground was increasingly firmer as the caravan headed north along the banks of the Euphrates and its canals. The forests along this stretch had been harvested by Babylon long ago, so there was little shade available. When they found themselves walking together later in the afternoon, Iannas took the moment to explore why Sai was still with them.

'Do not misunderstand,' he tried to be polite, 'I think you know how happy we are that you are still with us, Sai, but what made you decide to continue the journey? I was so sure you would leave us in Babylon and take the time you said you needed.'

Sai answered straight away, 'Babylon was simply not a place I felt connected to. The buildings are beautiful, and I have seen nothing like it, there is no doubt, but maybe it was our experience or maybe it was the people. I found it so crowded and busy. Everyone appeared to be rushing around and did not appear to have time for living. Right now, I need a peaceful place, somewhere like Sharuppak to meditate.' Sai wondered whether she should have stayed behind in Sharuppak, but the thought had not crossed her until now. 'I could not sense any peace in Babylon, and it occurred to me that if they are so keen on repairing the walls, I have to ask, who are they frightened of? Are they preparing for a battle?'

That was very perceptive of Sai, Husha thought.

'The walls of Babylon are so high,' Sai added, 'and the security so intense. I know it is for safety. The place reminded me of a little hamlet in the mountains near my village where a small group of people decided to live together with their own faith and customs, which, of course, no one on the mountain was concerned about. They were a private but peaceful community. Perhaps they feared intrusion, or maybe they thought the other villagers would persecute them. First, they built a fence around their hamlet, then they brought dogs to guard the gates, finally they built such a high wall that no one could see in or out. Every time I passed the compound to visit my grandma, who lived in a village nearby, I always felt sorry for them because she told me they never came out. They even had supplies delivered to them. I thought they were living in a prison of fear, and it really looked like a prison from the outside. They were free like us to enjoy the mountain, the sky, touch the nature and travel, but they chose a closed life. It would have been wonderful to get to know them and their faith and culture, but I think they felt threatened that the rest of us would erode their way of life. That is no way to live. This journey has revealed to me something special about the world and I am now keen to continue experiencing it.'

She brought a different way of thinking and the listeners enjoyed adding her perspective to their own experience.

Husha could not recollect having met anyone like Sai before, even in Egypt. How strange, where some saw security and order, others recognised it as oppression and confinement. Is this how empires end? Husha thought as he remembered Ur.

'Why Harran, Sai? Will you travel all the way with us?' Daniel asked.

'Because I have never been to Harran is the simple answer to your first question, Daniel. I know I do not want to return to India. Harran sounds like a good place and also,' Sai paused, 'because you two are heading there.' She looked at Daniel and Iannas. 'I am intrigued with the journey you have undertaken, and I want to see if you make it.'

Husha sensed the perfect invitation and Sai knew as she turned to Husha with a mischievous grin.

'You see!' Husha concluded. 'Even Sai is not sure if you will get there in one piece. Don't worry; Sai and I will make sure you do.'

Iannas unsuccessfully attempted his wicked look at Husha and asked before Husha could carry on, 'Now that you are a free man, what will you do, Husha?'

'You mean, after I have made sure you arrive in one piece in Harran?' Husha persisted.

'Will your papers be enough to get you through to Harran?' Iannas continued. 'You are free to do anything you want and go anywhere you want. Why stay with us?'

It was a good question that caught Husha. 'Yes, I am free,' replied Husha, more pensive.

Husha reached into his pocket and from a little pouch removed a tablet, placed it on his hand and proceeded to point out the Egyptian hieroglyphic shapes and patterns to Iannas, Daniel, and Sai, who of course, did not understand any of it; all three looked quizzically at Husha. Had Husha allowed them to inspect the tablet, Iannas and Daniel would have read the translation on the reverse and learned his identity.

'It is my Egyptian identity. I should have no problem reaching Harran, and indeed I can travel all the way back to Egypt freely.'

'That does not make any sense, Husha.' Daniel and Sai shared Iannas' puzzlement. 'Am I right in thinking you could have put the tablet on at any time and escaped from your slavery, even in Susa?'

'No,' Husha was quick in correcting Iannas, 'escaping from bondage is an executable offence in this land, and very few slaves ever escape and remain alive for long. I had no intention of meeting my end in that way. The way I see it, I was exactly where I wanted to be and exactly where I needed to be. Now, by some strange turn of events, I am free. I can wear my Egyptian identity for the first time, and I am with you on a journey I had never planned.'

Husha was reflective. Then he smiled. 'This tablet was only returned to me yesterday,' Husha confessed, and they all smiled as they realised Husha had left the truth till last; he had been leading them on. He had a well-developed sense of humour, thought Iannas. 'My owner kept this Egyptian identification tablet as security. It was given to him by the slavers, which added an extra price on my head. Ubi kept it in his private box with other personal tablets that he carried on his travels.' He smiled knowing he could have stolen it and escaped had he really wanted to, but being free was far better than being a fugitive. 'Let's talk about more important things. Sippar is only two days away. We need to be better organised.'

Iannas eagerly took over the discussion, and everyone was happy to allow him to oversee the next stop.

'Husha, have you been to Sippar?' Iannas asked, having organised everyone for Sippar.

'No.' Husha was always a man of few words when asked something directly. 'But you heard from Rabiat that there is a great treasure buried in Sippar?' he added.

Iannas, who loved the ancient tales, of course, took the bait and immediately wanted to know if Husha knew the story, could he tell them and if he knew of anyone who had searched for it.

Husha promised to be the evening's storyteller, as the shadows were already long and the sound of the horn would soon take charge of the caravan.

That night, the dinner menu had only had two items: the grain soup made with the recipe Husha had obtained from Rabiat, which everyone enjoyed.

'A little bit more practice and it will be perfect,' teased Sai.

Husha chose to ignore Sai, for he was enjoying the second item on the menu: music. The combination of drums, flute, and harps from tonight's impromptu performance by the band turned a still night into a gentle oasis of soft rhythmic beats allowing the imaginations to soar. Husha used the sounds to his advantage and proceeded to tell his version of the story of Xisuthros.

'The records of the world before the great flood are buried in Sippar,' Husha began. 'Who ever discovers them will know the secrets of the ancient world, a world of ancient gods, angels, mysteries, and magic. Whoever finds it will be the wealthiest person in the world, wealthier than the Pharaoh of Egypt.' Husha had clearly told this story many times before.

'I think you all know one of the most famous stories of Xisuthros, a great King of Sippar who, they say, was the tenth king from the line of kings that began when the first human was born, from a time when people decided that kings were necessary and needed. Since the world was so young, these early kings had knowledge of the creator of the world and the knowledge to communicate with the creator. They had a consciousness and wisdom of all the mysteries of the world, including where the gold and precious stones were to be found, the secret of life and death, and the secrets of the heavens and the animals and monsters in the oceans. They knew the languages of the birds, insects and animals, and they knew how to listen and understand the trees, flowers, even the wind, the mountains, the sea, the fire, and the very ground they walked on.

'One day, the tenth king was in Sharuppak and while there was commanded by the creator to make ready for a huge flood that would destroy not only the city, but all the cities of the world. In order to start the world anew, Xisuthros was asked to prepare for this inevitable disaster by building a huge ship for his family, friends and various animals and birds as well as many plants and insects who would become the life of the new world. According to some, these events occurred only four hundered years ago.'

Sai remembered the floods in Northern India and the devastation she had seen. She, Iannas and Daniel knew the story of Xisuthros, the flood, and the Ark.

'In this story, it is not the command to build the ship, which was later built in and launched from Sharuppak, that is of interest to us; maybe it was the ship Rabiat was referring to when she said Sharuppak was a place of all beginnings. There was another command that few people know of, or choose to ignore; Xisuthros was also instructed to save all the books in Sippar and write a History of the World containing all knowledge so that the people of the new world would have a reference to start their new lives. He was required to bury all the books including the History of the World, once completed, in Sippar itself.

'The problem Xisuthros faced was that in this era, writing was only just being invented and developed. Writing was a realm of the few. Only the high priests of the temples of the time had the knowledge of reading and writing, and they had become well respected and seen as wise leaders by the people. The priests had already written many tablets recording their prayers and rituals that only they could read and had access to. Since no one out of the circle of priests could access or read the sacred tablets, the prayers and rituals and even the written form was deemed a mystery.

'Xisuthros had a problem. The priests could have written the History of the World containing all their knowledge and that of the world, but there were so few priests for such a huge task, it would have taken them so long that by the time the floods came, only a small portion of the old knowledge would be recorded.

'So, against the wishes of the priests, the tenth king commanded that all the people of Sippar and the neighbouring cities who wished to learn how to read and write and help write the History of the World and all knowledge should report to the temples. All would be welcomed and be paid handsomely for their services. To start with, a few hundred people came, but as people realised that the king was serious, many thousands presented themselves and everyone who arrived was taught the gift of reading and writing. The priests distributed the teams of writers to all the temples in all the cities and invited all the people of knowledge to make their way to these temples where their knowledge was duly recorded with care. And so the History of the World and all knowledge was written and completed well before the floods began.

'The high priests were told to bury the collection of tablets of all knowledge and the History of the World in Sippar according to the instructions given to Xisuthros, so that the survivors of the flood could return and use the old knowledge to create a better life in the new world.

'Then came the floods, and many stories have been told of the events surrounding them. When the land returned, some of the survivors, including Xisuthros' family and friends, returned to Sippar to start a new life. Some of those who remembered dug through the mud and found the old tablets containing the old knowledge and the History of the World and made it available for the people in the new growing city. In time, a special dedicated library was built to house these tablets.

'A number of unexpected events occurred. Almost everyone who had survived had been a member of one of the writing teams that recorded the History of the World, and they taught their young ones to read and write. This was unexpected, and created a very skilled new young generation who, for the first time, could learn and teach in new ways. What was even more unexpected and created much concern was that very few of this new young generation came to the library to read and learn from the history and the old knowledge.

'The priests who survived tried to teach the young people some of the learning from the ancient books, but because the knowledge was so freely available in the library, they no longer came to the temples to listen to the old stories. The same priests who held all knowledge and power before were no longer held in such high esteem, for all the people had access to the histories and mysteries of the world, which they could read and use in the new world if they chose to at any time, but many made the decision not to.

'The new generations began to use their skill of reading and writing to record their thoughts, write stories from their new world, to pass messages, make contracts, and record transactions between them. Having learned the benefit of reading and writing, they taught their children and their children's children the written language, which began to evolve and spread throughout the lands as people travelled away or travelled through Sippar taking the written language to new homelands.

'As time passed, a small handful of the very elderly who had always used the library and read the History of the World began to learn the mysteries and even discovered the secret prayers to communicate with the world, the heavens, and the universe anywhere and at any time they wanted to. They understood that the whole world was holy, and the whole world was a temple. They learned the secrets of life and death, about spirits and angels, and wealth and poverty as well as the language of the birds, animals, plants, winds, the mountains, and the earth they walked on. Soon, of course, most of the elderly died, and only a handful still survived, and they continued to visit the library and tried to keep the knowledge alive, even though it was only among them.

'The youngest generation knew of the library of the ancients and never used it. They heard about the knowledge of this small group of elderly doctors and philosophers as they were known, labelled all their knowledge as superstition, sentimental stories, tales, myths, or legends and desired to learn only about the present and the new world. They wrote about their own lives and started new libraries containing their own stories and knowledge. When the last of the oldest generation died, the library with the ancient tablets and the History of the World was no longer visited, and the doors remained locked. With the passage of time, even the young people who walked past the unkempt crumbling library building forgot what it had been built for, and when the walls and the ceilings crumbled and the site where the library once stood proud became the city waste ground, nature came to claim the knowledge for itself and covered the site with sand and soil which became the home of wild vegetation and wilder animals, for they knew what lay underneath. The existence of the library was forgotten and the archives, still below ground, were never entered again.

'It is widely believed,' Husha concluded, 'that the library still exists under the current city of Sippar, and whoever finds it will learn all the mysteries of the world including the mysteries of life, death, and the universe. Many a king in this world would give you all the treasure they have and their empires for that knowledge.'

Husha finished, having completely enchanted his audience under the moonlight, stars, and the gentle breeze; they were quietly grateful all their other thoughts had been taken away. The music had continued and added to the drama bringing much of it to life, at least in their imaginaries.

'I had no idea you were such an amazing storyteller, Husha.' Iannas was the first to return to the present world and compliment Husha.

'It is not a story; many people believe it to be true.' Husha defended himself.

'In that case there is only one person among us capable of finding this treasure and has a nose for sniffing out valuable things-' Iannas pointed to Donkey.

They all laughed, not knowing that while he was carrying the book and because he had the purest of hearts, Donkey would have been able to find any treasure they wanted.

Daniel found the story entrancing. 'I am still learning to interpret the signals of the world around me, Husha. Having all of us together feels right,' he paused. 'I think the journey needs everyone of us and I do not want this journey to ever end.'

This time it was Husha's turn to make merry even though Daniel had spoken so sincerely, 'Wait till we get to Harran, Daniel. You will be so fed up of each of us and desperate to escape our company!'

Sai smiled with Husha and disagreed. 'I don't think that will happen.' Then she said to him, 'I noticed, Husha, you are in a good mood today. Tell us what happened in Babylon. Are you able to talk about it?'

Iannas and Daniel thought Husha had already told them what happened in Babylon, so they were surprised by Sai's question. Was there more to tell? Sai knew Husha very well and knew there was more hidden away.

This time, maybe it was because of the way Sai had asked unexpectedly, maybe it was the compliments he was receiving, or just that the door had been revealed in the world at that precise moment, Husha opened the door and told them some of what happened.

When they parted in Babylon, the busy side streets slowed them down. Donkey, in particular, did not enjoy the crowds, so Husha came off the side streets completely and decided to make his way to his owner's apartment in Babylon.

On the way he came across one of Ubi's servants who insisted they made a stop at a beer bar, as he had some urgent news for Husha. They had a drink together while Donkey drank some water and rested. It was in the bar that Husha found out about Ubi. Being told that Ubi had died had an impact on Husha, for Ubi had never mistreated him. In fact, Ubi had encouraged him to run the caravanserai and was always trusting of Husha in all affairs including finances. Husha had been provided with everything he needed but their relationship was always slave and master and while that was clear from the beginning, they respected each other, which was why Ubi had asked Husha to join him on the business trip to Babylon and Ur. Husha had proposed to Ubi to create a partnership with the caravanserais in these two places that would allow Ubi to trade and send supplies directly to each of them, empowering Ubi to act as a trading agent for them. Ubi was keen on the idea and wanted Husha to use his position to explore the possibility inconspicuously before he made any contracts with the caravanserai owners in Babylon and Ur.

According to Ubi's servant, when Ubi was severely ill and had woken up from his sleep, he knew he would die and insisted on settling his affairs. He asked the servants to bring the local official to record his last wishes. Of course, all his wealth was to go to his wife and sons, he left a small amount for each of the servants, and he also wanted to record his respect for Husha's trustworthiness and ability to run the caravanserai in Susa that had added much to Ubi's wealth. Ubi recorded that Husha was to be set free, given a small purse of funds, and that Ubi's son should employ him as Caravanserai Manager in Susa. Once these wishes had been recorded and duly marked by Ugibi, one of the servants went to the local governor's office and registered Husha as a free man and even obtained a small tablet in Husha's name declaring him to be free. From the beer bar the servant took Husha to Ubi's apartment and gave Husha the small tablet, the purse of funds allocated to him in the will and Husha's original Egyptian identification tablet. Husha described that he had no emotional reaction when he saw any of it but took it away.

'It was strange having a small piece of clay to signify my freedom. Was the clay worth just as much as a person's freedom?' he asked.

With the small purse, Husha spent the afternoon in the local beer bar thinking about his new options. It was in the bar that he learned everything he could about the caravan routes from Babylon and about Sargon the Builder.

Husha had not wept for Ubi. That was not his relationship. He explained that had he not been set free, he would have found a way out when the time was right. He explained that he was a free man in Egypt and had always planned to return as a free man when he was ready.

Husha finished his story and although everything Husha had told the group was true, what Husha did not tell them is that after the wine bar he went to see the Head Astrologer in Babylon. A very powerful man, who had expected Husha, opened his office to him and met him without delay.

Daniel, although fascinated by Husha's story, could not let go of his anxieties. It had started as an adventure, an ego that every young person boasts when he is trying to prove that he is an adult; his first journey without his father. The decisions he was making would impact on Alizer and the entire family. What if they needed more supplies, different supplies? What if they wanted him to slow down or speed up? What if they needed special items? Why did Alizer not make sure someone with more experience was given the task? His mind continued in circles all night and the next day. Daniel needed something to worry about. That was his nature. And he created many something's not realising that these doubts never solved any problems.

By choosing to travel together Iannas, Husha, and Sai developed a stronger bond, renewing their obligation and commitment to do everything possible to make sure that Daniel, Alizer, and the family made it all the way to Harran. The pact had already become a fellowship. Maybe now was the moment they became a family.

Donkey sensed the strengthening of this bond. He knew he was at the centre of this family. He understood that he was their anchor. Whenever they went in to the cities without him, they always came back to him. Donkey would lead the way for as long as he had life and strength and for some unknown reason already knew that his journey would last many lifetimes.

11 UDAMA OF SZAMASZ

The treasure of Sippar was the last thing on Daniel's mind when the caravan first glimpsed the walls of Sippar and the boat quays in the late morning from the distant hill rise. When they eventually arrived at the service station just outside the southern city gates in the afternoon, the shadows were still short, and there was plenty of time to sunset.

At dawn, Daniel had already transferred the book from the saddlebag into his shoulder bag while everyone was busy with their tasks. Therefore, on reaching the cedar tree that would be their camp and shelter for the night close to the service station, Daniel was able to forge ahead alone to find Udama while Husha gave Sai and Iannas a hand to unload Donkey. Husha too stepped into Daniel's tracks, and as he approached the gates, he watched Daniel ahead of him showing his identity tablet and paying his entrance tax.

The plans today hinged on Husha purchasing the supplies for the group and having it delivered to the camp, which Sai and Iannas would take delivery of and sort. Meanwhile, Husha would wait for Daniel, and together they would make the purchases for Alizer's group, have it delivered to the service station stand according to the new instructions, where Daniel would later make his way and label the supplies after booking the caravans.

Iannas and Sai both sensed an unspoken bond between them and, being alone, Sai took the opportunity to share with Iannas her fears about returning to India and why she decided to stay with them.

'I have to find a new life, Iannas. Right now, I feel safe with you, Daniel, and Husha, and the three of you are helping me to grieve for both my husband and my past life. This journey is giving me the chance to know myself as never before. I have never been free like this. The more time I spend on this journey, the greater my fear grows of stopping and finding my reality, whatever that is to be. I am scared of leaving the journey behind and looking at the new life waiting. I had never thought I would be leaving my family behind, and it would be the last time I would see them when I said goodbye.'

Iannas listened to Sai's heart and her aspirations and she to his compassion. They continued to talk as they unpacked and set up camp, and when the delivery of the supplies arrived, they began to sort it ready for the next morning's packing.

'There is an opposing force in what you say, Sai. Daniel and I are hurrying to move ahead and complete the journey while you are fearful of what the end of the journey will bring.'

As Iannas tried to understand himself and his new feelings, which he would not understand until he felt the love inside him for his first child, he sought to reassure Sai that he would see her settled when they reached Harran without realising the enormity of the commitment he was promising.

By the time Daniel returned to camp, Sai and Iannas had already received, finished sorting and packing the supplies, and were preparing the evening meal making the most of the fresh goods that had arrived.

'We are heading for Haradum, and the service station contact here is Nida,' was all Daniel needed to say.

Sai took over the preparation of the meal and Daniel and Iannas made their way to book the caravans and label Alizer's supplies at Nida's service stand when it arrived.

After the experience of Babylon, everyone was grateful to be sitting and enjoying Sai's wonderful vegetable stew and fish grilled on charcoal with much of the evening to spare.

Entering the city on foot without Donkey had made a huge difference. Husha and Daniel were able to avoid all the long queues at customs and enter through a separate channel for visitors without goods. The separate customs queues would have taken the other half of the afternoon had Donkey been with them, as the soldiers appeared thorough in monitoring the goods coming through.

Daniel waited and watched the guards check Husha's Egyptian identification tablet around his neck, this being the first time he had cause to use it. Daniel smiled as he watched the guard's reaction, noticeably one of respect as soon as he saw it and quickly ushered him onwards, despite the fact that Husha was dressed in the same simple clothes that did not distinguish him from the other slaves.

The atmosphere in Sippar was much more formal than Babylon. The pride of the formality was the huge volume of business enterprise that could only be found here. Neighbouring cities and visitors often accused Sippar of arrogance, but the locals took the comments as jealousy. Sippar enjoyed and took full advantage of being the central hub of business in all of Mesopotamia, having been designed and built as a river port across a junction of three rivers: one to the south, one from the north, and one from the west. Not always by river, but goods were arriving from Damascus, Nineveh, and Ur and being eagerly traded and sent in all directions. Every bar and every corner of the city hosted a business transaction. The trade taxes were a constant source of government revenue and meant that the city could afford to fund the many projects in Sippar that provided employment to almost every citizen of the city, be it administration, trade, scribes or schools. Since almost everyone in the town could read and write and only citizens of Sippar could officially be employed, there was much opportunity to create wealth. Sometimes with wealth grows a vanity, and although visiting traders found the pride objectionable, they often had no choice but to use Sippar as a gateway, contributing to its wealth, but were not offered any trade concessions in return.

But the compassion of Sippar was also legendary. No Sippar citizen or even visiting trader would ever go hungry or remain uncared for if injured or an illness overtook him or her. The city was well known for its public kitchens providing free food every evening and private hospitals all funded by the philanthropy of the wealth of Sippar. Daniel and Husha passed two temples facing each other on the way to the market, Husha pointed to them, 'These are some of the main employers, Daniel. I met a person in Babylon who is from Sippar and employed here. His job was to record the weather every few hours every day. His friend recorded the time of rising of the moon and the rising of the stars every night. They are making a huge historical library here. Just like in Nippur. They plan to make a record of the life of this city and the people here for the generations to come.'

'Could it not be that they just want people to have a living. Have a job for which they are paid?' Daniel thought out loud. 'Why would they create these huge projects? Who will be interested in the life of this city? Why would they be even interested?'

Before Husha could provide an answer to Daniel's questions they had arrived at the market. They agreed a meeting point in the market when Daniel had finished, and Husha immediately began to look for a farmer with a fresh stock of produce while Daniel went ahead towards Tel Habba to look for Udama.

Over dinner, they complimented Sai on her food and they heard about Udama. Daniel's meeting with Udama had cheered him. Having found the house quickly had helped. The gate was open and welcoming, so he knocked and went into the courtyard, calling Udama's name. He introduced himself to a lady wearing bright bold colours and a wonderful bright headdress to match, clearly from a distant land, Daniel thought maybe from Damascus by her accent, for he had seen and met people from Damascus, including Alizer of course, in Susa. She welcomed him inside as if she had been expecting him. 'Udama has been expecting you, Daniel!' She led him to another room where Udama was making his prayers and completing his chants.

Udama's chants were a sound that Daniel had never heard the like of before; melodic, musical. Although he could not understand the words, they expressed a poetry that Daniel found beautiful, and his soul reached out to touch and embrace the sound and feel its resonance and tranquillity. Both Daniel and Udama's wife sat and absorbed the sensations while Udama finished his chants and prayers. Daniel would always describe them as a trance, a meditation, a call to God. 'It was as if Udama was speaking with God!' Daniel exclaimed, 'and when I asked Udama, he confirmed they were the prayers from an ancient knowledge of Sippar and the chant was a connection to his God.'

Daniel could have easily been lost in it for the remainder of the day but too soon it had come to an end. When he finished, Udama stood and stepped towards Daniel, and gave him an embrace befitting a long lost member of the family. Udama told him he was a friend and they both sat.

'Daniel, your deed is noble, honourable and very generous. I wish I could be with you. I would very much like to make a record of your journey, but I have too much work and obligations here.' He smiled warmly at his wife. Daniel turned and noticed they were expecting a child.

'Your first?' he asked.

Udama nodded. 'Take this money.' Daniel tried to refuse it, saying that he had hardly spent the last bag.

'No, it is yours. This is from Alizer and he would not have it any other way. Last I heard, they were fine and making their way towards Babylon. Buy the same variety of supplies as before. Everything is going well. Which way are you heading, Nineveh or Mari?'

'Mari,' Daniel replied without hesitation.

'Given the size of Alizer's group, good choice. Your next caravan stop should be Haradum, but it will go via Rapiqum and Hit. Leave supplies in each of these places. Be careful in Haradum. I heard that there are bandits posing as caravans in Haradum. There is only one person to trust; her name is Susana, she is from Susa of course.

'Take your time in Haradum. Do not make fast decisions, Daniel. Stay safe. There will be lots for you to do there. It is good that you have made this time, I do not need to remind you to keep a good distance between you and Alizer.

'Leave your supplies for him with Nida at the service station.' Udama made to say goodbye and fare Daniel well. 'Be very careful what you do in Haradum and Hit,' he said again. 'Head to Mari and keep your head down. Alizer made the perfect choice in you. Very clever to have you leading the way.' Daniel was happy with the comment but did not know what it meant.

Udama embraced Daniel again. 'Now go. Take the first caravan in the morning, and Daniel,' Udama paused, 'God be with you.' Udama continued in the embrace, describing his God as all seeing and all knowing.

Udama's wife led Daniel back to the main door and gave him a pomegranate from the tree in the centre of the courtyard. 'I hope to see you again, Daniel. Enjoy your journey and pray for my child.'

Daniel felt a sense of joy, and maybe peace. Was this his first touch of contentment? Had he touched happiness in Udama and his wife? He realised something he had never noticed before, and the revelation seemed amazing. The people around him can make such a difference to his senses and his joy. Why was that? he thought. He reflected on his companions, and he appreciated Iannas for his endless positivity and Sai for her guidance, inspiration, wisdom, and independence. He had to work on Husha, he thought. But mother had always said that joy comes from within, he thought. So why do other people affect my joy? he asked himself, and he walked quickly past the Temple dedicated to the Sun God Shamash where the new historical records were being assembled and returned to the market to look for Husha.

Sai noticed that Husha was in a particularly good mood. Husha told her he had enjoyed the company in the wine bar by the market where Daniel had left him after the market purchases. Sai, however, was not so sure.

Husha had indeed met some good company in the wine bar, but only after he had been to see the Head Astrologer of the Sippar.

12 THE HEAD ASTROLOGER OF SIPPAR

Husha was in a good mood, but it would not last long. Everyone fell into their beddings very quickly after Iannas and Sai's stew and fish. Sai had finished off the stew with some extra herbs, a tradition from India, and the result had been well received by her patrons. The journey was taking its toll, and their bodies regularly needed a good night's healing. The human body sometimes has a longer memory than the mind.

Husha knew there was something amiss with his meeting with Zaros the Head Astrologer of Sippar, and as he lay down amidst the sounds of the cicadas that appeared to be local to Sippar - he had not heard the sound before - he recalled the discussion to find the clues of his unease. The small bag of gold had stimulated a temporary elation, and Zaros had been particularly generous, but Husha had allowed it to colour the rest of the discussion. Now, he could see that more was being said than asked. Being asked about Terah, the High Priest of Ur, had been unexpected, but not surprising. If he had made the connection with Terah, others were also likely to. The other questions Zaros had repeatedly asked had been the source of the disturbance in his mind. Now that the night was quietly buzzing with the cicadas, which somehow provided a comforting shield against the usual night noises of the animals and dogs, Husha looked at the stars and recognised that the world could not stop the events designed by the heavens. The realisation of his part in this drama being enacted began to haunt him and would continue to do so for the remainder of this life.

Each city, being its own state, had its own ruler, and in support were the ministers, governors, and, of course, the Royal Court, all funded by the city taxes. In almost all the cities there would be rumours or stories of power struggles and even gossip suggestive of the real power behind the throne; maybe it was the king's wife, mother, mistress, son, daughter, a favourite minister, and sometimes even an uncle or aunt if the king or queen was young. Occasionally the rumours were true but this was also the age of stars, and the stars had their own chronicles. Much of the time, it was these accounts that became the force that shaped the power behind the throne. The industry of astrologers had arisen and become powerful during this era of dreams when the significance of the heavens and the importance of the stars become synonymous with the gods themselves. For generations, the Sun God had kept the city and the world safe; then the Moon God came and did the same. The sky had fast become the canvas of almost all belief, and while the astrologers learned to read and paint the opus in front of them, the people that chose to hear the astrologers soon became servants to the stars. Two of the most devoted servants were the King of Sippar and his father, the former King of Sippar.

Observers employed by the Head Astrologer in Sippar for almost two generations had recorded the rise of every star constellation each night, hour by hour, and the tablets were kept in the city archives for reference, and for annual comparison, and then for later generations to study. In some cases when the archives were lost and then found again, many thousands of years later, they would be used again for the same comparisons and study of the old world. It was in the astrologer's suite of offices that the supremacy of Sippar was moulded. In Zaros' hands lay the future of the city and the empire, and Zaros already knew to weigh the significance of every action he took.

The King of Sippar did very little without Zaros. Nothing in fact, not even sleep, wake, wash, eat, or drink unless Zaros the Astrologer had calculated the exact moment for each of these events, so that the King and therefore Sippar would be in harmony with the gods and the stars in the heavens. To be sure, a sheep was sacrificed regularly on the holy day of each week, and the readings in the sheep's liver always confirmed Zaros' prophecies for that week or sometimes the entire moon. The present increase in wealth in Sippar was being ascribed entirely to Zaros' readings and guidance over the years. The King had trusted Zaros ever since his coronation almost 24 years ago. Only half a moon into his term as King, Zaros had foretold an attempt on the king's life, and the foretelling had been thwarted precisely on the day and at the exact time as portended, and only because of the additional security orchestrated in the palace. From that moment on, Zaros enjoyed an exclusive court with the King.

Needless to say, buildings were constructed according to Zaros' readings and designed according to his persuasion as guided by the stars; wars and battles were begun and concluded in accordance to the messages in the stars; peace treaties and trade agreements were agreed only in the presence of Zaros and signed only when he was satisfied. Zaros grew to be one of the most powerful people in Sippar under this king, just as Zaros' father had done under the previous king. Zaros had been mentored by his father very well and now he ensured that everything and everyone was positioned to serve him.

Almost nine years ago, the record keeper of the stars in Sippar alerted the astrologers that a new and alarming pattern in the heavens was being documented, and all the astrologers were summoned to study and learn the messages unfolding in the heavens. They all agreed with the Head of Astrology that the significance was a future event that would threaten all kings and all empires, but the details of the threat could not yet be ascertained. Because no one could understand the message in its entirety, Zaros convened the Guild of Astrologers, and they came from as far and wide as Egypt, Minoa, Afghanistan, China and India as well as Susa, Ur, Babylon, Nineveh, Urfa, Harran, and many other cities, for the Guild had grown since the time of his father who had founded it with its first five members. Zaros shared his findings and mobilised the entire network of the Guild to find out what they could and report back to him, as he was the Head of the Guild. Each Guild astrologer trawled through the ancient archives in their own cities and countries to look for any correlation between these new patterns in the heavens and past records, and attempted to read the mysterious movements in the stars. After five years, the threat still clear in the stars, Zaros and the Guild connected the patterns to a particular mountain region in northern Mesopotamia and then, in the past two years, Zaros himself began to focus on one particular tribe in that region, but he still could not identify the source of the threat or the individual - if there was one - behind it. He began a census of everyone in this tribe, an almost impossible task, since like any other tribe or community after the floods, they had migrated and the diaspora was very wide. But this did not deter Zaros. The stars, he was now convinced, had identified the threat would emerge from this particular tribe, so he began listing every chief, elder, priest, noble, and any important person of this tribe intending to bring the list to the attention of the King when he learned more.

Time was, however, not waiting for Zaros, or anyone else for that matter. The patterns in the stars were becoming more prominent with each moon, and in the last six moons the heavenly activity increased in intensity, and the activity around the world in the observatories increased to match the force of the movements in the stars. Zaros and his colleagues were in agreement that a threat to the kings and empires of the world was now imminent. Zaros also understood this to mean a threat to his very position and very existence.

Husha had been aware of the messages in the stars well before anyone in the region. He had already known the connection with the tribe in the north nine years ago, a full seven years before Zaros, and had arrived in Ur as a slave a year later. Since then he had been waiting. The first few years had been difficult, but then when Ubi saw that Husha was honest, had a natural talent for dealing with the traders, and was delivering so much extra business, Ubi taught Husha to run the caravanserai. This extra status helped enormously. A slave trusted and running a business was unheard of, but he remained a slave with no desire for a higher station. He made connections, not friends; slaves did not make friends, but through these connections he very quickly learned of something forgotten, an infant genocide a whole life time ago in the lands of Susa, Babylon, and Ur. All the deaths and misery in these lands was only to secure the death of one child, the one foretold in the stars at that time. For this rising of the stars, was not the first.

Husha's strongest, consistent, and most vital contact that was to provide the lead was the Astrologer of Susa. They would meet in the caravanserai regularly as there were always supplies to be ordered, collected, or delivered for the Astrologer's offices. Often they would sit and have a drink and their business talk slowly led to information that the Astrologer needed. Husha would seek and report back. It was usually general; who had come through the city and what was the talk in the market? Sometimes the requests for information were specific, such as the five elders of one particular tribe, and Husha extended his reach to many corners not accessible to the Astrologer of Susa or the staff in his service.

These new places that Husha was able to touch enabled him to learn for himself everything he could about the Eperu, a nomadic tribe, but it was someone within the social structure of this tribe that Husha soon learned he should be looking for. He had related all the events in the sky, and all the events in all the cities around him, to this particular someone. But who was it? How would he learn who it was? Would he find the answer in Susa? Maybe it was time to move, but where?

Four years ago, Husha was drinking a new hot drink with the Astrologer of Susa in the caravanserai. The drink was called tea and had been carried by one of the local traders from his travels to the north of India. The trader had promised almost everyone in the city who would listen that this was the new elixir of life from the mountains that reached the heavens in the Far East. Many did indeed listen, and the drink was growing in popularity. The caravanserai was not busy on that day. It had been raining early in the morning and when it rained the caravanserai was always quiet.

The Astrologer began reminiscing about his father who was of advanced years and had been ill for some time but was now close to death. The Astrologer recollected some of the stories told to him by his father from his younger days and how, while studying astronomy and still training for office, he would gather once in a while with the other trainee astrologers and trainee priests and sometimes get up to foolish pranks. Some of them he was embarrassed about and never spoke of them. One time his father and his friends had kidnapped the governor of Susa's private cook and held him until he cooked a feast for all of them. The cook refused to expose them only after one of the party, whose father was well positioned in the Royal Court, agreed to provide a written special commendation for the cook the next time he and his father were at the governor's house for a meal. The cook received a pay rise after the strong recommendation, and that was the only reason he never divulged the kidnapping.

On another occasion, the group raided the local high priest's wine store and carried off almost half a moon's supply of the best wine, which the local investigating soldiers never found apart from the one bottle which turned up mysteriously in the soldiers' mess one night and successfully diverted attention from the group responsible.

The Astrologer also remembered his father mentioning a celebration at the house of a more mature priest, one of their group, who had recently completed his training having begun his studies in his later years. It was a late night gathering to celebrate the birth of a son. Being more than a lifetime ago, certainly before the Astrologer was even born, the only reason his father remembered the night was because he and his friends had all come out of the house after the evening's celebration to find the cloudless sky lit by unusually bright stars. They all looked up in wonderment to witness five great bright Gods so close to one another that at first sight they had all mistaken them as one Divine Being in the sky. His father remembered it fondly, for this was the first major astronomical event he had seen in his novice years.

Some of his friends said that the stars were the sign of a special newborn in the land, but none took it seriously, for they had not yet studied the significance of such events. The next day, when they described the event in the sky to their mentors, they were told that this was an advanced event that could only be interpreted and discussed by wiser and more qualified astrologers. They were told that it was, in fact, such an important event that only the Head Astrologer and the King were permitted to discuss such messages from the Divine of such import. It had already been reported and was being interpreted and acted upon even as they spoke. The trainee priests were commanded to seal their lips and never discuss this event ever again unless they reached the highest position of astrology and learned the deeper secrets of the stars. With important skills to learn and tests and examinations approaching, the novices soon lost interest in the five bright Gods that had arrived and disappeared just as quickly, leaving no trace and, in time, almost no memory. But his father always remembered this moment, for he never saw anything as wondrous in the sky ever again in his lifetime. He made sure, however, that he never discussed it with anyone during his term as an astrologer. He had reminisced with his son, the Astrologer of Susa however, and Husha was now in possession of another vital piece of information he had been waiting for all these years.

The following day, while the Astrologer of Susa was in his office, Husha made sure to arrive at the Astrologer's home with a gift, a special embroidered cotton wool woven blanket for the Astrologer's father from the Ugibi family. It had some verses from the 'Debate of the Bird and Fish'; an ancient literary narrative embroidered along the borders of the blanket with thread coloured with a beautiful blue dye made from a particular variety of squashed rare snails. Husha was welcomed into the house warmly and asked if he would present it personally, exactly as Husha had hoped he would be allowed to. And so Husha was able to have a conversation with the old man about that night with the five bright Gods in the sky shining as one. Much to Husha's surprise, the old man remembered the detail and enjoyed describing the evening and at that particular moment and no other, he even remembered the name of the priest to whom the son had been born. This was the information Husha had been searching for all these many years. No one else in the room heard or even took notice of the name mentioned by the old man, for his voice was weak, cracking, and throaty, and Husha was leaning close to him. Then the old man mentioned something else seemingly congruous, that the Head Astrologer of Sippar, whom Husha knew as Zaros' father, had imposed the silence around the bright stars, and none who knew of it was allowed to mention or discuss it.

Husha now understood why it had been so difficult to find out anything about those events and most people who might have been witness to the events at the time would have been too old to remember, or have died. Husha took his leave and immediately began making plans to seek the priest to whom the son had been born on the night of the five stars. Now he had a name.

He mobilised his own network of contacts to search the records of Susa, Ur, Nippur, Sharuppak, Isin, Sippar, Babylon, and Nineveh under the pretext of having been asked to do so by his owner. Soon he listed one hundred and thirty nine priests in the region who shared the same name as the one he had been given, and from this group, forty-three were connected to the tribe. Things moved slowly to begin with as Husha began eliminating each of the forty-three priests. He had to wait until he came across someone, on their travels to Susa, who knew the priest personally. Some priests were too young or never married, and of the ones that did match the profile, Husha made sure to follow up carefully but always without a positive outcome, so he continued eliminating the names from his list. Over the last few moons, with only three people on his list and fitting the profile perfectly, he had focused all his attention on these three. One lived in Ur, one in Babylon, and the third was a wandering priest, more a temple overseer than a priest, who continued to visit many of the temples in the region including Susa. Not only did they all have a son that met the timeline, they were all alive!

By the time Husha arrived in Babylon the first time with Ubi, he had already made arrangements to meet with the priest under the pretext of delivering a message from the Astrologer of Susa, all of course, arranged by Husha at a time the priest happened to be celebrating fifty years of service to temple in Babylon. The meeting took place at the home of the elderly priest where Husha delivered the message of tribute, which not only recognised the great personal achievement but also helped to put the Astrologer of Susa in good standing in Babylon. In passing, Husha made conversation.

'My master, Ugibi of Susa, is also asking after your son, Sir. May I ask after his health and report back to my master?' The priest became angry and refused to speak to Husha about his son.

'You can tell your master he is not my son!' is all he would say. Husha was surprised. Was this angry talk? It was possible. Had he disowned his son? Unlikely, Husha thought. Or did he mean, literally, that his son was adopted? Husha already knew that his son was a minister in the Babylon court and had married with a wife from Uruk. Husha was looking for a birth son and if adopted, he was surprised as his sources of information had never revealed that the priest's son was not his own. Husha did not know how to reply when his son arrived to visit his father. Husha found this fortuitous and could see the relationship between father and son was not a good one. Husha was introduced but asked to leave by the minister's bodyguard, as they had family matters to discuss. Husha made to leave, but the priest intervened.

'He is a slave; there is no concern. He has a message from a close friend in Sippar and I should reply to it.' The elderly priest motioned to Husha, 'Wait in the next room.' The priest extended his courtesy, and Husha expressed his gratitude. 'Let me finish with my son here, and then I will prepare a reply.' From the adjoining room, Husha made sure to hear the entire conversation.

'I am angry, Father, but I am going to make it public. Sippar cannot get away with this. I am in a position of influence.'

'They will destroy you, Son. Your mother should never have told you that we found you in a small boat the same day we lost our son to the soldiers of that hateful Sippar King, but she wanted you to know before we reach our mortality. I am sorry you never met your real parents.'

'That is why I am angry, Father. Had you told me last year I would have met my real mother and father!'

The priest began to weep, 'Your mother and I are your parents, Son. We have raised you as ours. We are sorry too for not telling you. We love you, and you will always be our son. We are sorry we lied to you.' There was a lot of pain in the room.

His son calmed, and his voice lowered. 'I know that, Father. I am sorry. I am angry with the King of Sippar, not you. I have decided to go public, Father. I am not sure when but I will wait till I find the right time. No one remembers that they were child killers. You are the only witnesses I know. I was a victim. My birth parents saved me by putting me in that boat, and they never knew me. The King of Sippar should know what his father did. Maybe there were other survivors.'

'You only survived because our child was killed, and we remained in grief and kept you hidden in this house for years. These people are dangerous, and they will kill you, Son. They will never let you say anything. I do not want to bury you like our first born. You are our only one; you are our son.' The priest wept silently and Husha felt for him.

'I am a Minister of Babylon. Babylon will protect me. Like I said, Father, I will do this at the right time and I will make sure to protect you and mother.'

Husha was not one to get too excited too quickly. Had he found him? Was this man the one he had been looking for, searching for all these years? But something was not right. Here was a child survivor from that terrible day; but this was not what he expected. What if there was more than one surviving child to a priest with the same name? If so, this would make for an amazing coincidence. He had to follow up his two other leads in Uruk and Ur before being sure, but something still did not make sense. This Minister was the priest's adopted son, born on the same night, but who was he by birth? Which tribe did belong to? This was the strongest connection so far. He should be pleased but he was not; there was still much to do before he could be sure.

Husha could not believe the conversation he had heard. So a child survivor, now a Minister in Babylon, was going to go public with the story of the child murders at the time of the former King of Sippar. He was going to directly accuse the current King of Sippar's father of planning the genocide. Where was this going to lead? Husha wondered.

Just when he thought the conversation was over, it continued.

'Did you find anything more, Son, about your birth parents and their family? Did they leave behind any brothers or sisters? What is your birth legacy?'

'Father, yes, there is a sister in Ur, married and with her own children. I will leave tomorrow for Ur and see if I can meet her. I have some business meetings in Isin and Nippur, and I will stop over to see my wife's family on the way back. It seems my birth family lived in Sippar at the time of the child murders, but they were originally from Ur. My father's name we know; it was on the tablet mother showed me last week, and it seems that they were from a fishing village on the coast. My father was a fisherman. He was newly married, just like you, and he used his small boat and the river to save my life.'

Husha's excitement, if there was any, diminished very fast. He was looking for a priest's son, not a fisherman's son, and the priest had to be named Terah. He would not need to investigate this lead any further.

Husha listened to the heart-breaking story unfolding in the room next door and realised there were only two more possibilities in front of him. He listened to the father's quiet weeping while the son described the pain he felt for all those children. He heard the words 'killed because of a king's madness,' 'superstition', 'children who their parents never knew and had to bury and forget.' Husha was touched. He felt the deep pain and wondered for a moment if his search was in vain. How, in that madness, did any child born that day remain alive? That one had survived filled him with hope that there may be a second.

In Uruk, and on his return from Ur with Daniel, Iannas, and Sai, Husha met privately and briefly with Rabi to confirm the name of the minister from Babylon involved in the attempted assassination. Husha was not surprised to learn that this minister was the same one he had met in Babylon. The attempted assassination seemed vulgar to Husha, but he immediately knew something else was going on here.

Husha's main goal in Uruk was to meet the wandering priest, the second of the three possible parents. Again, he had a message from the Astrologer of Susa inviting the priest to a special meeting in Susa. On being received by the priest, however, Husha cut his meeting short when he realised that the priest was in grief. His one and only son had died less than a moon previously in a boating accident as a river ferry collapsed in the middle of a swollen river caused by the rains. Only a few young, strong swimmers had survived. This priest could not be the one he was seeking if the stars were still moving.

This left one more priest to meet - Terah the High Priest of Ur - and because of his very position, Husha had always thought the least likely. If the High Priest was not the one, Husha would have to start all over again, and that was what he wanted to confirm in Ur. Of course, Husha had investigated Terah and even discussed him with Alizer, but he was only a servant, and a recent addition to Terah's household, and claimed to know nothing of Terah's past. Was Terah the priest with a son born on the night of the five stars, and was that son still alive? How was the child kept alive? But the gates of Ur were closed. The High Priest had successfully avoided Husha's gaze in Susa and now again in Ur. If indeed he was the priest, and his son was alive, Husha could not explore any further.

By the time Husha met Zaros in Sippar for the first time that day, Zaros was already head of a Guild of Astrologers that had members in almost every important court in the world, including China, India, Persia, Mesopotamia, the land of the Hittites, Damascus, Pella, Timbuktu in Africa, and Memphis, as well as a small region to the west called Minoa. Zaros was not only proud of the Guild his father had founded, but particularly proud of the fact that it was his father in Sippar who had arrived at the significance of the convergence in his time and foretold the birth of the powerful magician who would challenge the kings of the time. Because of the nature of his interpretation, this information had been kept secret from all city ministers, governors, and the staff of the royal court including, and especially, trainee astrologers and priests, for they were the least trusted by the courts. The Guild predicted the date and time of birth of the magician based on the convergence of the five Gods in the sky. They even predicted the region where the birth would take place, but they could never agree the city.

Zaros' father shared this information with the King, and on his Head Astrologer's advice, the King ordered the death of every newborn child on that particular day and, to be sure, a day either side, in every city and village under his power, and those kings in the region, who also feared the prophecy and had a pact with the King of Sippar, did the same.

At Husha's meeting, Zaros was angry. Unlike his father, all these years and with his resources, Zaros had not managed to identify the specific meaning of the latest patterns in the sky. Zaros often gleefully told how his father had saved the former King from the magician child. Providence was repeating, and now it was Zaros' turn to save this King, and in fact all the kings of the world from this new threat. But who was the threat?

Zaros clearly was at a loss. He was also becoming concerned and increasingly worried with the latest movements in the heavens. All the signals in the stars pointed to a challenger to all kings. A king of all kings was due to rise imminently, and this leader would be from a particular tribe. By naming the man, his family and his tribe as the bringers of doom to the kings of this world, he would be the most powerful and the richest man in the world. He might even rule the world with such information. But why, with all his resources, did he not have the name or even the name of the family?

When Husha met Zaros, the conversation had begun the same way as it had in Babylon, Uruk, and Sharuppak with general questions about events, politics, noble families, the tribes in the region, and any information Husha was picking up about political and religious activity in the cities or the region. Both Husha and Zaros appeared practiced in the technique of fishing for information, and they were not willing to give too much away before learning what they could and needed from the other. Husha noticed that Zaros had not been interested in activity in Susa, Uruk, Sharuppak, and as the conversation progressed Zaros could not resist but hone in on

Babylon and Ur when Husha mentioned he was returning from Ur having found the city gates closed. Zaros was only interested in very particular neighbourhoods of Ur and Babylon known for a community from one particular tribe from the North.

Husha took a big risk but needed to know the reaction. 'The assassination attempt of the Minister from Babylon in Uruk, is that related in any way? I understand the assassin began in Ur.'

'No, a distraction if anything. A domestic dispute between the Minister and his wife's family. He is a wealthy man, and he was in Uruk to negotiate the terms of a divorce settlement with the wife. Her family thought that employing a thug to kill the minister would mean a full inheritance for the wife. It all backfired, of course, when the assassin was caught.' Zaros quickly returned to the subject of the tribe.

Husha did not explore this further. The Minister of Babylon had clearly not gone public yet. Husha wondered if Zaros knew that the Minister was a child survivor from the genocide. Husha also wondered if Zaros knew more about the assassination attempt than he was willing to tell.

Husha quietly agreed with Zaros. The Minister was a distraction, but in many more ways than Zaros imagined.

Zaros persisted. Husha already knew that Terah was from a very particular tribe, so when Zaros asked if the Eperu in Ur were involved in or even leading the uprisings in Ur, Husha chose his words carefully, having now learned what Zaros was thinking. Fortunately, having not entered Ur, Husha's lack of information was acceptable to Zaros. Husha was more interested to learn how far Zaros had reached and what his motivations were, so he continued listening to the questions. Zaros kept asking the same question in different ways, hoping Husha would know some snippet of information that would give him the edge over the other astrologers. There was a rumour that some of the tribe lived a long age, even two hundred years old or more. Was there more to the rumour? Who were the main chiefs of the tribe? Which villages in the north did they reside in? Where was the tribal centre? Did Husha know the tribe in Sippar and Babylon? What was the social structure? How many children did the chiefs have? Who were they? Who was the leader of the Eperu community in Ur? Who were the members of his family?

It was not an interrogation. Husha was there to sell information in return for other information. In fact, Zaros' focused attention on the tribe only served to confirm Husha's theories, but, if Zaros had come this far, Husha was very surprised that the name 'Terah' had not been mentioned. The only conclusion Husha could reach was that Zaros had not yet made the connection with the events at the time of his father. Zaros must be under the assumption this is a completely new and different threat to the

King. He must also have assumed that all the newborns on that evil day had been killed.

Husha also knew that the situation would change as soon as the Minister of Babylon became public. If he announced himself as a child survivor, Zaros would very quickly make connections.

Husha thought he had provided very little information to Zaros. What he did divulge he considered of no significance. He asked Zaros what the special interest in the tribe was to gauge his response, but Zaros was dismissive, quoting tribal rivalries and politics and wanting to make sure the uprising did not start in Sippar. When Zaros grew bored and Husha made to leave, Zaros asked if he knew of Terah the High Priest of Ur.

'Only to trade with when he comes to Susa. Usually his household deals with supplies so I have never met him.' Husha replied dismissively. This was true. The High Priest was rarely seen in public places.

'I have heard that he might still have links with the Eperu. I recently learned that his grandfather was born amongst the tribe in the mountains before he moved and settled in Ur. Terah is one of our High Priests and a good man. We have lost touch with him in Ur. We have lost touch with everyone in Ur, as it happens. Our High Priest must know something. He is always travelling between Harran and Ur, so if you come across him, talk to him, his companions, or his household. Let us see what they know about the Eperu. I need to know everything there is to know about them. My team are already meeting all the chiefs within the tribe. They are a very closed travelling community, and some of their villages in the mountains are extremely remote. We can find very little but have mapped what we can. Someone must know more. Where are you heading next?'

'I am returning to Memphis, my homeland, and I will pass through Mari.' Husha replied.

'I will send a message to the Astrologer in Mari to expect you. You need to have more to report there than you have done today. Take this.' Zaros threw a small bag, which Husha caught with both hands. 'I hear you have served us well all these years, and you are now a free man. You have been a great help to my friend in Susa. He asked that you be rewarded when I saw you. This is special gratitude.'

Husha was very surprised how little Zaros knew. He did not even know about Terah or that Terah had left Ur.

Husha expressed his gratitude for the small bag of gold.

It was this new and specific interest in the tribe that was playing on Husha's mind, making him increasingly uncomfortable and gave him sleepless nights. And through these nights Husha practiced what he was skilled at; putting pieces of information together. He began to understand that if Zaros' father had known the name of the family or tribe of the magician child born in his time, he would have suggested that every member of the family of the child and every member of the tribe itself be killed. He liked to do things thoroughly. Of course they did not know the name of the tribe. Zaros was now following his father's thoughts. If there was a threat, it did not matter which individual it was. The tribe where the threat came from had to perish. The infant genocide had already been forgotten. How many children did they kill? Infant genocides had occurred before at the time of the birth of King Sargon who only survived when his mother hid him in a small boat on the river Euphrates, only to be discovered and adopted by a gardener and later successfully challenged the throne of Sippar. Infant genocide would happen again. Who knew what type of wrath the present King would be capable of this time.

As far as Husha knew, only he had connected the birth in Terah the High Priest's home, the genocide a lifetime ago, and the latest events in the sky. Husha did not sleep that night or the next, or the one after that, and he became particularly quiet during the days. What was Zaros planning, and what would he do when he realised that this priest and his family were linked to the genocide at the time of his father? What would he do to the Minister in Babylon when he came out in the open?

Strange how Terah had distanced himself from his heritage, and there was only a loose connection between him and his tribe. Was this planned? Husha wondered.

The next day, Husha said very little. Sai missed Husha's sarcasm and patronising. 'What's up, Husha?' Husha ignored Sai. She saw his eyes and left him alone. 'He will talk when he is ready,' she told the others.

And every time Husha paused to think, he kept coming back to the same terrible conclusion; Zaros planned to exterminate every member of the tribe. There was no other conclusion Husha could make. Whether Zaros learned of Terah or not seemed immaterial right now. Zaros was preparing to remove every trace of the tribe by finding out where they were. Would he really go through with it? Husha was increasingly convinced that Terah's family was indeed the one he had been looking for all these years and his sole reason for having stayed in Susa all this time. Ironic, he thought, as he had unloaded Terah's goods in Susa at least once a year. What was going to become of Terah and the family, he thought? Why was he in this moment so closely connected to Terah and his family's future through Daniel? he wondered. And what part would he play in their destiny?

Destiny was what Donkey was thinking about too. He did not know what it meant but he did know he had a destiny and it was an important one, and everything would be all right in the end.

13 NIGHT OF READINGS

Days 27-30, 14 Beru.

In India, the people of Mesopotamia were known as proud and conservative. Stories of great temples, jewelled cities, and a complicated, sophisticated culture were commonly shared. They also had a reputation of being a warrior race with almost constant news of great battles and terrifying wars between the cities of Mesopotamia. Having never left India before, Sai's only experience of foreign lands had been through her mother's memories of China and then after marriage through stories of the Edin lands from her husband, whose family had traded in Mesopotamia for many years. Sai had now found herself as a refugee in a strange land that bore little resemblance to the stories and where she would always be a foreigner. To be able to count Iannas, Daniel, and Husha as friends meant so much to her, much more than she could ever say, and that they appeared to want nothing in return meant so much more. Mesopotamia was not the way she expected after all.

Most of all, and most unexpected, Sai had learned to relish and treasure her new freedom. She thanked Krishna for the moment and for these new companions. That second night on the way to Haradum, Sai felt comfortable and close enough to her new friends to ask Husha if she could read his hand.

Husha, as you would imagine, had heard many stories in the caravanserai of Susa of people in India who could read a man's soul through the patterns in the palm of their hands and faces. First, he did not believe a word of it, and second, he was not going to make himself vulnerable in case it was true.

'Tell me more about it.' Husha played for time. 'I heard you can see into a man's soul through his hands?'

Sai laughed; she had a calming laugh. 'The hand is important in the faith of Krishna. Our God is often portrayed with the palm of his hand in peace and facing the people.

'Many people, generations ago in India and China, decided that the patterns in the hand were marks of the universe and created an art form. They interpreted each and every line on the hand and matched it to the life of the person.' Iannas and Daniel looked at their hands.

'You mean like stars and the astrologers? But what information can you see in the hand?' Daniel asked.

'Like if you will marry, how many children you will have, whether you think with your heart or your mind.' She smiled as she said this. She probably knew the answers to these things without even reading the hands, she thought. Being playful with friends was always fun.

'It's only fun in fact,' she added. 'Some people in India follow the teachings very seriously, but they are the experts. They have studied the art of hand reading all their lives, having learnt it from their parents and grandparents. My family live on a mountain where the border crosses between China and India. My grandfather lived on one side of the mountain, the Chinese side where they practiced the arts, and my grandfather was an expert and taught my mother. She studied the art but never practiced it after she got married. My father lived on the other side of the mountain, which they said was in India, but I could never tell the difference. The people where I was born never believed in these arts, calling them superstition, but my mother still remembered the basics and she taught me some of what she knew as I was growing up, sometimes just to pass the time.

Husha gathered this would be harmless, Sai was not an expert, 'Go ahead, young one, read all our hands and see the condition of our souls. First, read Daniel's and let us see how many children he is going to have and if he will ever be happy.'

Daniel laughed at Husha's remarks nervously as Sai sat down in front of him, took his right hand in her left, and traced his palm lines with her right hand. 'Three children,' she announced straight away. 'Twins and a girl.'

Daniel raised his eyebrows. 'You cannot know that!'

'Just joking, you are right, but it does say here you will marry twice!'

Both Husha and Iannas made appropriate noises to both embarrass and tease Daniel. They knew he would do the same to them.

'You will live a long life, and you think too much with your heart, not your head, but as you get older this might change. You will not always be healthy, and your health line is short for some reason. You have a wide area under your thumb – you have much love to give and will have much love.' That was enough to make both Iannas and Husha imitate the noises of the little monkeys they had seen in the forests and in the markets. Sai kept her sweet, innocent yet sincere smile all the way through the reading, so they could never tell if she was inventing her readings, exaggerating or describing the hand as it was.

Husha was entering into the spirit, stopped his monkey noises, and intervened, 'Iannas next.'

Iannas sat impersonating a little lost child and stuck his bottom lip out as if he was about to be hurt and about to cry. Sai moved to sit in front of him. She knew Iannas really admired her and was always a little embarrassed to look into her eyes. She took his hand and forgave him his child-like behaviour that was obviously designed to protect himself from giving away his true feelings.

'Oh Lord Krishna! Oh my lord Krishna! Wow. Wait, wait, I will come back to you.'

'No, what's up?' Iannas was confused and even a little upset by this reaction, but before he could argue she had already placed herself in front of Husha and taken his hand. He shrugged his shoulders at Iannas.

'We always knew you were a problem, Iannas.' It was Daniel's turn to tease.

'No, hold on, what's wrong with my hand?' Iannas asked again, abandoning his child-like acting. Sai ignored both of them.

'It says here two children but the lines are faint. You will marry once. Do you know who she is, Husha?' Both Daniel and Iannas made the appropriate noises just as Husha had done to Daniel.

'Have you met her already?' Sai asked with a serious face. 'Are you already married?' Sai asked with a knowing tone. 'You will live a long life, and you think too much with your head, not your heart. You have a good health line, so you will always be healthy. There is love there, Husha, for you to give, but you will find it harder than most to accept it.'

Husha raised his eyebrows but said nothing.

'All right, all right, now tell me about me,' Iannas was impatient. 'What's wrong with me?'

Husha and Daniel came and sat close to the two of them as Sai began studying Iannas' right hand.

Sai explained to Daniel and Husha while pointing at the lines on Iannas' hand. 'Look at this line and compare it with yours. You see how you have two lines across your hand, one from the left and one from the right? They do not meet. Now look at Iannas' hand. He has one line. This is most amazing. In India and China, this is called the line of the head and the heart. Either you have no heart or no head, Iannas.' This brought both Daniel and Husha to heaps of laughter, but they both had to recover quickly and keep a straight face, for Sai remained completely sincere. 'Very few people have this in India. Where they do they are either mad or have the kindness of angels. Do you have angels in your faith?

'Yes we do,' replied Daniel. 'They are beings from the spirit world.'

'Iannas,' she continued 'I know you are not a bad person. You are not a mad man. According to the line, if you wish, you can be one of the most giving and the most powerful in the world. Your gift has an unlimited power if you can find it.'

'What about marriage and children?' Iannas asked, not wanting to be different from the others.

'Looks like one wife, four children, lots of health, a long life and plenty of love.'

Daniel and Husha let out a roar of praise for Sai.

'Well done, Sai. His hand is different, isn't it? Do the lines really mean something or is it just made up?' asked Husha.

'It depends on your beliefs, a little like the stars I suppose. Most people do not believe in palm reading, but some do consider it a sign from heaven. I just use it with my friends. For me, it's just fun, and we laugh together. And I wanted to say,' Sai seemed a little shy as she said this, 'that I am glad to be with my friends here in this place at this time. It means a lot to me, and I know, without needing to read your hands, you are all good people. The main thing is we laughed together, so palm reading has its uses!' Sai laughed and her friends joined her. 'I knew midwives on my mountain look at the hand of the child immediately after birth. They say they know if a baby is ill or has been damaged in the womb from the lines in the hand. So maybe our body has a link to the world and to our gods in some way. Maybe these are all signs that we have forgotten to see.'

Sai continued as if remembering another life. 'My mother described the most incredible zoo that she had seen in China where every animal that was known was being collected from every part of the world by the Emperor.' Her mother had seen and described huge white bears with black eyes and black arms found in the Chinese forest as well as the tree bears that keep their young in their belly pockets. She would say that these are some of the many signs from the Earth, the forces of nature.

'I even saw her pray in a forest amongst the plants and the animals, under the stars, wherever you see life and nature and the natural beauty at sunset, sunrise. She used to tell me that this was her way to be closer to the spirit of God than any temple.'

'Tell us more of this God Krishna, Sai?' Husha was intrigued.

'He is the father of all people,' started Sai, and spent the rest of the evening trying to explain her God Krishna and her faith of peace.

'Life was complicated on the mountain too,' Sai added. 'One day, two travellers arrived claiming to have studied the scriptures of Krishna and declared themselves as priests of the village so they could guide us, build a temple for us, and be our prayer leaders. But our village, having never had the need for priests and temples, did not accept them. Another time a group of astrologers visited the village and started telling us the meanings of the patterns in the sky. The village was dismissive of them too.

'My mother would tell me that our ancestors never needed to be told what to believe. She told me to look at the stars and make up my own mind. She told me to feel and try and recognise the signals of creation in our world. If you are blind to the world, you become like those in the towns and the cities who only see and feel their god in their temple. People created temples, my mother would say, and tell me that if we believe that God created the world, we should pray by standing in the world, not in the temple. My mother and father always disagreed over this, even after my father sent me to the temple classes in the town to learn about our faith.' As she spoke, Sai wondered if she would ever see her mother and father again. Sai realised that she would know the answer some day.

The walk the next day, a slight incline and every day increasingly so, was exhausting. Husha always tried to give the young ones a good start to the day by waking up early to make tea that Sai was more accustomed to and appreciated, and Daniel and Iannas had now been converted to, but Husha would also boil dates as usual for himself. He enjoyed starting the morning with a hot, sweet, date drink as he done ever since he was a child.

The next night, Iannas asked Sai to stay awake a little while longer. He wanted to discuss his palm reading without anyone listening. Iannas had learned to trust Sai and wondered if the dreams he carried with him had anything to do with the lines on his right hand. He had not told anyone of the dreams, but, for some reason, it seemed right to share them with Sai. When he described the dreams to her, she looked at him in silence and did not say anything. She thanked him for having the confidence to share something so personal and, in this era of dreams, something capable of being so potent and compelling, but she confessed that she did not have the answers for him, that he would have to seek them himself. She would try and guide him if she could and she needed time to think.

Sai told him to go to bed and that she would speak again with him in a few days. She needed time to meditate and reflect on the dreams Iannas had described. She returned to her bedding next to the supplies and, since there was no holding area for animals that night, where Donkey was already resting. This is where Sai always slept and was most comfortable and where she stayed awake all night and prayed to Krishna. Donkey watched over them and prayed with Sai.

A few days later, Sai was ready to speak with Iannas, and she did so after Husha and Daniel slept on one particularly quiet night, the first without any cicadas since Sippar.

In this age of dreams, powerful dreams were perceived as divine, celestial, or suspicious and even dangerous depending on who the dreamer was and whom one spoke to. Sai knew this and was concerned for Iannas.

Dreamers were often accused of being false prophets, imprisoned and even executed.

'Your dreams,' she asked, 'have you told anyone else?'

'Only you. They are very personal and remain a very powerful experience for me. Even now when I think about it I get a strange feeling in my stomach as if the dreams do not belong inside of me, that the dreams coming to me was an accident. I have no doubt about everything I saw, felt, and heard in the dreams, and I know they have much meaning, but I am too scared to consider the possible significances and the consequences. To be honest, Sai, I do not want to know and I do not want to understand. I only shared it with you after your reaction to my hand. I wondered if the dreams and the line on my hand are linked with part of me in some way. What you were telling me was just fun, wasn't it? But if it means more than that, I would like to know if you think I should be looking for the answer and where and how should I be looking?'

'It's a big responsibility, Iannas, to be the only one who knows about dreams of this magnitude. Sometimes it is not what you remember in the dream; it is what you do not remember that matters. Who else was there in your first dream? You said you were at the back, so who was in the audience? Who was the Divine speaking to? And why would a God ask, "Where is the love?" God does not need love!' Iannas had not asked any of these questions of himself.

'I cannot say if your hand and the dreams are connected, but your dreams suggest a tragedy, a tragedy in the future, not your past. But is it a personal tragedy to you? Or is it a tragedy for the world? Are you supposed to do something or prepare for something? There are too many questions, Iannas. You do have a purpose, Iannas; we all do, but your purpose may be intertwined with something greater than the rest of us. The purpose will not reveal itself to you, no matter how hard you try, until the time is right.' Sai paused. 'Remember life is what you choose it to be, not what others, your dreams, or the lines on your hand determine for you. You will always be responsible for your own choices,' Sai added.

'I am glad you mentioned choice,' Iannas retorted. 'I do not wish to have a greater destiny or purpose, Sai. I choose to remain as I am. I need and want nothing more.'

'Then maybe you should let the dreams go. Why return to them?' Sai challenged Iannas.

Iannas did not have an answer. He could not dispute Sai's wisdom. For a moment, he wanted to say he would think about the questions Sai had asked. He had a choice after all about what to do, but this returned him to what he had just said to Sai and he thought again.

'You are right, Sai. I do have a choice. I do not want this, and I choose to let go.'

Sai was not expecting this and was momentarily surprised, even shocked.

'You hold the power to be invincible with your dreams,' Sai reminded Iannas.

'That is exactly why I must let go of the dreams,' Iannas replied and Sai noticed Iannas visibly relax with his decision.

Sai smiled. She might even have been pleased and proud at his decision, but she knew that Iannas may never escape the dreams. 'It may be more difficult than you imagine,' Sai offered and moved forward with Iannas. 'Your mother knew about these dreams even though you never told her? Tell me about your mother.'

Iannas remembered his mother with Sai, and Iannas' descriptions returned Sai to her memories of her own mother.

'My mother believed in the God of nature,' Sai tried to explain. 'The natural mysteries of the world were her wonder, and the secret messages of the universe were her temples. That is how she taught me. I am only just beginning to understand what she really meant. The universe will always be a mystery, and we can never understand it.'

Iannas was amazed that he was able to have such a personal conversation with Sai, someone from such a far off land, so unalike and yet so similar.

As Rapiqum approached, the moon declared itself more confidently and majestically, reminding everyone on earth that it was still in charge of the night. The full moon ceremonies would be enacted in every temple declaring the passing of a whole moon since leaving Susa.

If the moon was a God, then the light of God shone on those that slept. If the moon was an instrument of God, the light of God still shone on all that slept.

14 HIT AND HARADUM

Days 31 to 32, 7 Beru to Hit.
Days 33 to 38, 21.3 Beru to Haradum.
Peace was quickly replaced with a quiet anxiety at the Rapiqum checkpoint, which was both an army garrison and a small town unhappily located within the border lands. As a result, often the town found itself surrounded, occupied, and changing hands and allegiances, much to the annoyance of the locals. Right now, being under the control of Susa, the checkpoint border guards were particularly friendly with Husha who swapped news with the captain of the guards while the checkpoint formalities and border taxes were being completed by Iannas. Daniel and Sai quickly arranged supplies for Alizer at the service station while Husha enquired about bandit attacks. The captain advised the caravan leader, who was standing with them, to cross to the caravan route on the northern side of the river until Hit, as bandit attacks were being reported on the south bank, and the north was more thoroughly patrolled by soldiers from Mari. The caravan leader expressed his gratitude and took the advice readily, leading the caravan to the north side of the river.

At the end of the next day, Hit could be seen across the river serviced by a local toll bridge. A new set of supplies for themselves was easy to organise, and they left more supplies for Alizer at the Hit service station as instructed by Udama. The journey resumed on the south side of the river, and Daniel kept his eye on the security guards who were noticeably on high alert, but few in the caravan had expected the sickness and nausea that were increasingly taking hold of the children and the elderly.

When Husha and Iannas noticed that everyone's appetites had reduced, Husha made a special effort by cooking fresh vegetable stew accompanied with some dried fish and grain soup. He even roasted a sack of grain on the charcoal to keep them all going for the next section of the journey. But they could not enjoy the food, and that is when Husha was the first to realise they had slowly become accustomed to the faint but ever constant sulphurous smell emanating from the distant naphtha fires. When he enquired, they all became aware of a light but continuous irritation to their throats. The smells accompanied them all the way to Haradum, sometimes during the day there were periods when the smoke and smells were intolerable and many in the caravan became physically sick.

The evenings were lightened by the moon and the music band who entertained eagerly in spite of the sickness creeping into the caravan, and this created a community spirit within the travellers providing courage to the sickly young, and strength and determination amongst the sickly elders. The down side was the increasing desire of the members of the caravan to talk with one another, which did not please Daniel and Iannas who were attempting to maintain a low profile. Thankfully, and maybe because of Iannas and Daniel's aloofness, travellers homed in on the more welcoming Husha and Sai for walking discussions.

Sai had no problem talking to the fellow travellers. 'Hello, where are you heading to?' was how most conversations began, and Sai enjoyed learning about their lives as well as taking delight in telling some of her audience she was travelling from India with her Egyptian slave and two servants. Sai created further mischief by telling others that she was travelling with her father, pointing to Husha, and two adopted brothers. Husha received quite a shock the first time a passing traveller came up to him declaring what a delightful daughter Husha had, and how wonderful it was of Husha to adopt two Mesopotamian orphans. Husha caught Sai's eyes and went along with the ruse, but the caravan gossip about Husha was confused as a result with most believing Husha was the father of the three teenagers and a few understanding him to be the slave of the Indian girl whom they thought a noblewoman. Husha never told Sai to stop her pretences. He took it in good humour, but Iannas and Daniel were not too pleased to be referred to as her servants and neither did they like to be felt sorry for as adopted orphans. Sai promised to clarify matters at every opportunity, which of course, she never did.

There was one particular traveller who, having congratulated Husha on his two well-behaved sons and delightful daughter, proceeded to ask if Husha had heard the latest news from Sippar and Babylon. The traveller's story turned out to be about a thief who had been caught with poison and a knife with the intention of murdering a minister of Babylon who had arrived into Uruk.

'I was in the queue in Uruk the day it happened,' noted Husha. 'He caused great delays for us in getting into Uruk,' Husha complained. 'I later heard that it was a domestic issue between the Minister and his wife.' Husha was wondering if the traveller knew any more.

'That is what they want you to believe. But think about it, why attempt to kill him in Uruk? Where his wife's family live? A little too convenient, would you not say?'

Husha agreed and asked the traveller if there were any more developments.

'The latest, it may just be gossip mind you, is that the whole assassination was a set up. Someone in Sippar wanted to threaten the Minister, scare him from making some damaging revelations. It appears that the Minister has publicly declared that he is one of the children that survived a massacre of newborns at the time of the previous King of Sippar. The night he was born was the time of the massacre. His parents, in the spirit of Sargon, placed him on a float covered with naphtha. After adding a small seal in the float so that the finder would know the name of the child and where he was from, they set it free. The boat, of course, was found and the boy survived. It seems the Minister has been digging into his past. He discovered his birth seal and now claims that the then King of Sippar ordered the killings, and he wants retribution. Relations between Sippar and Babylon have never been worse. In fact he is now seeking damages in the form of untold gold from the current King himself.'

Husha could not believe the news. So the Minister has gone public! he thought to himself.

'I bet the King of Sippar must be embarrassed.' Husha tried to gauge if there was more. 'His father, the child killer! What sort of heritage is he defending? Not good for a king to have to defend his father's vile actions,' Husha replied in the hope that there was more.

'Well, there is more,' claimed the traveller. 'The gossip has always been that the true power in Sippar lies with the Head Astrologer of Sippar. Actually it is fairly well known. Well, it turns out that the King is now publicly blaming the Head Astrologer's father for having started the mess. The Royal Court in Sippar is now in turmoil,' the traveller laughed, 'it always was. They have too much money, and power goes to their heads. Somebody new will slip in and take over soon.'

Husha could not help asking for verification, 'Where did you hear all this?'

'The soldiers at the checkpoints are the best people for good gossip. You have to buy them a good beer, mind. It cost me two beers to get this information in Rapiqum, but the news was worth it. It is good to know these things as a trader. Trading is all about opportunity. I can increase my fees for a while and make sure I am on the side of the stronger camp.'

'In that case, I owe you a drink, my friend, at the next station. I believe it is Haradum.'

'I stop before then. I make the trade for the naphtha for one of the boat yards in Sippar. I am here to make some purchases and see it delivered back in Sippar, so I will leave you tomorrow night.'

'So who do you think is the stronger side? The King or the Astrologer?' Husha asked.

'The stronger side might be a third group that creep in and take advantage. That is where you have to keep your eye.' The traveller exchanged more gossip and ideas of who the third side might be with Husha.

The Minister of Babylon was an interesting development that kept Husha occupied as he walked. That was when Husha noticed that the spirited mood had not spread to the entire caravan, and a group of traders continued to keep themselves to themselves at the rear of the caterpillar. If they do not want to be noticed, they usually have something to hide, he thought. Smugglers probably. He was right about at least one of them.

As the journey progressed, Sai was quietly satisfied when she realised that Husha never corrected fellow travellers in the caravan who had assumed that the three teenagers with him were his children. When some enquired about the purpose of his journey Husha extended the illusion by saying it was to join his family in Harran after the end of his employment in Susa. Sai might have noticed and would have been correct in sensing a pride in Husha at being seen as a parent to these young people he was growing to respect.

Meanwhile Sai and Iannas took advantage of the longer stretch with its routines by walking together and enjoying listening to each other's hopes and dreams while ignoring Husha's moodiness and Daniel's paranoia about the next impending disaster that would stop him from reaching Haradum.

Each night, Donkey also got to know his fellow travellers. He was always aware that the other donkeys were tired in the evenings while he was usually fresh even though he was carrying the same load as most of the others. There was one particular donkey that had been with the caravan since Sippar, and the two often ended up settling down for the night next to each other after sharing the animal feed. Donkey felt sorry for him. The other donkey appeared to be suffering, Donkey understood, and helped to calm him down each night.

Donkey also noticed that Sai needed greater care. There was something inside her he could not quite feel, so he always made sure to be gentle with her and protect her.

15 HARADUM

From time to time, seekers of tranquillity create their own settlements, oases invisible to the eyes of the cities, soldiers and bandits, and alien to taxes, identification tablets, and extreme bureaucracies. Not hiding from life but seeking a better life, a quiet existence veiled from attempts by people needing power to rule and organise the world.

Haradum was such a community. Attempting a quiet living from passing caravans and boats that, as Haradum grew, eventually treated it as a station on the way to Mari. From a settlement, it grew into a tiny little hamlet and then, as a consequence of increasing attention from passing travellers and traders, soon became a village. To many people's surprise, even now, there were no soldiers in Haradum, no customs, no checks, just settlers wanting a quiet life for themselves and their families.

Haradum was a place that most of the rulers had ignored, but now it was well-known as an ideal midway stop for boats and caravans, even during the annual river floods along the Euphrates. Being within the borders of Mari, it had already attracted the attention of the Governor of Mari, who saw it with new eyes, an opportunity for new tax income, and had promptly sent his city planners to Haradum. Without consulting the residents of Haradum, the planners designed a small town square, a temple, and even planned to turn Haradum into a walled settlement. The idea of a wall created much mirth among the settlers who had no intention of fighting with anyone or defending themselves against anyone, for everyone including vagrants, refugees, and exiles had always been welcome in Haradum. When the walls began to be built, courtesy of the Governor of Mari, the locals allowed it to continue and remained amused, for they had managed for so long without walls, without Mari, and without a town planner. But no one could deny that the new interest from Mari provided jobs that were otherwise hard to find in Haradum unless the younger ones worked on the boats, the caravans or the naphtha fields. But this was shortsighted. Soon the tax officials and the bureaucracy of Mari would rudely infect the simplicity of life in Haradum. For now, this was a community in the process of witnessing a silent, albeit violence free, subjugation.

It was the noticeably serene yet undisciplined atmosphere that gripped both Husha and Sai with a prickly sensation of being uncomfortable around the curious residents.

'It seems odd to feel vulnerable in a town where there are no soldiers when the opposite should be true.' Husha shared his thoughts as he stood with Donkey and Sai making sure that neither came to any harm. He simply did not like the way the people were looking at the goods on Donkey or for that matter at Sai.

One of the problems that the original settlers had not counted on and could do very little about was the never ending, sulphurous smell, and at times like today, the stench was oozing out from the hot black naphtha pools seeping from the ground on the opposite side of the caravan road immediately outside of Haradum. A few pools in the distance were actually burning, and the pungent biting smoke drifted into the village when the breeze was just right. On the day Daniel, Iannas, Sai, and Husha arrived, the breeze was just right and the smell so bad that all new visitors had taken to tying wet cloths around their faces, covering the nose and mouth. Iannas tied a cloth on Donkey too and it appeared to settle him.

The smell of tranquillity.

Daniel had already arranged to continue with the same caravan leader to Mari, leaving as usual at dawn. It was late in the afternoon, and they had no intention of staying any longer than necessary. Being a little village with so many eyes, it did not take long to find Susana of Haradum, formerly of Susa.

'Hello, Daniel, I got word of your travel last week. Alizer will be happy you brought them this way. He is always welcome here. You know, of course, everyone in Mari knows him?' Daniel had not known and immediately began wondering if Alizer's familiarity in Haradum would cause the family any difficulty. Daniel quickly managed to create his next comfort worry, being always in need of having something to feel comfortable.

'Are they making good progress? Are they receiving our supplies? Is there anything else they need? Should we be doing anything different?' Daniel asked all at once.

Susana, like Daniel, was a Susian and named after the city where she had been born and where her family still lived. As soon as Susana, a young woman in her fifth year of marriage, met Daniel, she was reminded of the first time she had set eyes on her husband. Susana's future husband had arrived as a boat assistant transporting clay bricks to Susana's father who was repairing a section of the wall at the time. It was at the wall repairs where they met for the first time when Susana was delivering food for her father. Now her husband had a boat of his own, a licence to work the river from Mari to Sippar, and was a riverboat man in his own right. His cargo was naphtha, and he was making a delivery to the Sippar boatyards. Susana was missing him.

'You remind me of my husband when I first met him,' she thought out loud and quickly changed the subject so as not to embarrass Daniel. 'Udama sent a message. Alizer and the group are on schedule and are finding your supplies invaluable, especially your extra plates and new shoes. Well done, Daniel. Alizer does not like the tea but apparently the family enjoy it. If my calculations are right they will have left Hit and should be here in three days.'

Daniel smiled, relieved.

'But do not slow down, Daniel. Mari is three days from here and even one day's delay will create problems for you later. In Mari, contact Erra Wasum. He is the chief tailor in the market. Ask any tailor and they will guide you to him.' Daniel accepted the customary bag of coins without any commentary. 'Sleep in my stable with your friends and tonight I will prepare food for all of you.' Susana spoke with the familiar Susa accent and this made Daniel feel particularly at home.

Daniel led Susana back to Husha and found Iannas and Sai also returning from a short inspection of the local market.

'There are a limited variety of supplies but we will make do.' Sai reported back before she and Husha left to purchase their supplies. Iannas and Daniel settled Donkey in Susana's stable, and then focused on Alizer's fresh supplies topped up with plenty of dried foods, some new pots and pans, and had them delivered to the small station at the entrance of the village where they were organised and labelled as usual.

Susana specially planned tonight's home cooked food, and Daniel was transported to the kitchen of his childhood as he smelled the aromas of Susa spread in front of him. Daniel suddenly expressed how much he had missed his mother's cooking at which Iannas, Sai, and Husha feigned offence and insisted he cook his own food in the future. Daniel had to admit that their food was almost as good. Susana came to the rescue and described how she had roasted the fish caught from the river that morning with an olive and date paste. The roasted brinjal was straight from the garden and coated with fresh eggs laid by her hens. For dessert, Susana spoiled them with pickled dates and fresh oranges. Sai took out her small purse of tea at the end of the meal and, of course, instructed Susana on how to make it. Susana had tried some before when a trader from India had fallen ill in a caravan and had remained a few nights in Haradum. He would make tea many times each day which he considered not only a remedy for his ailment but also an elixir for long life. He invited all who passed to try the drink, but the tea Sai had made was more to her liking than the taste she remembered before. Sai explained that her tea was a special mix of tea and herbs dried in a way that gave the special aroma that Susana found very soothing and calming.

'We see so many people passing through Haradum nowadays. Because of this, Mari has eyes on us. Haradum has no taxes or soldiers. That may soon change. I came here with my husband when we married and his father has lived here trading the naphtha all his life. They now want to use the naphtha everywhere and demand has increased so much. My husband makes a good living from transporting it in his boats. He has three naphtha delivery boats now.

'It is amazing what they use it for. My husband supplies temples where they use it to bind their clay for making figurines, the building trade use it to stop the water leaking through roofs, and most of the boats nowadays are coated in naphtha to protect them from rotting. We have new customers every week so we have enough money and are settled here for now.' Susana was contented.

'What will you do when soldiers arrive and bring the city with them?' Husha asked.

'Mari is my favourite city, and it is my dream to move there. It is so beautiful; you will see it in a few days. I would say it is better than Ur or Susa and that is saying something. But be careful of the people of Mari. They appear friendly and modern, but actually they are very conservative and protective of their ways. You might need the extra time in Mari and Terqa to arrange things.'

'Udama said the same thing about Haradum. He said to think carefully before proceeding from here, but I have already booked to leave in the morning. Why would he have said that, Susana?' Daniel asked.

'The city people think that because we are a small free community we are wild,' Susana confided. 'It's because we have no soldiers or security you see, and city people are often scared when they pass by here. Udama must have been worried about Alizer's supplies. I will make sure he receives them. Which caravan is he coming with?'

When Daniel told her the name of the caravan company she smiled, she knew them well.

'Not to worry. I know where they camp, and I will look after them,' Susana reassured. 'That was a good thing you did heading this way. Now, do not cross the river at Mari. Carry on to Terqa on the south bank caravan route. The route is busier and safer. Then cross in Terqa.'

'There is one last thing before you sleep,' Susana added. 'I heard some boat people talking about the King in Urfa and some big bonfire he is preparing for the festival of the shortest day and full moon. The astronomers have predicted a full moon on the night of the shortest day and the priests have announced it as the holiest of all holy nights. People around the empire will be celebrating the event.'

Daniel agreed. 'This will be a very special day to honour the Sin God.'

'Apparently the God-King is to be crowned on that same special night in Urfa and is announcing lots of celebrations. I do not think I have heard of a God-King in these parts before. Urfa is too far away to be our concern, but it is close to Harran so I thought I would warn you. You will have to travel through some of the Urfa district roads and checkpoints to reach Harran.' She paused, and Husha noticed that there might have been something more she wanted to say. 'Say hello to Erra Wasum in Mari and ask him where my dresses are. I want them ready for the festivals,' Susana finished before catching Husha's eye.

'Come on now, time for bed,' Susana instructed. 'It is good you are a small group. Make sure to appreciate your friends, Daniel.'

Daniel did. They were more than friends; they were family, including Donkey, who was eating his dinner and enjoying the company of some chickens and a few sheep in Susana's small barn which was protecting him from the terrible smell outside. Donkey could not wait to leave.

16 THE ROAD TO MARI

Days 39 to 42, 11.5 Beru.

The caterpillar grew fatter and longer in the morning as it swallowed tasty new morsels of families from Haradum heading for Mari to spend the festival period with loved ones. The extra footsteps breathed new life into the caravan community never ceasing to amaze with its new colours, sounds and fresh characters.

The relatively flat terrain made the walking easier, but the occasional tel and palm trees were welcomed to digress from the monotony of the journey. Often the caravan left the green scarf behind heading in what appeared to be the opposite direction of the river, but in fact, due to the meandering curve of the river, the caravan made sure to cut across two points of the river arch to reduce its travel. These excursions took the caravan away from the sound of the river and the calls of the birds so that the heavy echoes of the footsteps on the dry hard desert became the owners of the air. This northern part of the Euphrates was not as fertile as the earlier regions, and if anyone had not yet already done so, they would remember fondly the southern region of Edin, or Garden.

Husha and Daniel had both noticed the closeness between Iannas and Sai well before Sippar. Iannas and Sai were again walking and chatting together, and Daniel, who had tired of worrying about his worries for a change, along with a hint of jealousy, decided to interrupt their conversations.

'All right, you two. Enough talking between you, we exist as well,' Daniel said, hoping for some support from Husha which did not arrive. Husha would let Daniel fight his own battle today.

'What's the topic of conversation?' Daniel asked not expecting a decent answer, but when it came it caught him by surprise.

'Magicians, adventurers, travellers, stories of the gods and tales of the ancients!' Iannas proclaimed with appetite. 'I was saying to Sai we all want to be part of some great adventure, and I would count her journey from India as the making of a grand story that I will tell over and over again one day!'

Sai laughed. 'If you think that, Iannas, then I would say I am still living my adventure. My story is not finished!'

'In that case,' Daniel continued the thought, 'we are extremely honoured to be playing a part in your great adventure!'

'Daniel, you are right! We are part of Sai's amazing adventure.' Daniel's revelation was well received, 'I have never been in an adventure before.'

'So how do we turn Sai's adventure into a great story, like the one of Gilgamesh, how Ishtar became a God of Love from a God of War?' Daniel spoke animatedly and with his deep adventure voice, like the one Rabi had spoken with.

For a moment, the young ones became true adventurers.

'In my adventure, I shall be Princess Sai from the distant mountains of India come to the lands of Edin to restore law and order and bring peace!'

'And I will be your Protector. The faithful servant and magician, Iannas, who will call on the spirit world to protect you from the evil Husha, the bringer of war.'

Husha raised his eyebrows at Iannas, but did not rise to the challenge.

'And I will be the Guardian, the angel Daniel, sent by the Gods from the spirit world to teach the Princess the mysteries of the world so that she can become the first and greatest Queen of the Edin, the world and the universe!'

'And I will be the Queen of Peace,' added Sai. 'The Queen who restored compassion and love amongst the people of the world.'

'The Queen of Love!' Daniel joked.

'That sounds terrible,' Sai protested. 'Strike that from our story, servant!' she commanded Iannas.

'Why should I?' Iannas countered. 'We have a God of Love? Why not a Queen of Love? We say love the gods? We will say love the Queen!' Iannas was raising his voice.

Husha looked up as if he had just been woken.

'Iannas is right. We present our gratitude to the Gods for the patterns of the day and night that allows us to live our lives and rest. What is wrong with showing our appreciation to the Queen who brings peace?' Daniel decided this was so much better than worrying.

Husha emerged from his mood, joined the discussion, and attempted to steady their voices.

'I am able to hear you. Talk softly, young ones. You must be careful.' He was being very paternal, Iannas thought. 'In these times, God is the property of the king, his priests, his magicians, and his astrologers.

'It was not always like this,' Husha suddenly appeared to want to talk. 'But now, in these times, your debates about the gods could lead us into some grave consequences if someone were to hear you and misunderstand.'

They all agreed with Husha and allowed him to continue. It was good to see him out of his shell again.

'When I was young, we were taught of the Gods of Egypt, what they looked like, their purpose and their stories. These Gods united us. With age, my understanding of these things improved, but I also met travellers, artisans, masons and traders in Memphis and learned of an incredible new world out there waiting to be explored. I decided to join one of the Pharaoh's campaigns that would take me to the farthest lands, but before I had time to enlist, the slavers arrived.' Husha was not telling the whole truth. Sai was the only one who was perceptive enough to notice.

'In this land, just like in Egypt, if others hear you question the Gods you are seen as traitors, a threat to the king, his priests, the temples, the faithful, and the empire itself. In Egypt, the king is a God and any words challenging that notion is punishable by death. There is no question as to a king's power or divinity.'

That night they continued their discussions, grateful that Husha was with them again. Daniel was also grateful for the world as it was. He knew his place in it.

The next few days to Mari were filled with more conversations, Husha talked about the Egyptian Gods, Sai about Krishna, and Daniel more about Sin. Iannas listened and could not help but wonder how incredible and how separate each of these different beliefs were. He only wanted to listen and amaze at the differences, yet, here they were, friends walking together, sharing together and looking after one another.

Husha told stories of Egyptian kings, ministers thriving on power, coups, wars, death and enormous tombs, temples and the Book of Life and the Book of the Dead. He described how the dead pharaohs would be buried with his servants and animals whilst they were still alive.

'Why kill in the name of a God?' Sai asked. 'I heard the kings do this in Mesopotamia too. What will the king or the God do with the sacrifice of life? If God created life, why would we wish to kill it in the name of the God that created it?' Sai challenged, 'I can only describe killing in the name of any God as a perversion of a faith that is only dressed in the name of a God of creation.'

Husha also explained that writing in Egypt, unlike in Mesopotamia, was an act of profound holiness. 'The written characters themselves are a representation of life, and since life is a representation of God, all writing is a representation of God. Egyptian writing is holy as it is a celebration of all the creation of the world, and every time we write we celebrate God.'

As the discussion and debates continued, none noticed how freely accepting they had become of each other's beliefs and how this acceptance had brought them together, without them realising, towards understanding the nature of the world, and the very essence each was attempting to touch. Iannas was so close to touching the meaning of his dreams, but even if he had, he would not have understood what to do with the new understanding.

Then it was Daniel who, remembering a conversation between his father and Terah, asked a question that took Husha by surprise. 'Husha, do you know any more about the child killings? A lifetime ago I believe. I overheard my father talking about it in Susa. Do you know if it is true and why the babies were killed?'

Husha should have been expecting this question, but he had not. If he had seen how closely entwined he had become with Daniel and Iannas in the task of helping Terah's family reach Harran in safety, he should have realised that Daniel would have more questions to ask. Husha did not expect to be asked a question that he had spent so many years making sense of. Husha could not utter a word; in fact, he was so shocked he was lost for words. If he had been eating he would have choked. Husha's reaction puzzled Daniel.

'It's all right if you do not know, Husha,' Daniel assumed. 'I just wondered.'

'Let me begin by telling you what I heard about the Minister of Babylon from a trader on the way to Haradum.' Husha recovered quickly, collecting his thoughts and hiding his embarrassment for not replying to Daniel with what he knew. Sai noticed immediately and, as much as she liked Husha, she knew she would have to share her concern with Daniel and Iannas when an opportunity came. She could not understand what Husha was hiding and why.

Husha continued and reminded them of how their entry in Uruk had been delayed because of an assassin. They all remembered. Husha repeated the trader's version, narrated the two different versions of the attempted assassination, and then returned to Daniel's questions.

'Well, Daniel, this Minister, if the trader is right, is claiming to be a survivor of the child killings at the time of the former King of Sippar and now wants retribution in the form of gold from his son, the present King of Sippar. Somebody somewhere is trying to scare the Minister or even kill him.'

Daniel was very surprised with the news. He did not want to say that he knew that his Uncle Terah's son might be a survivor too. 'Is this really true? So the child murders did take place? It is not just a story?'

'No one is yet denying the allegations of the Minister.' Husha was speaking his thoughts. 'So, for now it seems so,' Husha answered casually.

'Do you know any more of the circumstances behind the killings?' Daniel pressed, keen to learn more.

'Let me find out more, Daniel. I will give you the news as I learn it.' Husha was glad that Daniel was satisfied.

The next day when Sai, Iannas and Daniel were away from any other ears, Sai released her need to share her concern.

'He is hiding something, Daniel, and I do not know what it is.' That is all she said, and it was enough.

Mari revealed itself in the distance with still half a day's travel to the city. It was early evening of the third day from Haradum, with the sun low, and the city walls were already lit like the ripe fruit of an orange tree. At the sight of Mari, conversations ceased. None of them had seen a city like this one before, and even from this distance and from the tel where they walked, Mari looked like a jewel. Perfect circular walls enclosed both sides of a tributary of the river, so that the city lay within and was effectively divided by the river flowing all the way through. It was ingenious. A second city wall lay within the first in expectation of new invaders in the future. Mari grew more impressive as they came closer, and when the horn was sounded for the night's camp, the weary travellers knew the caravan would reach the city gates not long after dawn the next day, which would be a generous day to enjoy the city and make plans for the next segment of the journey.

For tonight, however, the entire caravan attended its own music event. The drums held a rhythm until late into the night, the harps and flutes played every tune they could remember and then others prompted by their audience. The journey from Sippar had been long, and it was time to celebrate a safe arrival.

When Iannas lay down, their adventure story stayed with him. He had enjoyed the amusement of constructing a legend and how much they had laughed together. He had not felt so happy in a while and realised he had forgotten his mother in that time. And Iannas was content, for the sorrow of her last breathing had been replaced with different memories. He had not noticed the change until now. He thanked his friends, he thanked his God and he also smiled again at their playful words, especially Daniel's, which recalled some of the ancient legends he had been trying to recollect. The ones told to him by his Appa that mentioned a "watcher", a phrase Rabi had used, and the legends of the first ten kings of the world.

Donkey was nervous.

17 ERRA WASUM OF MARI

Less than a generation ago, artisans came together from the Amorite community and conceived new life into the abandoned city of Mari. The artisan love of culture thrived and continued to thrive through Mari's new leadership while the changing governments ensured that Mari had the military strength always at the ready to defend, if not to attack. Because it had been recreated in a new form from dust, Mari was proud to look forward rather than be stranded within the constraints of the old ways. Mari was a new city finding time to understand what it meant to be associated with culture, dress, art, drama, music and literature. As always, the atmosphere in the caravans reaching the city that fashioned itself as an icon of modern style and elegance was full of great anticipation and excitement.

While Daniel completed the city entry tax formalities, Sai, Iannas, and Husha were staring at the people around them. The facades of the buildings of Mari decorated the locals perfectly producing a feeling of joy and bewilderment. It was so unexpected. After allowing their eyes to be charmed by the architecture, they could not help but notice that the Mari around them were considerably taller and so much more smartly attired than themselves. The dress sense was extended to babies, children, mothers, fathers, grandparents, friends, husbands, wives, and especially the young people; teenagers who were planning to impress as much as they could as they walked, or took a seat along the temple steps either side of the street. This street was clearly a favourite for the locals to walk and meet, to watch others and, of course, the main activity of the street, to be seen. For the new arrivals, the elegance gave rise to a quiet suffering of feeling smaller, unkempt and messy until they chose to give each other heart by mocking each other's attempts to look smart. Both Iannas and Daniel had dressed into ill-fitting but clean hand-me-down clothes belonging to their fathers. Husha had his clean city clothes, but they were not too different to his travel variety. Only Sai looked splendid as she always did in a simple green dress styled in India, one of three she carried with her for city visits.

'It would have been better had we not tried, but I still look smarter than you,' Iannas teased Daniel, who ignored him successfully by finding eyes for the strikingly colourfully dressed and deliberately intending to be noticed by approaching group of young ladies with their long free dark brown hair complementing their long free flowing gowns. Sai suggested on a few occasions they should stop staring, but it seemed the young ladies of Mari were used to it and even enjoyed the attention. The men were less spectacular in their dress but nonetheless very smartly turned out, clean, manicured, and the hair and the beards were groomed to perfection in various different styles, some curly, some straight and some crafted.

'They remind me of the colourful fish we have in the waters of Egypt.' Husha looked to find fault. 'I am not sure if this is vanity, or they are so contented they actually have the time to think about their dress and just try to look good because they can!'

The more sophisticated women of Mari, so as not to be overshadowed by their younger compatriots, monopolised the head crowning to harmonize their vibrant wardrobes. Each head of dark hair demonstrated expert artistry and was framed with coloured ribbons or jewellery, the beehive hairstyle in all its different versions being the most fashionable to be seen in this season. Husha had listened to tales of Mari fashion and style from the travellers in Susa, but nothing had prepared him for the ornaments around him.

'Mari style will be a subject of legend one day,' Husha avowed. Daniel and Iannas made sure to point out the wildest fashion statements to each other so as to be able to describe them to unbelieving listeners one day and, naturally with appropriate adornments to the story, contribute to a future legend.

Arriving at the spectacularly situated central parade on the banks of the river, with an almost exact copy on the other side of the tributary serving the other half of the city, took longer than expected with all the distractions. Daniel appeared to have forgotten his purpose for being in Mari until Iannas gave him a nudge.

'Stop looking at the young ladies and find the tailor, Daniel. We will explore the market in the square and meet you at Zimi's here.' He pointed to the wine and beer bar just behind them. Iannas, Sai and Husha continued into the parade leaving Daniel behind.

Iannas had used the term square without even realising that the central parade they were strolling in was in fact one of two half-circles. They headed towards the familiar sound in the centre of the market and, as they approached through the variety of stalls, they recognised the music. Soon they were waving to their fellow travelling caravan band companions. The band had already been made welcome by their hosts and were celebrating their arrival in their traditional way. The marketers were grateful for the entertainment that they hoped would attract even more customers. The shouts from the mooring boats laden with fresh market goods being unloaded on both sides of the tributary, not far from the music, added to the whole medley of the parade. Despite the size of the market, the river granted the centre of the city an openness incomparable to any other they had travelled. Sai appreciated what Susana had meant about Mari being her favourite city, and when she thought about making a remark, she looked at Iannas and discovered that the city had already transported him into another world, for it was truly breathtaking.

Husha wandered off into the market leaving Iannas and Sai to enjoy the music and walk through the stalls admiring and sometimes enquiring about the goods, some of which had travelled far from Egypt, India, Europe, as well as Mesopotamia. The world was getting smaller, Sai thought, as she recognised some Indian and Afghan weavings and even spoke to a couple of traders from India. She asked for news from her birth country, and they told her that the northern lands were still recovering from the floods, which had now subsided, but whole towns and villages had been washed away, probably forever, and the smell and sight of death was everywhere.

The half-circles on either side of the tributary were almost identical even with facing temples and similar buildings either side of the temple. As Husha headed towards the government office buildings adjacent to the temple in his half of the parade, he noticed Daniel in the distance heading towards a tailor's shop. Husha walked through the main entrance of the government building and asked for the Head Astrologer's office and, after introducing himself, was not surprised to be both expected and quickly received.

'What do you have for me?' asked the Astrologer, even as his assistant was showing Husha into the study. The Astrologer, dressed in his familiar, smart, government-issued, plain tunic, and very stylishly curled and dyed black hair and beard, which made him look distinguished but not younger, was pensively standing watching the market activity through the window. He turned as Husha entered. 'We told you in Sippar to learn about the Eperu and seek news of Terah the High Priest of Ur. We have verified that he is no longer in Ur. In fact, we cannot tell where he is. We believe he is heading north. What have you learned? What do you know?' Husha was not asked to sit and gathered the meeting would be short. He sensed the tension and quickly calculated what information he might offer to prolong the information gathering.

'There is no word at all along the Euphrates,' Husha lied.

'Have you news of any other members of the tribe? Who they are? Where they live?' The questions were very clinically asked by a man who was particularly preoccupied and seemed not to have time for this supposed guest of the Astrologer of Susa.

'I only came because Zaros, the Astrologer of Sippar suggested I stop by. I am returning home to Memphis.' Husha avoided the questions for now.

'Say hello to my friend in Memphis,' the Astrologer softened a little.

'I heard there is trouble with the Minister from Babylon?' Husha was angling.

'What do you know of it?'

'A domestic affair, according to Sippar.' Husha knew that he would have to reveal something to gain something, 'But word along the road is that he is making accusations of a child killing at the time of his birth and placing it firmly on Sippar's doorstep. The King of Sippar, no less.'

'I know the gossipmongers have already started weaving their webs, and that damned Minister can claim what he wants. I am glad you alerted me to this. There is more going on in Sippar than we are being told. There is a conspiracy against Zaros' father. That is clear to us.' The Astrologer attempted to align Husha to his information. 'Even the King of Sippar has become involved and denounced the accusation as a slur on his family and Sippar. There was no child killing, and the Babylonian will not get away with this. This is the usual type of drivel Babylon sends out when they have eyes on another city. I would not be surprised if they try to take over Sippar, but first they will try and discredit the King and Astrologer and weave discord, just like in Ur and Isin.'

So here, thought Husha, was the official version from Sippar and the astrologers. Although he sensed that the Astrologer would reveal no further information, he still pushed a little more to see what could be gleaned

'What about the domestic matter, the divorce of the Babylon Minister? Was that just a ruse?'

The Astrologer did not answer but instead paused before responding, 'I am disappointed in your news. I thought you would have much more information for me. If you have nothing, then there is no point in your meeting the Astrologer in Terqa. I will send word that he is not to expect you. If you do not have any information about the tribe or the High Priest of Ur, you are of no use. Now go.' The Astrologer left the room leaving Husha to wonder if he should have said more. Husha was shown out by the assistants who, when by the door, whispered to Husha.

'We have reason to believe that Sippar is watching us. The Astrologer's Office is nervous and does not know where this will lead. I have heard of your work with us, and I know the Astrologer is grateful. Be careful in case someone is watching you. I know very little more. We have our people in

Sippar, and they report the Head of Security is behind this.' The assistant turned as if to re-enter the Astrologer's Office, 'One more thing. The Astrologer of Sippar no longer has the ear of the King of Sippar.' Husha watched as the assistant stepped back into the room and closed the wooden door behind him. Husha made to return towards the market in the parade and now understood the Head Astrologer's edginess.

Husha attempted to unravel what had been said and also how and why it had been spoken. They had clearly lost track of Terah, but there was no friendly concern for Terah in the voice of the Astrologer, not as in Sippar. Was Terah now a fugitive? Husha wondered, and what did this mean for the Eperu?

There was more. The Head of the Guild, the Head Astrologer of Sippar, had fallen from grace. What would Zaros do next? Who were his alliances and where would he go? And was this good news for Terah? If someone was watching the astrologers, it had to be the King of Sippar's men. Would anyone really be watching him? Husha wondered. He had been careful, but if they were already watching the astrologers, he would have been noticed. By denying the allegations of the Minister of Babylon, the Royal Court in Sippar was showing it was vulnerable and had something to hide. The intrigues were becoming more complicated than a spider's web. He would be happy to avoid visiting the Astrologer in Terqa, Husha thought, and clearly needed to put some distance between himself and the Astrologers. There was something else he sensed in the Astrologer. A fear. This was unusual. Had Zaros dragged the entire Guild into his own ignominy?

The only thing Husha was now sure of was that the Minister of Babylon had made his mark, and it was being deeply felt.

A mark of evil once made can never be undone.

Husha knew he would fall into a complex labyrinth if he allowed himself, and chose not to spare it any further thought. After all, he was heading home. A small part of Husha was hoping to be able to put all the deception behind him. He would miss the intrigues, but then there would be new ones in Memphis. As he left the building, he noticed Mari's City Library at the far end of the parade, and even from this distance, a copy of an Egyptian relief painting, almost as large as the library door itself, was placed at the very entrance. Husha knew that Egypt traded with Mari and wondered what he would find. He decided to walk across the parade to take a closer look. As he walked through the vendors' stalls, he asked himself if travelling with Daniel was now a threat to both Daniel and Alizer. It was with this thought he stepped into the library and followed the sign to a small 'Egyptian' room at the rear of the building, that housed a very limited collection. Even as he entered the room, he immediately recognised more painted reliefs from Saqqara, mainly copies painted on wood, some tomb artefacts, papyrus sheets, a mummified pair of cats, and even small statues of Egyptian Gods and old Pharaohs. He asked the lady museum curator, who had welcomed him and even asked Husha to translate some reliefs for her, how they had gathered such a collection. He wondered if he should have brought Sai, Iannas and Daniel so they could explore some of his heritage.

To meet the demand, there were a large number of tailor shops sprinkled all around the parade, and to be fair to Daniel, finding Erra Wasum was not as easy as Susana had suggested it would be. The first tailor Daniel spoke to pointed to Erra Wasum the Tailor's shop across the other side of the busy parade, and when Daniel wrestled his way across to Erra Wasum's shop, Erra Wasum was not there; the door was shut and the shop empty. The next tailor Daniel asked said that he had seen Erra Wasum heading towards a tailor's on the far side of the parade on the corner by the river. When Daniel fought through the market stalls again and reached the tailor's shop on the corner by the river, Erra Wasum had already left, and Daniel was guided to yet another tailor where, once again, he had already left. Daniel decided to return to Erra Wasum's own shop and sit outside thinking he should have done that in the first place. Sure enough, in time, and by now it was late morning, a tall distinguished-looking gentleman approached with a long and noisy entourage behind him. Daniel remained seated on the steps watching the procession march towards him.

Mari had a number of trading associations. Each issued a limited number of licences to sell and trade in Mari making sure that foreign traders did not take over the trade or the markets at the expense of the locals while still being well represented. The system was well organised and protected the local traders' interests and was paid for by a traders' levy collected by each association. Erra Wasum was in charge of the entire Mari central market traders' association, so when he arrived at his shop that was primarily his office, a small delegation of hopeful traders and agents lined up behind him looking for licences.

Daniel looked at this tall, very smart, and exquisitely dressed, well-groomed, elderly gentleman who exuded both confidence and command. He was clearly much more than a tailor.

Daniel recollected the market in Susa where no one had time for dressing up, and none at all for all this grooming and efforts to look good. In Susa, Daniel concluded, people were more preoccupied with making a living.

Erra Wasum's four assistants rearranged the chairs and tables inside the office in readiness for the traders to enter one by one; they also organised the traders into a manageable order. Before Erra Wasum decided to sit down and receive the traders, he noticed a young man standing, waiting, and trying to catch his eye just outside the shop door.

Erra Wasum left his assistants behind, even as they tried to protest, and approached the young man. Daniel instantly felt besieged by Erra Wasum's colourful garments as he looked up at this large being from inside Erra Wasum's shadow. Daniel felt both small and bedazzled as the sun sparkled from behind Erra Wasum.

'You are Daniel of Susa?' Erra Wasum enquired before Daniel had a chance to introduce himself.

'Susana from Haradum sent me.' Daniel felt slightly intimidated but gathered himself fast.

'No, she did not. Alizer did. Where did you last see him?'

'Ur.'

'Come, let us talk inside,' and much to the astonishment of the traders, Daniel was led inside and the assistants were told to wait by the door. Daniel's smile gleamed brightly at being treated as an important guest of Erra Wasum over the traders, who assumed it to be a family matter, and so no one complained.

Behind his veneer was a very well-informed and educated man. Erra Wasum spoke with confidence and import. This man was definitely not a tailor, Daniel thought, and he realised he was too nervous to ask.

Erra Wasum settled Daniel's nerves by opening the conversation and instructed one of his assistants to bring two boiled date drinks. 'Ur is still in curfew even after Susa has put a new Governor in charge. Demonstrations have turned into battles, and there are so many factions on the streets. I heard today that one group of protestors has taken the new Governor hostage. It is good that Alizer and the family left in time. People are not even being allowed to leave now. The Amorites will be taking over in Ur soon, mark my words. The safety of Alizer and the family are my responsibility, Daniel.' Daniel assumed this last statement was a figurative comment, which it was not. 'So far you have done very well indeed. I must congratulate you for reaching Mari without any incidents.' Erra Wasum's voice exposed a slight condescension that perturbed Daniel, but Erra Wasum explained, 'I must confess I was cynical when I first heard about you, but look, here you are. All the way from Susa! Terah made an excellent choice. You can go places I cannot and have done things I could not do. You can buy supplies and leave them for Alizer outside the city at the service station, and no one will notice you or ask any questions. If I try and leave even one jug of water at the service station, everyone wants to know who it is for, and the whole town knows my business even before I do.'

The hot drinks arrived, and both Erra Wasum and Daniel lifted a beautifully painted cup and sipped the hot sweet drink made from fresh, local dates from Erra Wasum's farm that had only been picked the day before. Daniel savoured the taste and the aroma, a fresh scented taste to the dry dull gritty dates he had become accustomed to. Daniel agreed with Erra Wasum, and it should have made more sense to him than it did as his attention wandered back to the drink. Even the cups are painted in Mari and the dates are scented, he was thinking.

'I see you enjoy the drink. It has a herb locally called menthe. Very refreshing.' Erra Wasum paused, drank and looked at Daniel intensely. 'Continue doing whatever it is you are doing, Daniel. Alizer needs you to keep his family away from the gaze of the officials, and you are helping with the task admirably. It may become more and more difficult as you approach Tuttul and Harran, but it is critical that you continue to keep a low profile all the way.'

As Erra Wasum paused and looked at Daniel, he had an admiration and affection for what this young man had already achieved and was unsure of how much to burden Daniel. The less Daniel knew the better, was Erra Wasum's first thought, but decided Daniel should know enough to keep his wits about him.

This large and imposing man intimidated Daniel. But Daniel also greatly respected the way Erra Wasum spoke about Alizer and the family. They had a common goal, and Daniel already knew that there was more here than he was being told. He resisted the temptation to ask and waited to hear what Erra Wasum would say.

'Let me tell you a little more, Daniel. You are old enough and you have come this far.' He looked at his assistants to confirm they were outside of earshot and the other traders well out of the way. 'If I tell you a little then you might understand your task, and it might help you accomplish it more gracefully. I have no doubt you will be tested between here and Harran.' Erra Wasum repeated looking for a reaction from Daniel as they sipped their drinks, but Daniel was too careful to provide one.

'You are a good listener, Daniel. You have been taught well.' Daniel was proud of the compliment that reminded him of his father in Susa. 'I am hearing that the Astrologer in Sippar and his colleagues in the north are spreading terrifying stories and making sure the kings in the region have much to be nervous about. Some of these astrologers want to bring harm to the family and the tribe. You know which family I mean, don't you?'

Daniel nodded. He knew Erra Wasum was referring to Uncle Terah's family but did not understand why.

'Some of them already know something they should not. They believe the family is heading to Harran. The eyes of the kings and the astrologers are everywhere. Talk to no one about Alizer, Terah, the family, or the tribe; no one must know your task, Daniel.'

'The best thing you did was travel along the Euphrates rather than the Tigris. That was a good decision. Although Terah has extended family in the north, and that is the route he normally takes, there will be many more eyes and ears there. He is safer heading this way. It is quieter, we can keep an eye on him and I do not think anyone at the moment is expecting him this way.'

Daniel was pleased with the decision. 'I was unsure at the time,' he admitted.

'I know, Daniel. Alizer wanted you to make the decision. He would have followed you whichever route you took. And you made the right one. Bless you, Daniel.'

Daniel was filled with relief even though he knew he would worry about the route again.

'These are your instructions,' Erra Wasum continued. 'Head for Terqa and look for Puvurum. He is a local fresh fruit and vegetable trader in the market square. Find his stall. If he is not there, his assistants will know where he is but do not discuss our business with them.'

Daniel was surprised that his next contact was a market trader. For the first time, he wondered what the connection between each of his different contacts was, and how Alizer could have coordinated the entire journey without even knowing what route Daniel would decide to take. What if he had decided on the Tigris route?

'Cross the river in Terqa. On the north bank, you will find a well-serviced station. From there take the caravan to Tuttul. From Tuttul it is a short journey to Harran. Repeat the route for me. I want to hear you say it.' Erra Wasum needed to be sure Daniel understood. Maybe he still did not trust Daniel after all.

Daniel repeated the route correctly and asked the question that was concerning him. 'Why does anyone want to harm Uncle Terah? He is just a priest, and why the tribe? You realise my family is related to the tribe?'

'When I see you in Harran, I will tell you, Daniel. Right now it is better for you not to know any more than I have told you. But you must not share your heritage with anyone. It is imperative for your safety.'

Daniel was not satisfied and had decided these would be his new worries.

Erra Wasum paused and continued to look at Daniel seriously. 'There is one more thing Daniel. One of your companions, the slave...'

Daniel interrupted Erra Wasum and did not realise until it was too late, 'He is Egyptian, and he is a free man now.' He had no intention to offend Erra Wasum and could not tell if he had. He relaxed a little but did not apologise for making the interruption.

Erra Wasum continued. 'Yes, I understand he is now a free man. He was seen by my contact visiting the Head Astrologer of Sippar.'

Daniel did not understand the significance and listened.

'No one sees the Head Astrologer in Sippar without reason, Daniel. Originally, I was concerned if he was passing news to the Astrologer until the same contact verified that Sippar has sent someone to keep an eye on the slave. They clearly do not trust him. At this moment, I know nothing more except it is something to do with his former owner, a relative of mine. I am looking into it. I will leave you to deal with him as you see fit. Someone has been following the slave... sorry, Egyptian,' Erra Wasum caught the look on Daniel's face, 'since Sippar. I cannot ignore this. Since I have no facts, we have to assume that whoever it is has inadvertently followed you.' Erra Wasum paused again for a reaction.

This last piece of news surprised and concerned Daniel. His instinct immediately wanted to learn more about Husha and ask questions of Erra Wasum. Husha had been part of the reason why they had made it this far, but Daniel's inner voice spoke another language. The voice told him to pause. Daniel trusted his inner voice. It spoke with his father's voice, it instructed him to focus on his given task and not be diverted. Erra Wasum had told Daniel everything he needed to know. Daniel was not going to react to this news and show any weakness. He remained impassive.

Erra Wasum understood. 'When I have further information, I will send it to Puvurum in Terqa. I am worried about the Egyptian. I want to know why he met the Astrologer, and you may wish to part with his company sometime soon, Daniel. I will leave you to decide when the time is right.'

Daniel listened very attentively and still made no response or reaction. If Erra Wasum was confused by Daniel's lack of a reaction, he did not show it.

'I know you have much to do today. I am sorry you carry so many burdens. I am honoured to share a drink with you. I hope I will become your friend one day. Here is the money you need. Leave your supplies with Johannum at the service station. I will make sure that Alizer receives them. Buy a little extra fresh fruit and vegetables. Here in Mari we produce many shade sticks. Buy some for the ladies and the young ones, as the sun will continue to get stronger till Harran. We are proud of you, Daniel,' Erra Wasum concluded. 'We love Alizer and his family and we are here to help you make sure they reach Harran safely.'

Erra Wasum knew much more than what he had told Daniel. In fact, he even worried if he had told him too much. Alizer would probably not approve. Soldiers from the north were already scouting the Tigris, and everyone was looking for Terah. Latest reports suggested that Urfa was sending a scouting party to the Euphrates, and they would be heading towards Mari. The issue with the Egyptian concerned Erra Wasum more than he had admitted. He would deal with the Egyptian when the time was right, but to do anything now might compromise everything Daniel had already achieved. Daniel was clearly much more impressive than Erra Wasum had originally thought and Daniel's lack of response to the news of Husha was a mark of experience. Erra Wasum knew patience was needed. Daniel had achieved more than anyone had expected, somehow he seemed to know what he was doing, and Erra Wasum had sworn to trust Daniel and all his decisions.

Erra Wasum was monitoring the reports from Sippar too. The Minister of Babylon's latest allegations, along with the King of Sippar's denial of any child killing by his father, had been a new and unexpected development. He wondered if he should have alerted Daniel but this had nothing to do with Daniel's mission. Let him learn about it on the road, concluded Erra Wasum.

Erra Wasum's plan to send Daniel to the other side of the River in Terqa had a purpose. He needed to keep the scouts busy with the hive of misinformation he was creating. Erra Wasum's network was already actively laying a seed trail signalling that Terah was heading north through Nineveh and through the mountains. Erra Wasum was also fearful but not shocked that the astrologers wanted more than Terah's immediate family. He had word from his contact in the Sippar Astrologer's office that motions were in place to determine the location of every member of Terah's tribe. Would Zaros' fall from grace accelerate matters, he wondered, and was this the reason for the Egyptian's meeting? Erra Wasum kept his options open. Would they actually go through with exterminating every member of the tribe? That would be tens of thousands of people across the entire region. They were certainly capable of it, but he could not accept the conclusions he was drawing. The region would sink into a huge battleground, for the Eperu had their own alliances with powerful kings throughout the region. The Protectors would do everything in their power for Terah and his family. He did not know, however, if his network would be capable of protecting the whole tribe, a tribe from which the original Protectors had themselves emerged.

Both Daniel and Erra Wasum were lost in their thoughts for a brief moment. As Daniel rose to leave, Erra Wasum noticed the shoulder bag.

'What is the book you are carrying in your shoulder bag, Daniel? Anything interesting?' Erra Wasum immediately realised his mistake. He was already feeling the weight of the meeting on Daniel's shoulders, and he regretted his comment. Erra Wasum was not coping with events as he might have wished. He was not proud as many thought. He was wondering if the time for the Watchers was coming to an end and if the future sat in front of him. If only Enaqim had not died.

Daniel let his hand rest on the bag, 'Just something for a friend in Harran.' He smiled but he did not like the fact that he had been asked about the book. The shoulder bag was too public, he thought. Later he would wonder how Erra Wasum had guessed the item was a book; the shape was not obvious, and it was rare for anyone to be carrying one. Why had Erra Wasum not thought it was a tablet? Erra Wasum and Daniel stood together. Daniel said his thank you and quickly departed so as not have to answer any more questions. Daniel stood on the steps outside Erra Wasum's office as the patient waiting traders made their way inside. He paused to breathe and take in the news and the views.

Nothing is at it seems, Daniel thought. He sensed danger, schemes and conspiracy. He had already accepted the magnitude of his responsibility and had increasingly become aware of the size of it. He parked his worries about Husha, and whoever was following Husha in another place for now, although not too far away. He knew he would have to come back to this place when the time was right. Like Erra Wasum, Daniel knew he could not afford to draw attention to himself or the group. If the spy was following Husha alone, that was the way it needed to stay right now. Daniel surprised himself at the calm, logical and reassured manner in which he was dealing with this new threat; a danger from within likely to break up their fellowship and jeopardise his mission. It was not going to be easy, and he hoped the course of action he had decided was the right one as he stepped into the bustle of the most beautifully situated market he had ever seen and allowed the noises of the vendors and the distant music to drown his fears.

By the time he found them, the group was already settled at Zimi's on a terrace table where they were enjoying the atmosphere and tasting a local hot sweet herb infusion, which included the taste of dates and a spice that Sai called cinnamon. Sai insisted on paying for the lunch and had already ordered the food for everyone in anticipation of Daniel's arrival, so when Iannas noticed him approaching through the market, they all waved declaring their good spirits. Iannas and Sai had clearly enjoyed the market and Mari. Daniel sat down with a heavy heart. He did not want to add extra anxiety amongst the group. They were family - or were they?

'We head for Terqa and look for Puvurum the market trader.' Daniel kept the remainder of the news to himself. He had already decided to take one step at a time. 'Tell me what you all found in Mari. Erra Wasum seems like an amazing man. He is not a just a tailor but in charge of the entire Mari Traders' Association.'

Husha was particularly impressed and increasingly intrigued with Daniel's contacts in each city.

Sai could not resist remarking on Mari's fashion status. 'The cloth and the dress designs are incredible, but no one in India would wear these styles. The ladies here are very interesting... confident.' Stylish was the word she was thinking, but for some reason she felt shy about saying it aloud for fear of being judged by her dress. 'The weaving is the finest I have ever seen. The traders said they make the cloth in the temples here.'

'What about the hairstyles?' It was Daniel's turn to express his measure of interest. 'You would look great in one of those styles, Sai.' Iannas and Husha smirked disjointedly which threatened to turn into wholesome laughter. Daniel glared at the two of them while looking around as if he were looking for someone and spotting a particularly fine and well-presented lady heading in their direction, he continued, 'I know the style that would suit you perfectly.' Daniel nodded towards the lady who had just stepped out of one of Mari's many exquisite jewellery stores. 'And I know the perfect hairdresser,' Daniel could not resist adding. He saw a lady walking past carrying a bag brimming with what looked like all the contraptions of hairdressing; probably unknown anywhere else and specially invented for the Mari hairstyles. They all gazed at the lady's hairstyle that looked no less like a network of birds' nests, with each 'nest' containing a small brightly coloured, polished stone attached to a bright, bowed ribbon. Sai looked at Daniel with a measure of contempt, and then all four of them burst out laughing.

Sai had to do what she always did after each city visit and asked Husha, 'Did you see anything interesting during your walkabout, Husha?'

As usual Husha did not answer directly. 'You are always so inquisitive, Sai,' Husha insisted. 'Like you, I walked around. There is a small collection of Egyptian artefacts in the library over there.' Husha pointed. 'I did not expect to see it here, so I spent some time there.' He was dismissive and did not feel like recommending the museum any more, and no one pursued the matter.

'Well, while you two were away, Iannas and I wandered through the market. The merchants may have their wares to sell, but they also have lots of information they give away freely. They told us all the latest from Sippar.' Both Daniel and Husha were very intrigued, and Sai and Iannas were very pleased with themselves.

'We knew you would be interested,' Iannas confirmed.

'It's about that Minister from Babylon,' Sai continued. 'Well, Husha told us about his allegations against Sippar. The latest news is that the King of Sippar has now publicly appeared in the city square and made a speech denouncing the Minister as a liar and accused him of attempting to sow discord in Sippar and discredit his family name. He denied that his father was involved in any child killings and has now accused Babylon of being involved in this charade. Then another trader gave us what he called privileged information, 'from the heart of the palace' he said, claiming to know a member of the palace staff. The King is blaming everything on the Astrologer of Sippar and his father before him who, he said, was also an astrologer for the court. The Royal Court in Sippar is now in a crisis, he claimed.'

'Even while we were talking with the trader,' Iannas was eager to add, 'one of the musicians from the band was passing and joined us. He added that the gossip in the market is that Sippar and Babylon are playing games. Word games. People are saying this has the stench of the usual politics. Babylon is strong for the moment, and the King of Sippar, since he felt the need to publicly deny any child killing, is obviously weakened and worried. Even if the allegations are not true, they seem to be working!'

Sai laughed. 'Politics!' she exclaimed. 'Thank the Gods that we are not politicians and may we never become government officials.'

Iannas had more to say. 'It seems no one wants to believe or even knows anything about any child killings. Everyone is watching the political tussle between Babylon and Sippar, and waiting to see who wins. Some are saying that the Minister is ambitious and simply trying to win popularity by showing he can stand up to another city state.'

Sai and Iannas were enjoying reporting the gossip. 'In the meantime,' Sai finished, 'no one with a Babylon seal is allowed in Sippar, and Babylon has retaliated by barring all citizens of Sippar. Just think, we missed all the fun!'

Husha and Daniel listened. 'You did very well, young ones,' Husha had a way of becoming paternal, 'but you should not get involved in idle gossip.'

'Husha's right,' Daniel added with a serious face. 'We need to stay clear of such hearsay and scandal.' Then he threw a mischievous grin at Sai. 'But it is great to know what is happening.'

Although the meal was much more normal compared to their surroundings, they enjoyed the joyous rhythmic music from the centre of the market and the thriving ambience that seemed to engulf the entire parade, while an eerie mirror image was being enacted on the other side of the tributary. When the food plates had been cleared of their contents and the cups emptied, Iannas quickly organised the group: 'Husha, you buy our supplies for the journey as usual and have them delivered to the stables at the station. I will join you, and together we will pack the bags for Donkey and set up camp. Daniel, you and Sai buy the supplies for Alizer, have it delivered to Johannum, pay for the caravans that I already reserved this morning, and then label the supplies. Sai, you have to make sure the supplies are clearly labelled when Daniel is finished.' Iannas was becoming increasing adept in his role. Since the afternoon was early, they took their time in the market and unlike the other stops, enjoyed for once a more welcome, leisurely pace.

As the afternoon grew late and having tired of the market and had their fill of Mari, which was now being taken over by flocks of swooping pigeons and crows and becoming increasingly annoying with their noise and mess, the group made its way back to the station to begin their chores.

Iannas and Husha set up camp as usual, slightly away from the service station, and waited for Sai and Daniel to return.

There was extra fresh produce purchased this time, some Mari sun-shading sticks - a local Mari product - and a number of colourful sweet items that caught Sai's attention. Daniel also bought extra blankets for the cold nights that he packed for Alizer and more for themselves. Daniel prepared a clay tablet with the name of Alizer clearly marked, the name of the next station, the name of the caravan leader to Terqa, and made sure to mark the back of the tablet as usual with his seal. Sai checked that everything was clearly legible on the tablet and that it was tied securely to the supplies.

That evening around the warming fire and wrapped in the new, soft, Mari blankets patterned with images of the river fish, Sai asked if one of them knew any stories of the city. Iannas remembered one his father had told him in Nineveh. He was reminded of it after Husha had mentioned the Egyptian items in the library. He remembered it well because, he claimed, he had met the wife of the Egyptian in the story who had once traded with his father and happened to live in Nineveh.

Iannas wondered if Husha might even know of the Egyptian in the story.

'It is said that an Egyptian soldier ran away from Pharaoh's army during one of Egypt's insurgencies into the northern green lands,' Iannas began.

'No Egyptian would ever run away from Pharaoh's army,' Husha protested.

Iannas ignored him. 'The runaway Egyptian travelled widely, and on one of his travels, he arrived and for a while settled in Nineveh where he became obsessed with the beautiful daughter of an ironmonger whose workshop and home was next to his lodgings. After presenting himself and his credentials to her father, he pleaded for permission that she be allowed to become his wife. It is said that the ironmonger only reluctantly granted permission, for he feared for his life believing that the former solder would kill him if he refused.'

Husha grunted, a feeble attempt to defend a fellow Egyptian against a slur on his character.

'After the marriage,' Iannas teased Husha with his cheeky smirk, 'the Egyptian was keen to see more of the region, and he set off again, this time with his new wife. It is said they travelled through many lands and city states until, eventually, arriving here in Mari. Fatigued with travel, they chose to stop for a while, and the Egyptian, having mastered many languages of the region, offered himself as a translator. His work included writing and translating contracts from and to Egyptian. This brought him to the attention of the city Governor whose office occasionally traded with

Egyptian merchants. When, as part of an official trade agreement with Egypt, the Governor was required to build a collection of Egyptian artefacts for the Temple of Ishtar Library, he approached the Egyptian to lead the project and made available many old cuneiform record tablets and other ancient local relics that none of the local historians considered significant and offered them for trade in Egypt where there was a growing fashion of owning artefacts from foreign lands. The Egyptian hired a small team to translate the tablets and trade them, along with the other relics, in exchange for Egyptian artefacts from various centres of learning, cities and temples. He also sent his own traders to Egypt to bring back special items for the Temple. The Egyptian was ideal for the job, and although he did not personally read all the cuneiform tablets he had been given, he was given some samples to read, and on one he found an ancient account of a siege of the city of Mari. The Egyptian gathered that Mari was probably not proud of the affair and was happy to dispose of it, but the Egyptian, when he read the details, kept this tablet for himself and would read it every night and study all its words. He became obsessed by it.

'An ancient King of Mari and his people had during his reign led a very contented life because the King was not a warrior, unlike all the previous kings, but a king of peace, a king for the people. The people of the city became wealthy without the burden of additional war taxes and built beautiful homes, palaces and temples and traded freely for the laws were benevolent. The King of Mari had an army, but its purpose was to guard and protect its citizens and was not designed for war. Instead of funding a larger army, the King spent the taxes collected on improving the city walls, water supplies, roads; he built libraries, free hospitals and even free schools for the young. He even implemented laws to keep the city clean, made sure the city waste did not mix with the water supply, and reduced the spread of disease. Some say he founded a school for the city's artisans and funded the study of art and music. The Mari loved their King and expressed their support by declaring him their King for life to stop anyone else trying to challenge him. Even after all this, most impressive to the people of the city was that the King had always managed to negotiate peace treaties and trading agreements with potential enemies of Mari for the benefit of all its citizens.

'When a new king was crowned in a nearby city, the King of Mari sent his ambassadors and personal messengers, but this new ruler would not receive any of them. His actions made it clear that he simply wanted Mari, the city, the spoils, and its taxes that amounted to ten times more than his own city. He was a warrior and his response to all the King of Mari's messages was to mobilise his entire army, the only thing he knew how, and march his soldiers to Mari where he surrounded the city and lay siege, first to weaken Mari then prepare himself for battle.

'On the eve of battle, as the invading army positioned themselves at the gates and around the walls across both sides of the river, the King of Mari instructed all the citizens of Mari to gather at the gates, on the walls, and in the public square so they could see, hear and take part in deciding their future. For once, all the ministers, high priests, generals, heads of tribes, heads of all the associations and representatives of the everyday citizens of Mari were one and gathered together.

'When every citizen was assembled, the King marched out of his palace and walked straight through the public square, greeting his people as he walked directly to the city gate.

'He commanded the gates to be opened, and the people were nervous, some even scared that the waiting army would charge the open gate. But the waiting army outside the gates remained where it stood and the King marched towards them alone, his bodyguards having been instructed not to cross the wall. Alone, the King stood midway between the gate and army. He demanded his audience with the aggressor King and waited, watched by his nervous people.

'From within the mass of the army encamped in front of the gate, there appeared one on horseback, and seeing the King of Mari alone, he approached alone and the two Kings met in front of the gate; the warrior King remained on horseback refusing to dismount.

"What do you want from Mari?" the King of Mari called out loudly so his people in the city could hear.

'The aggressor King spoke just as economically, "Make peace with your Gods. Prepare yourselves for death. I will be Mari's next king." The Aggressor King made to turn his horse, but the King of Mari did not move. The aggressor King stopped and looked at the King of Mari.

"We meet again at sunset!" the King of Mari announced and without waiting for a reply turned and returned directly to the city gate. The aggressor King, not having been given the chance to reply, returned into the safety of his army.

'The King of Mari stood in the public square. His people hushed, some weeping.

"I am your King", he addressed the citizens of Mari. "Our army is ready to fight to the death, and I may be the first or the last to die, and I am ready to die if it will protect you. Because of my lack of foresight, I built an army for peace. I did not build an army for war. For this I apologise."

'The people murmured. A buzz came from the crowds. The King raised his hands to silence them.

"Let me hear the voice of the people of Mari. Go and gather in your temples with your priests, elders, ministers, choose your spokesmen and women, and let us gather again when the sun is still high and when you hear the horns so I may hear your advice. Make your choice. We fight, or we surrender."

'With that, the people of Mari gathered in their tribes, associations and many with their priests, and when the city horns were sounded, they returned to the square where the King was waiting. The spokespeople, publicly and freely, gave their views. And the King listened to all.

'The King listened in silence and then, as the sun began to hide, he declared, "I have heard each one of you." The sun was setting, the crowd hushed, and soldiers cleared a path through the assembly to the city gates. All eyes followed the King as he made his way on foot through the public square. The gates were opened, and the King alone stood again between the city and the attacking army. He made a formidable sight in his brightly coloured robes and head dress as a lone beacon facing a dark storm. In his loud clear voice, he demanded an audience with the aggressor King to discuss the terms of surrender of Mari, and waited.

'Again, from within the mass of the aggressor army, there appeared the warrior King on horseback, and the two Kings met for the second time. Again the warrior King refused to dismount. The King of Mari spoke and offered a most magnificent concession that would be described by the people of Mari as the greatest of any king in the history of the world.

"I will renounce my throne and hand over the city to you on one condition; you will enter the city of Mari in peace. You will not damage the city, or plunder, loot or kill any of its citizens. If you agree, I will leave."

'The warrior King looked at the soldiers around him knowing they were listening, and they expected plunder as a soldier's right of war. He also knew that if he compromised this right, it would weaken his position and reputation. However, he was so impressed with the King of Mari's humbleness and magnanimity and concern for his people, he paused, waited, and to the soldiers disappointment, agreed. He gave the King of Mari two nights to settle his affairs, and take his family and court out of the city with anything they could carry.

'Just as the people of Mari and the King of Mari looked relieved, the warrior King raised his hand, the negotiations were not over. There was one more condition. The aggressor King demanded a guarantee that the King of Mari would not return with an army in the future. The two kings stood face to face and the warrior King waited for his answer. Then the King of Mari looked up to the terrace above the city gate where he saw his three-year-old son in the arms of his nanny, for his mother had died at childbirth, watching the proceedings. The King of Mari, with his heart heavier than at the time of his wife's death, and in a moment of incredulity amongst all who watched, offered the aggressor King his youngest son, his beautiful three-year-old boy, and suggested he take him, adopt him and raise him as his own son. This act would be his sign that both were bound in blood from this moment onwards, and the King of Mari would never return with any claim or army. The warrior King took an equally long time to think about the proposition. He had not expected this answer. He thought he would be offered money or gold to be distributed to the soldiers. But he decided this proposal was better. His respect for this King grew, and he looked up to where the King of Mari was gazing and saw the nanny and the child waving to his father. Seeing the child on the wall and remembering his own boys, the warrior King respected the sacrifice and also calculated that his acceptance would be both well received by his people, and add to his reputation as a warrior. He agreed. Had he heeded the moment, and without realising, this was the warrior King's first act of surrender. Peace had triumphed over violence, and the King of Mari stirred a peace movement among a small group of Mari, founded by the very same nanny holding the child who saw at that moment a sign from the God of nature in the form of a beautiful rainbow in the distance. The rainbow inspired her to sew many strips of cloth comprising all the colours from Mari to look almost like the colours of the most beautiful rainbow she had ever seen. She gifted this to the King of Mari from the people of Mari in recognition of his sacrifice and a symbol of peace that would last for millennia to come.

'On the third day, the King of Mari, with his three-year-old son with him, rode out of the city gates on his beautiful horse and with two personal guards, each carrying a Mari city flag. One Royal Barge on the river carried the King's family and some of his personal court officials who had sworn allegiance and chose to leave with the King for the last time. Behind them, stretched a procession of one hundred small boats laden with personal items and treasures the King had accumulated during his reign. However, since Mari had focused on peace and prosperity during his reign instead of war, and the city had become the richest in the world, the hundred boats could only carry a portion of the treasures of his palace, and the King did not want the gold and treasure that could not be carried to fall into the hands of the new king or his army. The night before his departure, he instructed the most trusted soldiers of the city to take the gold that could not be carried by the boats and throw it into the deepest parts of the river in the hope of washing it away to the great sea. It is a commonly held view that while much of the gold was thrown in the river, some of the soldiers kept a portion. When the new King found them out, the guilty soldiers suffered a terrible fate in the city prison for the remainder of their days.

'On his horse outside the city gates and with his son in his arms, the King of Mari watched the Royal Barge and the boats leave the city, and when the last boat had made its exit, the two guards with the flags and the King of Mari with his three-year-old son dismounted and stood face to face with the Warrior King. The King of Mari took both Mari flags from the guards and presented them to the new King who accepted them and gave them in turn to two of his soldiers who held them high in victory and all the soldiers cheered. But as soon as the transfer of power was done, each boat on the river raised a new flag, and all the people of Mari cheered as they saw one hundred and one multicoloured flags of the design sewn by the nanny, which proclaimed a second victory, this time for peace. The largest and original flag sewn by the nanny was flown on the Royal Barge at the very front. At this moment, the former King, as his time was now passed, commanded his son to bow to the new King of Mari. The new King did not allow it. Instead, he approached and lifted the three-year-old boy as any father would, and hugged the boy. The soldiers and people of Mari watched in silence. It was as if the child embodied the destiny of the city of Mari, in the hands of the new protector, a new father, as he became the son of the new King.

'The former King of Mari bid his last goodbye to his son, turned and never looked back. He mounted his horse and rode the short distance to the Royal Barge that was waiting for him, and where he joined his family. He had a premonition that his son was destined for greatness, and how he knew this no one would know, for the new King of Mari had two sons of his own, and both older than the new adopted boy.

'Many years later the King of Mari stood on a battlefield without his two eldest sons, for they both had been killed during previous countless wars involving Mari. The new King of Mari had remained a warrior and not a King of peace; he had chosen not to learn any lessons from the surrender of the former King. During this battle, the King of Mari himself was fatally injured and died on the battlefield. The heir to Mari was now his youngest adopted son, who, although he never knew his heritage until afterwards, saw and felt the pain of war with the loss of his brothers and father. As soon as he was crowned, he made peace with all the cities around Mari, and ruled his kingdom for many years.'

Iannas could see his audience was completely riveted and quickly continued.

'On reading this tablet, the Egyptian spent so much time searching for clues as to where the soldiers had dumped the excess Mari gold and where the river might have taken it, that he even followed the river south with the archaeologists and left his wife in Mari alone with little to do. After many moons, he lost all notion of time and forgot about her. He allowed this obsession to grip him like a fever with no cure. He spent all his time with the archaeologists looking for even the smallest clues along the river. Of course, when she discovered where he was and recognised his malady chasing his fantasy, she was outraged and left him. She returned to her home in Nineveh, started her own business and had nothing more to do with him. The woman and her family are well known and still live in Nineveh. In fact, her story has become a local traditional narrative. The last the family had heard, the Egyptian was living in a little boat, sailing up and down the river looking for signs of where the gold might have settled. The river we see in front of us is famous for swallowing this ancient gold, and there is even a story of a little boy who caught a river fish and found a golden amulet in its stomach.'

Everyone congratulated Iannas for his gift of storytelling. He had held them gripped all the way through like the Egyptian's fever in the story. Daniel asked if any of it were true, and they all laughed.

'What will you do if it is true, Daniel?' Husha teased, 'Look for the gold here in the river like my friend the Egyptian in the story? And by the way, Iannas, the only Egyptian I know who came as far as these parts is Sinuhe, who originally came with the Pharaoh. I asked in the Mari library where the Egyptian items had come from and the curator said they were collected by the city many years ago but had no further records. She was new and had only come across the collection recently, so maybe it is all true, Iannas. Good story but the gold sounds far-fetched to me like all these stories from Mesopotamia.'

'So the Egyptians are better story tellers?' asked Sai.

'Maybe!' replied Husha with an air of confirmation.

'True or not, I loved the story,' exclaimed Sai and gave Iannas a particularly encouraging and happy smile that everyone else noticed.

Iannas talked about how stories were valued in his family. 'The sharing of the story and understanding of the story keeps our connection with each other, and keeps our past and culture alive. My father often says that when people stop telling stories, as some of the younger ones are doing, culture and communities will die'.

Donkey had also found company and was spending a very comfortable evening in the stable. There were so many donkeys stabled tonight, and he remembered the feelings of being with his sister back home with mother. He missed them. He became friendly with one familiar donkey that had appeared at each of the stations they had stopped at since Sippar. He strolled over and shared the hay, fruit, and vegetables with him, but wondered why this donkey never walked past him even when he was going so slowly with Sai. Donkeys were always telling each other their stories and Donkey listened.

18 JOURNEYS END AT TERQA

Days 43 to 45, 8.6 Beru.

Daniel spent the first day from Mari looking for an opportunity to talk privately with Husha, and this did not present itself until late in the afternoon. Making sure the two were alone and out of earshot, Daniel quietly described his conversation with Erra Wasum, that someone was following Husha and that this person was probably watching them at that moment, but Erra Wasum did not know any more except that it had started in Sippar. Daniel and Husha both made extra attempts to behave casually and normally as they talked. Daniel neglected to mention that Husha had been reported meeting the Head Astrologer of Sippar, for Daniel wanted Husha to be the one to explain what was going on. This turned out to be a wise move. Husha thanked Daniel for alerting him and shared with him that he too was suspicious and had been monitoring all the other travellers in the caravan since morning, but he had not noticed anything untoward yet. Daniel said he would also be on the lookout in case someone or something unusual could be recognised as a clue. When Daniel pressed the matter further, Husha asked Daniel to wait till Terqa where he would try and find out more information and then tell Daniel everything he wanted to know. Daniel thought about Husha's proposal and agreed, but only after deciding that it was not wise to bring attention to themselves right now in the middle of the caravan with Terqa only two nights away. If Husha had thought one person was following him, Husha now knew that two people were watching him, Daniel's contacts and someone else, probably a security agent and, it seemed, not sent by the astrologers. If he was nervous or concerned, he did not show it and was grateful that Daniel had shared this with him the way he had.

Had Daniel been a proud young man, he might have felt he had behaved very wisely and clearly shown his trust in Husha, and, as it happened, this approach made a huge impact on Husha, as Daniel had intended. But Daniel was not proud, and he did not understand that he had been wise. He had followed his deeper knowing. Friendship was about trust, and Daniel had trusted his friend. He hoped Husha would now make the right decisions and not put the group, Daniel's task, or Alizer and the family in jeopardy.

By mid morning on the third day, they were already at the walls of the city, and neither Husha nor Daniel could point to any unusual activity amongst the travellers. Iannas, Daniel, Sai, and Husha, as usual, found shade under a tree, this time a young palm tree only thirty paces from the service station, to make camp and settle.

As usual, Daniel had picked up the package from Donkey's saddlebag that morning before the caravan had set off for the day and, therefore, was able to head immediately to the city gate to find Puvurum while Iannas left for the station to check the river crossing times. He discovered the crossings were very regular, as many as six between sunrise and sunset. He had yet to find out how well stocked the station market was on the other side of the river and where to book the caravans that travelled on the north side.

But events were overtaking him at the gates of Terqa and none of them was even remotely prepared for the cascade of fears that were about to open.

It began as Daniel reached the gate of Terqa, and three soldiers marched passed him even as he started to pay his entrance tax, and Iannas was still checking the crossing times at the station. The three soldiers headed without distraction directly towards the palm tree under which Husha and Sai were making camp. Husha noticed them, of course, and immediately knew something unwelcome was about to happen as the soldiers seemed to know whom they were looking for and were aiming directly for him. Husha saw Daniel continue into the city as soon as he received his pass. Husha only had time to catch Sai's eyes, but he did not have time to warn her. Then it was too late; the soldiers stood facing him.

'You are Husha the slave from Susa,' it was a statement, not a question, and declared by the largest of the three, a battle-weary warrior with his left upper arm scarred by an axe that had found the bone during his last battle, one of many scars hidden under his uniform. He stood in between the two younger unseasoned soldiers who were there more for show than effect. All three were intimidating, and Sai had time to be impressed with Husha's calm manner, as he continued his unpacking.

'I am a free man. I am Husha from Susa.' Husha did not look up but replied calmly and without the slightest concern as he unhooked the load from Donkey and finished placing it on the ground. Sai was already feeling nervous and even frightened for Husha. She searched his face for a sign that everything would be all right, knowing in her heart that there was something very wrong here. She felt even worse as the passersby began to approach the tree and gather round to ogle at the spectacle unfolding.

'Show us your identification?' Although demanding, the warrior was not aggressive and was the only one of the three who chose a voice.

Husha took the tablet from his neck and showed it to the soldier who only glanced at it, expressed contempt and remained unsatisfied. Husha took out the pouch containing the tablet from Babylon declaring his freedom from his previous owner, and this was met with the same look of derision.

The warrior took both tablets. 'You have to come with us.' This time the accompanying show soldiers took a step forward and stood either side of Husha so as to make sure he would not go anywhere. Of course, there was nowhere to go, and it was clear the soldiers intended to make a show of strength for both Husha and those watching.

Sai stood in between the warrior soldier and Husha and protested that his identification was fine and there was no reason to take him, but she knew not to take her objections too far. The soldiers assumed she was his daughter and threatened to take her too if she did not stop arguing. By now a rather large crowd had gathered around the soldiers, and then, as quickly as they had arrived, the crowd parted and dispersed as Husha was led away towards the city gate leaving Sai lost and forlorn with Donkey and their goods under the solitary tree. Iannas had seen the commotion from afar near the service stands and knew there was a problem, but the altercation had transpired so quickly, that by the time he approached the tree and made it through the large crowd, that was now already dispersing, he could only stand a few paces behind Sai and watch with horror as Husha was marched away by three soldiers without knowing why. He attempted to comfort Sai, and ask her what happened, but Sai knew there was nothing more she could have done.

Of course, all the travellers' camps in the service station knew of the arrest within moments of the crowd dispersing. As Sai and Iannas watched Husha reach the city gates surrounded by his guards, Sai became physically and uncontrollably sick. Iannas was scared as he had never seen her this way, and he did not know what to do. And then Sai became so very weak that she could no longer stand, and she fell to the ground. Iannas quickly found her bedding, and carefully settled Sai onto her blanket. By then, all the onlookers had disappeared as if nothing had happened. Iannas looked through their supplies for some water and food, quickly made the fire, and prepared a large hot date drink and some eggs for Sai, thinking maybe she had not eaten enough that day, and the stress of the arrest had made her sick.

Iannas kept his calm, unpacked the supplies, finished setting up the camp and was coaxing Sai to drink and eat a little when Daniel arrived.

Daniel had already heard rumours in the streets of Terqa of an arrest. He heard rumours of some father, apparently a slave with his daughter, but had no reason to relate the gossip to Husha and Sai. Daniel saw Sai resting, and Iannas recounted what had happened including Sai's sudden illness. When Iannas asked Daniel about Puvurum and saw Daniel's distressed face, he immediately knew that he was not having much luck either.

'He is not there; he seems to have disappeared.' Daniel sat down, looked around him and allowed the news of Husha, Sai and Puvurum to shrink his whole world into the size of a small cave that was about to collapse, but he made sure to recover quickly and put on a brave face for Iannas and Sai. He could see that Sai was clearly in pain. 'I tried the market, and they suggested I go to his house, but there is no one there either.'

Before Iannas even suggested it, Daniel knew he had to go back and look for him. There was still the afternoon and evening of the day to find Puvurum. Iannas reminded him. 'You find the contact. I will look after Sai, and we both know Husha can take care of himself. Whatever happens, don't come back until you have found the contact, and have the information we need.'

Daniel could not argue with Iannas. Although his instinct was to stay with Iannas and Sai, he also knew his responsibility, his task, his obligation, and he knew nothing was to come in the way of it. Before he left again, Daniel paused, removed the book from his shoulder bag, and returned it to Donkey's saddlebag. He remembered his experience with Erra Wasum, and Daniel did not want to draw any unwelcome attention to the book, especially when he found Puvurum. Having been asked about it, he did not want to lie and decided it would be safer in the saddlebag with Iannas and Sai. Sai was too weak to talk and clearly needed rest, and realising that matters had to take their course, Daniel left.

A little of Sai's strength returned after the drink and food, and when the hot date drink was finished, Iannas prepared some more, for this seemed to have a reviving effect on her. Sai sat up on her bedding. She had tears in her eyes, which shocked Iannas, and Sai shared with him something she had not suspected the first few times she missed her regular cycle, but only when she missed what she thought her third.

'I think I am with child, Iannas,' she whispered and then lay down, turned over and closed her weeping eyes.

Daniel had returned to the market in front of the Temple of Ninkarrak. One of the traders recognised Daniel from his first visit and relayed the same news; Puvurum had still not arrived. Being late was most unlike him, and the trader suggested Daniel try Puvurum's house again.

Daniel had been shown Puvurum's house behind the Temple and library complex, but no one had answered his door on his first visit. Daniel was already tired from the day's walk, he had not eaten since breakfast, and he was hungry and desperately worried about Husha and Sai, and that worry was draining him. One thing he already knew he did particularly well was worry. Of course, there was nothing he could do about any of his worries. He collected his thoughts and walked over to one of the local eateries, and bought a meat snack from a vendor by the Temple, and then returned again to Puvurum's house. He knocked again, no one answered, and so he sat by the entrance in the heat of the afternoon eating his snack; he was still there when the shadows were long and even in the growing darkness of the setting sun. Still no one came to the house and so, as the evening hunger and thirst caught hold, Daniel returned to the market and bought some more food and a hot date drink to keep him awake and recharged ready for the night. He returned to the house, sitting again by the door and knowing he was not going to leave until he found Puvurum. There was no moonlight, so the darkness impressed upon him. The neighbourhood was quiet apart from distant barking, which Daniel recognised as a pack of hunting dogs. Daniel closed his eyes to pray and without realising, he fell asleep in the late evening on the doorstep hoping, if not praying, Puvurum would return.

Husha knew better than to protest too much. He had enough practice and experience as a slave in Susa on how to act calm in the face of all sorts of threats and mistreatments in the early days. He wondered how he had gotten himself into this situation having never been arrested before in all his time in Susa. The soldiers led him to the offices of the Head of Security where they deposited him in a secure room, clearly a questioning room, on his own with a guard. Husha was glad he was not already locked up in a cell. There was nothing left to do but hope.

Husha adopted the appearance of patience while acting through all the potential scenarios, and only when the sun had gone down, did the guard outside the room receive an instruction from a soldier that Husha was unable to hear clearly. The guard turned and Husha was told to rise. This time he was taken to the floor above, which seemed to have many official offices for administration, and led into another room. Husha hid his surprise. After all the show of force at the camp, what was he doing in an administrative wing of the building? He had expected to be led to the cells for the night. As his eyes adjusted to this slightly darker room, Husha was even more surprised but remained composed after seeing the neutral expression on the official he recognised in front of him. The guard had allowed Husha to enter and then left, closing the door behind him but remaining on guard outside.

It was Husha who spoke first. 'What in Pharaoh's name is going on here, Uncle? You have completely destroyed my cover. What was all that about in the station? And that elephant you sent as a guard to arrest me, three soldiers? When all you had to do was ask...'

Husha was well into his tirade and would have continued for a good while longer, for he thought he had done very well in building the momentum for the colourful phrases he was about to discharge when Ejic, the Head Astrologer of Terqa, came up to him, looked him in the eye with the same blank expression which disturbed Husha even further, and then embraced him. Husha did not resist.

'That does not make it better.' Husha was still annoyed and was recovering from the shock of seeing his uncle. Every good friend of his father was an uncle, and Ejic was a very close friend.

'It's been a long time Husha. How is your father? I last saw you in Memphis with your father almost ten years ago. You have lost some weight, but you look good.'

Husha calmed.

'What's going on, Uncle? Why did they, I mean you, arrest me?' Husha asked.

'I had no choice. I received word from Mari that you were not intending to see me. You gave me no other option. My people...'

'You mean your spies,' interrupted Husha, 'so it's you who has been following me and you who had me arrested....'

Ejic held up his hand and signalled to Husha to calm down so as not to be overheard by the guard outside. Ejic sat down, inviting Husha to do the same, which had the desired effect, and Ejic explained. 'I have word that you were noticed, Husha, going to see the Head Astrologer in Sippar and asking for him by name was not a good idea. His power is feared by the Royal Court in Sippar, and he is being watched by the King's own security in Sippar. You have lost your touch, Husha. No one sees the Head Astrologer in Sippar unless there is a strong reason. You should have known that.' Ejic was clearly annoyed at Husha's ignorance.

'When the King's security in Sippar was notified of your visit to the Astrologer, they checked into your past and immediately had you tagged. That means followed.' Ejic waited for a reaction.

Husha had to accept that he had lost his touch. He pretended not to be shocked or concerned by the revelation that someone had followed him since Sippar, but how and who? Husha was thinking, expecting his uncle would give him the answers soon.

'Tension is high in the region,' Ejic continued, 'and because you had just been freed from enslavement, security in Sippar suspected you to be in the employment of a spy from Susa; they wanted to learn who it was. If only they knew the truth! Your slave attire is what saved you; otherwise you would never have made it out of Sippar. If you did not know that someone followed you from Sippar, don't worry. My Head of Security has learned who it is and will take care of him. My men will make sure he has nothing to wait around for and move him on in the morning.'

Husha had not noticed anything untoward in the caravan. 'Was it someone in the caravan?' he had to ask.

'The security has a network of traders and merchants for cases like yours. They are not spies; they are a little like you. They trade in information but, unlike you, have no idea what is going on. He is a simple delivery merchant for the temples. We have had dealings with him before, and there is nothing to worry about.' Husha was desperately trying to recollect the travellers in the caravan while Ejic gave his explanation.

'What did they find out about me, Uncle? Did this trader spy say anything? Do you know?' Husha hid his fears as he asked and insisted on using the word spy.

'That you were a slave in Susa, bought by slavers from Egypt and sold in Ur. Your owner died in travel in Babylon and set you free in his will. That much is clear. Sippar security could not figure why you visited Zaros, and then they found a connection between Zaros with Ugibi of Susa, your previous owner. It was inevitable they would find a connection given Ugibi's huge business network, but surprisingly, they then concluded that Ugibi was the spy from Susa. Why else would his slave visit the Head Astrologer of Susa? They want to learn what information your owner, the "spy", gave you before his death to give to the Astrologer in Sippar. Now they have focused on the son of Ugibi of Susa who claims to have no link with any astrologer or any knowledge of his father's business network, which happens to be true.' Ejic laughed; Husha scoffed.

Husha knew the son of Ugibi, of course, and added his opinion. 'He actually knows very little, and he is an idle creature. He has no business sense unlike his father, and has made a mess of every trade his father has tried to involve him with.' Husha was speaking his mind knowing that his uncle was not interested.

Ejic carried on. 'But much happened in Sippar after you left. Intelligence discovered records that you entered Uruk at the same time as the assassination attempt of the Minister of Babylon. Then the Minister went public with his allegations about being the only survivor of the child killings ordered by the former King of Sippar at the time of his birth and went one step further, he accused the King of Sippar of attempting to shut him up with a botched assassination attempt.

'The King initially laughed off the accusation, and then an emissary from Babylon arrived with a demand that unless the King publicly denied that the killings occurred, Babylon would rescind all trade agreements and close all diplomatic ties with Sippar. The reason? The King of Babylon's father was also complicit in the child killings, as was the King of Ur at the time. They were all in bed with each other.

'At the same time, Zaros came to the King and admitted that he had recently learned about the Minister's impending declaration, and it was he who had tried to scare the Minister with the supposed attempt on his life. He thought that the King would accept his explanation; he was trying to protect Sippar, after all. The King did not. Zaros must have been furious that one of the newborns from the killings had survived. He spent his life telling the King and all of us that his father had been instrumental in revealing the threat to the kings of the time and all the threats had been expunged. Not so, it turns out.'

Husha was smiling. 'I wish I could have been in Zaros' office when he first came to know that the Minister of Babylon was planning to claim that he was a survivor of the child killings orchestrated by his father with the King of Sippar at the time. Zaros must have believed, for a while at least, that this Minister was the threat his father never killed!'

His uncle replied with a rascally smile, 'You will be interested to know that my spies were present and told me about the King of Sippar's reaction. The Astrologer apparently mumbled his excuses and explanations, and then the King said, "Is this the threat your father was trying to save my father from? Is this it?" He added that if the threats of old to his father were all as dangerous as the Minister of Babylon, the one who survived, he would handle any future threats without his Astrologer. The King left the room and has refused any audience since.

'The King turned out not to be the fool Zaros had thought. My spies in Sippar tell me the King was so embarrassed at having to protect the honour of his father, his legacy, his family name, he has given instructions to strip Zaros of all authority and investigate all his activities. As well as refusing to see him, the King is unwilling even to listen to anyone from Zaros' circle.

'So the King of Sippar went ahead and made the public statement denying the child killings ever occurred and privately offered a chest of gold and precious stones as a measure of goodwill to the Minister and to Babylon.

'The Court of Sippar is quietly stripping the Astrologer of all authority; they cannot remove him outright, for he has too many allegiances and the King of Sippar will avoid a scandal at all cost. The Royal Court are now building a case against him in the hope they will find enough to force the Astrologer from office, and it seems you are part, albeit a very tiny part, of the case. Your visit to Sippar and your presence in Uruk at the time of the attempted assassination has implicated your owner Ugibi in the assassination attempt, and then your subsequent visit to the Astrologer in Mari has confirmed, as far as Sippar is concerned, that Ugibi of Susa was a spy and you are some sort of a slave-mule carrying information from Ugibi of Susa. They have extended the investigation to Ugibi's business in Susa,

Babylon and Ur. Of course, they won't find anything, and you clearly have led them on a merry chase.

'What has saved you is that you were, and to some still are, a slave. You are only a small fly to them. Nothing of significance, and their interest in you is already failing. By arresting you, it will dissipate entirely, and you can carry on your business without any attention.'

Husha should have been grateful but did not wish to express gratitude for having been arrested. He continued to listen to Ejic.

'Zaros knows he will not last long in Sippar. Zaros must be kicking himself for not going public earlier with this new threat on the horizon. He could have hidden behind it perfectly. Zaros is now trying to win the King's favour again with stories of the new threat from a new tribe.'

Husha interrupted, 'And he still has not linked the current threat to the child killings? Surely it must have gone through his mind!' Husha by now had calmed down but lashed out at himself. He should have known better in Sippar and he should have noticed the merchant in the caravan. Husha tried to remember. Was it the one always at the back with the donkey and cart full of cloth? Was it the trader with a cart full of temple statues?

'You are right, Uncle,' Husha conceded. 'I became too comfortable in Susa and seem to have forgotten some of the ways. I should have been much more vigilant in Sippar, and I should have noticed that I was being followed.' Husha only made this concession because Ejic was family.

Ejic appreciated Husha's personal rebuke. 'You are lucky that I know the Head of Security here very well. We work closely together, and he agreed to have you arrested on my word. The trader made his report in Mari and has already done so here. That is what I have been waiting for. We will see what he has to report. So far it appears that you are travelling with your children from Susa to Harran, and the only thing you have done of any significance is made a visit to the astrologer in Mari. That is all. Like I said, these traders pass on information, and we use them all the time.'

Whatever the case, Husha was relieved, 'How on earth did you become Head Astronomer in Terqa? I remember you were taking up a position in Damascus, and my father was planning to visit you. That was the year before I left.' Husha was gathering himself but still intrigued to know more of Zaros. What a fool he had been.

'Your father! This was his doing. I accompanied him to Terqa around eight years ago, when he came at the invitation of the Governor and the Head Astrologer. He recommended me to this court while we were here. A year later the Astrologer of Terqa died on his way to Aleppo, apparently murdered by the very same soldiers he had discharged earlier for bribery. I was invited here as an assistant to begin with, and I worked my way up from there. It has always been good to have your father's support from Egypt. So tell me, what do you know? What is the news?'

Husha told him about the uprisings in Ur. 'Last I heard even the new Governor was being held by the protesters. Is that true?'

'The latest is that the crowds in Ur have now heard of the Minister of Babylon. His family was originally from Ur, I suspect you already knew that.'

Husha nodded and told his uncle the conversation he had overheard in Babylon at the Minister's father's house. Ejic was astonished and continued.

'The people of Ur have been so impressed by the way the Minister has stood up to the King of Sippar, and when they learned his birth family was originally from Ur, they invited him to the be the new Governor of Ur. So now the powers of Babylon, Susa and Ur are negotiating.' Ejic paused.

'It is peculiar, because for a while, the Minister of Babylon and his father, Terah the priest from Babylon, were on my list as the ones we were looking for. When he declared who he was and claimed to be a survivor, I thought, this is it, the prophecy is coming true, and it was only when I realised he was the son of a fisherman from Ur that I understood he was a diversion. It is ironic that a poor fisherman's son may be the next Governor of Ur as a direct consequence of the actions of Zaros' father and the former King of Sippar who attempted to kill all the newborn at that time.'

'How much do you know about Terah, the High Priest of Ur?' Ejic got straight to the point.

'So it is true?' Husha asked 'It is someone from the High Priest of Ur's family? One of his sons?'

'Ah, you have come to the same conclusion?' Ejic's reply confirmed Husha's question. 'You and I had good mentors in your father and grandfather. My calculations and all the signs at my disposal are pointing to one of the High Priest of Ur's family. My colleagues have not reached the same conclusion and are focused, thanks to Zaros, on the tribe that the High Priest of Ur belongs to, not on Terah himself whom he knows quite well. In any case, there is news that Terah has managed to leave Ur and is now heading north to Harran where he has protection from the Royal Court. Now that Zaros is in difficulty and his position in Sippar is at risk, he has advanced his plans and begun informing all the kings of the region who continue to listen to him that the new threat is imminent and will emerge from the Eperu tribe. I have intercepted messages from some of the kings of the north who continue to respect Zaros despite his demise in Sippar. They feel threatened since the tribe resides in the north and messages say they are prepared to pay Zaros handsomely for all his information. Zaros has compiled a long list of key members of the tribe and intends to trade it, I am sure, for a powerful position in another royal court. Nothing good will come from any of this, Husha.' Then Ejic added, 'How much do you know of Alizer?'

'Only that he is from Damascus and Terah's manservant. I loaded and unloaded his donkeys when he was in Susa. He once bought dinner for me, and we talked of Egypt.' Husha did not mention meeting Alizer in Ur.

'He is of no interest to us. I know his father in Damascus.'

'Why ask, Uncle? Is he involved?'

'No, I do not believe so. I was surprised to learn he was Terah's manservant. I knew the family while I was in Damascus and just wondered if you had come across him. You realise he has family in Aswan as you do?' Ejic clearly was not concerned with Alizer but intrigued with his Egyptian heritage.

Husha thought of his conversations with Alizer and their common interest in Aswan. 'We talked of Aswan, but we did not make any family connections. What have you read in the stars recently, Uncle? Is there anything new, or different to what we already know?'

'Your father, when I last saw him, and I agreed that the stars and the dreams say the Messenger is alive. I thought we would only find one survivor, the one we have been looking for, and now we may have found two. Maybe they are both special in different ways. Of the true Messenger, once we learn more of him, I have no doubt we will discover an invisible army of protectors around him. Seems odd that he is on the way to Harran and must have walked right past Sippar without Zaros noticing. After Zaros' declaration, the kings of the north are now looking for the High Priest too. All the courts are intrigued as to why he has disappeared and are beginning to believe he knows something and has gone into hiding.'

Husha nodded in appreciation of the update. 'I was wondering if anyone else has connected the two events. I met one of the trainee priests just before he died, he confirmed he was one of the group at the house of a priest called 'Terah' the night of the birth of a son; the same night as the five Gods in the sky.'

'You actually spoke to a witness? So we have both confirmed it. His son, you say.' Ejic paused, thrilled, relishing in sharing the news with Husha. 'You have done exceptionally well, Husha. Your time in Susa was clearly well spent. As far as I know, only you and I have made the connection with the two events and have come this close. Others will soon.'

Husha interrupted Ejic's elation. 'Remember, there is still a supposition here. Neither you nor I have personally met the High Priest of Ur to confirm the events around the birth of his last born. Who is to say that there is no hidden story like the Minister of Babylon behind the High Priest? There may even be another survivor, one we both have missed.'

Ejic gave Husha the answer he already knew. 'Because there is no other. From what you say, we have both eliminated everyone else. Let us both agree this.'

Husha knew Ejic's words were true, and agreed. He wanted to be absolutely clear that his uncle had no other suspects he was investigating.

Ejic continued, 'The mad King from Urfa is the only one who has made a public response to Zaros' declaration of an imminent threat to all kings. The King of Urfa has declared himself a God-King and also protector of the God Sin and has promised to be rid of this magician who dares to threaten his kingdom, the Gods, his faith and his power. Most of my astrologer colleagues are followers of Zaros, and are convinced that the magician is a threat exactly as Zaros reports it. They have interpreted the stars to read that he will be more powerful than anyone in the history of the world. It is a surprise to me that Terah would head to Harran, for it will put his family in danger, even with the King of Harran's royal patronage.'

'Our interpretation is different,' Husha tried to answer. 'We have never considered the message a threat, just another sign from the heavens. If Terah's son is carrying a message, it is the message that will be all powerful, not the person. This Messenger will live and die like any other. If the heavens say the message is ready to be delivered then we have to make sure it is delivered and make sure it is heard.'

The Astrologer agreed. Husha was relieved that he had a chance to both catch up and share some of his news, but there were questions he needed answering. 'What is Zaros' intention in creating a list, a census of the Eperu?'

'It seems you know as much as I. His list is not complete, but contains all the elders, most of the leaders, chiefs, and power centres in the tribe. Zaros asked all the Astrologers of the Guild many moons ago to collect all the information they could about the tribe. Although Zaros is clear that the threat will emerge from the tribe, he has no idea who the Messenger is or even if the Messenger is born.'

Husha asked his question. 'The way Zaros was asking, I had every sense that he was planning to exterminate the entire tribe. He had a look in his eye, Uncle.' Husha described his meeting and wondered how Ejic would react to this supposition.

'He has not yet connected the current events with the genocide, he is a proud man and pride has blinded him, fortunately for us. You know all this, of course, and you walked straight into his court and asked for him by name.'

Husha looked sheepish and Ejic continued over Husha's sorry overtures.

'I believe he is planning an extermination of an entire tribe.' Ejic confessed his own fear. 'The kings who listen to Zaros - this God-King in Urfa for instance - have the resources and the will to attempt this genocide to prevent the Messenger rising from within it. These are dark times, Husha. The only other possibility is that Terah is heading to Harran for a reason. Maybe he knows what is going on and believes he can stop the genocide.'

'It is possible. I had not thought of that possibility, but you are part of the Guild, Uncle. Why do you not follow what Zaros, the Chief Astrologer of the Guild, directs you to do and say?'

'It does not work like that, but if Zaros had his way he would tell all of us what to think. No, the Guild is only a network. You should know that by now. It is not a gang with a leader who tells you what to do. That is what we have the temples for. You are due to come up to be a Guild member when you finish your training, and your father will introduce you, I am sure. Maybe I will suggest you be the next Astrologer of Sippar!'

They both laughed and wondered who would replace Zaros if his days were really numbered as Ejic suggested.

'I am worried,' Ejic continued, 'that this mad king will create a legend, a myth. We are in danger of giving substance to this Messenger by representing him as a threat and something to be feared. Zaros loves his dramas. It is only a message, not an army, and the Messenger seems to be getting all the attention right now, not his message.'

'Fear and pride is driving this. It happens now and will happen again,' Husha consoled.

'The latest news appears to be that the High Priest of Ur is moving along the Tigris, but no one can locate him. My spies, as you prefer to call them, only operate along the Euphrates, and everything seems quiet from this side, apart from some blundering Egyptian who chooses to get followed by a small scale merchant from Sippar!' Ejic paused, but Husha did not react.

'Whatever the case, the stars are very clear and strong. A message is coming, and there is nothing in the world that will prevent it. My colleague in Sippar is small-minded. He and his friends think ridding the world of the tribe, or the family, or, if they are lucky, the Messenger will erase the message. The message may already be written down. If the message has already been written down, then the deed is done, and it will spread like fire.' Ejic paused. 'But there is no news of any written message emerging from anywhere. We would have seen or heard something by now, but there is nothing, after all these years. Let's hope we are not all on a wild ostrich chase with our heads in the sand.'

'I will inform the court in Memphis of our meeting, Uncle. I know my father will be very grateful to know that we have met and we have shared this conversation.'

'Send your father my blessings when you see him.'

'So where are you heading? Is your work done?'

'We needed to know if the people of the Eastern lands were a threat to Egypt. It is clear they are not, at least not yet. If Babylon rises and becomes stronger, then it is possible, but that is a long time from now. Susa, Ur and Babylon are too busy with their own internal problems and do not have eyes for Egypt. In fact, I will recommend that they consider trade agreements with Susa, Ur and the new power that emerges, maybe Babylon.

'We also needed to know the name of the Messenger foretold in the stars that would challenge Egypt. It was written that the message would emerge from these lands. The Messenger has emerged, it seems. Now we know the tribe and even the family so they can be watched.' Husha concluded.

Ejic asked, 'So you are not worried about the possible threat to Egypt?'

'My work is done,' Husha declared. 'I will leave it for others to interpret it as they will. There will always be threats to Egypt. It might be one man from Ur today, and it will be an army from Assyria tomorrow. So no, I am not worried. I have learned that the world will continue without all of us, Uncle. I have played my part in this theatre. Now I will go home, rest and find a new adventure.'

'Heading back to Memphis or to your mother and family in Aswan?' Ejic asked.

'Memphis, to start with anyway,' Husha deliberated. 'I met Sinuhe in Susa, and he was adamant that I see Harran. I thought I would stop by since I am passing this way and take a rest there with my young friends.'

'You just want to see what happens to the High Priest and his family more like,' Ejic tried to mock.

'There is no harm in that. What is the road to Harran like?' Husha asked, expecting his Uncle to know.

'Busy and safe at the moment, but you will be travelling through the land of Urfa so be prepared for some disruption. He may ask for more taxes for his inauguration. The whole court of Terqa has been invited to the ceremony including myself, but we are too busy here to watch some king become a God. Harran seems to be a popular destination at the moment, ever since the King of Harran allowed the refugees from the famine areas to settle there, and he has asked that the grain reserves be used to feed the needy arrivals in Harran. You will enjoy it. I was there three moons ago. They are building a huge temple and library, and many artisans, scribes and writers are arriving.'

'Uncle...' Before he even started, his uncle answered him.

'No, no one knows about you except for me. It will stay that way as it always has done. Your father asked me to send word of you if I heard of you. In the circumstances I do not think that would be wise. Let us stay quiet about our meeting for now. Too many ears. Now, let's see what the Head of Security has to say.'

The guard outside was instructed, and the Head of Security entered the room a short while later with Husha's identifications.

'His tablets are fine,' the Head of Security turned to the Head Astrologer. 'I believe he is who he says he is. There is no record of him in our Susa lists or elsewhere as a risk. He is of no interest to us. The cloth trader mentioned that this man has visited the astrologer in Mari but says there is nothing more. Only himself and his three children.'

'Keep checking in case anything new turns up. Be sure to leave him locked up for the next two nights and send word to your colleague in Sippar that we will release him after two nights.'

Husha nearly swore at his uncle. The soldier and the Head of Security led him out of the room, down the corridor, and back to the ground floor to the back of the building where there were three cells, all occupied. He was put into the middle cell where a number of drunks and other notoriety welcomed him. He found a little space on the ground, made himself as comfortable as he could, and fell asleep. He could be annoyed at the entire situation, but he was resigned to his fate right now and expected Daniel and his companions to move on without him at dawn. He tried to set his mind to accept that his part in this adventure had reached its natural end.

When Sai and Iannas both noticed the blood stains on her skirt as she tried to sit up after a long sleep, just as the sun was planning its escape from the deeds of the day, Sai calmly explained to Iannas, who appeared shocked at the sight of so much blood, that she needed to see a midwife. Iannas gathered himself as quickly as he could, mortified at his reaction, and tried to be as calm as Sai without success. Iannas suggested he bring a midwife to her, but Sai insisted she not be left alone. Iannas quickly packed and loaded Donkey, then helped Sai gently onto Donkey, and slowly headed to the gate. The soldiers quickly ushered them through when they saw Sai's condition and pointed to the travellers' clinic only a few paces from the gate. The clinic had been set up by a local philanthropist widow in memory of her husband who had caught a fever and died in the rains while travelling to Ur many years before. Iannas left Donkey outside the building, a converted diplomatic residence belonging to, and donated by, the local Emissary of Ur, and assisted Sai as she carefully stepped into a large gallery where travellers with all sorts of ailments were resting on bedding. By now the patch of blood had grown to cover almost the entire front of her skirt; Sai promptly caught the attention of a female nurse who was delivering water to a patient. The nurse quickly called for a chair and rushed to help Sai. Two orderlies helped Sai onto the chair and carried her to a quiet treatment room; and Iannas was asked to wait outside the building. He reluctantly agreed, and Donkey kept him company.

It was not too long - to Iannas it had been an age - before the nurse came out smiling.

'Your wife is fine,' is all she said, and Iannas smiled with a huge relief, ignoring the comment of the 'wife' feeling it unnecessary to correct the lady. He sensed his eyes swell with a wetness which he attempted to hide from the nurse, albeit unsuccessfully, but the nurse knew how to handle the moment.

'I am going to take her home where my mother will make her some hot duck soup and treat her with some special medicines. All she needs is rest and more meats and vegetables in her diet. She will be fine in a couple of days. Follow us so you know my mother's house. Then you can tend to yourself and the donkey.

The sight of Sai, half delirious, the skirt still stained and being carried by the orderlies ahead of him in the chair, obviously designed for the sickly, from the clinic to a doorway twenty paces away along a side street was a raw and aching experience. The last time Iannas had felt this way was the first time he saw his mother in bed already weakened by her illness. Iannas could not see Sai's face, but he was comforted that Sai was being cared for and, when they arrived, the very friendly mother behind the door warmly welcomed her into the courtyard through which Iannas was not allowed. He realised it was time to make arrangements for Donkey and headed towards the stables he had noticed on the opposite side of the clinic towards the market. It would be more expensive than the stables outside the city wall, but Sai had provided him with some money and he was too worried about Sai to think of managing things differently. It was already dark in the stable with only a flicker of light from the torch outside the door. Iannas quickly found a space for Donkey, removed the load from Donkey's back, and returned to the doorway behind which Sai was being cared for, and waited for a signal that Sai was ready to see him.

Eventually the mother came out and found Iannas sitting on the stone bench by the door and invited him in without any fuss. She led him to a small room just off the courtyard where Sai was resting on a comfortable bed and where he was allowed a brief moment with her. Sai was weak, and they had barely exchanged two sentences when the mother of the house returned and insisted Iannas leave.

'She needs rest, lots of it.' There was no compromise in her voice or her heart.

Iannas managed to say to Sai that he would check on her in the morning and departed with a heaviness, but grateful to the mother for adopting her.

A mother from Terqa who had no compromise in her heart for the wellbeing of a young lady from a faraway land of India and whom she had never met was not what Sai had expected. The compassion was deeply felt by her. For a brief moment, she wept as she watched Iannas leave, and she remembered her birth mother, but then realised that the mother from Terqa was everything she needed right here, right now. She thanked Krishna for this new mother who made her less a stranger and more a daughter of this foreign land.

'Now you go and rest yourself. She will be absolutely fine,' the mother called to Iannas at the main door as he made to walk away. 'Do not worry. She is a little weak but I have the right tonics for her. Three of my daughters have been through this already. Young ones nowadays, always out and about and do not look after themselves.' The mother was very matter-of-fact and knew what she was doing. Iannas walked away dejected but reassured that Sai was in the right place. As he walked away he saw the nurse heading towards him and the house. He stopped to thank her.

'Check in on her tomorrow morning,' she suggested. 'Where are you staying in case she asks for you?'

Iannas described the hostel next to the stables, a place she knew. Iannas continued thanking her.

'Enough now, go and rest,' she stopped him and smiled.

He got the hint, walked to the hostel next to the stable where Donkey was spending the night, took a bed, and tried to sleep even though his stomach was demanding something else, but all he could picture was the blood on Sai's skirt and her weakness. He felt helpless. He had not seen Daniel since he had left camp. Had he met Puvurum? Would Daniel be leaving in the morning? Sai was not well and could not travel, Husha was probably in a cell, and he could not let Daniel leave alone, could he? Iannas began thinking of things he did not want to think about and in his exhaustion fell asleep.

Donkey could not sleep either. In his haste to return to Sai, and in the darkness, Iannas had removed the supplies from his back but left the saddlebag still attached to him. So when Donkey lay down it was very uncomfortable. The other donkey from the caravan was also in the stable so the two settled together and shared a meal as they had done the night before and the previous nights. After the restless uncomfortable night, Donkey was woken at dawn with the sound of the donkey next to him being made ready to leave, but unlike the other mornings, no one came for him. It was still dark as the sun was still thinking how it would surprise its hosts today. Donkey sensed someone trying to unhook and remove the saddlebag. It did not feel right. The person was not Iannas or Daniel; he could tell from the heartbeat and the movement and the touch. He knew what he had to do and made his loud unhappy noises that woke up all the animals in the stables and brought the watchman in. Donkey's call had its desired effect as the person stopped immediately, walked away from Donkey, took his own donkey and left.

It was early in the morning, and first light was slipping through the doorway when Donkey woke for the second time with the remaining animals to enjoy the fresh water and vegetables and also to wait for his companions. Donkey felt tired this morning; an unusual exhaustion he had not felt for a long time had already crept through his body. Donkey lay down again and his body went back to sleep.

19 PUVURUM AND THE RIVER CROSSING

Day 46

Husha had nothing but time surrounding him in the cell. Time to think. His silent cell companions were keener to sleep the night than have conversation and made no secret of their antipathy towards Husha having assumed he was a slave. Their aversion suited him. Husha listened to the busy snoring sleepers, but it was the stench of beer from one or two nearby that kept him from sleeping.

Alizer's planning impressed Husha. Even the spy following him - no matter how inexperienced or untrained he may have been - had failed to notice his young friends, and had not mentioned their activities to the Head of Security. No one, not even Ejic, had paid any attention to Sai, Daniel, or Iannas and their purchase of supplies. While he admired Alizer's plan, he continued to have many doubts. Placing a burden of such magnitude on a fifteen-year-old, a burden that neither Daniel nor Iannas could ever be able to understand was not something he approved of.

So much innocence, Husha thought, leading Terah and his family into the face of so much evil.

If the innocence of youth makes everything possible, then the caution of middle and old age limits the very same dream.

In between his restless sleep, Daniel thought fleetingly of catching the morning caravan to the next city, Tuttul, without connecting with Puvurum. But how would he know where to leave the supplies and whom to contact in Tuttul? He decided to wait. He could not afford to go ahead without the right guidance, and any mistake would jeopardise everything that he had achieved. Daniel had woken well before dawn, washed in the market square at the well, had some breakfast and plenty of hot drinks to revive him, and returned to Puvurum's house knocking again in case Puvurum had arrived while he had been away. Thoughts of Husha's arrest and Sai's sickness were demoted as Daniel wrestled with the options ahead of him today if Puvurum did not return. When the day's activities of the neighbourhood were already in motion, Daniel, from the shade of the bush next to Puvurum's doorway, watched market delivery boys arrive to the neighbourhood with pre-ordered goods for the well-organised homes. He saw husbands and wives making their way to start their work or begin their chores, pedlars knocking on the doors with all assortments and sometimes just one, children heading to the temple schools, and well-dressed young ones probably visiting grandparents. He also noticed an unusual character. He was dressed in old clothes, wore his hair loose and wild and looked very much like a homeless tramp, the type who would never normally be allowed into the city. This tramp was approaching the very doorway where Daniel was now standing.

Puvurum surprised his guest in the doorway by introducing himself first, Daniel quickly recovered from the shock and made himself known. Puvurum apologised. He omitted the details, but explained there had been an emergency, an incident involving a group of boat captains heading to Subir, from where supplies could reach the Tigris River. Daniel was asked to wait again while Puvurum went into the house. A short time later, Puvurum emerged after a quick wash and fresh clothes so he looked more like a market trader and handed a small pouch of coins to Daniel. Puvurum looked around him, clearly uncomfortable.

'Have you been waiting outside the door all night?'

Daniel nodded.

'Let's go somewhere else and talk. Follow me.'

Daniel followed Puvurum to a small gate, guarded by an elderly sleepy soldier, which led out of the city and directly to the river crossing where they boarded a waiting ferry. They appeared to be one of the last passengers for this ferry, and Puvurum watched if anyone boarded after them. After satisfying himself that only a mother and child had been behind them and as the boat left the south bank, Puvurum relaxed. The two found a quiet side of the large raft with rope barriers on all sides. They sat facing the river upstream allowing the river breeze to catch their faces, and encouraged the sound of the boat on the river to drown their voices.

'I heard about the arrest yesterday while I was with the boat captains. News spreads quickly here, and we have friends in many places. It appears your friend's identification was cleared, but he is still in the cells. You will need to confirm with security when he will be released. I understand it to be tomorrow.'

Daniel did not look surprised. Puvurum must also know about Husha being followed, he thought.

'The informer following your companion made a report to the security office here in Terqa. It seems they were not interested in his report. The informer was told to move on with the caravans this morning. My contacts confirmed that he joined the Tuttul caravan at dawn today. You do not need to worry about him anymore. The arrest, for whatever reason, seems to have dealt with the problem of the informer who has been following your friend since Sippar. We have come across him before, and we will keep an eye on him as he moves just in case he waits for you in Tuttul. Look out for a lone trader with a donkey and cart containing bundles of cloth from Mari bound for the temples of Harran. If you come across him, give him a wide berth. It is not my business who your companions are, Daniel. Our only interest is Alizer and the family. My contacts in Security could not tell me why they arrested your companion. It may have been just to check his identification. There are not many freed slaves on the roads, but you need to decide if he will, or already has, jeopardised your task. We have clear instructions to leave you to make the decisions, Daniel, and we trust your judgment completely. My only role is to give you the facts.'

Daniel appreciated having been told everything Puvurum knew about Husha. He appreciated even more that Puvurum had treated him as an equal, and allowed Daniel to make his own decisions. Daniel thanked Puvurum and told him he would leave Terqa at dawn the next day, with or without Husha. Puvurum understood.

'Are you still planning to cross the river here as suggested by Erra Wasum in Mari?' Puvurum asked. Daniel and Puvurum both looked around them at the glorious view of the river flowing to protect its green scarf and the green hills, filled with trees and vegetation, from the barren brown encroaching desert.

'We will cross here unless you have any new information.' Daniel was increasingly confident with his contacts.

'Since you are crossing the river here in Terqa, the simplest way to do this is to leave a very small set of supplies with Tabni-Sin for Alizer at the service station outside the main gate where you arrived. Leave instructions with the supplies for Alizer to cross the river and give him the name Eakubi, your contact in the north bank service station where we are heading now. They are sister and brother. Leave a full set of supplies with Eakubi for Alizer and arrange a caravan for him to Tuttul. It is a long journey, and it is certainly quieter on the northern side of the river. Most of the soldiers are still concentrated on the southern side due to the increasing numbers fleeing the drought in the west. I would agree with Erra Wasum that the northern side is still the better option. It is used more by the traders, and the stations are more popular with the boatmen.' Puvurum continued to be very direct and business-like, which Daniel appreciated.

The raft docked at the north bank service station, and everyone began to disembark. Daniel stood with the help of the side ropes in readiness to leave too, but seeing that Puvurum did not move, looked at him quizzically and sat down again.

'We are heading back, Daniel. I just wanted to show you the crossing, the north bank, and use the crossing to talk privately with you. I did not want to be seen talking with you at the house or in the market after the arrest. We can head back now.'

As they waited for the boat to fill again, Daniel and Puvurum watched the activity at the service station. They smelled the food cooking on the open stoves and meat being roasted on the coals; the aromas made them both hungry. It was very late in the morning and soon it would be time for the midday meal, and Puvurum admitted to not having eaten since the day before. The boat filled quickly, and they felt the raft free itself of the land, but it was not free at all as the rope guides, three on each side, pulled and led it back to the south bank, its original point of departure.

Puvurum used the return crossing to continue his conversation, his voice drowned by the river and the calls of the rope guides.

'There are growing numbers of scouts from Urfa along the river, Daniel. I am sure Erra Wasum will have explained this to you, but I have seen an increase even in the last few days. Be careful at checkpoints and do not trust anyone in Tuttul or even in your caravan. In Tuttul look for Sum-Ina; she is the assistant of the priest in the High Temple of Dagan. Be careful you do not fall in love with her!' Puvurum remained serious.

Daniel smiled and recognised the joke at the expense of his youth, and when Daniel looked at Puvurum's face more closely, he realised how exhausted Puvurum actually was.

'Is Alizer receiving everything he needs?' Daniel always had to ask this question every time he met a contact to reassure himself.

'Actually, yes. There have been no complications at all.' Daniel noticed a sense of surprise in Puvurum's voice as he spoke. 'In fact you have done the task so well that Alizer and the family have virtually disappeared. The situation has changed recently, Daniel, in that some of the Royal Courts now believe that Terah is hiding something. Why else would he be running like a fugitive they are asking? So many more scouts have been sent to look specifically for Terah in the last few days. Of course, we knew they would begin looking for Terah at some point, and we expected it to happen sooner. I think the Minister of Babylon helped divert attention. I assume you know about him?'

Daniel remembered him as Puvurum paused to look around to satisfy himself again that no one was paying any attention to them before he continued.

'Scouts are heading to Tuttul, Terqa, and Mari from Urfa tasked to find Terah and take him to the new God-King of Urfa. Terah will only be safe in Harran. We are now laying a trail of supplies along the Tigris to make it appear that is where he is. Yesterday, I was organising many supplies of foods and other travel items to deposit in the northern towns along the Tigris marked for Terah. I had to make sure the supplies were sent from different locations along the river and to different service stations along the Tigris. That is why I was late, and I have made you late. I was helping you and Alizer, so do not be angry with me for the delay. It took longer than I expected, for two boats collided and sank at a tributary junction not far from here yesterday evening, causing a complete standstill. The congestion today would have been huge had we not spent the night clearing up the mess. The deed is done, and I have made you late. I hope my actions will drive the scouts to focus their attention on the Tigris even for a short while giving you and Alizer enough time to reach Harran unnoticed. You have been delayed here so the gap between you is now reduced to two days. Make sure nothing delays you in Tuttul. If you cannot find Sum-Ina in time, leave a set of supplies with Hazil at the Tuttul service station, I have used him before but only if you do not find Sum-Ina. That is your last stop before Harran.'

This last statement was a realisation in itself. Only one station remaining, and Daniel was embarrassed to admit to himself that the thought had not even entered into his mind. How far they had come! As Daniel pondered, Puvurum looked at him.

'I think we both have much to do. We are arriving, and I have said enough.' Puvurum waited if there were any questions, but Daniel had already understood that it was better to know only what the contacts wanted him to know. Right now, his task was to reach Harran. Once Alizer and the family had arrived there safely, he would learn the rest. Daniel was constantly surprising himself with both his confidence and reasoning.

Daniel and Puvurum walked the short distance through the same gate that they had left earlier, and then, with a brief farewell, Puvurum set off towards his home, and Daniel headed towards the market square.

'All right. Stay calm, do not panic,' Daniel immediately muttered to himself as all his other worries began to peek and show themselves. 'Let's find Iannas first, and then worry about Husha and Sai,' he decided. 'The Gods are watching over me.'

It had only taken him a few paces to create his plan when he heard Puvurum's voice call to him. Daniel turned.

'Just wondered,' Puvurum had turned round and was walking towards Daniel as if having forgotten something. 'Did Alizer give you anything to carry? He was supposed to deliver a package to one of us along the way but nothing has arrived.'

Daniel watched Puvurum's eyes explore the shoulder bag as he asked, but Daniel replied without hesitation, 'No, nothing, just the money. Should he have given me something? I do have money left from the journey?'

Daniel played the naïve look rather well he thought and feigned surprise at the question for good measure.

'No. Nothing, I just wondered.' There was a short-lived hesitation before Puvurum turned again and left, and Daniel resumed his way.

Daniel was glad for his quick thinking. He was also glad he had not brought the book with him. It could have been stolen while he slept and he would have found it difficult to deny the book if it had been hanging round his shoulder. He had always carried the book when he had met his contacts but this time had left the book with Donkey; he had done well.

After the longest wait in the history of his memories, Daniel imagined that not only had he learned an extraordinary lesson in patience, but nothing more could go wrong. However, when he saw no sign of the camp under the tree where he had left Iannas and Sai the day before, he shook his head, allowing any brief elation at finding Puvurum to turn to despondency. He returned to the market square to look for a clue. Asking if someone had seen Iannas or Sai was not a good idea he thought, it would only attract unnecessary eyes. During his brief visits yesterday, he had become familiar with the market square, and he was looking in the direction of the traveller's clinic wondering if he should ask if Sai had been there. Even though he thought it most likely, Daniel had a sense like in Mari to sit in one place and wait. Having awarded himself the title as the world's greatest expert on waiting, he chose a small bar almost opposite the clinic from where he could see the comings and goings from the main gate entrance as well as the activity in the market. He sat outside, ordered his first hot date drink, and some food. It was lunch time after all, and was only just beginning to recall Puvurum's conversation when he saw Iannas emerging from the hostel almost in front of him next to the bar. 'The Sin God is shining!' Daniel called out. Iannas heard Daniel's voice and went bouncing to Daniel; both clearly delighted at seeing each other.

First, Daniel wanted to know about Sai. Iannas conveyed the news that Sai was with child to a speechless Daniel and described the events of the previous day, in particular when he and Sai noticed the bleeding and their visit to the clinic. Iannas calmed Daniel, who was clearly worried about Sai after the descriptions of the blood stains, after explaining that although there had been lots of bleeding, she and the baby were fine and being looked after by the mother of a nurse from the clinic opposite the bar. Daniel was amazed that Sai was with child. He only settled into the news after Iannas related his latest visit and described Sai as not only stronger, but also very happy indeed to be with a child.

'She is being fed hot duck soup, lots of tonics, and the mother of the house has the touch of an angel. Sai said she is almost fully recovered but is not allowed even to take one foot out of the bed.'

What Iannas did not share with Daniel is that his eyes had filled with tears of relief when he left Sai, after seeing her so well recovered overnight. He had let go of his fears through his silent tears from his nightmare of seeing, and then leaving Sai, in her deeply soaked blooded skirt and in half consciousness the night before. He wondered why he wanted to keep this feeling to himself and why he was ashamed to share it with Daniel. Iannas did not tell Daniel that if they were required to leave Terqa without Sai, his heart would be torn, but he would travel with Daniel, and without Sai.

'When can we visit?' Daniel asked straight away. 'I assume she cannot carry on…'

Iannas interrupted, 'You can ask her when you see her, but I think she is organising two orderlies from the clinic to carry her all the way to Harran with us in a chair if she is not well enough. She wanted to know where you were, so she will be very happy to see you. What about Puvurum?'

'Tell me news of Husha first,' Daniel insisted.

After seeing Sai well and recovering, Iannas had made Husha his next mission. He headed for the security office located at the end of the road where it met the market square, and Iannas enquired about his 'father' Husha.

'The soldier said no visitors were allowed,' Iannas explained. The soldier then went through the records, found Husha's name on the tablet, and told me "two nights" was written next to his name. I could not believe it. I told him that my sister was ill and even asked why he was locked up. What had he done?' Iannas paused, waiting for Daniel to ask.

'So what was the answer?' Daniel wanted to know.

'He did not know, and he was not even interested in finding out. Wouldn't soldiers know why people are locked up?' Iannas asked.

'Not really, they just guard them.' Daniel was not as concerned as Iannas. 'So when is he due to be released?' Daniel wondered if they would be travelling without Husha tomorrow.

'The soldier told me to return at dawn. He said it was written in clay, and that was the end of it. I returned from the security office and was checking with the lady at the hostel if someone had asked for me. No one had, so I was about to come and look for you. I knew you would be looking for us. What about Puvurum? You have all the information you need?'

They were both very energised having found each other again and ready to battle whatever the world was going to throw next, but Iannas could tell Daniel had not slept.

'You look worn out,' Iannas observed before Daniel answered. 'Do you want to sleep?'

'No time.' Daniel realised it had already reached mid afternoon, and there was so much to accomplish before dark, especially with the river crossing. He was drained and looked forward to the sleep tonight.

Daniel briefly described the meeting with Puvurum and the river crossing. 'Let's make the arrangements for the supplies and the caravans. We have to cross the river and we can talk more on the way. Do you really think Husha and Sai will be able to join us for the journey tomorrow?'

Daniel did not tell Iannas about the Puvurum's warning about Husha, about the false trail being laid on the Tigris, or about the scouts looking for Terah and his family. What they both talked about was that they were a day behind schedule and now only had a two-day gap between them and Alizer.

For the remainder of the afternoon, they organised the supplies and caravans as Puvurum had instructed, crossed the river, and returned on the last crossings before dark. Then Daniel, although he was wilting, insisted he needed to see Sai.

Sai was so glad to see the two of them together when they arrived.

Sai would have left the house there and then had she been allowed. She looked and felt so much better and stronger. Iannas and Daniel placed a new set of travel clothes next to her bedding, which they had bought in the market on the north bank after buying the supplies for themselves and Alizer and leaving everything with Eakubi. Sai was not only happy to see them but also very happy to be well and did not hide her delight at being with child. The mother was very clear when she saw Sai's eyes appealing to her.

'No, not tonight,' the mother was adamant. 'You have recovered well, dearest, but tonight I will give you more tonics, and you will rest. You leave tomorrow.' There was no negotiation, and Sai liked how she had been called dearest.

Sai secretly welcomed the extra night in a comfortable bed. She had slept most of the day and been fed lots of food, mainly duck soup and tonics. She made Iannas promise not to make any duck soup for her for the remainder of the journey. When Daniel asked her about the travel the next day, Sai showed them the supply of tonic she had been supplied with to add to her food. Daniel and Iannas showered both the ladies of the house with blessings and gratitude. It was clear the ladies wanted nothing in return, only for Sai to be well and the child to be born healthy. A mother and daughter who give so much in the service of others, Iannas tried to give words to his thoughts. If he had stopped just for a moment longer he might have found more words and these words would have been answers to his dreams, but the opportunity passed him by, for he did not know what he was looking for, or what love looked like.

To give Sai an early night's sleep, they quickly exchanged news about Puvurum and Husha, made arrangements to pick her up a little bit before dawn and then left to finish the day with a hot meal at the bar where Iannas and Daniel had met earlier. Over dinner, they both expressed their joy that

Sai looked so well. Iannas was particularly glad Sai would be able to continue the journey with them, but Daniel expressed his reservations.

'We cannot afford to let Sai slow us down, Iannas,' Daniel impressed, 'especially now.'

'I will organise another donkey for Sai tomorrow morning,' Iannas promised, 'and I will make sure she is fine and does not slow us down.' Iannas was going to make sure nothing would stop Sai travelling with them.

'Let's hope Husha is released in time for the first river crossing,' Daniel also worried.

Both would have slept immediately after dinner, but when they overheard a group next to them in the bar refer to the Terqa Bonfire as the 'biggest in the world', Iannas, to distract his worrisome friend, dragged Daniel even in his weary state to see the bonfire being made.

The partly-built large bonfire was situated outside of the city gate. It was traditional at the end of the solstice - the shortest night of the year - for bonfires to be lit in all the cities to honour the Sun and Moon Gods. This year was particularly special; there would be a full moon on the night of the solstice. The priests had already announced the night as the Highest Night of all Blessings, and even the magicians had declared it a night filled with Magical Moonlight. The King of Terqa had commanded the building of the large bonfire and scheduled many festivities for the night and also a number of nights preceding the Night of Blessing itself. Every temple in the land was going to hold services, and in keeping with tradition, all the cities had started their preparations a moon in advance.

By the time Daniel and Iannas returned to their beds, Daniel was worn out but relieved about Sai and too tired to worry about anything else, as Iannas had intended. Daniel crawled onto his bed and was immediately swallowed by the slumber hanging over him and went to sleep without even removing his outer garments or bidding goodnight to Iannas.

Donkey felt much better for the extra day's rest too. He could not escape the fear that something terrible had happened. Why had Daniel or Iannas not arrived today? Donkey believed he had done something very wrong.

20 THE BIGGEST BONFIRE IN THE WORLD

The God-King of Urfa, having proclaimed himself both a God, and King, and having been supported and defended in his proclamation by every one of his astrologers, magicians, the Royal Court, and members of his government, declared the coming longest night full moon solstice ceremony to be the inauguration day for his Divination. In the meantime he summoned the Royal Court and the citizens of all his lands to bow down to him as a God. Since so many thousands were expected to attend, the Court arranged 'Daily Bowing Ceremonies' that the court, nobles, and citizens of the lands of Urfa duly attended, and where they swore allegiance to the new God-King. It was an incredible sight that would not be forgotten for generations. The temples and palaces on top of the hill were a blaze of colour with banners, flags and the Royal Urfa Insignia. The citizens of Urfa on the opposite side of the valley to the hill had a grand sight. He was the first God-King in the line of Urfa Kings, and the Court made sure everyone in the land of Urfa knew by sending out messengers to every town, village, hamlet, and farm in the kingdom. The entire court gathered each day at sunset where the proclamation was read and the new God-King was formally introduced to the day's new worshippers who had journeyed from the many distant parts of the lands of Urfa and filled the palace grounds. More worshippers would come the next day and the next, and each day the size of the congregations grew.

To mark the Divination Ceremony on the longest night full moon solstice celebration, the God-King declared that Urfa would build the largest bonfire the world had ever seen, a burning wooden colossus the world would never see again. A bonfire fit for a God-King. He commanded, 'Build me the biggest bonfire the world has ever seen. Bring all the wood from the empire. Cut down all the trees of the land, let no wood be seen outside of the bonfire, let the fire consume the fuel of the land so that the land may be blessed anew and Urfa may be born again from its very ashes.' The astrologers and magicians bathed under the shower of the power of the God-King and absorbed his power and encouraged him. This Divination would be remembered forever, and they would be powerful forever.

Now that the King of Urfa was a God, the lands of Urfa would be strong. There was nothing to fear, and no one could ever defeat the God-King.

'Nothing is more powerful than a God-King,' he declared, but the God-King was angry - angry that a threat still existed. The message from the Astrologer of Sippar described a terror, a menace, a danger to him and his Gods, and his own astronomers and magicians had confirmed this.

'Find this threat to our kingdom and Divinity and bring it here!' was the God-King's command. 'Let the Astrologer of Sippar make his home with us, so that he can lead the search, and we can learn from him.'

The Astrologer of Sippar, an expert on all dangers to kings, especially God-Kings, was even now speeding his way to Urfa to his new benefactor, to personally update the God-King, and protect him with his life if needed. He would supervise the search for the High Priest of Ur named Terah who held key information and was heading to Harran. Urfa now took over the lead in the search for the High Priest and extended the range of the teams of scouts from the Tigris across to the Euphrates.

Zaros the Astrologer, supported by the astrologers and magicians of Urfa, pointed the finger at a tribe from the mountains to the east.

'The magician will emerge from this tribe and no other,' the Astrologer declared.

'Find the High Priest of Ur and his family. Let him bow down to the new God-King! No magician can threaten us,' the God-King commanded.

'While the eyes of Urfa watch, let them see what a God-King can do to those that do not worship us,' the God-King told his court as he marvelled at the activity below in the valley where the greatest bonfire in the world was being assembled.

All timber in the city, all doors, chairs, tables, any item made from wood not just in the city but in all the towns and villages, in all the God-King's lands of Urfa, was arriving by cart, by basket and even by foot on the shoulders of loyal citizens, day and night. The God-King would bless every citizen who gave freely and contributed the food of the bonfire. Some of the older residents had already harvested all the wood from the roofs of their homes and even from within the structure of the walls. They were proud to serve and receive blessings from the new God-King. 'All he wants is a big bonfire!' some said. 'This is far better than the burden of more taxes,' many said quietly. 'The new God-King's blessings will put us in the court's favour and make us rich,' others hoped.

The bonfire grew, and soon became a mountain of wood situated in the deep valley, in the very heart of the city of Urfa.

21 THE CARAVAN TO TUTTUL

Day 47 to 54, 27.2 Beru.

Husha delighted at the first touch of the light of the rising sun and the cool breeze effortlessly stroking everyone in its path, accompanied by the fresh waking sound of the river ferry splashing on the strong flow of the water as it approached the north bank of the river. Husha allowed Daniel to ask the same question for the fourth time that morning, but on this occasion Sai was not going to permit him to finish.

'Enough, Daniel, and will you two stop looking at me like that?' It was a warm hearted demand rather than a question. 'We are going to hire an extra donkey, and I am going to let our friend Donkey carry me when I am tired. Thanks to the mother of Terqa, I am as fit as a goat now. I know I am with child.' She was clearly so happy, never tiring of these words, 'I have three wonderful future uncles to look after me, and I do not want to be anywhere else and with anyone else right now. I can rest in Harran.'

Sai had made the most comprehensive and formidable answer she could have given, and only because they were all enjoying a moment of respite from the activity of the morning, which was about to begin again in earnest. Two ferrymen jumped onto the north bank and commenced tying down and securing the ropes of the ferry, allowing the passengers and animals to disembark. Sai certainly looked as healthy as ever. Iannas was thinking that Sai looked even better than she had done in Ur when they first met, as he steadied Sai by taking her hand as she stepped off the ferry.

Iannas and Husha hurriedly led Donkey to Eakubi. He had been holding their supplies along with Alizer's from the night before. Donkey was unloaded and the supplies repacked with the new ones bought the day before. Daniel rushed to the caravan leader who had been waiting for the ferry to arrive with the last of today's customers, hired a donkey, and arranged for it to be returned in Tuttul. Daniel had to put up with comments about people always leaving things to the last minute and not informing them when making their bookings.

Within a few moments one of the caravan assistants arrived with the hired donkey, and while the caravan was absorbing new life and waiting for it to organise itself, Daniel led the donkey to Eakubi where Husha and Iannas were quick to transfer the freshly packed supplies to the new help. Sai was already settled on Donkey with a makeshift saddle. Only Donkey was trusted to carry Sai. As the caravan finally consumed all its devotees, the caravan horn was sounded. The caravan leader made his usual announcements reminding the large group of nearly forty people and an equal number of animals to stay together and not walk behind the rear security guards. Then the second horn signalled the front groups to lead the way.

There was so much news to share, and each was keen to hear the other's account in detail. Daniel had particularly primed himself to hear from Husha and with everything else going on that morning had not yet informed him they were rid of the spy, but the caravan had not yet settled into a routine to accommodate any conversations. The caravan quickly arrived at a bridge where they crossed a small tributary heading north off the Euphrates and where Puvurum had been delayed the day before from having to salvage and clear two half-sunken boats with their loads from almost under the bridge blocking the river traffic. The caravan soon spread into its familiar and comfortable caterpillar. Husha led the hired donkey and made sure it kept pace with Donkey who was for the first time accommodating and getting used to Sai. Iannas made sure to lead Donkey at a gentle pace, but he need not have worried. Donkey knew that he was carrying more than Sai alone, and he set the correct pace in symphony with Sai and the extra force he could sense inside of her. Daniel walked between Husha and Iannas and was curious who would start the conversations. When he could not wait any longer, he did.

In his keenness to tell the group his story, he described his long wait for Puvurum and Puvurum's vigilance when they talked on the river crossing. Daniel explained the reason for Puvurum's delay and the false trail to the north that was being laid. He chose to leave out the information about Husha, and did not mention the question Puvurum had asked at the end. He was concerned why he had been asked about the book a second time. Even as he thought about the book he quickly cast his eye behind him to Donkey and the saddlebag. Daniel recognised the bulges and outlines in the saddlebag straight away even as Sai's legs were partially covering the pouches. He felt relief, and he would leave it there until Tuttul. Daniel's story only stressed the gravity and seriousness of their task, and, as usual, it appeared extraordinary to Husha how these young people seemed to take the information in their stride as if it were simply part of another normal day. He hoped that when he shared his news, it would be received with equal pragmatism.

Husha told a very condensed version of his arrest and his two nights in the cell. He tried to focus his attention on descriptions of his cell companions. Daniel knew, of course, that Husha was not sharing the full story. Husha attempted to shift attention away from himself by congratulating Sai, but she too knew he was holding things back and pressed, 'The way the soldiers came specifically for you – there is more to this, Husha. What are you not telling us? Is it that you do not know, or you do, but you are not ready to tell us?'

Sai had asked the question in such a way that forced Husha to open the door to his fears.

'Sai, you are wise and right.' They all looked at each other while Husha paused and collected himself. 'I am not proud of many things that I do and have done, and this is not the place for the longer conversations. So give me till the evening to recover myself from the confinement and the smells, including those of the inmates in the cell. I do not want to experience that again, so give me the day to find my heart again and make peace with the knowledge I have collected. We will talk this evening and in the evenings to come. I have much to say, and you can hear my story.' For the first time, they saw vulnerability in Husha through his voice that they had not felt before; it attracted some concern. Husha had been and continued to be a keystone on the journey, but Daniel was clutching many serious doubts and wondered how long he would need to wait before reaching any decision regarding him.

'It must have been dreadful in the cell, Husha. Take the day to recover and let's hear your story tonight,' Sai became the voice for all of them. There were many evenings between Terqa and Tuttul for Husha's tale.

Sai used the short midday rest break to confess that she had not realised she was with child until just before Terqa. She was too embarrassed to divulge more until Husha asked her directly how many cycles she had missed and she quietly replied, 'Three, Husha.'

She described the shock but also the delight. She described the fear at what the bleeding had meant, had she lost the child? Had she suffered an internal injury? She had known this to happen to young mothers-to-be in her village, and some had not survived. She had focused only on being strong, healthy and completing the journey with them. There was no other option for her. Now that she was here, with them, and still on the journey, she contemplated out loud how the child would change her life and her decisions. The others expressed their own delight that she was with them, and each had his particular advice about not walking long distances and resting.

'Remember your tonics,' added Daniel, 'and let's cook lots of duck soup, Husha. It's the best thing for her.' Husha agreed, and while wondering where he would find a duck, he did not understand why Daniel and Iannas were laughing until Sai told him how many pots of duck soup she had eaten in the last two days.

Daniel did not speak of the decision he had made in Terqa to travel without the group if Sai or Husha had not been ready to travel that morning. He did not believe they needed to know. When he and Iannas were alone a few days later and he mentioned the decision to him, Iannas approved and supported him. Daniel felt better and they never discussed it again.

Only Iannas did not speak at all on this first day out of Terqa. He knew what Husha meant when he said he needed the day to collect his thoughts. He had believed for a moment that Sai was dying in front of him, and the moment had awoken a memory of his face touching his mother's face as she breathed her last after she had whispered her last words to him. Today, all Iannas needed to know was that each of them was well. Iannas questioned his own lack of strength at dealing with the anxieties and stress of the previous days. It was a hard lesson to learn, and he was ready to learn.

The companions spent most of the day walking close or a least nearby to one another, like a pride of young cubs seeking comfort after a close encounter.

Later in the evening they regained their strength over a meal of fish and bean soup that Husha cooked, and Sai insisted on spicing, of course. Sai was reminded three times to take the tonic with her food. The group camped near the animals to mask their voices, eager to hear Husha's story, but were questioning the virtue of this strategy now that the number of animals in the overnight enclosure had increased so dramatically, and the animal smells emanating were becoming pungent and unsettling.

'I know you are keen to hear what I know,' Husha started, 'but first I need to hear that Sai is well and more of what she is thinking now that she is with child.' Sai appreciated this. 'What will you do now, sweetheart?' Husha asked. It might have been the first time Husha had addressed her with a tenderness. Sai had endeared herself to him, and he now felt a particular responsibility for her, and, being the oldest, it seemed right for him to take on the role of a surrogate parent for Sai rather than an uncle for the child. 'It will not be easy raising a child alone. You are so far away from your home and your parents,' Husha finished, and Iannas and Daniel appreciated the questions he was asking.

Sai appeared slightly embarrassed. 'I am sure I will meet someone.' Husha and Daniel may have taken that as a reference to Iannas, but Sai had not intended it, nor did Iannas react to it. 'For now, I want to reach Harran and then rest. Perhaps I will have my child there, and then I can think about a home and, if or when I meet the right person, marriage. I have loved being on this journey, all of us together, and you may laugh at my beliefs, but I sense, I feel, there is a destiny between us. I want to discover what that destiny will lead us to.'

They each took it in turn to ask her if she felt stronger, what more could they do, what foods she should be eating, what they should be cooking, and again was she taking her tonic? In the end she was so overwhelmed and she told them to stop.

'If I need any extra help, be assured, I will ask. Now stop worrying. I am taking the tonic, and I feel fine.' She actually was, and being with her friends made her feel so much stronger. In fact, being with each other was another tonic and the fulfilment of another destiny that only Sai had sensed.

'So tell us your story, Husha. Start us off tonight and then you can share more each night until you finish,' Sai invited Husha.

So Husha began narrating his story, a small part each night over the next few nights heading to Tuttul, but only after Sai encouraged Husha a few times this first night. 'Tell us everything, Husha,' she would say soothingly. Somehow, she could anticipate when he was holding things back or was thinking of doing so. She wanted to reassure Husha that whatever he would say, they would not judge him. Daniel and Iannas would probably not have agreed with Sai, certainly not Daniel.

It was strange, Husha thought. Maybe an irony? Here he was, with three teenagers of an age where they could be his children, and he would be so proud if they were. Yet, here he was sharing with them dark realities of the world that normally he would have done everything possible to shield his children from. But to protect themselves and each other, he knew they needed to know what he knew.

And whatever Husha knew, Donkey seemed to know even more.

22 HUSHA THE EGYPTIAN

'When my grandfather left Aswan to take up the position of Head Astrologer in Thebes, it was the first time anyone in our family had moved away from our home town and the first time anyone in our family had such a prestigious posting.' Even Husha's first sentence drew surprises as he continued. 'Because he knew he would miss his family he asked his eldest, my father who would have been your age at the time, to consider leaving Aswan and settling in Thebes with him as his assistant. My father agreed instantly, and in time, after proving himself worthy, he became Grandfather's understudy.

'When my father had learned all he could as an understudy, he began his studies with the elders in the school of Astrology in Thebes. He completed his studies soon enough, showing great promise, and so the time came for him to specialise as all students had to complete their training with one expertise. My father chose a topic that had captured his interest during the time when he was an assistant and had very occasionally heard extraordinary descriptions of outer earthly, or 'extra terrestrial' events. He could only marvel when he listened to descriptions of eclipses, comets, alignments and events that might only be seen once in a lifetime.'

'I do not understand all those words, Husha.' Sai admitted, so Husha spent a whole evening mesmerising his audience describing eclipses, comets, and the alignments of beings in the heavens, and then continued his story the next evening.

'To conduct his research, my father was introduced to the central archives in Memphis where, to his surprise, he came across many ancient records of the type of rare astronomical events he had been studying and others he had never heard. My father began cataloguing every rare event he came across in the archives in the hope of using his index to study patterns and interpretations over time.

'One day in the Memphis archives, he came across a record that bore my grandfather's signature, stored and forgotten, about a very rare astronomical event that he had witnessed around the time of my father's birth. My father recorded it in his index like any other, but remembered it not only because it was his father's record, but because it was particularly unusual as it involved five heavenly beings uniting.

'When he completed his studies in Memphis, my father returned to Thebes and began teaching. His reputation grew, and he began to be invited to speak and lecture in Memphis, Damascus, Nubia, and the land of the Libu. That is when the Royal Court of Memphis heard of his unique work and invited him to join their team of Royal Astrologers. By this time, I was approaching my teens and, as his father had done before him, he asked me to leave our home in Thebes to accompany him to Memphis and become his assistant. My mother refused to bring up my younger siblings in a big city like Memphis and returned to our family home in Aswan where my brothers and sisters had their schooling. My family would visit regularly and stay with us for long periods in Memphis, so I did not miss them too much. Like my father before me, I too proved myself worthy and soon became father's understudy at which time he introduced me to his research detailing some of the strangest events in the heavens.

'These rare heavenly events remained with me and continued to fascinate me, and I began to appreciate my father's index, the patterns he analysed, his predictions and the scale of his research. My interest began to focus not on the interpretation of these rare phenomena but on the study of human behaviour around each of these phenomena. I became entranced by how these rare events were regarded as holy or magic, a language of the creator or a myth, an ancient sign from God or even a sign of destruction. I began to study how celestial events and their interpretations or even misinterpretations sometimes had massive impact, transforming societies. Like my father, I too entered the field of Astrology, and in Memphis I found little-known and rarely accessed astrological records of interpretations, stories and beliefs from India, China, Mesopotamia, of course, as well as Assyria, and many other empires, cities, and even individual tribes. I found it remarkable and even marvellous that the one heaven above us does not change and yet people see so many different stories, legends, myths, messages, and so many different gods.

'So when it was my turn to specialise, I chose a little-known subject after a phrase I had read on a fragment of a Mesopotamian tablet stored in Memphis. Its origins I could not find except that an Egyptian trader travelled with it from Harran, and it was a rescued item from a raided tomb in Mesopotamia. It mentioned an ancient king who travelled to the God in the Heavens and spoke the Language of God. So I chose to specialise in Astrology and the Language of the Universe.

'Anyway, I am rambling. Do tell me if I bore you,' Husha apologised.

But the stories never became wearisome. Husha spoke with a new confidence and he filled the evenings with another world, transported Egypt to their present, to the Euphrates and towards Tuttul.

'It was during this time that the senior-most position in Astrology became vacant in Egypt, and my father was called to become the new Head Astrologer of Memphis, one of the youngest who ever held the post.

'When I graduated from Memphis, almost twenty years ago, my father was so proud and thrilled with my research that in our zeal, we spent one week pouring through a set of records that my father and I had collected, from which we calculated that the stars told of a sage who would be born two thousand years from now, and another six hundred years after that. Of course, we never made a presentation of our calculations in case we became a laughing stock, and if we had, we knew that no one would ever take the Astrologers of Memphis seriously again.

'It was just after I had graduated and my father was still settling into his new position that a special invitation by personal messenger arrived inviting my father to a secret meeting in Damascus. It turned out that my father had inherited, by virtue of his new position, membership of a secret Guild. It was the Guild of Astrologers founded in Sippar and, in fact, founded by the current Head Astrologer of Sippar's father.

'My father attended his first Guild meeting in Damascus and as part of his initiation, the Head of Guild, Zaros, took pleasure in narrating a story of how the Guild, ten years after it had been formed by his father, had identified a convergence in the stars and foiled the coming of a sage, a magician who, according to the stars, had he survived would have become so powerful that every king and every god that came in his way would have been destroyed. It was a huge claim that drew my father's interest as I expect it was intended to. My father found it surprising that he had never heard of this before since rare phenomenon was my father's specialist field.

'Zaros was only too happy to supply the details of the heavenly convergence to my father and other new members of the Guild. He revealed that the convergence was first predicted in Egypt, and it was brought to their attention by the then Head Astrologer of Memphis who wanted to understand its meaning from the collective wisdom of the Guild. When Zaros described the astronomical event, my father recognised it as one of the records he had indexed in Memphis as part of his early research. He was sure he was hearing the very same record inscribed with my grandfather's signature, but he did not say anything. Instead, he listened as Zaros even went as far as boasting that it was his own father, the then Head Astrologer of Sippar, who interpreted the threat, calculated the possible locations and the date of the birth and broke the news to his king of a powerful magician about to be born in his empire, one who would threaten every king and every god in the world. My father learned that immediately on hearing about the threat, the King issued a secret decree that every newborn in the empire on that fateful day, and to be sure one day either side, were to be found and killed. To be certain that the threat was completely neutralised, Zaros' father was dispatched to other kings with whom Sippar had allegiances to present them with the evidence and convince them to do the same. Each king so feared the prophecy, thanks to the Head of the Guild, they obliged and they became complicit in the genocide. Fearing that the child killers would be traced back to them, the kings and the Head of the Guild ordered all records of this event to be destroyed from all archives across the entire Guild and full secrecy was maintained by the Royal Courts so only a few knew of it, and no one was allowed to speak of it. These three days were the darkest days in the history of mankind when no child born in the region was allowed to live. Of course, in time even the child genocide became folklore, a tale, and was forgotten. Most of the people alive at the time have since died, and only a select few people know about it even today.'

'So it is all true?' Daniel asked, 'It really did happen?' Daniel was clearly shocked even though he had known deep down it was true ever since the conversation on that rainy day between his father and Uncle Azhar. But never for one moment did he want to believe that a king would kill every newborn in his realm. Daniel said nothing more. He did not trust Husha. He wanted to hear more of what Husha had to say.

'This is why, Daniel,' Husha attempted to explain his concern over Daniel's inexperience, 'we have to be vigilant. The people we are dealing with are very powerful. They have the power to commit the greatest of evils.'

Husha made his point and quickly returned to the story. 'On his return to Memphis, my father and I travelled to Thebes where my father shared what he had learned with my grandfather and me. My grandfather was already extremely old, but still remembered the night he first predicted the convergence of the five Gods in the stars and his record of it. My grandfather told us he had recorded his observations and informed the Head Astrologers' office in Memphis as per protocol for major observations, and Memphis not only verified the convergence but also ordered him to archive his record and never speak of it again. He also told us he only archived the one observation and prediction he sent to Memphis. To our surprise, my grandfather then led us to a dust-filled storeroom at his home, actually under his home like one of the tombs, where he had stored all his private records. Thanks to a habit among all astrologers, nothing had been discarded and the records had been so well catalogued that the three of us were able to find all his original observations and research about the convergence that he had not sent to Memphis thinking it unimportant. By working with my grandfather's original research and my father's latest records, we were able to piece together the sequence of the original convergence to the present day. Our findings were startling and unexpected. According to our interpretations, it told of a great sage who would be born three times, first from the mother, the second from death, and third, many years later, from fire. We even tried to calculate the gap between the second and third births and decided it to be one life span between fifty to seventy years. Some religious people would call this a prophecy. Prophecies are dangerous, so we kept this information amongst the three of us.

'We then scanned the patterns in the stars and with my grandfather's help just before he died, we saw certain key stars from his original observations moving again, and everything indicated that the sage had not died in the child genocide. The sage was alive; the patterns in the sky were moving.

'We were so excited, and you should have seen my grandfather. He helped us conclude three things. First, if the sage was born at the time of the convergence, the first part of the prophecy had already come to pass, but there was no evidence in the archives in Memphis to confirm the birth of any sage in Mesopotamia or indeed the child killings of the time. The second part of the prophecy, born from death, indicated that the child sage had survived the killings, the genocide in Mesopotamia. We believed this to mean the fulfilment of the second part of the prophecy, but there was no evidence of any baby having survived the genocide. In fact, Zaros had told my father that in his king's empire, where all the experts were convinced the child would be born on one particular day, no child born on that day survived. Zaros was so sure. Could this sage have been born outside the empire? Not according to the heavens.

'Grandfather died in Thebes, and we buried him in a valley on the west bank. My father and I remained in Thebes for a little while longer and continued our readings and soon came across another clue; a sign that the sage had a message for humanity, a message from the heavens. While Zaros' father had interpreted the signs as a warning and as a threat, my father and I were convinced this was not the case. The ancient force of creation was communicating with mankind with a message, and my father insisted it would be a message of hope and guidance. I did not support my father's notion of 'guidance', but we did agree that when we added up all the evidence in front of us, particularly the original records my grandfather had kept, all the signals pointed to one conclusion. Mesopotamia was the region where the sage was living, where the final 'birth from fire' would occur, and where the message would begin to unfold.

'The two of us could not believe what we were seeing before our eyes and that this was happening during our lifetime. The messenger, sage, magician - however we are to describe him or her - was alive, living in Mesopotamia and we knew this only because we had my grandfather's original records of the first alignment, and saw the Messenger was being followed by the stars in the heavens.

'On our return to Memphis and over the next few years, my father and I worked together to increase our knowledge about the sage; we made sure to do this secretly and discreetly. This time we wanted to be certain that no one would seize and usurp our research for their personal benefit.

'If the Messenger was alive, we wanted to know who and where he or she was and also, for the protection of our Pharaoh, in case there was any threat to Egypt. We saw no threat in the stars; otherwise, why would the gods of the heavens announce this arrival? My father and I made it a personal mission to find this message, listen to it, make up our own mind about its authenticity and develop our understanding and connections between the stars, our beliefs, our societies, and the language of the heavens. As Egyptians, we believe everything written is a manifestation; a celebration of the world. Something written by the stars was therefore by nature a manifestation, a celebration of the humanity that would see it, and the universe that created it.

'A number of years passed, and my father received another invitation to a secret meeting of the Guild. This time in Ebla, where he met astrologers from faraway lands such as India, China and Minoa. Zaros loved his drama and started the meeting with his proclamations.'

Husha attempted a speech in the likeness of Zaros. "My father protected these lands and his generations from a threat foretold by the stars during his time. It is now our turn, friends, colleagues. My astrologers have alerted me that the stars are moving, and a new threat to our kings and empires is coming. The gods are with us. They send us warnings. This is the chance for the Guild to be great. It is our duty to protect our kings and our lands from this pretender. Let us mobilise our efforts and find him together. If we are successful, we will be the most powerful people and the greatest Guild the world has ever known."

Husha continued, 'After Zaros made the speech, one elderly guild member asked if this new warning was any way connected to the old convergence Zaros had so often talked about. Zaros' reaction was aggressive and defensive. Either the question had been innocently asked, or Zaros did not appreciate the implication. Zaros made it clear that this was a new threat, a new pattern. In fact, Zaros went on to confirm and insist again that his father had removed every possible threat, but he was angry too, and said something in the heat of the moment that he probably regretted. What he said sickened my father.

'Zaros proclaimed, "My father personally supervised the purging of the newborns to make sure the deed was done". And Zaros was not finished. He had one more instruction. "Help me identify the location, the tribe and the people of the tribe from which this new monster will emerge". My father realised that Zaros had not and would not link the new heavenly movements to the original convergence at the time of Zaros' father. Both pride, and the destruction of the archives related to the original convergence would stop him.

'When my father returned to Memphis and told me the news, I was shocked at the horror unfolding in Mesopotamia. Being convinced that the Messenger was among us and living in Mesopotamia, I planned and volunteered for a secret mission after convincing my father that this would be the only way. We had to verify any of our conclusions; see firsthand and be at the very heart of events as they were revealed.

'At this point, the only person we brought into our confidence was the Head of Security in Memphis whom we knew as family, but even then we told him nothing about our secret research, only that we had discovered a possible security threat. On hearing this he was eager to help. Then one day, my father, by chance after a long meeting, happened to find himself alone with the Pharaoh, except for his bodyguards who were too far away to hear. He grasped the moment to quietly and briefly mention our research, our main conclusions, our plan to seek the message, and establish if there was any threat to Egypt. Apparently the Pharaoh listened intently and agreed that the mission should remain secret. Who knows what he was thinking, but he bestowed his full blessing. He then called the Head of Security and instructed him to give us his full assistance in the completion of our mission and that the matter should not be discussed with anyone else; Pharaoh would wait for news.

'So I implemented my plan, and the Head of Security in Memphis sent me to work in the quarries near the coast where he had traced a new and active group of foreign slavers targeting the quarries and transporting their captives to be sold in the coastal city of Ur, at the very heart of where I needed to be. My task was to be captured as a slave, spend my time in Mesopotamia working on the identity of the sage, wait to see if the sage declared the message, if not, to seek out the sage, learn the message and also assess the threat, if any, to Pharaoh and Egypt.'

At the end of each day under the evening light, the narrator and his audience eagerly prepared camp and dinner as quickly as possible so that they would hear more of Husha's epic saga, which they found extraordinary. He was not a slave after all, and at this time, without intending, Husha captivated his audience and transformed them into his own slaves - slaves to his own story.

Husha asked if he needed to describe how he had been captured with the twenty-three other stonemasons and transported to Ur to be sold as slaves. Iannas and Daniel moaned having heard it before many times in the

Susa market but Sai, who had only heard potted versions, encouraged Husha, told him to ignore Iannas and Daniel, and so he recalled it once more. Iannas and Daniel noticed a few embellishments, such as a storm and pirates that had to be fought off, but the story was essentially the same as the one they knew.

'There were no pirates, Husha,' Daniel challenged. 'Sai, he made that up. I have heard this story so many times, and there have never been any pirates in any of the versions I remember'.

Husha smiled and reluctantly admitted to Sai that Daniel was right. 'There were no pirates, but there was a storm.' They all laughed and retired under another clear star-filled sky. Husha wondered if it was true when his grandfather had told him that if he tried to count every star he could see, he would count no less than forty thousand stars, and wondered if his grandfather ever made his teams of observers count each one of them. He closed his eyes feeling a force lift his spirit, and Husha believed in both the forces and the spirits of nature. Maybe the Spirit of Truth has come to visit and is glad with me, he thought, having forgotten what truth feels like after all these years in hiding.

As they lay down in their beds, Iannas' voice reached Husha, 'I saw how a soldier reacted to your identification tablet in Sippar. What does it say, Husha?'

'It says, Husha, son of the Head Astrologer of Memphis and under the protection of the Royal Court of Memphis. Then it asks for the cities of Mesopotamia to grant me free passage. It is written in Egyptian one side and Mesopotamian on the other. I did not let you read the other side.'

The next evening Husha told of his time in Susa. 'I had no idea who I would be sold to but knew it would be someone wealthy. I hoped to remain in Ur, but knew that I could find myself in any city. Making connections as a slave would be difficult, but I planned to use my father's connections with the Guild to the maximum.

'When I realised I would be based in Susa and not Ur, I was disappointed. I sent a coded message to my father with one of the travellers heading to Memphis. One day, almost a year later, the Astrologer of Susa bought a hot date drink for me in the caravanserai. I realised Memphis had asked him to assist me, and I learned that he had been led to believe I was an informer for the astrologers.'

Husha told of his time in Susa, of waiting to learn the identity of the Messenger, of eventually running the caravanserai, and of his relationship with the Astrologer of Susa, through which he learned what the Guild were thinking, and confirmed the Guild had still not linked the events of the first convergence with the new movements in the heavens.

'That is what I was doing in Susa. What better way to watch the world as a slave where those around me see me, yet I am invisible and of no consequence?'

Daniel and Iannas pressed Husha for more details. 'What did you learn? How did you pass messages to Egypt?' they asked. 'Not once did I suspect anything, Husha,' Daniel admitted, having seen him so often in Susa. 'Have you discovered the identity of this sage? Is it the Minister of Babylon? Are you a real spy?' asked Iannas. 'Would we be good at it?' he asked, little thinking that, to many, he already was a spy.

Then Husha took his revelations to another level; to the identity of the Messenger. Husha knew he was taking a risk. He had promised Daniel he would tell him everything and he decided they all needed to know. Now he made sure they camped well clear of others, kept his voice low and insisted the others did too.

Husha began by describing his meeting in Susa with the Astrologer's father that not only confirmed the first prophecy and the date of the birth of the sage, but also the name and profession of the father of the child. He even described how he systematically identified every priest with the name given to him and went through the process of how he patiently eliminated each priest and their families. Husha also spent some time discussing the events surrounding the announcement by the Minister of Babylon claiming to be the only known survivor of the child killings and how this had been a great diversion.

'But are you sure the Minister is not the sage? He appears to be making declarations and threatening the King of Sippar? Will he not be a greater threat if he becomes the new Governor of Ur?' Daniel insisted.

'What we are certain of,' Husha explained, 'is that the sage will emerge from the tribe of the Eperu. While the Minister's adopted parents are from the Eperu, and his adopted father's name was the same, that is, 'Terah', a common and popular name, the Minister's birth parents are a tribe of fisherman from Ur, and his birth father is not called Terah. He was caught up in the original killings in Sippar and by a strange coincidence adopted by parents, the father of whom was called Terah, from the Eperu tribe who had already lost their own child in the massacre. The Minister has created a strong diversion, but the astrologers are no longer interested in him now that they know his birth background.'

Husha explained how he reached the conclusion that Terah, the High Priest of Ur, was the last and the only possible father of the child. 'The child that would be the sage, magician, and messenger, and foretold as the challenger of all kings and gods.'

All three of his audience felt an instant deep heaviness in each of their stomachs as Husha said these words. The heaviness grew deeper and stronger as they attempted to understand the ramifications of their role on this journey and the larger puzzle; the maze that was unfolding, their destiny as individuals and as a group within the enigma which had encircled them.

Donkey knew that he was responsible for the message and something terrible had happened.

23 THE GOD OF BIRTH

Had Sai been at home, her mother, mother-in-law, sisters and extended family would all have been around her to make sure the baby was born healthy. That was before her husband died. Now if she returned she would be asked to leave the house. Maybe her house had already been divided among her husband's family, her being with child or not would make no difference. Where did Sai want her baby to be born? To grow up? Sai listened to the sound of her baby as she journeyed, knowing that the life inside her had already decided where it would enter this world, but she had not yet learned where that place would be.

When they entered the tiny settlement of Zelebiye, nestled amongst the palm trees as if an oasis, Iannas and Husha quickly purchased more bedding and a comfortable saddle for Sai. Donkey was grateful to be carrying Sai and not the supplies as he was finding the journey, the weight and the heat increasingly arduous as if a piece of him had been taken away, but everyone still looked after him and none noticed his distress.

Husha imagined and smiled at the vision in front. A young Indian widow with child, riding on a donkey being led by a doting sixteen-year-old from Nineveh, and a fifteen going on sixteen-year-old from Susa - already blessed with the responsibility of a man twice his age - and all accompanied by an Egyptian former slave; the most unlikely sight anyone in the world would expect. The caravan viewed him no less than a father travelling with his three children. In either case, they were a group of nobodies, the unseen.

Husha was uncovering the genius of Terah's - or was it Alizer's - plan. Could they have foreseen this image he had in front of him? In the words of another time, 'the universe was conspiring in every possible way to make Daniel's journey a success.' Daniel was not even aware how much in step he was with the world, and Husha was grateful to the invisible force for the place he had been granted in this very special journey, a trail that could lead him to the very message he had been seeking all these years. How had any of this happened? What was his purpose?

Husha questioned if he had revealed more than they needed to know. It was too late; he had spoken, but he was still worried about the impact, so he asked Daniel, Iannas, and Sai the next evening.

'Alizer was planning to tell us as soon as we met him again in Harran.' Daniel was still grappling with the information about Terah and also grateful that Husha had told them the truth. 'All the things Erra Wasum and the others were saying to me about someone wanting to harm Terah, so the sage is not Terah?' Daniel asked for confirmation.

'That is correct, Daniel,' Husha confirmed having guessed what Daniel was thinking, 'but it is more complicated. Zaros has not yet learned the identity of the sage. They know that the message will emerge from the Eperu who are based in the mountains to the north of Sippar and east from here. Terah, the High Priest of Ur, has always been a loyal servant and friend of Zaros, and Terah is from that tribe. Since he has now disappeared - let us say, gone into hiding - they now believe that Terah has information that will lead them to the key people in the tribe and the sage himself.'

'In the mean time, Zaros has been identifying key leaders of the tribe,' Daniel said, trying to understand.

'What would they do if they do not find the sage?' Iannas asked. He was thinking the same as Daniel, and the thought was shocking.

Husha picked the reply and turned to Sai, 'Every time you saw me disappear in Uruk, Sharuppak, Babylon, Sippar and Mari, Sai, I was visiting the Head Astrologer in the city. These are the contacts that I was referred to by the Head Astrologer in Susa. I have been finding out what I can from each astrologer, piecing together the facts I was learning about Zaros' plans.'

Husha paused, almost afraid of saying the words, 'There are evil and powerful forces involved who fear the message greatly, and have the predisposition to kill the entire tribe if the sage is not found. I believe Zaros has attempted to identify the whole tribe not only to find the identity of the sage, but also to extinguish the tribe if the sage is not found. But it will take the resources of a king, an empire to put the genocide into practice. Right now, Zaros no longer has the ear of the King of Sippar. '

Iannas shared his thoughts, which echoed what Husha had been thinking that morning. 'And we are part of this key, this puzzle, this madness, let us say. We are the group that no one notices leading Uncle Terah - Uncle Azhar - to safety, at least as far as we can. We have been insignificant and invisible to those who pass us as you say, Husha. It all makes sense what Alizer did when he arranged for Daniel to lead the way. But what more can we do to prevent Terah being caught? Is there anything more we should be doing? Is there anyone else we can tell to help prevent any killing? This is like one of those ancient stories on the tablets, like Sargon, yet it is happening right now, and we are part of it.'

'Let us remember that we are not the only ones guiding the way for Terah. This journey has been meticulously planned,' Husha pointed out, and the others agreed. 'Terah has protectors. Let us do our part for Daniel, for Daniel has done his part in leading Terah this far, and we are nearly at Tuttul.'

'You almost gave it away, Husha, by getting arrested,' Sai lectured.

'I have not finished, there is still more.' Daniel knew what Husha was about to say. 'I was arrested because I was followed from Sippar.' Sai and Iannas reacted with disbelief. They turned to Daniel, his lack of reaction gave it away.

'You knew?' both Sai and Iannas accused him together.

Daniel described him, 'A merchant, I do not know if you noticed him. He was always at the back of the caravan with a donkey and a cart. I think I noticed him after Mari, but I am not sure. There was a cart loaded with bags of cloth.'

Neither Iannas nor Sai had noticed him, and Husha was impressed with Daniel.

'He is no longer following us,' Husha added.

'How do you know that?' Daniel asked, puzzled. Puvurum had told Daniel, but how would Husha have learned this? He had been in a cell in Terqa?

'My uncle is the Astrologer in Terqa, and he made sure to move him on.' Husha shared more secrets.

'Husha, I have no idea what you will say next!' Daniel was shaking his head and could not believe his ears, but he listened intently.

'He is not my real uncle but that is what I call him. He had me arrested to throw the spy off my back and then sent his men to make sure he left the following morning. According to my uncle, he is now heading to Tuttul and wanted me to know in case we come across him again. He is probably a day ahead of us.'

Husha then described his meeting with his uncle and how he was the only other one who had connected the convergence at the time of the child killings and the current movements in the heavens with Terah the High Priest because his mentor happened to be the same as his own, Husha's father!

'My father trusts him, and he is the only other person to know that I was situated in Susa. My father asked him to look out for me.'

Iannas and Daniel looked worried. 'What will your uncle do with this information? Does he know about us? Did this spy find out anything about you or us? What do you suggest we should do, Husha?' Iannas asked a lot of questions and showed his concern. 'Maybe you should have told us all this earlier.' He did not want to recriminate, but it was how he felt.

'I know you are upset. I was also trying to protect you. This spy turned out to be an informer, not a professional. He found out very little about me and reported nothing of you. It was as if none of you existed. Even my uncle has not noticed you, and I can confirm that no one has connected us with Terah at all. That is how it is, and how it needs to stay.'

'You mean, not even your uncle? You did not even confide in your uncle about us?' Daniel asked incredulously.

'Of course not! No one. Those were Alizer's instructions, were they not? It is better for my uncle not to know. You must remember he works for the royal courts.'

It was Daniel's turn to be the mediator. 'You did put us at risk by visiting the astrologers, Husha. Of that there is no doubt. But what you found out from the astrologers was critical, and it has helped to know and understand what they are thinking. We should pass this information onto my next contact in Tuttul. I knew in Mari that you were being followed, but I did not know how we were going to lose the merchant. I was scared that anything we did out of the ordinary would have made things worse. So your uncle, the Astrologer, has intervened and solved the problem for us. We owe him a debt of gratitude.' Daniel weighed up the information he had just heard and Iannas and Sai agreed. Husha felt better.

'And you are sure your uncle knows nothing of our task?' Daniel repeated the question.

'Nothing at all. He thinks I just happen to be travelling with three young friends from Susa.'

The conversation was a little surreal for all of them except Husha. It was as if they had been talking about something supernatural, otherworldly, about other people and not themselves; talking about events that had nothing to do with them.

'Husha, you do realise that Daniel and I are distantly related to the tribe?' Iannas asked.

'I knew about Daniel, I did not know about you, Iannas,' Husha admitted. 'As to how I got involved with this journey with each of you, even I cannot understand. None of this was in the stars, I can assure you.'

'And what about me,' Sai chipped in, 'I appear to be just a witness to this destiny of yours. I cannot see any purpose for my presence in this.' Sai seemed disappointed but also mystified.

There was no answer to Sai's comment, only gratitude to know the truth, grateful that Husha was a friend, and appreciation that they had each other. Trying to figure out if the universe really did conspire to bring each of them together, at that Station in Ur, at exactly that moment in time, would be thought of many times for the remainder of their journey together.

Even with Husha's disclosures hanging heavy, Iannas reminded Daniel, 'Tuttul is the last main settlement between here and Harran. What will we do once we have delivered the last set of supplies to Harran, Daniel? Shall we head back home? Shall we go to Nineveh?' Iannas attempted to bring everyone back to the journey.

Daniel was not sure. 'We should offer our help to Alizer, Iannas. As you said maybe there is more we can do to help.'

'You're right of course,' Iannas agreed.

Husha and Sai were close by and heard the conversation. 'You have done more than enough already,' Husha reassured. 'Alizer and Terah, I am sure, are already immensely grateful. They would not have reached this far without you. Whatever happens next may be far bigger than all of us. We may not be able to help.' Husha had a premonition but thought it best to keep his thoughts to himself.

'And you, Husha, what will you do when we reach Harran?' Iannas was intrigued.

'I will head down to Memphis once I have seen Harran,' Husha did not mention the sage. 'My father is there and, I am sure, eager to hear my news. It has been a long time since I have seen him. But,' Husha promised, 'I will stay in Harran for as long you need me, and I will see you all off wherever you are travelling before I head to Egypt. Who knows, events may overtake us and lead us in different directions than the ones we have planned.'

'What about you, Sai?' Daniel was the one to ask, but they all wanted to know.

'Let me see what my child says when we reach Harran. I will let him or her decide.'

Sai's remark softened the air and everyone laughed. She pretended to be upset by the laughter and had a response ready. 'No, it is true!' she insisted. 'Sometimes young ones know exactly where they want to be born.' Because they all looked at her quizzically, she told them to wait till the evening. It was the last evening before Tuttul, and she related a story she had heard from her mother when Sai was coming of age.

'As she closed the door behind her and stepped into the one and only street of the tiny village in the mountains of Nepal, a young mother-to-be, expecting her first child, thinking of nothing other than crossing the street to visit her sister who lived in the house opposite, saw a movement out of the corner of her eye. She recognised immediately the God of Birth at the door of the neighbour's house where a child was due that evening. The God of Birth was always present at every birth to bless the child and, if the child died, to take the baby's soul back to the heavens.

'The God of Birth happened to be making his way out of the neighbour's house, and as he turned his head he, for the shortest possible moment of time, caught the eye of the young mother-to-be, and even as their eyes met, he could not hide his surprise at seeing her.

'The young mother-to-be was instantly terrified, not because she had glimpsed the God of Birth, but because of the look in his eyes. In her terror, she called out to the God of Birth, "Why are you so shocked to see me? Is something going to happen to my unborn child?"

'But the God of Birth did not answer. Instead, he turned and in that instant disappeared.

'The young woman was so afraid and so convinced that something terrible would happen to her unborn baby, she and her husband decided there and then to head as far away from the mountain as they possibly could. The next day, they sold all their possessions, purchased a pack animal and cart, loaded it with supplies, and left the mountain. They travelled five moons through mountains, forests and deepest jungles eventually arriving to a city called Rangoon where, because the baby would be due soon, they ceased travelling and made a new home. The husband even found well-paid work in the local boat yard, for he had been a carpenter in his home village.

'On the night the baby was ready to enter the world, the God of Birth stepped into the room. The woman smiled and called out to the God of Birth, "It is too late. My baby is already coming into the world and is well and healthy."

"Yes I know," replied the God of Birth. "I am here to bless the child."

"So why did you express so much shock when you saw me in my village on the mountain in Nepal?" the new mother asked.

"Because," said the God of Birth, "I knew I had an appointment with you in Rangoon in six moons. I could not understand why you were in the village in Nepal. I thought I had made a mistake."

Sai's story created an abundance of laughter and diversion from their thoughts. When Husha laughed, he could not remember ever laughing so much, and the muscles on his face hurt afterwards; he was glad and filled with hope.

And Donkey was glad for the laughter, for he was losing all hope.

24 TUTTUL, THE LOSS OF ALL THINGS

Instead of commanding the junction of the River Euphrates with the River Balikh, a tributary leading to Harran and Urfa, Tuttul, normally a city reminiscent of Mari, was coping with, if not attempting to command, one of the largest refugee crises the region had ever known. The city was bloated and open-mouthed as it digested both caravans from every direction and increasing numbers of refugee arrivals from the drought-stricken lands in the west, attracted by the promise of refuge and food in both Tuttul and Harran.

Dishevelled Tuttul could not offer the best of welcomes to today's caravan-weary travellers. Even the Temple of Dagan had suspended its stately activities of oath swearing, treaty signing and loyalty pledging, normally available to all new kings of any faith from any land. To empty the saturated walled city and calm its complaining residents, the city entry tax had now been increased seven fold. The entry tax had, for the most part, barred almost all refugees and caravan travellers from entering the walled city, and created an unexpected and spectacular calm inside the eye of the refugee squall.

To the caravan arriving in Tuttul in the early afternoon, the encircling refugee camp emerging out of the city walls into the organised mass mayhem of the aid workers was daunting. Newly arrived refugee crowds were waiting to register for bed space and food at temporary stands at the service station. It was gratifying to see that Tuttul was making good its humanitarian commitment to the needy.

'This is not going to be easy!' Husha said out loud, but they had a task to complete and nothing would stop them. Iannas said it once more for effect and self-satisfaction. 'This is our last stop before Harran; in four days we reach our destination! But it is not the sort of stop I expected!'

Everyone had already forgotten the lion sighting the evening before, the pack of hyenas and the herd of elephants sighted two days out of

Tuttul, but Husha was not encouraged by what he saw. This is a perfect place for scouts and spies to masquerade and lay in wait, he kept thinking and knew they would be waiting for Terah.

Husha led the group well away from the buzz of the service station and the attentions of the refugee camp to a little palm tree to unload and set up camp. The hire donkey was unloaded first and returned to the waiting caravan leader at his stand in the service station. Daniel had been debating the virtue of having Husha travel with them. Erra Wasum had warned him, but Daniel knew the answer deep down. Right now, however, after seeing the refugee activity at the city gates and the camps surrounding the walls, his attention had returned to the book as he watched and waited for Sai to dismount. This morning, after his experience with Erra Wasum and Puvurum, he had already decided to leave the book in the saddlebag, out of sight and out of mind. But now, seeing the mass of commotion at the city, he was having second thoughts and was inclined to trust his intuition. He decided he would carry it in his shoulder bag and risk being asked about it by Sum-Ina, his contact in Tuttul.

While Husha was returning from having delivered the supply donkey, and everyone else was busy with sorting the supplies and the camp, Daniel untied the saddlebag and pulled out the cloth-wrapped item from its pouch. It took a few pauses to register, the cloth was not familiar, it was not tied, and did not feel as it should. Being so loosely folded, it came undone quickly, and Daniel quizzically looked at the item; a long piece of old wood which had carried the shape of the book. With the growing realisation that the book was not in his hands, any flame he had had in his mind a few moments prior immediately flickered away to be replaced by a new, giant, heavy fog that completely immersed his mind, his heart, and every single bone in his body. He rechecked the saddlebag hoping to retrieve the packaged book. Maybe he had pulled out the wrong item? He sensed his arms and legs attempting to fold away under this new weight, and realisation suddenly thrust down on him that the book was not in the saddlebag. He had no time to disintegrate and gathered himself as best as he could, concentrating on his memory, ignoring his shivering body and lack of breath. Where and when was the last time I touched it? he ask himself.

If Daniel felt his world had fallen apart in Terqa, he now believed the world was consuming him. An inner strength that he had never been conscious of before had kept him going through the slings in Terqa, and this same force revealed itself again, taking over as he walked up to Iannas, the only other person who knew he was carrying the book. Iannas eyed the cloth with the wood in Daniel's hand and immediately realised, "The book!" he felt like screaming. No words came out of his mouth as Iannas shook his head to confirm he did not have it or know anything more. In the future, neither of them would remember this moment, this feeling and fear of tragedy they shared, no matter how much they tried; Husha would be the one to retell the events that occurred.

And it was to Husha that Daniel and Iannas instinctively turned. Husha was with Sai beginning to unpack and making ready for the camp when he, like Sai, knew that something was not right. He looked up and saw the pale faces and limp bodies of these two lost young men approach them. Husha quickly prepared himself for some terrible news. While Husha and Sai listened, Daniel told how the book, given to him by Alizer in Ur, had been lost, hoping against hope that Husha would know what to do. Speaking the words made the loss a reality, and saying them also increased the realisation of the significance of the loss. Daniel spoke with Husha with a new level of need, friendship and trust, a fellowship that Daniel would never question again.

'A book, Daniel? Describe it.' Husha was calm, but he was already leaping many steps ahead. Despite what he was thinking, he was relieved it was not a fatal injury, and when he later recollected this moment, it was this thought that kept him calm. At least his young friends were alive and well.

'A book; a roll of papyrus, as thick as three of my fingers, in a skin sheath, wrapped in a simple cloth of no colour and tied with string. Not this cloth. This is the one it has been replaced by.' He put out his hands again containing the cloth and long piece of wood. He had spoken clearly considering that he was now feeling physically sick and grimacing.

'Alizer gave it to me in Ur. He told me never to show it to anyone. Only Iannas knew about it, and every time I left the group I carried it with me in my shoulder bag. When we travelled or camped I let it remain in the saddlebag. Each night, when we unpacked Donkey, it stayed where it was, and I made sure the saddlebag was under the supplies. Everything went wrong in Terqa. I left it in the saddlebag. Now it's gone.'

A near tearful and desperate Daniel looked at Husha, Iannas and Sai, hoping one of them had moved it.

Husha intervened. There were people not too far away, and a few were looking in their direction having sensed something. Husha spoke in a riddle just in case.

'We have to find the money,' emphasising the last word. 'Go through the supplies again. When was the last time you saw the money, Daniel?' They all understood straight away.

'In Terqa, I took it with me to find Puvurum. I could not find him, so I returned to camp. When I came back you had already been taken, and Sai was feeling unwell and resting. In Mari, Erra Wasum had asked me if it was.... money I was carrying in the shoulder bag. I was so annoyed that he had noticed and that I had been asked, so before I left to look for Puvurum again, I replaced it in the saddlebag where it has always been safe, and I expected to return soon anyway. Iannas and Sai were with Donkey at the camp, so I had no reason to worry about it.' Then he added, almost to make himself feel better, 'And Puvurum did ask me if I had been given something by Alizer to carry. I was glad I did not have it upon me, and he did not see the shape of it in my shoulder bag. At the time I was glad I left it on Donkey.'

Iannas remembered and began to feel responsible, 'The saddlebag remained on Donkey's back for the two nights he was in the stable in Terqa, the one opposite the travellers' clinic next to the hostel where we slept. To be honest, I was so worried about Sai I did not even think for one moment about the saddlebag and only realised it had stayed on Donkey's back when I collected him the morning we left Terqa. It must have happened when I settled him immediately after leaving Sai at the mother's house. It was dark in the stable room, I was in a rush and I could not see. When I packed Donkey, the saddlebag was still tied to him. I thought nothing of it assuming that Daniel was carrying the … *money* in his shoulder bag.' Iannas almost erred and two people, scouts or just inquisitive refugees, were approaching to figure out what the distress or argument was about. Iannas lowered his voice, 'I am sorry. I should have taken it off and checked.' Iannas was desperately sorry.

Husha dealt with the approaching curious onlookers explaining that he had lost his money and dismissed them, thanking them for their concern knowing that they were more likely to be scouts than traders or refugees. Iannas, Daniel and Sai began combing the supplies and each other's bags, and by the time they finished they had unpacked and repacked everything twice.

'Daniel, it is not here. We need to retrace our steps.' Husha was desperate to escape the prying eyes that appeared too interested in their business. Husha quickly loaded Donkey and just as quickly deposited Donkey in an extended stable at the station on the way to the city gate.

'Let's get into the city and find somewhere to talk.' Daniel paid the entry tax, and Husha led the way towards the market square, each quickly accepting of the contrasting atmosphere inside the walls but without the time to appreciate the peace being lost in their own worlds of lost possibilities and consequences. Husha noticed a busy and fairly loud beer and wine bar in a back street, still away from the market. He stopped and found a corner, ordered drinks and snacks and quizzed Daniel. They huddled with their heads close together, for they would not have heard one another over the other voices in the loud bar, exactly as Husha had planned. He reminded them to smile as he asked Daniel,

'What is this money, Daniel? Did Alizer tell you?'

Daniel did not have a clue but now, armed with Husha's knowledge, he had a thought he was unwilling to share. 'He told me it was precious,' Daniel began, and even this was enough to confirm what each had already begun thinking. 'I never opened the package. Alizer told me not to. He said it should not be seen by anyone and that it contained....' Daniel almost choked as Husha stopped him.

'Enough.' Husha did not want Daniel to say any more. Could this be the book? The Message? Did they have it in their hands all this time? Were they now responsible for losing the Message? Husha felt a shiver, and he felt his skin on his arm shrink as he thought how close he had been to the Message itself, but he managed to keep his perspective. He was still glad they were alive and well. Husha swallowed, attempting to regain his voice.

'Tell me about these contacts you have been seeing in each city.' Husha had never asked Daniel this question, having left it as a private matter between Daniel and Alizer. Sai and Iannas, like Husha, now wanted to understand who the contacts were, and if they were part of the puzzle that might help them discover a way to finding the book. Husha was thinking fast.

Daniel explained who each had been, and Husha listened intently. Could these contacts be the Protectors or Watchers he had read about in Memphis? But they were myths. His father had told Husha that every Sage or Messenger had a group of guardians who would die to protect the Message. The Watchers were not just normal guardians. According to some legends, Husha had read, heavily exaggerated no doubt, the Watchers held the ancient and forgotten knowledge of the world and the world of spirits. He remembered the word "Watcher" being mentioned by Rabi in Uruk. Could it really be? He could only help but wonder.

'Daniel, it sounds like even they did not know about the money. From what you and Iannas have described, there is only one conclusion. It has been stolen. And there is only one place it could have been stolen from,' Husha looked at Iannas. 'The stable in Terqa.'

Iannas nodded feeling painfully guilty as he described again the events after Daniel left him and Sai in Terqa at the camp by the tree.

Husha listened and still could not accept his presumption. Was it really the Message? Was it with Daniel and Donkey all the time till Terqa?

Husha followed Iannas' description of events and interrupted him a few times.

'Did you notice anyone following you? Was Donkey ever alone outside the clinic? For how long? Was anyone in the stables with you when you unpacked Donkey? Did you see anyone behaving unusually inside the stable? Can you remember anything about the stables? Describe everything you remember in the stable.'

Iannas tried to answer all the questions as clearly as he could. Donkey had been alone only while Iannas left Sai with the nurse, then he came out, it had only been a moment, and he had waited at the entrance. Donkey was right there, and no one was nearby. Since the supplies covered the saddlebag, it was hard to reach. No one could have taken it then, he suggested. He was alone when he deposited Donkey in the stable and had the impression that Donkey might have been one of the last to find a space there. Iannas removed the supplies, left them next to Donkey where he was tied and then rushed to Sai. Iannas remembered that the supply bundles looked untouched when he returned to pack Donkey the morning of their departure. It was in the torchlight that the stable guard had lit for him that he noticed the saddlebag still on Donkey, but it too looked secured, and he had no cause to think different. Iannas felt responsible even though no one was blaming him. He had the inevitable feeling that had he brushed Donkey down the night before or even the day after he would have recovered the saddlebag, and Daniel would have known straight away if the book was no longer there.

Husha asked more questions, 'What about the road from Terqa? Could anyone have taken it during the night?'

Iannas had a question for Husha, 'Could the man who was following you have discovered the book?'

When they exhausted all their questions and had discussed each one after a second round of drinks Husha realised they were progressing no further.

'I think we have explored every possibility for now. What is certain is that the value of the loss cannot be underestimated. We have to get the money back. I have no doubt, Daniel, that you were entrusted with this money for a reason. The problem is that it has been eight days since you last saw it, since you last held it in your hands.' They all knew what Husha was about to say. 'But it is no longer with you and, if it was taken eight days ago, it could be anywhere, it could be one day ahead, or eight days away from us towards Damascus, or, if the thief headed towards Sippar, it could be a full sixteen days away from us.'

The words were distressing and cut deep. Only that morning, when they were walking at dawn, they seemed to have left all their problems behind on the path to Tuttul, and now, so suddenly, everything was covered with an endless mist of stabbing darkness which was striking deeper with every moment.

Husha kept calm and tried to be clear-headed as Daniel had been hoping, 'Daniel, see the priest's assistant. What is her name?'

'Sum-Ina,' Daniel remembered.

'Tell Sum-Ina about the money. Tell her everything about Terqa, the stables. Let us see what she has to say. Your contact in Mari knew I was being followed.' He thought about Erra Wasum. 'If they have been watching us, they may have seen something.' Everyone nodded.

'But also', Husha continued more sombrely, 'be careful. I do not yet understand why some of these contacts asked you if you were carrying it.

Why would they do that if Alizer had entrusted it to you? Why would they say that Alizer was supposed to deliver it to them if Alizer told you only to hand it to him and keep it out of sight? I am troubled. They may wish to claim it for themselves, Daniel. But there is nothing else to be done. Your contacts must be told since Alizer trusted them, and they have helped you all this way. I also have another thought, a hunch.' Husha turned to Iannas. 'I am thinking of what you said earlier, and I will need your help, Iannas. Let's follow the few options we have. It is all we have right now. Sai, let us take you to a hostel where you can rest, and we will meet together again when we have our information. ' Sai objected almost immediately, for she wanted to help, but Husha insisted she rest and a short battle ensued. In the end, Sai won. 'This is too important, Husha. We stay together. If I get tired I will tell you.'

Daniel stood, leaving the others to settle the payment, left the beer and wine bar seemingly calmly, and then ran. He arrived at the small daily prayer Temple off the market square just as three assistants, dressed in the traditional white cotton dresses and no masks, which were only worn during the ceremonies, were making preparations for the moon rising service. The youngest of the three finished pouring the wine into the cups on the altar and looked up at Daniel while the other two continued organising the altar and lighting the torches and candles. She put away the wine casket and walked the length of the temple to the lone figure just inside the entrance. Before Daniel had a chance to ask for Sum-Ina, she introduced herself. When Daniel did not reply, he looked confused for some reason, so she spoke again.

'You look confused. Maybe you have travelled from Susa and left your voice behind somewhere on the long journey?' Sum-Ina decided that she needed to remind this young man who he was.

Daniel nodded and was still lost for words, so Sum-Ina persisted, 'I see we are playing guessing games today. Do temples have this effect on you?'

Temples, priests and their assistants always had an effect on Daniel, and he gathered himself as quickly as he could. 'Daniel of Susa,' Daniel whispered at last.

'I have been expecting you,' was an answer Daniel should have been expecting. 'And I heard that Husha is still with you.' It was an observation not a question.

Sum-Ina was about to say that she would see Daniel after the service, but before she could speak and leave as she had hoped, Daniel, quietly - so that others in the temple would have difficulty catching his words - but firmly, blurted out that he had lost all his money, he had no idea where it was, and he was in trouble. Sum-Ina stopped in her tracks, looked at Daniel's pleading eyes and paused. If she realised the magnitude of Daniel's distress by looking at his face and the firmness of his voice, she did not show it. She looked at him once more, reassured him with a smile that again made Daniel speechless, and led him to a quiet room on the left side of the prayer hall, normally reserved for pilgrims in need of solace and silent prayer at any time of the day and night. Right now, the room was empty. The other two assistants ignored their colleague, it was normal to have local people and travellers seek help from the temple. They watched Sum-Ina lead Daniel into the quiet room and carried on with lighting the candles, for the congregation would arrive soon.

'It's a book Alizer asked me to carry from Ur to Harran, Sum-Ina. I have lost it.'

Daniel watched Sum-Ina's face, which he had already observed a bit too closely when she introduced herself, change from a serene calmness to a composed urgency, but a smile remained to reassure Daniel.

'A book from Alizer?' she repeated, almost as a question to herself and her eyes widened. She wanted to know where he had last seen it, and Daniel described the events in Terqa as briefly as he could, he could see members of the congregation beginning to arrive for the service and gathering at the entrance waiting to be invited in.

'One question before you join the congregation, Daniel. Do you trust Husha? Would he have the book?' Sum-Ina was entirely sincere.

Daniel should not have been shocked by the question, and he certainly was perplexed. He should have thought of this himself.

'I trust him completely, Sum-Ina,' Daniel replied. He spoke the truth as it came from his heart.

'Stay in the temple, join the congregation. Let me see what I can find out for you.' Sum-Ina quickly returned to the altar, correctly positioned the wine cups in readiness for the service and disappeared through a door to the right and behind the altar. Daniel stayed in the quiet room for a few more moments taking in the moment of peace to offer his own prayer before joining the congregation. A few moments into the service, Daniel noticed Sum-Ina make a discreet entrance through the door behind the altar and stand to one side so almost no one noticed her. The service did not last long, but it seemed like an age to Daniel who could not remember anything about the service as he watched Sum-Ina while asking himself how he could have allowed the book to be stolen.

Husha led them out of the bar while Iannas wanted to discuss the virtue of one of them heading back to Terqa to search for the book, but Husha calmly stalled him. 'I have a hunch,' he said again. 'It may not lead anywhere, but we have to start somewhere. Think again, Iannas, could this spy or informer have followed you from the camp in Terqa?'

Iannas went through his memories again, 'He would have had to follow me to the clinic with Sai, but I am sure there was no one else with me at the gate or behind me.'

Husha said, 'If he was following me, he would have seen that I had been taken to the security office. I bet he even asked about me in the office, and that is how he must have been identified so quickly, and why my uncle was able to tell me who he was.'

Iannas worked with the notion. 'And the Security Office was only a short way from the stables, just up the road. He might have watched where you were taken and deposited his donkey and cart in the nearest stables before returning and asking about you.'

'The same stable where you left Donkey,' Sai finished off Iannas' sentence.

'If I am right,' Husha continued, 'and we are dealing with a simple informer, not a spy, then he may have left a trail.'

Sai concluded for all three of them. 'If he had been asked to leave by the security as your uncle told you, and he saw Donkey in the same stable with his saddle bag still attached, he might have tried to take the bag or the contents. We are discussing chance. This is all very incidental, just a coincidence. As you say, Husha, we have to start somewhere. It could have been anyone, but if it was this spy, how do we know where he went?'

Very quickly they arrived at the Tuttul Security Office. Sai and Iannas were too tired to ask Husha why they were there and chose to follow his lead. Thefts were often reported here, and the soldier on duty patiently listened and even made a record of Husha's reported loss of money on a clay tablet and expressed surprise at the detail of Husha's description of the suspect. The soldier was even more surprised when he read Husha's Egyptian identification tablet after asking for his name and identification.

'How do you know the trader stole your money?' the soldier asked for clarification.

'I noticed he was on the same caravan as my family from Sippar, and he must have been watching us, watching where I kept the money. I saw him, without fail, in every caravan we took,' Husha lied, 'That is unusual to say the least.'

The soldier disagreed. 'Not necessarily, groups often travel to Harran or Damascus from Sippar, but it is suspicious for you to change caravans and for him to still be there.' The soldier took Husha's well-dressed bait.

'He suddenly disappeared after Terqa when we discovered the money had been stolen, and he is the only one we can think of. If you find him, and he has a lot of money on him, then he is the one,' Husha continued.

'You could have dropped your pouch?' the soldier insisted.

Iannas stepped in. 'No, we kept the money in three separate places and all three pouches have been stolen. They had to be taken while we slept.'

The soldier seemed more convinced by the extra decoration provided by Iannas and thankfully did not pursue the matter by asking exactly where the pouches were when they went missing, for they would not have been able to sustain the confident furnishing of answers for too long. The soldier submitted, wanting to close the matter as soon as he could. He was hoping for a quiet night tonight.

The soldier finished the tablet record and put the small clay item near the fire to dry.

'All right, let's look at the customs and records of traders. If he came ahead, he may have arrived here yesterday.'

All of them were surprised by the response from the soldier. He really was taking them seriously and not just telling them to return the next day as almost always happened with crime reports. The office was quiet today. It was only then that they realised the lack of people and commotion in the streets.

The soldier asked Husha, Sai, and Iannas to follow him to the Customs Office next door where he told the duty soldier to find the records for the day before and look for a trader with twelve bags of cloth from Mari heading to Harran with a donkey and cart.

'Yes. I remember him,' and it was the security soldier's turn to be surprised at the speed of the response and the progress he was making. 'He arrived yesterday late and left early morning. I was on duty at the gate both times.' The customs soldier checked the records tablet from the day before and saw the name near the bottom, almost the last entry on the list. 'His name is Dazatu of Urfa.' The customs man checked another tablet, 'and I can see that he left early morning today with the caravan to Harran. He still had twelve bags of the cloth with him. I remember him because he had a problem with his donkey outside the gates this morning. He was beating the donkey without mercy, because it was refusing to move. Some of the families and children became very upset, and one of the gate guards had to intervene and stop him from beating the donkey. He was even told he would be arrested if he carried on with the beating. I watched him leave with a bale of cloth on his back. His donkey was very weak. I am not sure it will last. Someone should have arrested him for animal cruelty, but we have enough to do here with the refugee camp outside.'

'Well, that was easier than I expected,' the security officer confessed. 'I will inform our soldiers on patrol duty to pass the information on to the checkpoints. Let's see if we can catch up with him in Harran if not before. If we find him, he will be brought back here as we have an agreement with Urfa and Harran, and this is where the complaint is filed. Check with the security office in Harran. I will send a message if there is any news.'

'Thank you so much,' Husha expressed his gratitude. 'May I buy some beer for you, sir? I want to thank you for your help. Is it allowed?'

Iannas could see how Husha operated with the right people. 'Thank you, but I will be off duty soon. I wish all the complaints I received were as easy as yours.'

They thanked each other. Husha quickly found a place serving beer only a few doors away and told a waiter to deliver a pitcher to the soldier in the Security Office. Husha paid, and they waited while the waiter made the delivery. The soldier, seeing Husha walking past, came out to thank him.

Husha was satisfied, and Iannas had an urge to leave at that instant to look for the trader. Husha persuaded him to slow down, for the trader was only one of many possibilities.

Sai mirrored Husha's thoughts. 'If we leave now, first we have bandits to contend with, never mind the night animals, and second, what if Daniel learns something new tonight? What if Daniel's contacts were watching and saw who took the book? What if it was not this spy or trader after all? We have to keep exploring all possibilities before we act.'

Husha always knew she was the wise one. 'This is all we have right now,' Husha concluded. 'If it is a professional thief or spy who was actually looking for the money, then we have very little hope.' Making sure that despair did not occupy them, Iannas, Sai and Husha hoped and hoped for some encouraging news as they made their way back to the still busy beer and wine bar to wait for Daniel.

It was not too long a wait. After only one sweet hot date drink that calmed them, Daniel returned with a young lady who was there 'officially' to visit Sai with child to see how she was at the request of Daniel, a clever way of getting permission from the Temple for Sum-Ina to accompany Daniel. Sum-Ina seized the role of assistant priest and blessed the young mother-to-be. She asked Husha to settle the bill, which Daniel stepped in to do instead, and then led them to a dedicated small hostel for temple guests where all four could stay, eat fresh food, and Sai would be given a special room just for her to convalesce for the night. What's more, the hostel was empty so they had all four rooms to themselves.

While they waited for dinner to be prepared, Sum-Ina wanted to learn more, as well as to reassure them. 'I can tell you one thing, everything will be all right.' Iannas heard the words of his dream being echoed and was a little taken aback. 'I want to hear from each of you what happened in Terqa.'

They recalled the events once more, trying to remember any detail they may have forgotten before, and Sum-Ina would have asked them to start all over again had it not been for a young messenger who asked to speak with Lady Sum-Ina privately.

'Don't worry,' Sum-Ina replied, 'this is Daniel.' She did not introduce anyone else to the messenger, and he looked at Daniel with some surprise, almost as if he expected someone older. The messenger was not introduced by name either. 'Go ahead and make your report to all of us. These are Daniel's companions.'

And a little invisible! Iannas thought to himself; Sai and Husha would have agreed.

The young messenger, no older than Iannas, came closer to the dining table, stood and made his report in a formal, official manner. There was obviously a rank system amongst these Protectors or Watchers, if that is what they were, Husha observed.

The messenger's report was surprisingly accurate. 'According to the caravan records, only one caravan arrived from Terqa yesterday. The caravan registered twenty-seven arrivals in Terqa and listed having begun with twenty-one at Tuttul. Eighteen of the twenty-one who started in Tuttul travelled the entire distance from Terqa, and the other three completed their journey in Zelebiye. Nine travellers joined the caravan at various stations along the way between Terqa and Tuttul. We are also in the process of inspecting the records of the travellers that arrived in today's caravan from Terqa. But that will comprise my second report later this evening, My Lady.'

Sum-Ina was following meticulously and nodded.

'Of the eighteen who arrived yesterday and travelled the full distance, seven of them are known to us in various capacities and there are four amongst them that I would like to describe and report.' The messenger paused as if seeking approval.

'And the three that stopped in Zelebiye?' Sum-Ina asked.

'They are not known to us, My Lady, and appear to be local farmers. But I will send someone to Zelebiye to inquire further.'

Sum-Ina nodded in approval.

'The four individuals where I would like to focus our attention are known to us as thieves or spies, and at least one of them is known as both a thief and a spy. All four have donkeys, are merchants, and two of them left their donkeys in the same stable as the one you reported in Terqa, and had opportunity. I will describe all four to you.'

The numbers were getting smaller. This is a good sign, Husha thought.

'The first two did not use the stable in Terqa. One is a known thief, wanted in Sippar, and left for Damascus this morning. He was carrying temple statues. The other is a thief and a spy known to us heading to Ebla with six bales of cloth. He is working for the temples and security in Mari and is known to purchase stolen items on his journeys and sell them at this destination. Now, we turn to the two who used the same stable as reported in Terqa. One is a merchant and informer reporting to Security in Sippar who left for Harran this morning with twelve bales of cloth. He supplements his income by trading in counterfeit goods and he often visits our temples.' The messenger paused again and looked at Sum-Ina, hesitant to say any more.

'My young friend is embarrassed to add that this is the culprit who was following you, Husha,' Sum-Ina stepped in. 'We tried to check on the content of his report in Terqa, and it appears he had very little to report, but we cannot be too sure. We know he is an informer from Sippar. We can only guess why he followed you, but we have people working on it in Sippar and as yet I have not heard.'

The messenger did not wait for any response but continued as soon as Sum-Ina had finished. 'He leaves an interesting trail behind him. In the Tuttul entry and exit records, he is listed as Dazatu of Urfa. In the Terqa stable, he is listed as Meskalum of Sippar. With the descriptions of his supplies and number of bales of cloth he was carrying we are convinced he is one and the same. The second suspect is still here in Tuttul. He has left his donkey at the station and is selling musical instruments in the market; some are stolen and some purchased legitimately. We do not believe this last trader is a spy, but we can never be sure in these matters. With your permission, My Lady,' he looked at Sum-Ina, 'I will have our network shadow all four.'

Sum-ina was not satisfied, 'Send a message to Terqa and ask our friends to trace everyone else who used the stable that Daniel used in Terqa for the two nights he was there. Any one of them had opportunity. You have done well in tracing all those who arrived in Tuttul. There will be others who travelled to the south towards Mari, and another one or two may still be in Terqa. For now, we will continue the premise that the thief took the item from the stable, and we need to eliminate every possibility.'

'I have already sent the message, My Lady.' The messenger thought he was one step ahead, but Sum-Ina was still not satisfied with the response.

'I know the owner of the stable in question works with us; he regularly sends us lists of everyone who stay in all his stables. Have him scrutinised again even if he is Puvurum's family. His stable watchmen had opportunity too. Get a list of everyone on duty over the two days and have them investigated in case we missed something before.'

Husha realised that Sum-Ina was part of a very talented group of people. He should have expected to have been impressed if they really were who he thought they were.

The messenger made a note and asked if they required him to describe other details he had collected so far about the four suspects, such as where they slept the night in Terqa and where they spent their time. Sum-Ina looked at Daniel who shook his head.

'He should go and continue his investigations and find out where this Dazatu is,' Sum-Ina suggested.

'Not yet,' Husha interrupted. 'Let us add a little to what you know about the merchant Dazatu from Urfa.' Husha, Iannas and Sai related their activity at the Security Office. The messenger was grateful and sought permission to leave and hurried out just as food was beginning to arrive.

Sum-Ina made an impression on everyone. How she and her team had organised all this information in such a short space of time baffled them. As soon as the messenger had left and the food delivered, she dismissed the waiters so they were alone again and turned directly to Husha and, firmly but politely, spoke to him.

'I have already asked Daniel, and he tells me he trusts you completely.' Husha was embarrassed at being spoken to as a governess would with a child who was being chastised. She could have been his daughter. 'If he trusts you,' she looked at Daniel, 'I do too. I do not need to know your story or why Daniel has confidence in you. The merchant Dazatu followed you and is the strongest key we have. What else can you tell me about him and the reason he was following you? I want to understand if he was tasked to look for the book. All this time, we believed he was following you.' Sum-Ina was so direct, single-minded and chilling with Husha, no one else dared interrupt their conversation. Husha felt reprimanded, but also knew she had the right to ask questions of him. In turn, Husha was not going to jeopardise his uncle's position or any of his other contacts and mission. Daniel, Iannas, and Sai sensed this.

'As we all know now, he was originally sent by the Head of Security in Sippar. It is related to my previous owner, Ugibi of Susa, and connected with the Minister of Babylon who we accidently crossed paths with in Uruk. Sippar thought that because I met with the Astrologer of Sippar and was in Uruk at the time of the attempted assassination of the Minister, my owner was somehow involved, some sort of a spy, and I was a messenger for him. I believe they lost interest in me when I was arrested in Terqa.' Husha knew Sum-Ina would not be satisfied.

'Yes, Puvurum informed me that this Dazatu was almost thrown out of Terqa. I do not understand why he was thrown out if he is an informer for Security. But you do not believe he was looking for the book, that his only interest was you?'

Husha nodded, 'If he did indeed take the book from the saddlebag, we can only speculate that it was chance. He will try and sell it in Harran. If he did not take it, then we are looking at someone more professional who might have been looking for the book. He or she will be difficult to find.'

Sum-Ina appreciated Husha's insight, and Husha could tell she wanted to know much more.

Daniel took the pause, 'Sum-Ina, let us eat and discuss the various ideas we have. As Husha said, Dazatu is a lead but is there someone else? Let's go through what we have learned and I still need to organise supplies.'

The food was getting cold and over dinner they expressed their gratitude to Sum-Ina and discussed every possibility and every clue over and over again until everyone could not see or say anything new. Husha was embarrassed to admit he remembered all four of the suspects by their description but not once had cause to doubt them. He also expressed his surprise at how much Sum-Ina knew.

'This means there are other people whom we do not see, and yet they watch us? I am impressed, Sum-Ina. I do not know how you gather so much information so quickly. Now I think I will have to behave.'

Sum-Ina smiled at Husha and held his hands. 'These are the hands that have been protecting my friend, Daniel,' she said to him. It was Daniel's turn to be embarrassed as Sum-Ina looked at him again. 'We are eternally grateful, Husha.' But Sum-Ina was sincere. There was no blame or accusation in her voice, although she had not yet dismissed the probability that directly or indirectly he may have been the reason and cause for the loss of the book. Husha was well aware that Sum-Ina did not trust him.

When Sum-Ina left, Iannas arranged for the group to buy the supplies for Alizer, have them delivered as instructed by Sum-Ina to Hazil at the service station, and book the morning's caravan. This time they insisted that Sai rested and she did not object.

When they had completed their tasks and were back together again in the hostel, Daniel was reminded again how important it was and the difference it made to him being surrounded by people who seemed to understand the world in a different way from himself, understand it and accept it as it is and be guided by it. He wondered if the heartening and hopeful force from these people affected the universe in the same way it had provoked him to step away from the gloom earlier in the afternoon. He thought not and decided that the universe was constant and did not have negative thoughts. He appreciated his friends for their positivity and thanked the God Sin for Sum-Ina.

'So what do you think of Sum-Ina?' Husha asked Daniel as they sipped another calming hot date drink to which Sai had added some fresh root ginger she had asked Husha to purchase for her. Sai had finished her drink and was already in her own room as the three of them were preparing to fall into their beds.

Iannas looked at Daniel before attempting a very poor imitation of his voice and accent. "I am going to marry her one day", Iannas tried.

Daniel looked at them sternly. 'Is that all you can think off. I have lost the book, and all you can think of is the priest's assistant.' He paused and allowed a smile to creep onto his face. 'She is beautiful, isn't she?' he added with a sense of wonderment. 'And she asked me to attend the midnight service. They will be performed during each of the seven nights leading up to the big service on the special full moon winter solstice, the night of the shortest day.' He had already decided to attend the midnight ceremony with Sum-Ina.

'But the priest in Susa is beautiful too.' Daniel found himself admitting with a wide smile. They all laughed which helped to release some of the day's tension. They continued to tease, and the humour lowered the tension until Daniel blurted, 'Not sure if we will find the book again. How could I have allowed it to happen? Alizer trusted me. What if it is a special book? And how is it that I am the one to lose it? Why me?' and it was hurting Daniel.

Husha took hold of the moment to settle the atmosphere again. 'We do not know what the book is, Daniel. Let's be clear, we have to carry on our journey to the end as we have been tasked. We have to leave the book to providence now. There is nothing more we can do. Perhaps we will come across the merchant Dazatu in Harran, and who knows, he might even have it,' Husha added for good measure.

Iannas and Husha heard Daniel leave his bed and disappear just before midnight for the service. Daniel saw Sum-Ina and she was glad he came and he was glad for her company.

Daniel would have effortlessly fallen in love with Sum-Ina and she made it so easy but he knew better. He was becoming wiser. If he had lost a book of great importance to the world, it had been too easy to lose. He should have protected it and yet, as the journey had progressed, he had taken it for granted. He returned to sleep only to be haunted into another sleepless night. He could not see how the book would be found. He had to listen to and trust the universe like the others. But they seemed to find it easier and he did not yet know how.

Sum-Ina's smiling face met them at the Terqa station at dawn, and just in time to see them off. 'Go to Harran. All my people are on the lookout on all the routes. There is no contact for you to find in Harran, Daniel. If there is any news we will find you.'

Sum-Ina came up close to Daniel and gently placed the back of her right hand on Daniel's right cheek and he immediately felt her spirit through her soft cold hands and saw courage sparkle in her eyes. 'It has been an honour to meet you, Daniel. You do a great deed, far larger than any of us, and you have carried a great burden with such ease, you are an inspiration to us all. Continue being who you are and don't try to be anyone else.' She removed her hand, turned and left without looking back and Daniel watched Sum-Ina walk away wrapped in her dark heavy woollen coat used by her mother, grandmother and great grandmother before her for the cold early morning temple duties.

Donkey sensed the loss of something special. He also knew what this something special felt like and he also knew he could help Daniel find it.

25 MESKALUM THE PIRATE

Ever since he had run away from his guardians in Kanaan and found himself in employment at a boat yard at a southern port on the mouth of the sea known as the Red Sea, Meskalum could remember something following him, and he knew it lived inside his shadow, and his shadow was called Greed. Meskalum had spent his whole life absorbed by his shadow. From the boat yard, his shadow had drawn him into the world of piracy. After so many years on the seas, being shipwrecked after a very unexpected cyclone on a tiny, bare and empty desert island known as Shrau off the coast of Katara, and being rescued by a passing trading ship who found him near death, Meskalum settled into a slightly quieter and better paid life on land. He now transported goods from various temples between Ur, Mari, Nineveh, and Harran. Of course, his shadow had contrived ways of making extra money over and above what he was paid, and after nine years no one had noticed, so he was glad to carry on with his schemes.

On this trip, having already received a basic fee for expenses along the way, he had been contracted to move twelve large sacks of Salalah Frankincense from the shipyard in Ur to the High Temple in Sippar, one of the few temples in the land that could afford such high-grade incense. In Sippar, he was to pick up nine specially commissioned temple statues by the renowned Sippar artist Id-Nivic and deliver them to the High Temple in Mari. Finally, twelve sacks of the finest Mari temple woven cloth, the best in the land, coveted by many, and so fine that it was only used by the temple priests for their holy gowns, were to be picked up in Mari and delivered to the newly built High Temple in Harran. The King of Harran had commissioned the Temple, and the cloth would be used for special temple inauguration ceremonies. Only when the contract was completed, would Meskalum receive the remainder of his fee. And there was always a new contract waiting with a different set of goods and new destinations.

Greed had ensured that on this trip, like all the others, he supplemented his income. On his way to Sippar, he had convinced a temple official in Babylon, competing with others for a larger congregation, to pay a high price for one bag of the rare Salalah Incense. He then found two of his old pirate colleagues in a beer bar located in the market square of Babylon from whom he obtained a sack of normal grade quality frankincense at a very cheap price, which he was able to repack to look like the other eleven bags. The twelve bags were delivered in Sippar as instructed. Meskalum had already earned more than his transport fee for the entire journey.

In Sippar, Meskalum had loaded the nine exquisite Id-Nivic statues for the Mari Temple delivery and was ready to leave, already calculating about how much one of the statues might fetch in the market in Hit.

In addition to his temple services, Meskalum also received payments from the Royal Court Security Office in Sippar for providing them with simple information. He had volunteered to be one of their informers almost eight years ago. Anyone who pays me for saying a few words is worthy of my attention, he had thought. Meskalum's information was usually restricted to the number and location of checkpoints on different routes, location and numbers of soldiers between cities, and the cost of the tax levies at each checkpoint and at his destinations. Being asked to keep an eye on someone had never happened before, but since he would be paid almost six times his usual fee for valuable information, he had agreed. He, of course, had no idea that he was only being given this task because none of the royal court spies would accept a slave as a target, even a former slave. As far as the court was concerned, the informer was sufficient for this particular lowly task.

Greed, however, had its own shadow, a darker shape growing and now surviving in the form of Hate. Ever since he had found himself alive but with no food and no water after the shipwreck on a small barren desert island, Greed had met Hate and Hate grew to consume every part of Meskalum.

Meskalum abandoned any fleeting thought he had for the gods after the shipwreck. Once he had felt close to the God Sin, for being looked after by the moon almost every night on the ship had always been a comforting and spiritual experience. But stranded, lying on the hot desert sand and stone, half alive, he could draw no other conclusion than that he had been fooled, and there was no Sin God, no fate, no goodness and certainly no such thing as love. When he woke in Ur in the clinic, he began to worship his good luck. He was forced to draw a new conclusion: a few good people did exist, notably the ones who rescued him from the island and the ladies of this clinic who tried so hard to nurse everyone back to health. He had already decided that there was nothing in this world he could love or care for.

He thought about his parents who had chosen to die when he was so young that now he could not even remember their faces or their voices. He remembered the neighbours who tried to raise him and beat him because he would not tend to the animals as well as they liked and told him he was anything but useful and should have died with his parents. When he was nine years old, he remembered running away and meeting a traveller who worked in a boatyard who befriended him and told him he could work for him, Meskalum hated him too. Meskalum did everything he was asked and his payment had been food, a bed and lots of empty promises of wealth. He sailed on the pirate boat for more than twenty years, and still he was always the last and the lowest. He learned that there was nothing else, and now, although he had never cared to see himself, he looked twice his age. A young man with an aged, huge shadow.

Greed meant that he carried out any actions asked of him, and even if he had felt any remorse afterwards, Hate now meant that he felt none. Luck meant he was alive and had to look after himself, for there was no one else in the world who would. He faked some tablets so that he had the recommendations for a first class licensed delivery agent for the temples, having arrived at a clever scheme to increase his profits tenfold. He was now doing very well, no thanks to anyone at all.

Meskalum had watched Husha from a distance and asked about him. None of the travellers knew anything of him, and he did nothing interesting except buy supplies. He got bored of Husha quickly and turned his attention on finding a good temple statue to replace the one he had sold in Hit for a very good price to a passing trader heading to Damascus, where the price would be considerably more. This trip was proving very profitable, and in Haradum, as he expected, he caught up with some of his old acquaintances who supplied him with a good statue at a very low price by dawn. He, of course, did not ask where it came from and left Haradum in the same caravan as Husha. In Mari, he delivered his nine statues and picked up his twelve bags of Mari temple cloth for the temple in Harran, after having noted that Husha visited the Astrologer in Mari. With no other news to report, no wonder they gave him this task, he concluded and expressed his hate and disgust for Husha for not being worthy of anything interesting. Interesting might have meant more money.

When Husha was arrested in Terqa, he had waited in a nearby beer and wine bar. Then late in the afternoon he made his report to the Head of Security and used the opportunity to ask what would happen to him. 'You are not going to see him for a while,' was the answer and Meskalum managed to extract enough to realise that he was arrested on the orders of the Royal Security Office and decided that Husha was not just a slave but also a scoundrel, a brigand, just like himself except that he was too clever to be caught. He realised his mission with Husha was over, and he was glad.

Early dawn the next morning in the torchlit stables, Meskalum had been surprised to see Husha's donkey next to his, and when he saw the saddlebag on Donkey, what an opportunity to replace his own crumbling and decaying saddlebag! When Donkey would not stand and part with it, he decided to empty its contents, at the very least to pay Husha back for having been asked – actually, told - to leave Terqa or pay additional taxes by the soldiers who were even now waiting outside to escort him to the city gate. Seeing the carefully wrapped package that he had removed from the saddlebag and realising the value in the attention of the wrapping, his shadow gleefully sneaked it into his own shoulder bag. To ensure it was not missed, Meskalum quickly found a piece of wood roughly the same size amongst the waste in the corner, wrapped it in his own wiping cloth to make it resemble the same shape and feel, and placed it in the saddlebag, tying it up carefully to make it appear untouched.

Almost forgotten, the book remained in Meskalum's shoulder bag for the journey to Tuttul, and from there it searched the mind, the heart and the body of its new keeper and found nothing but Greed and Hate and darkness. It searched again for even a glimpse of light, as the journey was seven days and the book would never stop looking. Eventually, after a few days, it found a tiny memory as small as a mosquito bite that the darkness in Meskalum's shadow, both Greed and Hate, had not been able to reach, and inside this miniscule memory was the remnant of a moment of tenderness and where the book began its work.

Over the next few days, Meskalum recognised a new feeling; it was small and it was distant, but then he recalled it as a familiar sensation from a long time ago. The feeling guided him to a memory of a ship's port where he had been eating some snacks and waiting for his colleagues to return. A tiny wet, lost and cold shivering kitten wandered over to him, found his long overcoat touching the ground, and clambered up the coat unaided to Meskalum's side where it found the dry warmth of his coat, curled up, and went to sleep. Meskalum had ignored it, for he was busy finishing his snack, and when his colleagues returned, and it was time to leave he looked at the sleeping, comfortable, recovering kitten and rather than stand and destroy its moment of peace it had been craving for, or move the kitten, which would have had the same impact, Meskalum gently removed his overcoat and left it where it was so the kitten remained sleeping in the warmth of the overcoat on the seat while Meskalum returned to his boat.

The feeling of tenderness, as small as it was, was accompanied with a sense of hope, which grew each day, just as a mosquito bite grows until that he could no longer ignore it, for it kept returning even as an itch, and Meskalum had never enjoyed a journey more than the one from Terqa to

Tuttul. When the journey was close to the end, and the caravan was a day from Tuttul, he even began to consider what hope might look like, but the next day he arrived in Tuttul and was thrown into such hordes, a mass, a swarm of people, that fear emerged, fear that these people would steal his valuable cloth. He fought his way through the hordes to the city gate where he paid his entry tax, recorded his goods and made his way to a stable inside the city of Tuttul, as he had done in Terqa, where his goods would be safer. And fear kept hold. It latched on and remained with him all night. Meskalum could not manage the nightmare of suppressed hope uncovering itself as it had for that moment, and he hid himself from it during the evening and night in Tuttul. It was a fear of hope.

At dawn, as usual, Meskalum led his donkey out of the stable into the courtyard, where he attached his cart and lined up behind the other travellers leaving at the main gate where Meskalum saw that the customs were being very thorough, and all the goods were being recorded for the exit tax. Normally Meskalum would never have been concerned, but today his fear was for the package around his shoulder that until now he had not thought of or even opened. For some reason, he believed it would be noticed and he had a sensation that the package needed to be hidden. So while he was waiting, he made it seem he was checking his load, and in the process he removed the package from his shoulder bag and placed it in the middle of one of the Mari cloth bags on the cart being pulled by his donkey.

When it was his turn, the customs officer recorded his load and did not charge exit tax as he was leaving with the same goods. Meskalum was relieved and led his donkey through the gate and outside the city where the donkey stopped and nothing would shift him. Meskalum would miss the caravan and wanted to get away and tried everything; he pulled the donkey, even beat him until the soldiers from the gate came running, stopped him, and warned him he would be arrested if he carried on beating his donkey in this manner. When Meskalum unhooked his donkey from the cart, the donkey was fine and moved freely. The cart is too heavy, he thought having forgotten that his donkey had pulled it all the way from Mari, but he wanted to get away and his fears had confused his mind. He removed one bag and reattached the cart. His donkey was now satisfied and started pulling the cart. Meskalum cursed the donkey and accused him of pretending to be a "lazy, good-for-nothing, utterly useless, motherless rat", a phrase he had forgotten and now remembered being beaten with in his younger days before he had run away. Meskalum decided to carry the bag himself and reach the caravan. He did not have time to argue with his animal. Of course, everyone who was awake enough to notice pointed and laughed at the sight of a merchant with a donkey and cart having to carry his own bag of goods.

When Meskalum joined the caravan to Harran in time for the second horn, he quickly registered his arrival and started moving at the very back. He allowed his donkey to lead the way, and while at the rear of the cart, he attempted to return the bag; the donkey sensed the extra load and immediately stopped, refusing to move. Meskalum was given no choice but to carry the bag again, for only then did his donkey agreed to move forward. Not to be outdone by the animal, he tried once more to outwit his donkey, this time by removing individual rolls of cloth from the bag he was carrying and dropping them onto the back of the cart, one by one, as his donkey continued walking. Eventually he had no cloth left, and the bag was empty except for the hidden package. Meskalum quickly placed the package into his own shoulder bag, glad that he had outsmarted the donkey. He threw the empty bag into the cart and would repack the cloth another time.

The day passed quickly. Meskalum had remembered to introduce himself as Dazatu of Urfa in Tuttul, having changed all his identification the first day out of Terqa with a new set of contract tablets to match his second identity. After the skirmish with the security office in Terqa, when they had escorted him out of the city, he was always glad to be prepared and had avoided being arrested on past occasions in this way. He had no problems at any of the checkpoints travelling as Dazatu, and he made a mental note not to use Meskalum again if he was back in this region. He reminded himself to have a new set of identification tablets made in Urfa with a new name, and he knew exactly where to go.

That night Meskalum, even that was not his real name, repacked the cloth into the empty twelfth bag, and everything was now ready for Harran. The next day, as usual, he remained at the back of the caravan. Somehow he always felt comfortable there because he could see everything happen ahead of him, such as checkpoints, soldiers, bandits or even wild animals. In this position, he would have enough time to take appropriate action depending on the threat. Fear had made him nervous today, and his mind was not at ease.

During the midday break, Meskalum had enough of the shoulder bag and the outer coat he had worn since morning. He was increasingly hot and bothered. He removed both and placed them both in his donkey's saddlebag.

When the caravan started, his donkey refused to move forward even a step. He pulled the donkey, beat him and even untied him from the cart. The caravan security had to intervene and stopped him from beating the donkey and swearing. All the children and families passing were clearly alarmed by his behaviour, his curses, and how he was treating the animal. Meskalum pleaded with the rear guards, but they would not wait and told him to find some shade in the nearby hills and wait for the next caravan.

They left without him; it was not the first time he felt abandoned and vulnerable to the elements.

Meskalum swore he would buy a new donkey in Harran. He unhooked the cart, removed the saddlebag, and with the donkey walking again, led him into the shade of a small hill not too far off the track. Here, he even found a small cave set in the hill which acted as a good shelter and view point, and from where he could see the caravan trail while remaining hidden in the dark shadows. After returning with the cart and the saddlebag, he found little or no wood, but he had no plans to attract attention to himself with a fire.

As he waited, he saw two soldiers on horseback heading towards Harran from Tuttul. He made sure they did not notice him, and there were no other travellers. There was no second caravan today. He would have to settle down in the cave tonight. Fear reminded him of his shipwreck; no wood, no fire, no signal, no rescue and eventually no water. He looked at his cart and saw that he had enough food and clean water for many days. In fact, the river nearby looked fairly clean along this stretch, but he had been warned on a previous occasion not to drink the river water here, for the waste from Harran and Urfa being dumped into the river further up always accumulated in this section. He had seen pockets of waste on the river with his own eyes, and they were not pleasant. He never touched the Euphrates river water again when he saw that all the cities were doing exactly the same. He relied only on the tiny little rock streams that came out of the ground and fed the river. He became cold in the evening, unpacked his outer coat that had been in the saddlebag, and noticed the shoulder bag with the package he had been carrying since Terqa. He felt safe in the cave but still checked that no one was nearby and used this moment to unwrap the package and discover its secret.

Like many, Meskalum could not read. So when he unwrapped the package and saw the leather sheath and unrolled the tediously long papyrus with writings on it, he was disappointed. Nevertheless, papyrus was in demand in Harran, this much he knew. He hoped it would be of value to someone in Harran where there were a number of tablet and papyrus book sellers. He had even heard of a book collector and seller called Lau-Sin of Harran whom he had made deliveries to before. He returned the papyrus to its sheath, wrapped it again, tied it with the string and returned it to his shoulder bag.

He spent the night cursing his donkey and bestowed as many Mesopotamian descriptive words as he could remember on the animal. But Meskalum knew he was vulnerable here, and so he was relieved to see the dust of another caravan in the distance the following day during the midday sun. First, he saw two caravan security scouts, went out to meet them, and told them his woes. They checked his credentials and told him the caravan was not too far away. They advised him to wait and join the caravan when it came by, and they would let the caravan leader know to expect him.

He returned to his cave, made his donkey and cart ready and let the caravan approach, relieved to be back in the safety of a crowd and even more relieved that his donkey was behaving again. He made his entry to the caravan without any fuss at the rear. In fact, it was a large group so hardly anyone noticed him except the rear security guards who had already been expecting him. When the caravan made ready to camp for the night, he released the donkey from the cart, removed his saddlebag, and settled him with the other animals in the night pen in the middle of the camp, where the animals would be fed and watered. Meskalum always left his cart of goods at the rear edge of the camp where he would sleep soundly away from the noise. There was no campfire tonight, and he wondered why. He did not care, for he had plenty of fruit, bread, vegetables, dried meats and beer.

Luck was looking after him again, he thought, and yet, for the first time since his shipwreck he felt a slight niggle, which turned out to be self-doubt. He quickly swatted it away like the flies around him, but it kept coming back, like the flies around him.

When Meskalum woke, the caravan was already a hive of activity. He had slept a little too long on his comfortable cloth bales in his cart. He quickly brought his donkey back to the cart, attached him and returned with the cart to the other donkeys that were still being fed so his donkey could finish feeding with them. Meskalum was pleasantly surprised that the donkey moved the cart this morning without any hesitation and thought that his shouting and cursing the previous day may have had some effect. As he began his wait for his donkey to finish feeding, Meskalum noticed a traveller nearby drinking some cold date drink. He threw his overcoat and shoulder bag into his donkey's saddlebag, not worried about them, for he would only be a few paces away, and went to see if the traveller could spare some of his morning drink.

26 DONKEY, THE MAGIC BOOK AND HARRAN

Days 55 to 58, 15.5 Beru.

As soon as Sum-Ina disappeared, the teasing began. Did he meet Sum-Ina after the midnight blessing? Had he arranged to meet Sum-Ina in Harran? The teasing did not cease until they joined their caravan with the new pack donkey just as the first horn was sounded. All the travellers listened to the caravan leader make the usual announcements about keeping up, safety and so on. There was an extra announcement today, and the leader raised his voice to ensure it carried to the groups standing furthest away. It seemed important, and everyone hushed more than usual.

'The area you will enter during the day belongs to the city of Urfa. There are new additional checkpoints on route where extra taxes have to be paid. The King of Urfa, or should I say the God-King of Urfa, has made a new proclamation that affects us all. We only received it last night, so listen carefully. There are to be no fires in the lands of Urfa until after the winter solstice festival is over. All firewood is to be collected and transported to the great bonfire in Urfa. We have a special cart with us today, and we will collect firewood along the way to hand over to officials at the checkpoints. All wood in the territory is to be collected only for the big fire and for no other purpose. Anyone starting a fire in the land of Urfa will be charged with treason as an act against the God-King of Urfa.'

Everyone groaned. No hot food. Thank the Gods it was only four days to Harran, everyone thought. 'I have no intention of waiting for you if you get arrested, and there are plenty of soldiers watching,' the caravan leader warned.

'There is one more announcement,' he waited until everyone was quiet again. 'Normally, we allow four nights for this journey arriving early morning on the fifth day. Because we will be travelling without fire and hot food or hot drinks, I propose we travel through and out of Urfa territory as quickly as possible. I will set a slightly faster pace than usual. Keep up and we will only spend three nights on the road and arrive in Harran in the late afternoon or early evening of the fourth day.'

The caravan cheered in support and the leader finished with his final call, 'Be ready to go!' The caravan guards took their positions at the head, sides, and rear, the second horn was sounded and the front groups moved forward to lead and head the caravan.

As they moved into the heat of the morning, an eerie emptiness welcomed them, and it was only later during the mid morning break did a voice call out from the caravan and everyone noticed, 'Where are the trees?' Not one tree could be seen. Not even a root. The trees had been ripped from the ground and taken away.

Husha, Sai, Daniel and Iannas were glad and reassured to know that Sum-Ina's entire network was on the road searching for the suspects, one of which was a day ahead of them. The afternoon and the next day revealed a monotony of the same empty terrain, the lack of shade making the journey hotter and more uncomfortable. When the caravan made ready to stop for the second night and with the knowledge that there was only one more night to go, they tried not to be too despondent and helped each other accept the reality as it was and not as they might have wished it. They did the same as they had done before and camped close to the animals. In fact, they felt comfortable next to Donkey who, as usual, was enjoying their company too; he always missed them when he was left in a stable.

Each tried to be as enthusiastic as possible at the prospect of arriving in Harran. Two more days of travelling, the end of their journey, but none of them was looking forward. The loss of the book had cast an uncertainty and they were unclear what awaited them.

Sai knew she needed to stop and settle in Harran, but being unsure of what to expect, she steadied the reality and asked if they would mind if she stayed with them until their journey was over, whatever that meant and wherever the path took them. With the impact of the loss of the book, the thought of separating had not been at the forefront of their minds but for Sai, she did not want to be abandoned by her child's new uncles in Harran in case they had to move on.

'Let's see what tomorrow brings,' Husha said calmly, attempting to soothe the group's anxieties, especially Daniel's; everyone had noticed his agitation as they came closer to Harran. Daniel would never accept that his task was over until the book was found. Arriving without the book in Harran was a pain too difficult to bear, and he could no longer see that everything else had proceeded so smoothly. They all could feel Daniel's hurt. 'Let's sleep,' Husha tried, knowing that each of them would be trapped by their thoughts and anxieties for the next two nights.

In the morning the camp was almost ready to go, and Sai was already sitting on Donkey, waiting with the last few animals to be collected. Iannas noticed that no matter how much he pulled Donkey, Donkey simply refused to take a step forward even as the other animals were one by one being led away without difficulty. Sai suggested it might be her weight, and Iannas helped her dismount. Still Donkey did not wish to move. Iannas checked Donkey's feet and legs, everything seemed fine.

Donkey's world had stopped. No matter if the other world continued, he would not move until they listened.

When the whole caravan started to advance and with most of the camels and donkeys from the temporary night pen stepping away, only Donkey, the hired donkey which Daniel and Husha had packed and made ready, and another donkey with a cart remained. Donkey stepped closer to the donkey with the cart as if obstructing his path. A trader came running up and tried to pull his donkey to move and moaned, 'There is no hot drink in this camp, and why won't this donkey budge. It's been like this for days,' he grumbled. 'There is something wrong with him.'

Iannas gently tried to convince Donkey to walk while the other trader was getting increasingly angry with his. 'Not again, you're not leaving me here!' the trader shouted to the approaching rear guards as he reached for his stick.

Husha was holding on to the pack donkey and getting impatient with Iannas who was trying to lead Donkey away from the donkey with the cart.

'What's wrong with them?' Husha called as he stepped in between the two clashing donkeys. He quickly assessed the problem and asked Daniel to bring him a blanket to cover Donkey's eyes and head. It was only then, as he was waiting for Daniel who was pulling a blanket out from the supplies on the pack donkey that Husha's attention turned to the other donkey and the cart laden with bales of cloth, and immediately his mind launched into an involuntary sequence of acts. It all happened almost instantaneously.

The other trader started to beat his donkey, and Iannas immediately stepped in his way.

'Don't beat him; something must be wrong!' Iannas pleaded, and the trader switched to shouting insults, curses and expletives that were no different to the ones in Egypt, Assyria or even India, except the comparison with the cow, much to the entertainment of some of the travellers who had decided to stand and watch rather than join the slowly moving caravan.

One of the rear security guards screamed, 'Get a move on, or we leave you here!' His tone encouraged the onlookers to return to their pack animals and families and leave behind the three donkeys, their keepers and the rear guards who were clearing up the camp as they edged forward.

Meskalum was so preoccupied with his donkey he had not yet noticed Husha who signalled to Iannas and Daniel with four words so only they would understand, 'The money is here!'

Daniel, who was now approaching with the blanket, understood, immediately feigned anger and joined Iannas between the donkey and the trader who was still in the middle of his tirade.

'Do not beat the donkey; something's wrong with him. Get that cart off. Let us check the donkey to see if he is hurt,' Daniel roared, hoping Husha would understand.

Since the other trader had no intention to comply with this demand and carried on attempting to pull and beat his donkey, Husha understood, stepped towards the cart, and unhooked it from the trader's donkey. Meskalum was still swinging his stick, Daniel and Iannas were attempting to prevent the stick from striking the donkey, Donkey stood firmly in the way refusing to move.

With the cart untied, the trader was now distracted and turned to the cart and Husha. 'Why did you do that?' he shouted, and stepped towards the cart. Husha signalled to Daniel and in the scuffle Daniel searched through the donkey's saddlebag. He pulled out an overcoat and let it drop to the floor, and then a shoulder bag emerged. Daniel turned to Iannas who immediately untied the flap of the shoulder bag while Daniel held it steady with his back to the trader who was now frantically shouting at Husha to tie the cart back onto the donkey. Meanwhile, Daniel instantly recognised the cloth-wrapped book. He grabbed the package, let go of the shoulder bag allowing it to fall to the ground, and turned to Husha with a nod. Iannas and Daniel rushed to join Sai next to Donkey, and Sai led Donkey away from the mayhem. Donkey was happy to move now as Daniel opened Donkey's saddlebag and returned the package from where it had originally been taken. Donkey immediately felt as if he had been lifted and was walking on air. He began to run forward to the cheers of Iannas, Sai and Daniel, but Iannas caught the rope from Sai and slowed him down.

When Daniel had given his signal, Husha immediately let go of the trader's donkey and cart, and as he did so, the trader reacted by raising his hands and stepping away recognising Husha for the first time. Husha responded by shaking his head and turning to his pack donkey that had been patiently waiting and had done well to add to the confusion by virtue of simply being there. Meskalum watched Husha lead the donkey towards the moving caravan and the rear guards still picking up the last of the camp litter making a pile, but unable to burn it.

Everything had happened so fast that Meskalum and his donkey were left standing. In fact, his donkey sat down, and Meskalum now saw his overcoat lying on the ground next to the open shoulder bag. He threw down his stick in exasperation. You thief! he felt like shouting but came out with 'Who cares!' and then added, 'I will still get my money in Harran, if I get to Harran that is.' It took him some time, but he encouraged his donkey back onto its feet, tied the cart onto the donkey's harness, picked up his coat and shoulder bag, only to realise that the caravan was now too far away. He watched Husha in the rear catch up and merge and disappear into the emitting dust of the caravan. He felt an energy ebb away from his body. There was an almost burning desire to leave his donkey, leave his cloth and run after the package containing the book, but it extinguished just as quickly as Meskalum turned and reacquainted himself with his cart full of cloth, which was certainly worth good money. He looked again at the dispersing dust of the caravan and wearily began to lead his donkey and cart towards it, almost surprised at the good fortune that his donkey was moving.

Meskalum was watching the caravan escape further and further away as he slowly trudged towards it when two soldiers approached on horseback from behind him. As the two reached him, one of the soldiers moved in front of the donkey and cart forcing Meskalum to slow down and stop. Meskalum's donkey was not having much luck this morning. Meskalum thought to strike up a conversation, but before he could do so, the second soldier approached him on horseback. 'You are Dazatu of Urfa?' he called as he dismounted.

Meskalum's morning shadow grew longer and darker as it filled his heart, mind and body and projected his hatred to Husha. Was he the cause of this? he loathed.

In the distance on top of a hill from where the river valley could be clearly observed, Sum-Ina's nameless assistant watched as Dazatu was apprehended, and stood in wonderment at the sight of Donkey effortlessly striding away carrying Sai. He savoured that hypnotic vision, and like Rabiat who had captured that moment too, the nameless assistant smiled a knowing smile and turned his horse towards Tuttul.

After Meskalum had served only two nights in a cell in Tuttul waiting for his conviction, the Governor of Tuttul decided to pardon Dazatu along with ninety-nine other inmates in celebration of the occasion of the longest night full moon ceremony. Meskalum decided that providence or something other than luck was watching over him. The soldiers had found money on him, more than he should have had, and the city judge had convicted him for stealing Husha's money, but for some reason Meskalum no longer blamed Husha. It seemed to him that he deserved his conviction even if it had occurred for something he did not do. He did not know why, but he felt calmer than he had ever done before, and this feeling was new to him.

He decided there and then to give up his life of temple deliveries. He would head to the region of Emar, Alep and Ebla. A huge drought was taking hold in that area, and within a few moons, with the failure of the season's crops, the situation would be desperate. As a former pirate, Meskalum knew that where there was adversity and desperate people, there was money to be made. Maybe even legitimate money. He sold his cloth, his donkey and the cart in Tuttul to some keen refugees with money to spend in the Tuttul Refugee Camp, and he, of course, kept all the proceeds, even though the cloth had never belonged to him. He had no intention of working in the region again and left Tuttul a rich man. He sneaked away, crossed the river to the south bank and headed for Emar, the main stop before Alep. Something told him Alep was the place he needed to be.

Waiting for the caravan to Alep to depart, he thought about his life, his life of never enough's: never enough money, never enough people he could trust, never enough friends, a donkey that could never carry or pull enough stock, and never enough of what other people had. Somehow none of that mattered any more. He needed to feel that book again. He needed to be close to it again. He did not know why, but he needed to find out what was written in the book and why it made him feel this way. It was an uncontrollable, unexplainable longing he would never be able to explain or describe it to anyone. Besides, there was no one to try and describe the longing to in his life anyway.

Luck would have it that Meskalum and the book were destined to cross paths once more before the end of his time. Meskalum would touch and feel its magic. He would find himself sitting with a small group of travellers, and he would taste a special tea and a spicy hot date drink under a tree in a distant land and remember the seven days that he carried the book and also his life's deepest regrets.

Donkey had the urge to move faster, but Iannas stopped him, and when Sai sat on Donkey he immediately sensed the need to be careful, slow and gentle. Donkey was so enjoying the lightness and was moving as if on a cushion of air. Even Sai commented on how smoothly Donkey was moving. The two donkeys, led by Husha and Iannas, one carrying Sai, made their way slowly in the rear of the caravan and watched Daniel many paces ahead walking tall and alone.

When they were all together again for the short mid-morning break, they looked at each other and laughed and hugged. They laughed and laughed and laughed and the other caravan travellers laughed with them, glad to join in the laughter, to take their minds away from the increasing heat of the day, the lack of hot drinks and the lack of cooked food.

'There is something about this donkey,' said Husha, more as a fact than a feeling.

'He is not a donkey,' explained Iannas. 'He is one of us. He found the book.'

Daniel was ecstatic. He too had seen the lightness in Donkey's walk. 'The book is magic,' he declared.

Husha shared his quizzical look, but everyone had noticed the 'magic' and knew what Daniel had meant, but did not comment.

Donkey was the happiest of all. He felt a certain power again. He felt invincible.

27 THE DECREE OF THE GOD-KING

Using the fastest royal boats made available to him by the God-King of Urfa and the fastest horses and carriages that the Royal Palace of Urfa could commission, with a troop of soldiers that guided him through the military zones between the empires so as to avoid the cities and the crowds, the former Head Astrologer of Sippar arrived in Urfa within seventeen days instead of the usual thirty-three caravan days.

The new Head Astrologer of Urfa, who was now also the Deputy Prime Minister of Urfa and the most important title of all, Protector of the God-King of Urfa, for God-Kings need protection particularly from other Gods, briefed the God-King and his court of the impending threat; and the former Head Astrologer of Sippar was an expert on threats.

If resources were needed to exterminate an entire tribe, he now had the power to mobilise them.

The God-King expected nothing less if the Magician could not be traced. 'If he is not found by the end of the seventh day after the full moon celebration, my inauguration, you will implement your plan, my Astrologer, Deputy, and Protector, and you will not fail.'

Zaros would wait for this trickster and charlatan, Terah, the High Priest of Ur, hiding like a rat and travelling concealed from all his scouts and spies. What is this High Priest - and he would not be one for much longer - hiding from? What does he know? What could be so important that he has to disappear? He knows where to find the Magician? Maybe he has discovered who it is?

The God-King's new Astrologer, Deputy and Protector made one last attempt to extract the High Priest from his hiding place. He sent out a private message to all the temples between Urfa and Ur anticipating that someone within that circle would ensure that the High Priest received the message. But there were very few days left if the God-King wanted the

Messenger to be brought to him during the longest night full moon solstice celebration.

"To the High Priest of Ur, Terah.
Blessings of the Gods.
We invite you and your family to the inauguration of the new
God-King of Urfa
and lead the prayers for the
Longest Night Full Moon Solstice Celebration Mass.
You or your family's refusal will offend the great God-King and the tribal consequences
will last forever."

Head Astrologer of Urfa, Deputy Prime Minister of Urfa,
Protector of the God-King of Urfa

Zaros took a risk; he had nothing to lose and he knew that the High Priest would understand the meaning of the words.

So it came to pass, as Zaros had intended, that immediately after Sum-Ina received and read the message from Urfa, she broke away from her Tuttul Temple duties and sent the message with one of her courier's to Terah who was even then on the road between Tuttul and Harran.

Terah made himself known at an Urfa checkpoint only one day away from Harran and from there was given a military escort with his family to the Urfa Royal Court.

'He will be here tomorrow!' chimed the new Protector of the God-King of Urfa. 'And tomorrow he and his family will bow and swear allegiance to the new God-King. He will lead us to the Magician.'

Meanwhile Zaros had gathered the generals of the army, the head of the spy network and the head of the new assassination department. With his army of killers, he shared his precious census of the Eperu, the reason for his elevated high position.

'What a marvellous plan,' Zaros praised himself, 'to invite all the nobles, elders and tribal chiefs of the Eperu to the inauguration where they may be watched, followed and then if necessary eliminated in one strike. What an inspirational idea,' he commended himself. He bathed in his new power. If the High Priest did not lead them to the magician, he would exterminate all the Eperu tribal elders and then the entire tribe.

Zaros would make sure that the new God-King of Urfa would come to be known as the most powerful - even more than any other magician, monarch or god from the heavens.

The new God-King celebrated the news of Terah the High Priest of Ur's imminent arrival with a new decree. 'The bonfire in Urfa is to be twice as large as the original decree,' he commanded, for he was not satisfied and would never be so. The original decree to make the world's largest bonfire was not good enough. Now he decreed that every piece of wood, every branch, every tree should be harvested, collected, including furniture, doors, windows, cups, every piece of wood from the walls and roofs of homes from all the lands of Urfa. This fire would surpass all bonfires in the past and the future and be a message to the world that he was the greatest God-King – indeed, he yearned to show his subjects that he was a God as well as a King. And the people of Urfa obeyed. They worshipped him and began to bring all they could find to Urfa to add to the pyre, which would not be lit until all the last pieces of wood from the land of Urfa had been gathered.

28 THE GREATEST BONFIRE IN THE WORLD

'The line of the ten kings that reigned before the flood and taught the world the "Laws of Goodness" and watched over humankind, and who became known as the Watchers, ended with the tenth king, so Xisuthros was the last; there was no eleventh,' Iannas began. It was the last evening before Harran and Iannas recalled a story which had taken many evenings to assemble, with the fragments of the memories of the evening many years ago when his father, the one and only time as far as he knew, told a story of the Watchers. He spoke confidently the parts of the story he could remember and equally confidently the parts he filled with his own creation to good effect.

'Each king had ten protectors called the Warriors of Peace. However, having served and protected the original ten kings or Watchers, the protectors erroneously became known as the Watchers themselves after the tenth king passed away, for it was thought that they now watched, waited for and protected the kings or messengers who would come from the heavens to continue the work of the first ten kings, the greatest of all kings.

'The Protectors were never kings, had no desire to be, and never wished to be known as the Watchers. They remained together, as a group, a society, as the Protectors of the Seal - as that was their real name - and some who knew very little or were suspicious of them even described them as a cult or a sect. As time passed, they each dispersed to lead their own lives. They were free to travel and settle in any land they chose to but with a covenant that they would meet once every ten years. Some remained in the service of a king, if he was deemed just, and others led a more simple life. Some travelled afar while others stayed in the heart of Mesopotamia. The Society of the Protectors of the Seal survived for centuries, and there continued to be ten in number and each held one golden seal in memory of a secret tomb. And ten there has always been and will continue to be until, it is foretold, the seals will be lost, one by one and the Watchers will vanish one by one, and the Protectors will become a memory, a legend and a myth, just a strange story told by an old man to a young traveller who would retell the story to a small group of adventurers on the trail to Harran.'

Iannas was not too surprised the listeners did not appreciate his little embellishment at the end.

'The Watchers were not immortal but lived long lives just like the first ten kings, as they were from the same tribe as the first tribe ascribed with long life. Before a Watcher died, he or she was required to pass their knowledge, the Golden Seal and the Secret Oath they had protected all their lives, to their first born, a child who would consent freely to accepting a new life and responsibility as a Protector and be prepared from a young age.

'There are those that tell stories, there are others that believe them, and, of course, there are many who would do both. From the ones that believe, many say that one seal is already lost, the chain of the ten Protectors is already broken and one of the lines of Watchers is already no more. But since this story was first told, who is to say how many more seals have been lost and if any Watchers or Protectors remain at all?'

'That is all we have time for tonight. I will tell you more in Harran!' Iannas told the disappointed listeners. 'Time for bed,' he commanded, excited about reaching Harran the next day.

'And tomorrow,' Daniel reminded them, 'there is no contact to look for. We should be able to relax for a change.'

'Iannas,' Husha asked inquisitively, 'I have been remembering the Watchers too.'

'Did you hear about them in Susa?' Iannas assumed.

'In Egypt,' Husha corrected, 'when I was studying in Memphis. You remember I mentioned a small fragment of a tablet that inspired me to specialise in Astrology and the Language of the Universe?'

Iannas nodded.

'There were a number of tablets in Memphis brought back as plunder from raids by the army and some bought from traders. One of them recorded the story of a Queen of Harran called Zugalum. That is where I first came across the term Watchers. Maybe I can tell the story tomorrow and we can compare notes,' Husha offered.

Iannas agreed. 'Does that mean you are one of the believers, Husha?' Iannas suggested almost mockingly.

Husha laughed, 'Belief? I do not know what to believe any more!' he admitted.

'Have you checked...?' Husha began asking Daniel, wanting to be sure. He did not need to say any more.

'While we were unloading.' Daniel confirmed. 'Nothing lost is lost forever!' He echoed words from Sharuppak and smiled. Sai, at least, still remembered the Instructions.

'It is almost as if Rabiat knew something,' Sai commented already lying on her night bed.

Soon they all slept in anticipation of what would be found in Harran.

It was Enaqim's younger brother who waited to meet Daniel at the service station just outside the gates of Harran. Ibi-Faru had been waiting impatiently since the morning when he had received the message from Sum-Ina. He did not wish to be there but would comply only in memory of his brother, for he had been at the request of the Watchers ever since his brother had passed away. He already had his own life and did not need the weight of having to fill his brother's sandals to add to the challenges of his own life as a struggling artist. There were many jobs for artists, but for someone who specialised in surreal and fantasy, it was either painting tombs in readiness for dead people or frescos in a nobleman's home. He had never been inspired to paint images in temples or on gates or even statues. He wanted to create new art; small paintings of beauty on wood or leather just to place in a simple home, mobile frescos, and illustrations on the new papyrus books and even paintings depicting the past and the future. Not in my lifetime, he was thinking, and this is why he had arrived early. To sit at the station bar, sip his favourite warming infusion of Jasmine and Ginger, engage his creative ideas and allow them to flow. But the only thing he could see flowing today were the caravans arriving from different directions, and the one heading towards him from the south was the one he knew he had been waiting for.

It was approaching sunset, and the extra pace set by the lead teams had come to fruition and everyone in the caravan praised the leader for his good planning and management. They were delighted to arrive and even more thrilled at not having to spend another night under the stars. The whole caravan was very enthusiastic to find the nearest hot meal and hot drink. The bars and inns at and near the station had been experiencing exceptional business, thanks to the blessings of the God-King of Urfa. Most of the bar and inn keepers also ascribed their good fortune to their own King of Harran for sending one hundred cartloads of wood as a gift on behalf of the people of Harran for the Urfa bonfire.

'You are Daniel of Susa?' Although Enaqim's brother recognised Daniel from the description sent by Sum-Ina, he still asked nervously and added, 'Sum-Ina sent me with a message.'

Daniel appreciated being met at the station and quickly introduced his friends. Enaqim's brother, however, was not one for polite conversation or any social occasion; he liked to keep himself, and his life private. He was sent to deliver a message, and that was all he wished to do. Daniel took the initiative and signalling for everyone to follow him walked away from the service station towards a stream of running water noisily making its way to quench the thirst of the walled city. Daniel had already learned from Puvurum to take advantage of the sound of running water to distance unwanted ears.

'I am the brother of Enaqim.' He did not feel the need to use his name. 'He would have met you himself had he not passed into the next world. I am temporarily dealing with his matters. Alizer is still two days behind you, but tomorrow he will bypass Harran and travel directly to Urfa under military guard on a more direct route. The plan is changed. You are not required to stay in Harran. Sum-Ina asked me to give this to you.' A pouch of money was handed over as usual to Daniel. Enaqim's brother understood from Daniel's expression that he was confused.

'Military guard?' is all Daniel came out with.

'The King of Urfa issued a decree commanding that Terah and his family immediately present themselves to his court and bow and pledge allegiance to the King, I mean God-King of Urfa. Terah will by now have received the command and has been advised that he must attend the court as instructed, and I understand, he has no option for there may be serious consequences to many innocent people if he does not. A local battalion of soldiers is on its way to meet them and escort them to Urfa. Your task is to leave tomorrow morning for Urfa. It is usually a day and half by caravan, but Sum-Ina asks that you take a private guide and reach Urfa tomorrow evening. With a strong donkey and a good guide, you will be fine.'

Daniel, Iannas, Husha, and Sai were already anxious and concerned by the news, but Enaqim's brother did not stop, keen to finish delivering his message.

'When you arrive in Urfa tomorrow night, leave a small set of supplies, enough for one person for three days, in a cave at the foot of the cliff below the temple. You may stay in Urfa tomorrow night but not beyond. The following morning make your way to a hill they call Gobekli Tepe and wait for word from Alizer.'

'Have we failed? What did we do wrong? We have let Alizer down?' Daniel was already confused and distressed.

'This is all the information I have. From what I understand, you have fulfilled your part. This is the only way for the safety of all concerned.' Enaqim's brother said something that lodged with Husha's fast-moving thoughts. Husha remembered a passing comment by his uncle in Terqa about reasons why Terah had chosen to head north in the path of the God-King of Urfa.

'Is there more?' Husha asked. 'What do we do after Gobekli Tepe?'

'As I said, wait for Alizer. That is all I know,' Enaqim's brother concluded.

'No, no, no,' Daniel insisted, 'this is not right. Alizer is meant to meet us in Harran.'

'This means we stay together for longer.' Iannas pointed out the positive in an attempt to take away some of the anxiety, but his words had little effect.

'What about Terah and the King in Urfa? Is there anything to be done?' Husha pressed.

'I have no further news other what I have told you. I should not be here, but there is no one else to take my brother's place, and I am not privy to the full details, so I cannot help you anymore.' Enaqim's brother turned, waved, stepped away towards the main Gate of Harran, and headed back to his home on the slopes of the hill overlooking the city temple complex.

'This is all different to Alizer's instructions,' Iannas repeated the obvious sharing Daniel's pensiveness and insecurity but remaining calm. 'I thought we were trying to keep Terah away from this King and everyone else!' he exclaimed. 'Now the family is heading into the hands of the people who wish them harm!' Iannas could not help but express his shared anguish.

Husha spoke calmly and slowly. His words changed the mood. 'It seems that Terah and his family are destined to face the final steps of this journey alone. This is their destiny and it always was, Daniel,' Husha was reading the signs. 'This journey, your journey, Daniel, was never about Alizer or Terah.' Was Husha seeing things clearly all of a sudden? Even he was not sure.

Daniel was puzzled, but Iannas quickly gathered what Husha had implied, 'Alizer has been protecting you, Daniel. By travelling three days behind us, they have always made themselves the target, the distraction.'

Sai could see too. 'There is another purpose here, you have been carrying it, Daniel. A greater purpose. Even greater than Terah and his family.'

While Husha waited for Daniel to respond, he could not help but dive into his thoughts and spoke so the others could hear, 'And secrecy will now be even more critical for our safety as we move to Urfa. Our lives will depend on it.' Husha had one more thought. The future is in the hands of a fifteen-year-old! Husha did well to keep this last thought to himself. Sai looked at Husha oddly, as if she had heard him in her mind.

'The book is with me, with us,' Daniel was processing and finally acknowledged and grasped what had been said. 'The book is not with Alizer. Sum-Ina and the others are watching out for the family. We have our role and must now do our part.' Daniel spoke wisely and confidently. Husha was very impressed but did not say so.

Iannas organised the group quickly as the shadows had already disappeared. 'Daniel and Sai, you organise the caravan for the morning and also a personal guide to help us reach Urfa by sundown. Choose a good donkey for the supplies, Sai. Husha, you and I will buy some fresh supplies from the station market to get us through tomorrow. We will probably not need much but it is best to be safe. Let's all meet at the caravan stand.'

If Harran was not yet ready for Terah and the family, Harran was not yet ready for Daniel, Iannas, Husha, or Sai, and if there were another force keeping Daniel from entering Harran, only the storytellers of the future would ever claim to know.

They met as planned and impatiently traced their way back a short distance in the growing darkness along the route they had arrived to a rest house, an inn they had passed while still travelling with the caravan; a favourite of Iannas and Daniel's fathers. They entered through an open gateway into a walled square courtyard which, after such a long day's travel, could only be described as welcoming and enchanting with its large central fire and outdoor sitting areas scattered around the central beacon and nested with their own single small warming fires. Opposite the gate stood a stone building structure lit with evenly spaced torches along the top of the facing wall, illuminating the three surprising stone beehive domes typical of Harran. The owners welcomed them even more warmly after Daniel and Iannas introduced themselves, for their fathers were two of their regular customers. Donkey was quickly unloaded and settled while Sai found a place for them all to rest in the courtyard where a lady was preparing a hot infusion for the new arrivals to taste.

The extra donkey, guide and guard had been booked from the caravan leader, and they would leave with the caravan at dawn. Their guide would set a faster pace and allow for shorter breaks to ensure they arrived in Urfa by the end of the day.

'The road is flat and...' the guide had hesitated when he saw Sai with child, 'you all look young and strong enough. The lady will travel by donkey, I assume. We will enter the city as the sun goes down, but that will be through the outskirts of the city itself so it will be safe and as a precaution, we have a guard.'

Planning their departure before even arriving at the city gate was not the way they had expected to experience Harran.

'So it seems Sai and I will have to delay our visit to Harran,' Husha looked at Sai as they settled with their hot drinks and Husha watched Sai add a little red chilli powder to her sweet infusion. He knew Sai was disappointed after everything they had heard about Harran. He was concerned about her. She needed to stop and rest.

'Let's have a hot meal, or two, and rest.' Husha made the two hot meals sound enticing. 'You are eating for two, Sai!' he tried to justify himself keeping the mood as positive as possible.

The hot meal of soup, stew, grilled meats, and fresh baked bread was accompanied with an interrogation by one of the charming ladies of the house. Whilst serving dinner, she was persistent in enquiring about Husha and insisting on learning if he would consider an educated lady from Harran as a wife or, if he was married, as a second wife. While her attentions were particularly entertaining for Daniel, Iannas, and Sai, Husha seemed more in a hurry to finish the meal than the others.

To accompany the food and distract from the unwanted attentions of the lady of the inn, Iannas suggested to Husha that he tell the story of Zugalum, Queen of Harran. Husha was delighted to be reminded and quickly launched into the story, successfully avoiding any further overtures.

'Harran was nothing more than an outpost of Ur when it was founded as a small settlement, some say under the guidance of astrologers and priests from Ur who calculated the exact location of where Harran should be. There is even talk of a mysterious tablet, supposedly an astronomical calculation that binds the two cities as twin centres of the Sin God. Some say that the tablet even identifies a third centre, but I know nothing more of this.

'Harran and Ur, two cities linked forever, buildings and temples constructed at the same time and dedicated together. The Temple in Harran is the most important place of celebration of the God Sin in the whole world and positioned exactly where the astrologers and priests calculated that it should be.

'At the time of my story, Harran was already growing and becoming increasingly independent and wealthy by virtue of its trade with Persia, India, the lands to the east, Damascus, and the lands to the west, including Minoa. Zugalum, Princess and daughter of the King of Ebla, Irkab Damu, was visiting Urfa, Armani, Tuttul, and Harran as part of a diplomatic and trade mission. She was eighteen years of age they say, not yet wedded, and since the age of fourteen her mother and father had arranged for their children to accompany the official delegations to learn the art of politics, trade, and diplomacy.

'Zugalum had no intention of being a diplomatic bride like her older sister who had married the King of Elam. Zugalum was enjoying her life, learning to be independent, just like her brother, and her latest fascination was ancient tombs, an activity that occupied much of her time with her teachers at the temple where she studied and which held a collection of eighty ancient tablets in its museum and library.

'She and her assistant Sin-Nada secured and catalogued an ancient Royal Tomb in Ebla that had been raided many centuries earlier, so all that was left were the wall paintings and fragments of tablets which, when restored, described the location of three other Royal tombs. Zugalum and Sin-Nada followed the clues only to find the locations bogus, designed to mislead future tomb robbers. Zugalum and Sin-Nada restored one more tablet, coded and written in an ancient language, Eblaite, which Zugalum had learned to read as part of her studies. The code, coupled with the wall paintings in one part of the tomb, illustrated the journey of an ancient king two thousand years earlier, called Enmenduranki, also referred to as the Watcher. The writings also briefly mentioned an immortal language of God and a journey that Enmenduranki took to the heavens to walk with God.

'Of course, tombs are always filled with so many myths and legends of the Ancients, but new myths always captured Zugalum's interest. As she was translating and recording the story of Enmenduranki she found a reference to a fourth tomb. Even though the other three references to tombs had turned out false, for some reason she was convinced this one was genuine, and located in or around Harran.

'The story of the fourth tomb read as a fantasy, and it was precisely the fantasy that caught Zugalum's attention. The tomb, she translated, belonged to Anunnaki, one of "those who from Heavens to Earth came". Zugalum could only assume that the reference meant a heavenly being. But what would the tomb of a being such as this be doing here on Earth?

'Zugalum became intrigued and remained so for the rest of her life. She seemed to enjoy the fantasy of the search. She wanted to visit the archives of Harran, but she knew, as a Princess of Ebla, that it would be almost impossible, so she jumped at the chance of joining a delegation to Harran, led by the Governor of Ebla himself, to negotiate trade and tax agreements.

'Of course, the Governor of Harran, not much older than the Princess, became totally infatuated by this educated and progressive young lady and opened the doors of the Harran temples, museums and libraries to Zugalum and even invited her and her entourage to remain in Harran as his guests after the diplomatic visits were completed to study for as long as she liked. With her father's permission, Zugalum accepted and naturally, after all the time they spent together, the Governor of Harran and Zugalum grew very fond of each other, as her father had secretly hoped. When he asked for her hand, and much to the surprise of all her family, she accepted, and her father was, of course, delighted.

In time, Zugalum became the Lady of Harran and was credited to have sowed the early seeds that transformed the town into a liberal, tolerant and free society as it is now. When Harran severed links with Ur, it was not the Governor but Zugalum, probably because of her royal blood, who declared Harran an independent, neutral state and it was she who became Queen of Harran. She negotiated treaties with all the neighbouring city-states which, in return for generous trade and tax concessions and long-standing peace treaties, agreed to recognise Harran as a free, independent and neutral city on condition that Harran never interfered or intervened in their politics. The reign of Zugalum was considered the greatest and wisest of the time. As part of her peace agreements, she created joint archaeological societies that brought together the greatest field historians of the time and she had a reason, a very special task.

'Zugalum had never forgotten about the Tomb of the Heavenly Being and sent out many teams of archaeologists to different locations in and around Harran. Archaeologists even dug around the caves of Sogmator after Zugalum wrongly translated one part of the puzzle. Zugalum's reign as Queen ended when she died without a record of her having made any significant archaeological discovery. This is strange considering she had so many archaeological teams working for her and probably explored so many ancient sites,' Husha paused. 'At least,' he added, 'there is no record of any finding. But some say, if she had found the tomb containing a being from Heaven, no doubt she would have kept it a secret, never revealed it to anyone, and maybe even hidden it so it would never be found again.'

Iannas and Sai clapped at the story. 'Great story,' Sai approved. 'A tomb of an angel. It is a very romantic idea but there cannot be any such thing,' she announced.

'I did not say angel. Could be anything,' Husha played with his audience. 'What else comes from Heaven?'

Iannas was less taken by the romanticism. 'It could just be a rock that has fallen from the sky! That is also a heavenly being!'

'It could be a Jhinn!' suggested Daniel.

'And why not?' Iannas changed his mind or just tried to argue and see how far he would get. 'Maybe this Queen Zugalum saw something, a clue, something no one else could see, like Husha and his father with the stars and the Messenger. No one would search for something if it did not exist, would they?'

'Everyone is always searching for something,' Husha commented, 'I wonder what we will be searching for once our task is completed.'

As soon as Husha had finished his last words, he noticed that Daniel was already submerging himself in worry over Terah and the family. Iannas attempted to rescue Daniel, if only for a short while. Everyone was feeling the anxiety.

'Daniel,' Iannas proceeded, 'tell us about your first time in Harran. Your father purchased your first Egyptian donkey from here if I remember.'

The request had the desired effect, and Daniel smiled as if remembering a different time. It did not take him too long to recollect his first experience of Harran and begin sharing his memories. He knew what Iannas was trying to do and welcomed the diversion; and it felt good to remember his father again.

'My first journey to Harran was with Papa and the stock he carried was particularly unusual; animal skins the like neither of us had ever seen before. The skins were from India and China and purchased from a weary traveller from a place he called Mongolia whom we met on the way to Harran. By the time my father met him in Nineveh, the trader was desperate for anyone to purchase his load and provide him with much needed funds. He told us he had spent all his reserves after barely escaping with his life; first, from particularly harsh snow blizzards in the northern Indian mountain passes, and then absconding from a group of bandits in Afghanistan who had taken all his supplies and stock after discarding the skins considering them worthless. He later retrieved the skins and was appreciative of the offer that Papa made, and accepted it readily. Papa was always generous that way.

'We displayed the skins with our other wares from Susa in Harran's main market, and that is where I noticed this Egyptian trader, sipping his drink as he sat in the stall next door, looking at the skins. I knew from his eyes he was interested, so I alerted Papa.'

'His name was Taros, the Egyptian. He had just sold his complete stock of best Egyptian stone-mason tools and the highest quality Egyptian papyrus, and had already spent most of his proceeds on a range of tablets from the tablet sellers and libraries to sell to his exclusive noble clientele in Egypt. He told us that the current trend or fashion in Egypt was the possession of foreign artefacts.

'Taros also told us that he had only just discovered the skins by chance, and the guilty party was the new hot drink and beer room just next to the spot where the skins were being displayed. He could not afford the skins having already spent most of his money. But he told me afterwards that he knew he had to have the skins, they would be the talk of the town in Memphis and make him considerably famous, as well as, he hoped, very rich.

'Taros had brought with him three donkey loads of goods from Memphis to Harran. He ordered a boiled date drink with cinnamon, his favourite, to replace the tea, having decided it was not to his taste, and calculated that he only needed two donkeys to return to Egypt with his goods even if he bought the skins. Maybe he could trade one donkey, he pondered. Taros gently caught the eye of one of the skins knowing that he would be noticed. He knew the art of negotiation but, of course, so did Papa. Taros commenced the theatre of trade by feigning a lack of interest, and then interest for just one lesser item as he introduced himself and, as we exchanged pleasantries, Taros added more skins to the deal so by the end of the afternoon Taros had closed the transaction with a combination of local currency and one donkey. As a pack animal, Papa and I knew the donkey was worth more than all the skins together in Susa, but neither Taros nor we were aware that this particular breed of Egyptian donkey was very rare, and would command an even higher price in the province of Susa.

'When the deal was done, and it took most of the afternoon for eventually he bought all the skins, I even asked Taros if I could see one of his Egyptian parchments, and he was so proud to show us. I was amazed and awed by the patterns and pictures, the language of the Egyptians. "How many different languages, religions and customs were in this world," I remarked, and how wonderful to discover and meet people like Taros from such distant lands in this city. The whole world all in one place. It made me love my time in Harran all the more.

'I made sure the donkey received an attention-packed and unreasonably pampered journey back to Susa. Papa said that it was certainly one of the most lucrative journeys he had ever undertaken after he sold the donkey having obtained five times the value we bartered in Harran. Papa put it down to my presence as his amulet. The next time Papa made the journey to Harran again, this time with Uncle Azhar, Papa returned with another Egyptian donkey, the same breed as the first and in healthier condition and better attitude from a gentleman called Alizer!' Daniel paused. 'This donkey had been bred in Damascus, and Alizer taught Papa how to breed the donkey and look after the young.'

'I remember!' Husha picked up the story. 'So back in Susa it was the result of the union between this second donkey and the male donkey belonging to the Egyptian Sinuhe, a match that I arranged that created the two heavily indulged donkeys.'

'Yes,' Iannas added excitedly much to Sai's amusement. 'Both a malt coloured brown, and whereas one had four white feet and a white tip on the tail, the other had three white feet, a completely brown tail and a white-tipped ear.'

'And I can see which one caught your affections, Iannas and Daniel. I love his three white feet and white-tipped ear,' Sai caught herself in the round.

While the stories of the evening had the desired effect in settling everyone to the realities of the moment, Daniel could not help but return everyone's mind to Terah. 'What will happen to Uncle Azhar and his family in Urfa?'

Sai reconciled, for there was no answer. 'Let us complete our task in Urfa and move on as quickly as possible. Like Husha, I have a bad feeling about the bonfire and the new God-King. Must we spend the night there?'

And Donkey did not want to take the book to Urfa, nor did he want to approach the bonfire. Donkey had read Sai and Husha's thoughts. He too wanted to stay in Harran.

29 HARRAN TO URFA

Day 59, 5.2 Beru.

Those that would consider a monarch's popularity to be a measure of a king or queen's greatness would also measure the greatness of the God-King of Urfa by the size of the bonfire to be lit at the inauguration of the longest night full moon solstice ceremony. The greatness of the bonfire would be determined by the loyalty of the citizens, and the loyalty of the citizens would be weighed by the quantity of firewood each individual collected and added as their sacrifice to the bonfire. The checkpoints on every road and every entrance to Urfa ensured that every item of wood carried by citizens and visitors was collected and deposited on the growing bonfire.

Husha, Sai, Iannas, and Daniel watched as the soldiers seized all their wooden plates, wooden spoons, and wooden goblets as a contribution to the bonfire. Daniel remembered he still carried the piece of wood the thief had replaced with the book; he rummaged through his saddlebag and gladly donated that too.

But Husha was not glad as they repacked their supplies. 'This is not a bonfire; it is a cemetery for all that is nature, for everything that signifies life. There is something very wrong in this.' He spoke quietly so only they would hear his comments, but Donkey felt them too and for the first time in the entire journey Donkey felt as if he was walking into a darkness, a place where fate would be decided.

Both the guide and guard who had led them to Urfa were surprised how well Donkey travelled, and Donkey, in turn, knew to encourage and made sure the hired pack donkey kept up with his pace. Having forged ahead at their own pace, fed by their already well-developed stamina and fitness, and without being detained by the routine motions of the caravan, none was too surprised at covering the distance in the light of the day. Sai sat in comfort on Donkey and travelled as a queen encouraging her subjects with various regal phrases.

'Do keep up, citizens. We do not have all day!' and 'I do not know why you need rest, Iannas. If it weren't for all your resting, we would be there by now!' and also 'Please stop your wallowing, Daniel, and pick up your feet.' She kept everyone's spirits high with her jesting, and thank goodness none were offended by her remarks.

With hardly any supplies to carry and all wooden utensils and items commandeered by the God-King of Urfa, the extra donkey had been a luxury in Sai's opinion.

'Donkey could have carried both the supplies and me, you know?' Donkey agreed with Sai. The others were not too sure.

She and Donkey arrived in Urfa, at the central caravanserai, as fresh as they had been at breakfast, keen and ready to complete their task in Urfa and move on. But the others had not fared as well, and Iannas, Husha, and Daniel's tiredness was keen to rest for the night.

Husha felt a familiarity and remarked that the same architects must have designed the caravanserais in Urfa and the one in Susa, for both were so remarkably alike.

Remnants of daylight still in the sky were quickly disappearing into the night, and the town was making its final preparations for the next day that would herald as the greatest day, marking the commencement of the annual seven-day celebration. This year, however, there was a different anticipation; the night of the Solstice Ceremony would not only be marked by the full moon but also as the day the God-King of Urfa was born.

Daniel and Husha quickly purchased the supplies from the market surrounding the caravanserai while Iannas and Sai used this time to learn the route to Gobekli Tepe. They quickly discovered there was no caravan to Gobekli Tepe, being no more than a morning's walk from the centre of Urfa. Iannas learned the route to the Tepe and also asked about the caves in Urfa, particularly the ones in the valley.

Husha and Daniel returned with supplies for themselves for two to three days, not knowing what to expect in Gobekli Tepe, and the rest to leave in the cave as instructed: fruit, dried foods, nuts, olives, and roasted corn, foods that would last, for they had assumed the food in the cave would simply be a store.

'Sounds like emergency supplies for Alizer or one of your friends, Daniel, for I cannot see any other purpose,' suggested Husha.

Sai insisted on walking, and Donkey carried the supplies as they walked the short distance through the market and then uphill towards the edge of the valley.

'We do not need another donkey tomorrow,' Sai insisted. 'I will walk some of the way, and Donkey can carry me when I am tired. Believe me,

Donkey will be fine,' she added, sensing the others would express their reservations.

It was on the uphill that Daniel's attention was caught by a torch illuminating a painted sign on the side of a wall, pointing to a villa letting rooms for the night. Daniel asked everyone to wait while he followed the torches to a well-lit building just off the main road, ran inside, and very quickly reappeared after securing the most comfortable rooms the lady owner had available. Although no one questioned this impulsive decision, Daniel insisted on justifying himself by explaining they deserved the comfort after the long journey from Harran, but also informed Sai that the villa only accommodated men and since the journey had not tired her, she would be sleeping in the stable next door with Donkey. The owner would give her bedding if she needed it.

Sai understood immediately Daniel's attempt to return some of her jesting that she had forced on them during the day. She allowed him the pleasure and smiled without comment welcoming the affection and warmth in his teasing.

As they continued walking, the valley began to appear and open in front of them, their eyes accustomed to the torch and moonlit surroundings. But it was the distant temple in the fortress, perched on the cliff facing them, lit by what seemed like a thousand oil torches along the entire wall of the fortress and lighting up every pillar of the temple, that would dwarf even a moon's splendour. It was a beacon in itself to mark the preparations for the celebrations to come. In the night light they approached the lip of the valley and for the first time acknowledged the full height of the facing cliff that dominated and held the illuminated crown of the fortress and temple above.

It was not the glory of the pinnacle on the cliff that held their attention, for they were lost for words as their eyes grew accustomed and recognised the construction of the most massive bonfire they, and possibly the world, had ever seen, and with all the activity surrounding it, it was not yet finished; it was still growing. The sea of wood already hid the entire width of the valley and more than half its depth, and the wooden waves lapped the cliffs on either side.

They were imperceptible as they joined the myriad of devoted servants carrying offerings to their new idol.

When they reached the valley floor and looked up at the solid coral wall of wood in the star and torchlight, it was as if a sea had parted leaving the coral behind for everyone to stare. And it was the life in the wooden coral they saw as each one spotted a strange or bizarre creature. Sai pointed to a whole tree with roots and branches and wilting leaves lying on its side but almost suspended in mid air half-way up and in the very centre of the wall, Daniel pointed to a door that had fallen as if it would open and lead into a room, except that it was at a height at least as tall as the wall in Babylon. Iannas pointed to a lone empty chair positioned as if it were ready to welcome a weary guest. An entire wooden roof lay over it, providing protection from the massive tree above waiting to crush the one who sits.

'The cave is not far from here,' Daniel said, interrupting the vision as he pointed to the base of the cliff face opposite. They sliced their way through the constant stream of devotees heading to the pyre. Approaching the foot of the cliff face almost directly below the temple, they searched until Iannas discovered the cave behind some boulders with a narrow entrance into what appeared to be a small grotto. Daniel went to the entrance and had to take his time to adjust to the lack of light, not daring to light a torch, for any fire was forbidden at this time, except for the oil torches being used to light the fortress and the temple, which was providing ample radiance. He took advantage of the light, but it was too dark to explore any more than one step into the cave. In the cold silence, Daniel could hear what seemed like an underground stream running through the cave. The ground at the entrance was dry and hidden from view by the boulder so no one in the valley paid any attention to them as they formed a chain for the supplies. Daniel placed the last bundle of supplies on the ground at the entrance and paused. He had not finished. He removed some wet clay and in the dim light wrote four names, Daniel, Iannas, Sai, and Husha, and on the reverse made his mark for Alizer, placing it on the top of the stack of supplies. Daniel was pensive as he left, and Iannas was the first to reach over and embrace his friend.

'What we have been asked, we have done, Daniel. Now we pray for the safety of Terah and the family.'

'It is well done to all of us!' replied Daniel as he reached out to Husha and to Sai with silent gratitude of the most humble kind.

The former slave, the book keeper, the dreamer, and the mother-to-be were of no consequence. Invisible in their humbleness and normality, yet they were nothing less than the greatest force, the humility of humanity.

They turned, their load lightened, and marvelled at the solid, wooden, mosaic mountain under the brightening moonlight and the shadows of the torchlight cast from the fortress and the temple. Daniel's voice asked the question again, 'Why are we leaving food in this cave?'

'Now that I have seen it, it is strange,' agreed Husha. 'This does not make sense. It looks like a hiding place.'

'It looks to be for one of Sum-Ina's friends,' suggested Iannas. 'But how would they keep an eye from here?'

'It is nothing more than emergency rations for Alizer in case needed,' Husha returned to his original suggestion.

'We have been on the road two moons.' said Sai. 'The journey is close to an end, and the time has passed too quickly. Husha began the journey as a slave and has arrived a free man. I was lost in Ur, alone, and I arrive here with three friends, brothers, and a new family for a new child I carry. You have carried the book all this way, Daniel. There is always a plan, and you have done as you were asked. Let us rest now and allow events to unfold.' Sai watched the activity on the wooden mountain and around her as they retraced their steps through the continuous feeds of devotees with their offerings. She was relieved to see the path ahead that rose out of the valley and would lead to tonight's beds. 'Sum-Ina is right. Husha, you were right. This is no place for us. This is not a bonfire. It is much more. Let us reach Gobekli Tepe in the morning. It is not too far away and make a distance between this madness and us'.

Husha suddenly and unexpectedly stopped to help an elderly lady worshipper pick up a load of wood that she had dropped onto the ground. Stopping among the masses of loyal citizens still bringing more wood, even a small handful in some cases and cartloads in others, there was nothing else to do but be lost amongst the frenzy of faith. Husha asked the lady why they kept coming when the bonfire was already the biggest in the world.

'Our King will become a God tomorrow. He has demanded it, and he will bless each one of us. The fire has to be the greatest that the world has ever seen. He is our God and King, and his blessing will bring us, our city, and our lands much fortune.' In the face of such zeal there was no response.

The only activity of interest to the people of the city was this bonfire, and through it to see the new God-King content, for only in his pleasure would the citizens find their blessings. In the fervour, the citizens from the lands of Urfa would now surge through the night. Almost half the population of the land of Urfa would arrive tomorrow in the hope of witnessing a King become a God, and they would bring with them additional, huge cartloads of wood from the furthest lands of Urfa. No one would expect the speed at which the bonfire was about to grow. The cave with the supplies would be completely immersed in the bonfire by the end of the next day thanks to each visiting king's gift of one hundred carts crammed with wood, and there were many kings. The soldiers were still arriving from village to village collections, house to house searches removing every item of wood, every tree, every shrub wherever it was found. The bonfire would almost double in size within the span of one night and one day.

Having settled Donkey, Husha wanted to return to the familiar caravanserai and invited the others to join him. It was a good suggestion even though they would only be served cold food and drinks, but it was enough to be in the company of one's friends where Iannas would one day stand on a chair and shout a different name to find almost all the men turning and looking at him before bursting into laughter.

Donkey settled in his stable, distressed by the bonfire and their presence in Urfa. He sensed a cold suffering in Urfa, and he would not sleep until they put distance between them and the cruel mischief, a new speck of evil, being plotted. He would have preferred to leave this very night.

30 POTBELLY HILL

Day 60, 2.4 Beru.

After a hearty but cold breakfast in the villa courtyard with the fresh and waking alarm of the fountain, Daniel, Iannas, Husha, Sai, and Donkey made their own way northeast towards Gobekli Tepe, and for the first time since they had travelled together, they were immersed in an expanse of freedom, and with every step away from Urfa, floated in liberation.

'Some sort of site for ancient temples,' Iannas was explaining, 'far more ancient than anyone could imagine or even remember is what I kept hearing from those we asked. One man made me laugh; he believed that some ancient foreign beings from the stars came to our world and built a temple of life and worshipped there.'

'He was only playing with us,' Sai laughed.

'No, it's true,' Iannas tried to build the drama despite Sai's rebuff. 'He believed it. Then another Urfa trader told us that the hill has the shape of a belly, and is called Potbelly hill because there is an ancient being trapped inside it, waiting for the moment to be born again! I am telling you, these stories are wonderful. I could make up loads of tales and entertain people with what we heard.' Iannas calmed a little from his excitement. 'Anyway,' he concluded, 'most people agree that the place contains ancient mysteries, and some said it contained ancient gods that have now been forgotten.'

Daniel found the statement curious. 'I cannot see how gods can be forgotten and lost,' he remarked.

Iannas finished off his report, saying, 'There is a small village near the Tepe where we can look for lodgings while we wait for Alizer. It seems we can see Urfa from the Tepe, so we should have a good view of the bonfire tonight.'

The talk of forgotten gods reminded Daniel that it had been exactly two moons since he was in the temple in Susa receiving the blessings of the Sin God. He remembered the image of the Priest of Susa with her moon mask, standing in her beautiful flowing white dress, pointing to the full moon in the sky, and smiled.

'What are you thinking about, Daniel?' Sai captured Daniel's smile and was being inquisitive as usual.

'Sum-Ina,' he teased with his normal cheeky smile and walked ahead knowing that he would not be caught, for Donkey had no intention of walking too fast with Sai resting on his back, and Sai would not be able to inquisition him any more.

They had walked away from Urfa without a heavy heart or any trimmings of regret. The stifling, unbearable, king-obsessed, sanctified, divine mood of Urfa, and its eerie bonfire were lifted and scattered into fading fragments. As they stepped further away, the joy of walking on this fresh cool morning was rekindled, but this time without a caravan, guide, or guard. The moment revealed a freedom they had not realised had been missed so much. They were glad to be away from Urfa, and now they would wait for Alizer's instructions, always there when and if they were needed.

Too soon - for they wanted the freedom of the trail to continue - they arrived at the small village with Gobekli Tepe only a few hundred paces further uphill. At the village, they enquired what lodging could be found. Daniel immediately thought the village was a safe distance and very separate from Urfa and must have been the reason why Alizer had chosen the Tepe.

A shopkeeper directed Husha to a couple, elders he called them, who lived in the village at the end of the only path in the village leading to the Tepe. They were the Ng-Lista family, and known as the Keepers of the Tepe. Husha walked ahead of Iannas and Daniel who stayed with Donkey and Sai, and by the time they caught up, Husha was talking to an elderly lady and her husband who worked the land on the Tepe.

'Since the beginning of time itself,' claimed Grandpapa Ng-Lista as he told Husha how their family had owned the land on and around the Tepe for generations, 'my family have been Keepers of the Tepe, and we make sure it is well looked after and accessible to all who come.'

Husha introduced everyone, and the elders were happy to be called Grandmamma and Grandpapa by these new visitors.

'There is magic here,' Grandmamma Ng-Lista tried to add a little sparkle to the Tepe. 'None of us know what is buried inside the Tepe. Maybe our ancestors have forgotten, maybe it was no longer important at the time, but it has a strength, a power. If you spend the night on the Tepe, as I have done on many occasions, you will feel it. Many women believe the force has a power to heal, and young childless mothers often arrive from distant lands and spend the night in prayer on the Tepe in the hope of bearing a child one day. I can see one of you is already a mother. You look beautiful, my child.'

'What do you think, Grandmamma?' Sai was testing. 'Does the magic really heal?'

'Only if you are in touch with the world.' Grandmamma did not explain what she meant. 'What it does, how it works, I do not know.'

Grandpapa was more absorbed by the Tepe. 'The Tepe is more than magic. It holds the power of an ancient belief. I prefer to believe it to be the first temple ever built for the Gods. My great grandfather told me what his great grandfather told him; temples lie deep in the Tepe, and they were buried, not destroyed. He said the ancient temples were buried as a sign of respect for the Gods of the time, and a belief that the Gods would one day return, and when they do, the faithful will restore the temples.'

Husha was intrigued and enchanted by the belief system Grandpapa described, recognising there was so much more here than met the eye, but before he could ask something more, Iannas asked if there was lodging in the village. Grandmamma and Grandpapa did not reply, immediately insisting they stay with them; they had a barn and much space.

'Stay with us a few days. We like to talk of the Tepe. You can meet our children and grandchildren who will be the next Keepers when we pass on. And we want to look after this beautiful young mother-to-be. I will make you duck soup tonight.'

Sai smiled and told Grandmamma that she loved duck soup and would be delighted to stay with them.

'We hope to hear from our friend soon, but we do not know when,' Sai added. Grandmamma was so happy to have guests in the house again.

'Go to the Tepe,' Grandpapa insisted. 'Go and enjoy the views. You can see Urfa in the distance and make your way back when you are ready; we will be waiting.' And with that the Ng-Lista's headed back home to make preparations for their new guests.

Husha led the short walk up the hill where they stumbled across a number of long, half-buried horizontal stones, and Sai chose one on which to rest while the others made a temporary camp around her. At the highest point of the hill, only a short distance away, an abandoned mud shelter marked a viewpoint.

Husha and Iannas prepared a cold lunch, but there was also some leftover roasted grain and a raw meat dish that Husha had bought from Urfa for everyone to try.

'Everyone must try this,' he was insisting. 'Since the last full moon, it has been unlawful for the locals in Urfa to light a fire. Can you believe it? Anyway, in the market this is what they are serving. This meat has been pounded with salt and herbs and even some vegetables, all because they are not allowed to cook the meat. I tried it; trust me it was delicious. Now it is your turn.'

Only Sai absolutely refused and Husha did not pressure her, but Daniel and Iannas grew to enjoy it only after shutting their eyes the first time they tasted the pounded raw meat.

The temperature fell further as the shadows began to lengthen, so they found their overcoats and wrapped warmly while Iannas retrieved some bedding so that Sai could lay down on her flat rock in comfort. They decided to stay and watch the sun go down.

'This is the last sunset of our journey together,' Husha pointed out. There is something else in the air, he thought, but he could not describe it.

'What was your best memory of the journey, Husha?' Sai was in a reminiscing mood. Secretly grateful the travelling had stopped, even if it was going to be for a short while, she too felt so relaxed but had not understood why.

'Meeting all of you in Ur and hearing your wonderful news, Sai.' Sai smiled back at Husha. 'But the best part was when I realised that I was on my way back home after all these years and that somehow, I still cannot believe it, my journey became entwined with yours,' Husha looked at Daniel and Iannas, 'and that of the High Priest Terah and the Messenger. I have felt a greater force guiding the way, even towards a new destiny. It is a new feeling for me, and I do not know how to describe it fully.'

'What about each of you? Daniel? Iannas?' Sai wanted to know.

Iannas took to answering first. 'You are right, Husha. It was like we were meant to be together. This journey would not have succeeded without each of us.' Iannas paused, but before Daniel could take his turn, Iannas picked up again. 'One of the best things for me was meeting you, Sai. I have enjoyed learning about you and the life you left behind in India. I have never met anyone like you, or from your part of the world. I am glad you stayed with us.'

Sai and Iannas shared an embarrassed smile, which Daniel dissolved quickly.

'To start with,' Daniel began, 'being on my first journey without Papa was the best part, but then it was your strength and friendship, Iannas, your guidance, Husha, and your inspiration, Sai, that became my centre.' He looked at Sai. 'No matter how difficult things became, you gave us hope to make the impossible possible.' Daniel paused. 'I did expect that finishing the task given by Alizer would be the best feeling, but it is not. Now? The best feeling is being among a group of friends sitting here, together. I hope we will know each other forever!'

'What about you, Sai?' Husha picked the moment to ask Sai.

'I think you all know the answer. Each of you is a part of my child's destiny in some way, but the child is the greatest gift this journey has given me. Having each of you with me at this time and being part of your journey is another gift, a second one. Because I am greedy, I like to have two gifts.

You have become my new family, and I hope my child and I will know you for the rest of our lives.'

They watched the approaching sunset and could not help but recognise and grasp the contrast between the mood of Urfa and the peace and the spirit, maybe even some hope on the Tepe.

'Are we simply relaxed because we have nowhere else to go tomorrow?' Iannas tried to explain.

'I expected this in Harran,' Sai meant more but could not explain. 'It feels good and right to be here.'

'Maybe this place does have a force for goodness,' Husha whispered, surprising even himself by his contemplation.

Sai stroked her tummy. 'Let us hope so. What was that you said in your story, Iannas? The Laws of Goodness?'

'It is only a story,' Daniel rebuffed, 'no one knows what they are or even if they existed.'

'I like the thought anyway,' Sai protested. 'I like the words, their meaning, what it might stand for.'

'This moment,' Iannas tried, 'maybe it is all right here. Goodness is what everyone lives for and fights for.'

'Not everyone,' Husha touched reality. Husha was also thinking the "Laws of Goodness" might even be in the saddlebag.

'I want my child to touch goodness,' Sai hungered. 'I want each of you to promise to teach my child the Laws of Goodness.'

'We will seek them out, and we will be the best teachers!' Iannas promised on behalf of each uncle.

Sai laughed at his offer. 'You do not need to seek anything. Just be yourselves,' Sai played with a compliment.

'Do you know what you will call our newest member of the family?' Husha wondered. He wanted to ask more, but he hesitated, recognising the uncertainty of the future, and did not want to spoil the magic. This was incredible, he was thinking and feeling, but could not see why.

'Well,' Sai began, 'if it's a boy, maybe Husha.' This made Husha blush. 'But why not Daniel or even Iannas?' she quizzed.

'And if it's a girl?' Iannas wanted to know.

'To be honest, I have not even thought about names,' Sai confessed. 'It has been enough to arrive. It feels good to stop. In fact, this place is unexpected in so many ways, but I feel safe here.' The remark surprised Sai and she accepted it for what it was.

'But when the time comes,' Sai announced, 'in keeping with the tradition from my home mountain in India, we will celebrate with a naming ceremony. You will travel to me wherever I happen to be from wherever you happen to be. And at the ceremony you will add the name of my newborn to your identification seals, and we will name each of you as family on the baby's seal.'

They all thought the plan perfect, ignoring the unknown future ahead and the challenges it would bring.

'I will have a new seal made for the occasion.' Husha removed his seal from around his neck and examined it. 'This one has no more room.'

Iannas lifted out two seals from around his neck. 'This seal belonged to my great, great grandfather. He survived the floods.' He showed Sai the symbol of the fish on the seal. 'And this is my own.' He lifted a second plain seal. 'I will have the name marked on both seals, and you will bring the baby to Nineveh so my Appa may meet the newest member of the family.'

As Iannas finished, Daniel removed a pouch and emptied its contents onto the stone that Sai lay on.

'I have a gold Amulet Seal here.' Daniel lifted it by its string, and Sai looked at it with interest. It appeared to have a soft blue glow around its golden reflection in the moonlight.

'What is the story behind the gold amulet, Daniel?' Iannas asked.

'It is an Amulet Seal my father gave me in case I ran into trouble,' he laughed remembering some of the troubles they had encountered; the others enjoyed the irony too. 'Apparently, my father has the protection of the Royal Court of Harran, and this was a gift to him, but I am not allowed to use it.'

'But your father gave it to you!' Iannas tried to be convincing. 'I think you now have Royal protection, Daniel.' Iannas teased, and they all laughed with him.

'This will belong to the newest member of our family, Sai, and with it the protection of Harran!' Daniel declared.

Sai appreciated the sentiment and readily agreed, 'An extended family and Royal protection! I cannot say we will always be the happiest, but we will be the most loving and loved family in the world.' Sai smiled with a fresh contentment, grateful again that the travel had ceased for a few days. She needed to stop moving. Stop the motions of her body. She watched Daniel return the Amulet Seal to the pouch and to his tunic pocket; and suddenly felt a cold shiver.

They all felt the cold; there was no campfire tonight. In fact there were no fires at all in the land of Urfa.

'We need to pack and return to the village. Will Alizer and Uncle Azhar be all right?' Daniel spoke the second half of the sentence out loud not intending to. They all looked at each other as reassuringly as they could but did not need to answer as they packed and headed back to the village.

'Tonight is the Full Moon Solstice Ceremony. We return when the moon is at its highest and the bonfire will be lit,' Daniel announced with a hint of regret that there was no temple in the village for the prayer ceremony.

They packed and walked to the place of Grandmamma and Grandpapa Ng-Lista who would hear nothing other than making the group their guests in their own home for the first two nights.

'If your friend is late, and you need to stay in the village after that, you can have full use of the barn for as long you like,' Grandpapa insisted.

'The barn is not for you, dear,' Grandmamma took Sai's hand. 'You will have your own room with us in our home until you hear from your friend.'

They also had some good news for Daniel.

'Our temple is the Tepe, Daniel. We will have the Solstice Ceremony Blessing there tonight. We have a village priest. Who told you we need a temple to pray, young man? I hope you will join us,' Grandmamma was looking forward to the ceremony. 'Our new King will be declared a God during the ceremony tonight, and they will light the bonfire of Urfa immediately afterwards. It should be a sight.'

There was much celebration and festivity in the air throughout the entire village, and then again on the Tepe that night as everyone gathered in front of the priest, a young lady from the village clothed in the familiar Mari cloth dress and mask that Daniel had famously fallen in love with back in Susa. The full moon on this particular night was a special sign for the year ahead, and all the villagers shouted with joy as they gazed in awe at the moon at the zenith in the sky.

During the evening, the gentle disk had quickly flowed through its colours from a deep waking orange to a temple cotton cloth white knowing that it had the largest audience in its entire history. The priest stood on the pinnacle of the Tepe and presented the moon with her right arm pointed upwards and towards it, and her left palm facing her heart. She spoke the ancient prayers of thanksgiving, hope, and safety, as well as health and food on everyone's table so no one in the land of the God Sin would go hungry. In Urfa at this moment, in the Temple in the fortress on the cliff, the King was being divined, becoming a God.

On the Tepe, the village choir stood on the hill below the priest facing Urfa under the beaming moonlight, and performed a gentle soothing melody with a voice and words that haunted the heart and captured the tears of the night. Words of hope singing the voice of loneliness, accompanied by one harp, delightfully expressing the comfort of the moon. Everyone joined the soft chorus raising their eyes and voices to the glowing guide in the sky. An ode to the moon. A moon that was predictable, had no conditions in exchange for sharing its light, and kept them safe.

Some on the Tepe shouted when they glimpsed the flicker of light and shadow from the freshly-lit bonfire in the distant city of Urfa nestled in the valley. It began as a little glow, and then when it grew brighter and more confident some claimed they saw a small flame. Very quickly the small flame sprang into life as it enjoyed the taste of its fuel and devoured the wooden sacrifices from the people of the land of Urfa. The villagers shouted in praise of the new God-King and the Sin God, and the villagers remained on the hill till early morning watching the bonfire grow from an essence into a small wave and then a turbulent sea. All the people of Urfa and the lands around the city began to see and feel the size and might of this powerful fire. The God-King must have been satisfied, they hoped, counting on their offerings being accepted and blessings being granted as they stood in awe of this bonfire, which held within it a symbol of the power of this new God-King who had commanded it. There was so much joy and celebration to be felt among the locals as the fire burned brighter, stronger and higher.

The second night, the whole village congregated again as they would again every night for the next five nights completing the period of the seven night celebrations. The flames had yet to reach their peak on the second night, and all this time the sky had been polished and clean and the moon and stars had appeared especially dusted for the solstice. Now the fire smoke began quietly to create a layer in the sky and blanket the stars and the moon, so only the brightest stars and only the softest image of the moon could be seen.

On the third night, the flames were even larger and higher. It was early in the evening and the sun had set, but the sky was not yet completely dark and a blue tint remained, a bright white flame with a blue hue emerged from the intense strong yellow inferno, like a tower reaching for the clouds. It happened suddenly, and did not need a voice to proclaim itself in charge of the rage. Some would describe it afterwards as an angry flame attempting to escape from the heart of the fire. Others saw it as a travelling flame speeding up towards the sky, like a tornado, a beam, and for an instant, connecting the Heaven and the Earth. Many said that it was aiming at the moon, and some were even scared that the moon would perish.

At almost the same time, the villagers saw dark grey and black clouds gathering exactly where the white tower had been. The clouds multiplied and swelled over Urfa, eventually creeping towards the village, and over the Tepe. The black clouds continued mounting, relentlessly covering the remnants of the moon so it lost its battle to be seen, and the last of the night stars. Finally, the only light remaining in the night was the majesty of the light of the bonfire of Urfa being reflected down by the dark clouds. Some saw the clouds as a symbol of the new God-King, for the scene was without doubt a splendid manifestation. But others saw a wretched glow approaching from the inferno. Grandmamma and Grandpapa Ng-Lista were the first to realise that something extraordinary had happened.

'It is time to return to your homes,' Grandpapa Ng-Lista turned, stepping towards the village. 'This is no longer a dream, it is a nightmare.' And all the villagers including Husha, Sai, Iannas, and Daniel who heard Grandpapa and respected his voice dispersed and returned to their beds. But those who were not from the village and did not know the Magic of the Keeper of the Tepe, they did not hear his voice, for they were deaf to the sound of wisdom. They stayed and allowed the darkness to enter them, and they and their offspring would always see the darkness even amidst the light.

Daniel, Iannas, and Husha would only find out many moons later that the cave with its supplies had by now been completely covered and consumed by the blaze.

The moon would not be seen again by the villagers or in the land of Urfa until the spring as if it was too embarrassed to show itself. Grandpapa had understood, and Donkey lay on the ground in prayer and hope.

31 THE FIRE, THE BIRTH, AND THE DEATH

Some reported that the fire burned for one moon, but the effects of the bonfire lasted much longer. When the moon revealed itself again, the young who had forgotten what it was would explore it with their eyes in awe. They would reawaken that distant memory of the moon and its comforting shadows in the night.

While all the villagers continued to gather on the Tepe for the fourth, fifth, sixth and seventh nights according to requirement, many did so as a courtesy to the festival, to the Sin God, to the God-King, and only for a few moments for the mood had turned sombre. The dark clouds united with the black smoke of the fire so that by the seventh day, the tormented clouds cast a gloom into the weakness of the day. Storm clouds without rain. Angry clouds without emotion. On the last night of the festivities, the village elders gathered, and Husha, Sai, Iannas, Daniel, and Donkey were given permission to move into one of the abandoned houses in the village, which was duly repaired and made comfortable with the various donations, many in kind, by almost every household of the village, led by Grandmamma and Grandpapa. The village had warmed to the former slave and the young travellers and, recognising their predicament, invited them to live among them. They were welcomed and respected, for they paid their own way and were not a burden to anyone.

The fire was now so huge with its endless fuel that even though the festivities ended, most of the villagers continued to make their way to the Tepe in the evenings to touch the immensity of the flames. The heat, the noise, the reflection of the fire in the darkening clouds, and the smell of the burning fuel, all had a power to capture the eyes of those who watched, as if the fire wanted to be seen and be remembered for eternity.

The refugees began appearing on the eighth day of the bonfire, but the inferno continued to grow and devour until it towered to its most majestic on the fourteenth day. By the time the flames of the fire waned after twenty-eight days, to be replaced by a hot orange flameless glow over Urfa, the land around the village was already scattered with numerous makeshift camps and settlements. The orange glow was now accompanied by a growing cloud of endless thick black smoke oozing out of the glow, and collecting as a wide mushroom above Urfa forming a new cloud. With no wind to carry it, the black smoke cloud grew so large that it encompassed the whole of Urfa like an inflating stomach. Within a few days, it wrapped itself around the villages and consumed the whole valley. From the higher ground of Gobekli Tepe, some watched the black smoke rise and creep across the valley towards them. When it finally reached the village doorstep, it entered without knocking or waiting for permission. The orange glow of the fire in Urfa disappeared entirely when the thick black smoke filled and packed every possible gap in the harsh air. The gloom of the days grew so dark that day and night resembled one another, and the birds, trees, flowers, and the animals remained asleep or in hiding throughout. The air became a mass of smoke and ash, the entire village coughed, and many could not breathe if they ventured out. When it was necessary to collect food supplies, they resorted to tying rope to one another and to their homes for fear of losing one another and one's soul in the black fog.

The elderly and the young ones despaired, unable to even walk as their lungs became coated in the fine burning ash, and there was nothing anyone could do to relieve the suffering.

The heat, invisible now, remained deep inside the bonfire and had become so hot that no one could approach it for many more invisible moons.

The few people who strayed into the village brought with them tales from Urfa. They described how their homes were no protection from the heat or the smoke. They described an ocean of refugee camps in the valley between Urfa and the village, which in the darkness the villagers could not see. It was as if the world had disappeared.

Other refugees claimed to have been present at the solstice celebrations and spread rumours that the God-King was now indeed so powerful he had thrown into the fire, with his own hands, anyone who had refused to bow to him. Some even claimed they had seen the God-King throw a whole family into the fire, others claimed he had burned an entire tribe, and the smoke in Urfa was heavy with the smell of burning flesh. These rumours pierced the silent distress Daniel, Husha, Iannas, and Sai could not discuss.

Days and then weeks moulded the stories again to the burning of one man, while some said two, others said three, and yet others included a woman among the victims. None, however, could name those supposedly consumed by the fire, and none knew what to believe.

It was the refugees entering the village two invisible moons after the solstice festivities, who brought a growingly common rumour that was turning into a tale. They told of one who had been thrown into the fire and emerged from the intense heat alive and well. The news soon identified the man as a magician, a miracle man who had challenged the God-King, was thrown into the bonfire, and had survived.

When the rains and the winds came at the approach of the third invisible moon after the solstice to wash away the deeds that had been done, the air began to clear. But the rains only succeeded in making all the roads impassable with a soup of mud, while the winds revealed the brown dirty carpet of refugee camps and tents on the floor of the valley and in every direction from distant smouldering Urfa. But at least the coughing ceased.

Husha, Daniel, Iannas, and Sai learned and knew not to believe any rumours they heard. Husha kept the conversation in check while discouraging any fears, explaining almost every day the harmful nature of gossip and the virtue of truth. His inclination was to mention the prophecy, but Iannas and Daniel were so deeply engulfed by the anguish of the wait, not knowing the fate of Alizer, Terah, and the family, that Husha knew they would have no room for it in their hearts. Husha knew something. He felt it every time he went to the Tepe. He still did not recognise hope.

Sai refused to listen to any more stories after the first few rumours. She attempted to turn her and her friends' attentions to being calmed and contented with each other's company, while she became stronger with her child.

When the clouds began to lift, and the views began to return, Daniel spent almost every waking moment at Gobekli Tepe waiting for Alizer.

Sai went into labour much earlier than expected, and Grandmamma took Sai into her home to see Sai through her time. The whole village knew Sai's story, and they were always trying to encourage Iannas to take her for his wife before someone else.

Grandpapa who had stayed indoors for the entire time since the solstice celebrations began to venture out, but when he was asked how he was, all he would say was, 'Much evil has been achieved, yet something great has occurred.' Husha resonated with Grandpapa's words, recognising his feelings on the Tepe.

It was during this time when Daniel stood on Gobekli Tepe and it was like being on top of a mountain gazing out over a sea of mist covering the valley, with Urfa peeking through the fog in the distance, that Sai's birthing began, such a long and difficult labour that Grandmamma called on her daughters and granddaughters to help.

Sai was so exhausted from the birth that she fell asleep while feeding her tired first born at her breast. As the day grew old, Sai grew weaker and weaker, for no one knew a way to stop the blood flow from inside her; she never woke, even for a few hours, to enjoy her first-born and only child. And Iannas, in his intense grief, took the child as his own and named her Sai, in memory of his love, for he now understood love. He gave the child to a wet nurse and then cried inconsolably for five days and five nights while Husha and Daniel mourned Sai as they would have mourned their own flesh.

The whole village gathered together for the burial, and everyone felt the sorrow, for they had grown to love Sai. They wept as they watched Husha and Daniel dig the earth with their own hands, for there was no wood to burn her body in accordance to her custom, and then they lowered Sai into the waiting refuge. It was Iannas, and only Iannas, who covered her body with the soil of the Tepe as the choir of the village sang their mourning hymn for the afterlife. And this is where Iannas stayed and shed his tears and from where he did not move until his eyes could not release even one more tear.

It was on the seventh day after Sai's death and the birth of the orphan, when every breath and every waking moment still cut deep, and every blink of the eye cut even deeper with the memory of the loss of Sai, that Sum-Ina arrived with a message from Alizer.

'We have to leave, we are due in Alep, but first we are to meet Terah in Harran. He is ill, and he will not live long.'

HISTORICAL NOTE

Although a story of fiction, some of the backdrops have historical references that may be of interest.

Terah/Azhar is mentioned in Jewish, Christian, and Muslim scriptures and the two names are commonly considered as a reference to the same person. Many different narratives of Terah/Azhar exist and the Torah, Old Testament, and Quran might be good starting points for further exploration of this interesting and sometimes controversial character.

Alizer, more commonly written as Eliezer of Damascus, is the other borrowed character that makes an appearance in our story. The Targums of Onkelos, (trans. Etheridge 1862) clearly describe Eliezer as a 'Manager' of the household. Given the journeys undertaken by his household, Eliezer would have been a very loyal, strategic and efficient organiser and would easily have arranged a trip from Ur to Harran for an entire household if required. There is, however, very little to learn about Eliezer outside of the Pentateuch, except that he remained in the service of the household for a long time. Therefore, no doubt he will make another entrance in the sequel, and we will wait to learn a little more of his loyalty and commitment to the family as well as his talents.

The names of the two friends Daniel and Iannas originate from Susa and Nineveh respectively.

The astronomical event of 1953 BC is a reference from Pang and Bangert (1993) The Holy Grail of Chinese Astrology: The sun-moon-five planet conjunction in Yingshi (Pegasus) on March 5th 1953 BC, Bulletin of the American Astronomical Society.

The 1887 (J.H. Parry and Co.) edition of the Book of Jasher was used for the original quote in the introduction. Connecting the description of the birth of a Messenger and relating it to the astronomical event from 1953 BC is not new, a number of blogs on the internet have already done this, although the timeline for Terah/Azhar and the key events during his lifetime lack consensus.

There are many narrations of child genocide in history. The Mesopotamian story of Sargon and the story of Nimrod are two. The one in this novel is an adaptation of a Nimrod version.

There are two possible routes from Ur to Harran. One is through Nineveh on the Tigris, and the other through Mari along the Euphrates. Some sources state that the Ur of the story is not in the south at all but in the north. In this novel, our hero, fifteen-year-old Daniel, chooses to journey from Ur in the south and along the Euphrates to Harran. Both routes are likely to have been used widely at the time.

The map shows the location of the archaeological sites where each city and town mentioned existed and where they lie buried today. The path of the rivers Euphrates and Tigris, and the coastal area to the south of Ur has obviously changed with erosion and sedimentation. The river, land mass and coastline is an approximation to the time of Sai, Daniel, Husha, and Iannas. The descriptions of the ancient towns and cities have been taken from various sources and adapted for the purpose of this story. The locations of the city-states were recorded on a satellite map, and the walking trail shown follows actual paths and routes available today, thus mirroring the journey as it might have been taken at that time almost four thousand years ago. The maps will be updated with details after the first walking expedition of the route that will take place as soon as the political challenges currently in the region allow - updates will be posted at yeosola.com.

The Mesopotamian caravan probably covered between twenty-five and thirty kilometres a day. The Mesopotamian 'beru' is the distance travelled in two hours (one twelfth of a day), but it varies in span depending on the source. If we allow for five hours walking from dawn to midday and a further three hours in the late afternoon before sunset, the caravans may have settled with eight hours (four Beru) of walking a day. Thirty kilometres is possible in eight hours even with a caravan pace, and the Mesopotamians were far more used to long-distance foot journeys than we are. Time was also money. The caravans would not have been pleased with a slow pace or any delay. I have listed distances in 'beru' in the chapter headings using a commonly accepted 8.45 Km (5.25 miles) as a measure for one beru. The approximate walking distances have been calculated using detailed satellite mapping software and are listed at the end of this section.

Life in ancient Mesopotamia, including Harran, Mari, Sippar, and the other city-states has been studied and written in countless books on all topics. Some of the more interesting descriptions may be found in, for example, Pritchard (1969) Ancient Near Eastern Texts as well as the writings of travellers including Benjamin of Tudela and Ibn Jubayr. For a personal understanding of the people of that time, the best way is to go directly to their records. Read some of the translations of the hundreds of thousands of tablets and cuneiforms that have been discovered. They describe marriages, divorce, trade, tax, checkpoints, protocols, crime including thefts and murders, contracts, stories, complaints, and some of the most interesting are the personal letters. I would recommend starting with the Cuneiform Digital Library Initiative, The British Museum and Oracc but many academic institutions and museum websites have hidden treasure chests, the Ancient History Sourcebook, a Collection of Contracts from Mesopotamia c2300-428 BCE at Fordham University, is one example. Read these personal accounts and make up your own mind about life during this incredible era.

Very little is written about the floods that occurred in India around 2000 BC. A few passing references can be found in web searches.

Various folk tales, tablets, and written and verbal sources have inspired the campfire stories, but, in the manner of the ancient story tellers, they are all fictional creations of the author and are not intended to resemble any events in history. This includes the Gilgamesh rendition told by Rabi and the burial of the 'History of the World'. There are at least five different versions of the story of the floods and although the two in the British Museum are often frequented, the one adapted in this book is taken from the tablet where Xisuthros is asked to gather the 'History of the World' and bury it in Sippar. For more details see Verbrugghe and Wickersham (2001) Berossos and Manetho, Introduced and Translated.

A good source that references 'Watchers' is The Book of Enoch. The version that reads particularly well, although controversial, is the Schodde, 1882 version translated directly from Ethiopic. The term 'Watchers', according to this book, was originally ascribed to the angels who came to teach mankind. This book inspired some of the stories told by Iannas and Husha about the Watchers and Protectors.

Zugalum was indeed a Queen of Harran and a Princess of Ebla. The story of Enmenduranki is inspired by the incredible journeys of the seventh antediluvian King (Enoch or Idris). Zugalum was been trained as an archaeologist and tomb explorer for the purpose of this novel only.

The 'Instructions of Sharuppak' comprise sets of tablets dated to 3000 BC. The best source for this wonderful record is Black et al (1998) The Electronic Text Corpus of Sumerian Literature (http://www-etcsl.orient.ox.ac.uk/). Some would suggest the 'Instructions of Sharuppak' are a precursor to later theological writings. The lines from the 'Instructions' used for Rabiat's quotes are, in order, 274, 255, 257, 128, 134, and 264.

The event of the fire is frequently written and narrated. One of the possible locations of the fire is a massive pilgrimage site to this day in San

Li Urfa, better known as Urfa, in southern Turkey and which has inspired the location of the final chapters of the novel. Gobekli Tepe is a nearby site currently being excavated by Professor Klaus Schmidt with the help of the

German Archaeological Institute. It is an extraordinary place, and Professor Klaus believes it to date as far back as 10-12000 BC.

What becomes of the Book? Does the Book contain the original Laws of Goodness? The journey is not over, and Daniel will have to carry it into the next adventure.

The Dreamer and the Orphan
To be published soon.

Distances travelled in 'The Slave and the Book Keeper' by Daniel, Iannas, Sai and Husha

Susa to Ur	300 Km	(35.5 Beru)
Ur to Uruk	86 Km	(10.2 Beru)
Uruk to Sharuppak	66 Km	(7.8 Beru)
Sharuppak to Babylon	152 Km	(18 Beru)
Babylon to Sippar	78 Km	(9.2 Beru)
Sippar to Rapiqum	118 Km	(14 Beru)
Rapiqum to Hit	59 Km	(7 Beru)
Hit to Haradun	180 Km	(21.3 Beru)
Haradun to Mari	97 Km	(11.5 Beru)
Mari to Terqa	73 Km	(8.6 Beru)
Terqa to Tuttul	230 Km	(27.2 Beru)
Tuttul to Harran	128 Km	(15.15 Beru)
Harran to Urfa	44 Km	(5.2 Beru)
Urfa to Gobekli Tepe	20 Km	(2.4 Beru)
Total	1631 Km	

The Slave, the Book Keeper, the Dreamer, and the Orphan

The Slave and the Book Keeper
Daniel is about to begin his first adventure. Voices of innocents caught in the shadow of a battle to protect 'Goodness' from evil.

The Dreamer and the Orphan
The newly formed company of Assassins is determined to find and slay the magician who survived the great bonfire of Urfa. The sequel to 'The Slave and the Book Keeper' follows the epic journey through the lands of Assyria, Kanaan, Memphis and Arabia. But shadows wait on every path and it is not only the assassins Daniel and his companions must navigate through; there are also those they had counted as friends and would take the book and its secrets for themselves. And within every shadow lies new treachery. Due 2014/15

Walking the Book: A Companion and Guidebook.
A record of expedition that will walk the ancient route described in 'The Slave, the Book Keeper, the Dreamer and the Orphan'. The expedition will follow the steps of the ancient and first Pilgrimage that begins in Susa and Ur and through ten countries across the Middle East and Arabia

One of the last challenges on Earth

YEOSOLA.COM

www.ingramcontent.com/pod-product-compliance
Lightning Source LLC
Chambersburg PA
CBHW022025240626
47154CB00007B/2271